# THE BILLIONAIRE BACHELORS TRILOGY

R.G. ALEXANDER

THE BILLIONAIRE BACHELORS TRILOGY

Copyright © 2014 R.G. Alexander

Editing by D.S. Editing
Formatted by IRONHORSE Formatting

**The CEO's Fantasy**
Copyright 2014 R.G. Alexander
**The Cowboy's Kink**
Copyright 2014 R.G. Alexander
**The Playboy's Ménage**
Copyright 2014 R.G. Alexander

All rights reserved. Without limiting the rights under copyright reserved above, no part of this publication may be reproduced, stored in or introduced into a retrieval system, or transmitted, in any form, or by any means (electronic, mechanical, photocopying, recording, or otherwise) without the prior written permission of both the copyright owner and the above publisher of this book.

This is a work of fiction. Names, characters, places, brands, media, and incidents are either the product of the author's imagination or are used fictitiously. The author acknowledges the trademarked status and trademark owners of various products referenced in this work of fiction, which have been used without permission. The publication/use of these trademarks is not authorized, associated with, or sponsored by the trademark owners.

ISBN: 1500767557
ISBN-13: 978-1500767556

# CONTENTS

The CEO's Fantasy     1

The Cowboy's Kink     123

The Playboy's Ménage     235

# THE CEO'S FANTASY

2

# PROLOGUE

Our favorite Billionaire Bachelors were spotted this weekend at Warren Industry's annual charity gala.

Yes, the country's most eligible bad boys are all in town again and they each decided to go stag—that is, sans their usual sugary arm candy—signaling to single Cinderellas everywhere that these princes are on the market once more. Surprised? If you are, you haven't been paying attention. This fierce foursome goes through women like...well, let's just say if I had a nickel for every time a heart was broken by our charming scoundrels, I'd be a billionaire too, and between globetrotting and manicures, I wouldn't have time to fill you in on every last detail of their infamous adventures.

I dare you to send Ms. Anonymous your nickels.

But potential sudden windfall for yours truly aside, this relationship update leads me to today's question:

We know every debutante's mama wants a piece of their action, but if you could choose without repercussions, which of the Billionaire Bachelors would be your fantasy? The true hardcore cowboy who has enough land and employees to start his own country but no dancing partner for his *special* kind of two-step? The musician with a royal pedigree, a wild streak and a vast fortune at his disposal, who's never been seen with the same woman twice? His best jet-setting buddy who can claim no less than five estates, four degrees and three charges of lewd public behavior on his record? Or the sweet-talking, picture-perfect tycoon-cum-philanthropist who used to be the baddest of the bunch but put those days behind him when he took over as CEO of his family's company? (Or did he?) His public image has certainly been polished to a dazzlingly dull shine, but is the strain of the straight and narrow getting him down? If his grim countenance and lack of companionship of late are any indication, perhaps it is.

So ladies, pick your fantasy lover—rocker, rancher, rebel or reformed rogue. Glass slipper shopping is a dangerous sport to be sure, especially with prey as slippery as these particular animals, but I'll still wish all my readers happy hunting.

Dean Warren crumpled up the gossip page of the newspaper he'd been handed and drank the rest of his scotch in one go, reaching for the bottle that had been left for him at the table.

"Happy hunting, my ass." Someday he was going to find Ms. Anonymous and tell her what she could do with her column. In graphic detail. As it stood, he'd be spending more time at his office, and his assistant would be busy for the next month fielding personal calls and invitations instead of working, the way he did every time the columnist mentioned Dean in her article. He'd ask for another damn raise and Dean would give in, because he would rather pay the man more money than allow his secretary, Mrs. Grandholm, to take on the burden alone. She was a national treasure and too close to her well-deserved retirement to start worrying about his love life again.

"I don't think reformed rogues are supposed to swear,"

Peter Faraday admonished, grinning at the others around the dining table in the private room Dean had reserved for the four of them. "But then, I'm not sure his image would keep its sparkle if Anonymous knew where he was right now. This place is more my speed, according to her. Speaking of, did you notice how she always finds a way to use the word lewd in connection with me? Every damn time. What's that about?"

"She obviously knows you well," Henry Vincent offered helpfully from his chair. "Maybe you got her mother arrested, you cad, after convincing her an orgy in a public fountain was harmless fun. Now, because of your indecency, we're being punished with this flagrant example of stereotyping. Rocker, rancher, rebel, reformed rogue…" He snorted. "As a writer, I commend the clever alliteration, but she makes us sound more like Ken doll collectibles than men. I'm not just a piece of beefcake performing on a stage, you know. I have feelings. I'm a complicated man with a dark, mysterious soul. I'd be more than willing to show her, if she'd like."

Peter groaned. "Dude, give it up. Co-writing song lyrics doesn't make you a writer. And there's nothing mysterious about you other than why you brought *that* to dinner and why we're here instead of Dean's townhouse. I thought you wanted to stay under the radar this trip."

"I picked the restaurant," Dean assured him. "Henry told me he wanted real food, Tracy always enjoys a show with his meal and I didn't think you'd care. To put your mind at ease, Franco's is the best kept secret in the city. He wants privacy to work on his gastronomic masterpieces, and I have a fondness for his seared scallops, so it works out perfectly. No one who comes here discusses it, and no one who hasn't knows it exists. It's about as under the radar as I could manage on such short notice."

"Your pick, huh? For us? And I'd been told you'd lost your touch." Peter leaned back in his chair and smiled wickedly. "I'm not convinced your chef was thinking about his culinary art so much as his personal sexual fetish when he designed this place." He waggled his brows. "You have to admit crème brûlée and whips and chains don't normally go together."

"Few interesting things do," Dean murmured, glancing toward the floor-to-ceiling one-way mirror Peter was gazing through—the one giving them a private view of an erotic exhibition. And it *was* pure exhibition. A nude woman, her nipples pierced and her arms and inner thighs covered in irezumi—Japanese tattoos—was chained to a St. Andrews cross, being thoroughly and patiently played by both a male and a female dominant. She was writhing in pleasure, her body artistically marked with welts from the man's whip and bruises from the female's pinching fingers. She had given herself over to them, but she was the one in control.

There was a time he would have wanted to capture this moment with his camera. To frame the ecstatic submissive's expression that told him she was as excited by the knowledge that strangers were watching her as she was by her partners' actions. It was the only reason she played here instead of in the privacy of one of the more secluded dungeons. She wasn't doing it for money—participants here volunteered—but for the thrill.

Sadly, he was neither thrilled nor aroused in return. He felt no twinge of curiosity. No interest—sexually or otherwise.

Hell, he *was* grim.

Dean lifted his glass toward his friends as a distraction. "To things that don't usually mesh."

The other men hoisted their drinks in response. They were an unlikely group personality-wise, each leading very different lives. It had been a year since the four of them were last together, so when Henry let him know they were going to stay in town for a while after his company's event, Dean had streamlined most of his month's schedule in order to accommodate them.

He hadn't realized it, but he'd definitely missed having them around—the three people he trusted completely and could be himself with. His friends.

Henry Vincent had been touring more on than off for years, Tracy Reyes was often neck deep in maintaining his land and cattle empire, and Peter rarely stayed in one place long enough to meet for drinks. Dean had known Henry and Peter since they were children, but it wasn't until they met Tracy in college and rented a house together off-campus that they'd bonded over beer, basketball and their love of trouble.

Those days they'd been wild and careless—and Dean had, indeed, been the baddest of the bunch. The one to introduce quick-study Tracy to all manner of vices, the one who rivaled Peter for public spectacles and Henry for his luck with the ladies. Back then he would have laughed over a harmless article like this. Or paid someone to write it. Back then he hadn't cared what people thought or why a woman wanted him, as long as he got his way.

The last fifteen years had changed him, the last five even more—not that anyone had noticed. The knowledge left a trace of bitterness on his tongue and in his heart. No matter how straight the path he walked or how many accomplishments he had under his belt, he would always be seen as the baddest of the bad. To the board of directors, his uncle who pulled their strings, and to any woman he found remotely attractive, the thoughtless words of one loquacious gossip columnist would always matter more than his actions.

It made him wonder, not for the first time, why he tried to so hard to toe their line. To be better than his father had been. To be known for something other than his social life or his grandfather's success. To win the board over to his side. The task was Sisyphean bullshit.

He stared at his glass morosely until a heavy sigh made him look up. Tracy was studying him with concern. He took off his ever-present hat and ran his hands through his short, thick waves before he addressed Henry and Peter. "If you two would just settle down, start thinking with the head on your shoulders and stop fucking your way through the phone book like Dean and I have, the gossip would die off pretty quick."

Wishful fucking thinking.

"Don't play the gentleman hayseed everyone seems to think you are. *We* won't let you get away with it." Henry reached into the ice bucket filled with beer he'd requested and pulled out a new bottle. "We know what she means when she says *special* two-step. Case in point, Dean picked this place with you in mind, and I'd be willing to bet you're on speaking terms with at least one of those lovely kinksters in the other room."

Tracy responded with a lazy, sideways smile. "The difference between us is that I understand the meaning of the word discreet."

"I know what it means." Henry took a drink and licked his lips. "You have no idea how discreet I can be. But if I wanted to *settle*, I'd have let my mother pick her favorite blue blood while I was away and I'd be rocking a white picket fence and a wife obsessed with tiaras by now. Settling sounds like an appetizer. I want the whole meal. One I have an actual craving for."

"Oh, the problems of a royal rock star." Peter laughed. "I suppose that's the benefit of being the genuine bad boy of our club—I have zero familial expectations and no particular skill set, and women rarely think of settling down when they see me. I don't get much sleep, or that much respect in the morning, but if I die, it'll be with a lewd smile on my irresistibly handsome face."

That was Peter's favorite line, but Dean knew better. Faraday had earned four degrees in little more than the same time it took the rest of them to snag one, and he'd still managed to get into trouble between finals. He was a certified genius, and between his highly publicized dalliances and cock-ups, he spent his time in ways that would surprise the hell out of the gossipmonger and the rest of his friends. Peter didn't like people to know what kind of man he really was. Dean wasn't sure why. Maybe *playboy* had a better ring than *polymath*.

Tracy muttered something in Spanish under his breath. "You joke all you like, but some of us care about our family legacy and having someone to pass it on to before we die."

"Then get busy," Peter countered, his irritation clear. "What's stopping you, *Patricio*? *My* sex life or yours? Afraid you'll have to stop practicing your roping skills on long-legged city girls who don't know horns from balls about country living? Worried the woman who's willing to put up with your schedule and your family to make a mini rancher or two will only do it with the lights out and no handcuffs in sight? I'm sure there's a good, wholesome girl out there secretly yearning for a controlling cowhand. Track her, tie her down, make a baby and quit bitching about it."

"It's not that simple, smartass." Tracy knuckles went white as he clenched the brim of his hat. Peter had struck a nerve.

"Why not?" Henry raised a brow. "Sure, dating is pain in the ass, particularly when every woman you meet for coffee gets a four-page spread in Sleazy-Gossips-R-Us—but it isn't impossible. It's just a poor little rich boy problem. We're all intelligent, most of us are good looking and we aren't exactly wanting in the financial department. To a man, we're all a better catch than Anonymous makes us out to be."

*Poor little rich boy problems.* It was what Dean's mother had said to his father every time he complained about his lot in life. If she were still alive, she'd agree with Henry, but Dean wasn't sure he did.

"Which one of us are you calling ugly, you tattooed, bearded hippie?" Peter glared.

"Guess." Henry caressed his full beard to show off his sleeve of tattoos. "But don't change the subject. Anonymous is getting famous making us targets with her talk about the Billionaire Bachelors. Some of us are fine with the speculation and bad press—hell, it's done wonders for ticket sales—and Tracy is the Teflon Cowboy, the kinkiest of us all but nothing sticks to him. I'd guess the head of Warren Industries doesn't get off as easily. He's spent the last five years being a sitting duck in a suit."

Dean shook his head, taking another drink. "I'm a big boy, Henry. It's nice to know you care, but I do just fine. I don't need to be your between-tours project."

"Bullshit," Henry challenged. "You're not doing fine, and everyone knows it. And not just because it's time for another damn performance review. When was the last time you took a trip that wasn't for business? Had such mind-blowing, earth-shattering sex that you couldn't move your legs? When was the last time you did something you wanted to do without thinking about how it would look to that damn board? To Ms. Anonymous and the rest of her ilk?"

"Fuck off, friend." Dean's smile took some of the edge off his words. "When was the last time you kept your nose out of my business?"

"I can't believe none of us have found out who she is," Tracy grumbled, breaking the tension. "Tracked her down wherever she holes up to write and paid her off. I'm tempted to buy the paper just to fire her and be done with it. If we were the kind of men she believes we are we'd have done it already."

Dean had thought of that, but the results would be disastrous and impossible to contain. Suing the paper for defamation or firing the columnist would only draw more scrutiny to his personal life, call into question his capabilities and remind them about all the worries they'd had when he took over. If he couldn't deal with one basically harmless gossip columnist, how could he handle a multi-billion dollar corporation?

"I have something in the works on that front, but she's

not the real problem." Henry leaned forward, his elbows on the table. "If she was, I'd have convinced Peter to hack into her computer by now. Gossip happens. She doesn't help, but she isn't the only one who shares every detail of our private lives for money. At least she's honest about what she's doing."

Then she was a rarity, Dean mused, his fingers tightening on his glass. People lied all the time to get what they wanted, and everybody wanted something. A merger instead of a relationship. A scandalous chapter in an autobiography. A picture on the front page of their favorite tabloid. Money in exchange for silence. Everyone had a price.

No one could blame him for deciding to focus on the business for a while.

Henry studied Dean's reaction. "We've all got horror stories. But this article… She plays to her reader's fantasies about who we are. Who they want us to be. The way she worded it started me thinking."

"That sounds ominous."

"Thinking is not what he's known for," Peter agreed with Tracy smugly.

"Just some harmless dinner conversation, Tracy. And I'm surprised at you, Peter. You used to think my ideas were brilliant." Henry swigged his beer. "Question. If you could have any woman you wanted—"

"Audrey Hepburn." Peter interrupted swiftly. "Or Lara Croft. Let's be safe and say both at the same time because I refuse to choose between them."

"They have to be alive and not characters in a video game." Henry kicked Peter's chair with his booted foot. Hard. "I'm serious. What's your idea of the perfect woman? Librarian, gymnast or candlestick maker?"

Exchanging amused looks with Dean, Tracy shifted in his chair and leaned over to steal a bottle from Henry's bucket. "Aw, hell, this isn't what men talk about when they sit around drinking and watching a woman get well and truly played. This is a Cosmo quiz."

"Save us from our sensitive musician," Peter intoned dramatically. "I feel like we should hug it out now and really share our feelings. Maybe Henry will co-write a song about it full of angst and alliterations."

"No, this is logic. Strategy." The guitarist persisted. "Something Dean has had to learn a lot about in the last few years. Humor me for a minute. Tracy's easy so we can start with him."

"I am *not* easy."

"He wants a family. So a woman who loves children and old-fashioned family values, can cook and is probably as comfortable in the country as he is. And we've known him long enough to know he prefers blondes."

"That description makes his dream girl sound like Auntie fucking Em." Peter joked. "Daisy Duke in chains is more his speed. Someone athletic, open-minded and obedient. Preferably discreet. The last of his friends he introduced us to spent the entire evening enlightening me on his stamina and how she needed vitamin b shots and energy drinks to keep up with the stallion. Even showed me her rope burns. I wasn't sure if she was bragging or offering me a challenge."

"Not playing this game with you, Dick," Tracy warned him.

"Suck me," Peter snarled in response, and Dean took a drink to hide his smile.

When would Peter realize the only reason Tracy kept using that old gag was because *he* kept rising to the bait so beautifully?

"Well I'm playing," Henry declared. "To make it fair, I'll go next. I know exactly what my ideal woman is like." He rolled his bottle back and forth between his palms and glanced across the table with a defiant smile. "But I don't think Dick will approve."

"Ganging up on me, I see," Peter growled. "I thought we agreed not to talk about her anymore."

Dean and Tracy looked at each other, both knowing immediately who they were referring to.

"Holly Ruskin," Dean chuckled for the first time all evening. "I haven't thought about that name in a while."

Peter and Henry had both been in love with the brilliant, vivacious Holly in college. Competed for her affection as if it were an Olympic sport. She didn't seem to mind. Dean distinctly recalled how often she encouraged the competition. For a time.

It seemed the one that got away was their fantasy. That made sense—everything came too easily to both of them. It was the challenge they loved.

"What about Dean?" Peter's voice was gruff. "Does he get a pass because we're worried about him, or are you going to tell us what kind of woman *he* secretly longs for so he can feel just as uncomfortable as the rest of us?"

The words came out of Dean's mouth before he had a chance to consider them. "Curvy redhead. Smiling green eyes. Luscious."

*She likes cinnamon on her strawberries.*

"Wow." It was Tracy's turn to laugh. "This conversation is officially interesting. Helluva lot of detail for a fantasy, my friend."

Too much detail. Too revealing. And currently impossible. "This conversation is pointless," he said restlessly. "I don't need your worry. I'm perfectly capable of handling my own affairs."

"*I* can manage my own affairs, too," Tracy agreed, "but however much I hate to admit it, Peter's right. It's time I took charge of this the same way I would anything else. Make it happen."

Peter's eyes widened. "I'm right? Did he just admit I was right?"

"Shut up, Peter. We're talking about Dean." Tracy pinned Dean with a piercing look. "About why you know what you want—sounds like *who* you want—and you're not going after her. Does the bastard finally have something on you? Ready to let us take care of him?"

"My uncle makes a play for the company following each review, but after five years he still hasn't gotten what he wants. Unless pissing me off is his only goal." Dean's laugh was hard. "As to why I'm not dropping everything to chase a momentary thrill? It's called facing reality. Henry can be a wicked rock star like his father was before him because his mother married him despite the backlash. Rebelliousness runs in his family. Peter's from old money that not even he could work his way through or scandalize his way out of in one lifetime. And you have more relatives than any of us, all of whom could pick up the slack if you let them—if you really wanted to start a family. But that's your choice. You *all* have a choice. I don't."

Peter whistled under his breath. "It's really getting under your skin isn't it? The will didn't stipulate that you *had* to be in charge of running the company, Dean. You could be traveling the world right now, taking dirty photographs, falling in love and sleeping in."

He slammed his glass down on the table. "You're right, Peter. I could have said fuck the business my grandfather built from nothing. I could have grabbed my substantial inheritance and let my uncle take the reins at any time since he refuses to sell me his shares every year. Of course, he still wants what he wanted five years ago—to break up the company like a jigsaw puzzle and ship the pieces he can't sell overseas." He swore under his breath. "Shit, I'm sorry, guys, but I don't have time to play in Fantasyland. I have rules I have to follow. Rules I don't break."

*Poor little rich boy problems.*

"Hell, man," Tracy murmured. "I shouldn't have said anything."

"Ignore me, Tracy. I'm in a rotten-ass mood."

"Like hell we'll ignore him," Peter declared. "At least he's finally opening up and getting some of that inner jackass out. That is the first step to healing, and it was very informative. We can discuss this company business later, but right now I'm more interested in the redhead." His smile was enigmatic. "She works for him. He has the hots for someone at Warren Industries. No wonder he's tense, Henry. He takes that shit seriously."

Dean shook his head. That *would* be what they took away from his rant.

"I know he does," Henry sighed. "About as seriously as he's been taking himself lately. But I think it's time for him to drop the Daddy issues and break his rule. Fuck this board bullshit. The world isn't going to end if you grab a little ass in the copy room. In fact, I think it's the only thing that will cure your current mood."

"That's your advice?" Dean scoffed. "Stick to your songs, Vincent. You suck as a therapist."

Henry shrugged. "Everyone believes that's what we do anyway. That we're spoiled deviants who use the fame and fortune at our disposal to get our way. You've been living like a hermit and following your rules and they still report your every move. I say if they're going to talk about you, you might as well give them something to talk about and get what you want in the process. Think of it as a challenge, Dean. I will if you will."

"Don't you dare," Peter warned.

"Afraid I'll find her first?"

Tracy's laugh boomed through the small private room. "Jesus, you two are dogs over that bone. What if she's taken? What if she's married and she's spent the last fifteen years having a dozen babies?"

"She hasn't," both men said in unison.

Dean was no longer paying attention. He was still too thrown by what had come out of his own mouth. They'd been friends for so long now his bitter venting hardly made a dent. What *they'd* said, however, had. They were right about him being a jackass, right that he was avoiding life beyond work. Avoiding what he really desired.

*Curvy redhead. Luscious.*

Sara Charles. The accountant on the twenty-third floor had tempted him for close to two years with a smile that always reached her eyes, full, succulent breasts that would overflow in his hands, and that sweet, delectable ass that would look even better bent over his desk.

She'd woken needs in him he thought he'd buried a long time ago. Desires that were more than most women could handle. Insatiable desires. Not pressing her against the wall of the elevator and reaching for the bounty she offered on a daily basis, or joining her in the atrium where she always had her lunch and spreading her legs to feast on her until she screamed loud enough to alert security, had been his own personal torment. A true test of his willpower and a silent testament to the fact that he was nothing like his father, who'd practically invented sexual harassment during his tenure as CEO of Warren Industries. He may be guilty of wanting someone he couldn't have, but he never acted on it.

He'd come close. So close there was a file in his desk with her name on it that he'd shamelessly requested but never opened. If he wanted to, he could find out everything about her. Where she was born, how many men she'd slept with. He could satisfy some of his curiosity and see if she was, unlike most of the women he'd dated over the last few years, what she seemed to be.

What kind of asshole would he be if he read it? If he used it to get her where he wanted her?

*The kind Ms. Anonymous readers think you are.*

Instead of succumbing to that temptation, he'd started watching the damn clock in the mornings, timing his arrival so it would coincide with hers. He tortured himself with fantasies while he soaked in her scent, occasionally giving in to harmless small talk to hear her voice until the elevator reached accounting and she left him.

He never thought he'd come to loathe the non-fraternization policy he'd implemented the day he took the job. It was the one thing that held him back from pursuing her.

That and the thought that she might not be what he'd imagined her to be. As interested in him as he was in her. As passionate as her swaying hips, rebellious curls and curious green eyes implied.

But what if she was?

Could he do what Henry advised? Break his own rule? Take a chance on dating again, one of his employees no less, and to hell with the fallout?

Dean's only other option—to maintain his personal and professional status quo indefinitely—was untenable.

Something had to give.

# CHAPTER ONE

The elevator was going *up*.

That had to be the cherry on top of the most dramatic exit Sara had executed in her thirty years on the planet.

"Well, hell." She sighed and shifted the heavy box in her arms, uncomfortably aware of the raspberry soda drying down her back. She didn't dare glance at the mirrored walls along the small moving room. It was one of *those* Fridays.

Perfect.

She could take comfort in the fact that today's events would live on in infamy at the water cooler on the twenty-third floor of Warren Industries. At least until Monday afternoon.

The Clown Catastrophe. That's what they would call it. Mainly because Terry Anne, the woman who'd worked at the desk across from her since Sara started the job two years ago, had a thing for collectibles. Specifically clowns.

Smiling clowns. Sad clowns. Bear clowns. Ballerina clowns. Scary, strange Stephen King clowns that followed you with their painted, beady eyes and plotted your demise.

Sara had seen those damn things in her sleep for years and they'd been the start of all her trouble today. Or more

18

accurately, accidentally knocking one of them on the floor with the stack of files she'd brought to her desk had started it.

She'd already been in a mood. Her day had started without its usual pick-me-up, aka the company's owner, Bossy McHotpants, joining her in the elevator. She'd spent ten floors wondering why she hadn't seen him at all this week when she knew he was in the building, and the other thirteen chiding herself for thinking about him at all.

Then she'd been passed over for the special projects spot she'd been angling for in order to escape life in the beige accountant cube, and given the workload of the two men who'd been assigned to the projects instead.

Hence the pile of files set down a little too roughly, which cracked the clown and set her own personal Rube Goldberg hell into motion.

When the collectible fell, Terry Anne had let out a scream that was impressive enough to belong in one of those late night horror movies. That terrifying noise was followed by the wail of a mother who'd just had her baby thrown out the window. She should have been an actress. And Sara, of course, was cast as the villain. Every accountant on the twenty-third floor stopped what they were doing and turned to watch the show.

Sara closed her eyes and rehashed the episode in her mind. Maybe she shouldn't have said anything about the clowns or office space or professionalism. And perhaps she should have walked away to clean up when Terry Anne had gestured defensively with her open bottle of raspberry soda and coated Sara's white blouse and neck with the sticky, sugary liquid, causing half the room to gasp with barely suppressed glee.

And yes, she definitely shouldn't have broken more of Terry Anne's collection in response while telling her that she desperately needed to get laid and stay off the Home Shopping Network. That had been a mistake.

She'd never been in a slap fight before. But when Terry Anne smacked her cheek with the palm of her hand, Sara's had come up of its own accord to pay her back in kind.

It was more satisfying than she'd ever admit out loud. Even under torture.

Their supervisor had been no help. "These things happen" was one of his favorite phrases whenever a conflict arose, and today was no different. He hadn't fired her *or* Terry Ann, despite the physical altercation. He hadn't compared all the times Sara had worked late and her consistently stellar performance reviews to the weekly complaints Terry Anne lodged against her fellow employees and all the times she was late because her cats/aunt/cousin/cousin's step uncle/favorite grocery store clerk was sick and declared Terry Anne had to go. Instead he'd offered a compromise—Terry Anne would pay to have Sara's shirt professionally cleaned and Sara would replace the missing pieces of the clown collection. They would agree not to officially file complaints, would both apologize for the things they'd said, and then they'd go back to work, better friends than before.

Her supervisor was a wuss.

And Sara couldn't do it. Oh, she could apologize, and maybe swallow her pride and go back to her desk for the day coated in pure cane sugar and raspberry food coloring…but she just couldn't replace those damn clowns. She wouldn't spend another two years feeling their accusatory stares as she hunched over her small desk across from them.

The realization made her decision easier. Despite her supervisor's panicked suggestion that giving two weeks notice would be the smart thing to do, she'd quietly found a box and packed the few personal things she kept at the office.

Fuzzy slippers to wear under her desk. A small plant so she wouldn't forget there was a world outside. A stress ball she could squeeze instead of Terry Anne's head. Her collection of postcards filled with beautiful black-and-white photography that she'd sigh over when she had lunch in the building's peaceful atrium, her second favorite part of the day.

When she carried her box toward the elevator, she'd had the sensation of being in a scene from *Norma Rae* or *Jerry Maguire*. She'd half expected a slow clap to mark her epic exit, but she shouldn't have. Accountants, as a rule, had no sense of humor. Everyone had simply watched with unblinking, mildly curious stares as she stepped inside. As the doors closed, no one even waved goodbye.

She was so busy fuming she hadn't noticed she was going up instead of down.

Thirty-three.

Thirty-four.

There were only forty-two floors in the building. When she saw the number thirty-nine light up she started to panic. Quitting her job didn't worry her, being labeled a clown killer didn't worry her...but the sudden realization that she could be on her way to *his* office, where his secretary and assistant were usually stationed like guardians at the gate? It would be weird if she *wasn't* a little tense.

She'd only been there twice. Once when she'd been sent up to personally deliver a file after her supervisor screwed up and brought the wrong statistical analysis report to a meeting, and once for the annual review—which had given her hours of good, solid drooling-over-the-boss time. In both instances, she'd been seduced by the smile of welcome she'd sworn was in Bossy's hazel eyes. She'd also managed to say something off color and inappropriate enough to earn a warning glare from the kind but formidable Mrs. Grandholm.

Sara never knew when to keep her mouth shut. It wasn't very accountant-y of her, but other than her obsession with numbers, not many things about her fit the mold. Maybe it was because she'd worked two jobs for so many years, as a waitress and then as a party host for a very lucrative sex toy manufacturer, while saving up to pay for school. Spending time with normal open-minded people gave her an affinity for things like colorful clothing, chaos and boisterous laughter. Spending evenings discussing kinky positions and demonstrating "marital aids" gave her an affinity for, and an admitted preoccupation with, sex.

Accountants hated chaos and—at least in her office— rarely mentioned the S word unless it was about who was having it with their boss.

She supposed it was a good thing she was going to miss this year's review. In five weeks another accountant would be standing between the delicious Mr. Warren and his dragon lady, and that one would probably refrain from wondering aloud who'd created the unmistakably phallic statue in the lobby, or asking for a second piece of Mrs. Grandholm's triple fudge decadence, which she'd brought for the review, because it tasted "like warm, rich make up sex in her mouth."

She adjusted her box so she could hold it in one arm while trying to straighten her stained, clinging shirt with her free hand—but it was pointless. She was a mess. And, unlike every other time she'd gotten on the elevator since the day she began working for the company, *up* was the last direction she wanted to go and *he* was the last person she wanted to see. Not when she looked like this.

Dean Warren was the "he" in question, otherwise known as Bossy McHotpants. He was the second-generation billionaire, philanthropist and walking sex god of all of her wildest, raunchiest fantasies. The first time she'd seen him step into the elevator, she'd had the sensation of falling.

He was clearly as out of her league as he was out of her tax bracket. Men who looked as if they'd stepped out of a GQ magazine rarely went out with anything less than a Victoria's Secret or the Sports Illustrated Swimsuit Edition—and Sara didn't rank any higher than the TV

Guide.

She could have sworn that once or twice she'd seen something in his expression that reminded her of interest. Desire. But even if she had, as the owner of the company, he was off limits as well. Officially and unequivocally forbidden.

It was a trigger word for her. Anybody who knew Sara knew that, while she had some wonderful qualities, she had a hard time resisting a dare, keeping her thoughts to herself and staying away from things that were forbidden. But she was a professional. About this anyway. Even if it weren't against company policy, it was a personal line she'd always promised herself she wouldn't cross.

*Don't lie. If he offered, you would cross it in a second, and you'd be naked while twirling flaming batons and singing the national anthem.*

Dean Warren was the signature at the bottom of her paychecks, she reminded herself firmly, ignoring the graphic image. And now, he wasn't even that. If his wickedly talented and sadly imaginary doppelganger visited her in the shower until the hot water ran out, or slipped under the covers with her to personally deliver her monthly bonus until she begged for mercy... Well, that was between her and her overworked vibrator. Oh, and her other new favorite toy— the one that had been worth the week's worth of groceries she'd paid for it to take some of the pressure off her old faithful.

Just thinking about that oral sex simulating gadget made her squirm, now in even more of a hurry to get home than before. It was exactly what she needed to forget this day. She would spend the weekend with it, extra batteries and her favorite ice cream, putting herself into a self-induced sugar/climax coma. And now that she had time, she might take her friends up on their repeated offers to go out dancing. She needed an outlet for all this career-enforced sexual repression. In other words, she needed the S word.

She shifted again and it was one time too many. A stream of swear words started escaping from between her lips as the bottom of her box opened up and everything in it landed on her feet. "Fuck." She dropped to her knees, her skirt tightening around her thighs as she lunged for her stress ball and scooped up a handful of dirt from the potted plant. "Son of a dog, mother fucking bit—"

*Ding.*

Don't let him be there, she silently begged the universe. I'll never kill a clown again.

Sara looked up and sighed in relief as the doors opened on the forty-first floor. In the space of a racing heartbeat she noted the fact that the front desk was unmanned and no one was waiting to step in. That was strange. Good but strange. Could she be this lucky? Or did someone up there just really love porcelain figurines?

And then she saw Mrs. Grandholm walking out of his office, Mr. Warren right beside her.

Nope. The universe hated clowns as much as she did.

The doors started to close and Sara willed them to move faster, giving her the ride down to stuff her things back into the wilting box and retain what was left of her pride.

He looked up suddenly and shattered her hopes with three words. "Hold the elevator!"

Office manners too deeply ingrained to resist, she put out her free hand and stopped the doors from closing. She closed her eyes and tried to slow her breathing. She could do this. It was just like any other day she had to share the elevator with the sexiest tycoon alive.

Sure it was.

Mrs. Grandholm's voice sounded closer and seemed to agree with her silent sarcasm. "Ms. Charles? What on earth are you doing on the floor? And *what* happened to your blouse?"

She felt him kneel beside her. She hadn't opened her eyes but she knew it was him because of the way he smelled.

Delicious. Memories of all the times she'd stood behind the lean, six-foot-two CEO when the elevator was full filled her mind. While she enjoyed those rare moments when it was just the two of them and he'd say good morning or ask about the weather, she had to admit she liked a full elevator even better. She didn't get to hear his sensual baritone, but if it was crowded, she'd move closer to him than she would ever dare if they were alone. How many times had she leaned in and breathed in that clean scent that reminded her of the forest and sex and him?

And sex *with* him in the forest...or anywhere he wanted.

God, she was a stalker in the making. She needed to rein in her imagination and inappropriately overactive libido.

"Ms. Charles?" His voice was low, deep, soothing and sexual at the same time. Concerned. "Can you open your eyes? Are you hurt?"

She opened her eyes, embarrassment tightening her throat. She could open her eyes—she'd just been hoping she wouldn't have to. "I'm not hurt, sir, I was just saying a few last words over the box. I'm not sure he'll ever recover, but I hear he was old and lived a full life."

He laughed and she found herself riveted to his sparkling hazel eyes. She hadn't realized there were so many flecks of gold mixed in with the brown and green. Or that his laugh would make her think of sex again.

*Big surprise.*

His gaze lowered to her lips. "Do you need any help?"

Mrs. Grandholm made a noise of frustration. "Of course she needs help, Dean Warren. She's on the floor covered in dirt and...what *are* you covered in, dear?"

"Raspberry soda, Mrs. Grandholm," she mumbled, wishing she could disappear. "And shame," she added in a whisper to herself.

Mr. Warren laughed softly again as he grabbed a handful of dirt and one of her fuzzy slippers. He'd heard her. "Will you tell us what happened or should we guess?"

The phone rang at the secretary's desk and Mrs. Grandholm turned and headed away from them to answer it. Sara bit her lip. "I made the wrong turn in the elevator. I was trying to get to the parking garage. Now Mindy will hate me for leaving dirt all over her perfect floor."

"Mindy?"

"Mindy is the reason your lobby, bathrooms and elevators are always so shiny. And don't try bribing her with chocolate. She'll never tell you her secret."

He nodded absently, staring at her postcards. "So you're leaving early then? Big plans for the weekend?"

She couldn't help but notice that his some of his hair had fallen onto his forehead, making him look younger. Touchable. The golden strands seemed so soft, she wanted to reach up and brush them back. To tangle her fingers in it and pull him closer.

Instead she forced out a chuckle. "No, sir. My only plan is to run into as few people as possible until I can strip naked and shower. I think I have raspberry soda in my cleavage."

She probably could have worded that differently, she thought when she saw his jaw tighten. He didn't want to hear about her cleavage. "As Mrs. Grandholm pointed out, I'm a mess."

"*What* about clowns?" The secretary raised her voice and Sara flinched. "Well have security escort her out." She paused. "The building isn't that big. Find her. She's an accountant not a child, and these things simply do *not* happen at Warren Industries. Not on my watch."

Security? *Find her?* Shit. "Mr. Warren, I appreciate your help, but if you could just wait for the next elevator…I *really* need to get to my car."

Bossy McHotpants, who'd been listening to his secretary as well, turned his head to snare her gaze. "What exactly did you do today, Ms. Charles?"

She sent him a pleading look. "Nothing illegal, I swear. I just…I quit."

"You quit?" He stared at her for what felt like an eternity. "Mrs. Grandholm?" he spoke without taking his eyes off Sara. "I'm going up and I don't wish to be disturbed for the rest of the afternoon."

His secretary covered the phone with her hand and nodded distractedly. "Of course, Mr. Warren." Then her voice hardened when she returned to her call. "Young man, you do not want me to come down there. I'm old, my feet hurt and I can't promise not to send you packing as well."

Sara watched as the man she'd just been daydreaming about stood, allowing the doors to close while opening a small panel on the bottom and punching in a code.

There was only one reason to do that. The forty second floor. Employees weren't allowed in his private suite. It was…well, it was private.

"Mr. Warren, don't let me keep you from wherever it was you were going. I assure you I didn't do anything wrong." Her voice was breathless. "Nothing that security needs to be concerned about. Not really. At least, I didn't start it."

Had Terry Anne decided to press charges as soon as she left?

"Can I help you off the floor, Ms. Charles? That can't be comfortable."

He held out his hand without acknowledging her comments and she shook her head ruefully at his cool. "Have you ever been embarrassed, sir? In your life?"

A cynical smile hardened his handsome features momentarily. "Don't you read the tabloids?"

The door opened with a soft whoosh and Sara struggled to her feet without him, clutching her plant and the remnants of the box to her chest. "I meant fly undone, food in your teeth, raspberry soda and plant parts all over you in front of your boss embarrassed. It's not the same thing as an article expounding on your limitless sexual prowess, no offense."

He took the box from her, his lips twitching subtly. "I suppose it isn't. Come inside." He headed into the penthouse without waiting to see if she'd follow.

She held the doors open and swallowed hard. "I'd rather not."

*...if I'm going to be arrested,* was how she wanted to finish that sentence. She barely held her tongue.

He looked over his shoulder as he set the mess of box on his glass coffee table in front of the oversized black leather couch. "I'm surprised, Ms. Charles. You never struck me as a woman who's easily intimidated. Or prone to criminal activities."

"Oh, I can be intimidated," she corrected him. "And wary of most law enforcement, though I've never even gotten a parking ticket and my cousin's husband is a..." She noticed him smiling and stepped inside, all too aware of the elevator closing behind her with a disturbing finality. "I *am* guilty of talking too much when I'm nervous. I suppose you could arrest me for that."

"There's nothing for you to be nervous about. I have no intention of calling security. At the moment. We're reasonable adults, you and I, and I believe we can discover the truth and deal with this situation on our own."

What did *that* mean? Did he actually think her leaving in such a hurry had to do with her duties in accounting? Maybe. She was acting like a guilty party of one, mostly due to embarrassment. But she'd rather be embarrassed than have him think she was capable of something criminal. "This situation consists of a girl on girl slap fight, some spilled soda and a clown fetish. It has nothing to do with my job performance at Warren Industries. Does that satisfy your reasonable curiosity, sir?"

"Hardly." When he headed to the kitchen, she found herself momentarily distracted by the beautiful wall of windows that gave her a view of the entire city. Her fantasies would now have the perfect backdrop. She could easily imagine Dean Warren pressing her against the glass, lifting her skirt and taking her like a man possessed while she moaned and begged for more.

A shiver raced through her.

She should turn around and go home before she asked him the question that instantly came to mind. *How sturdy are those windows, Mr. Warren? Want to get naked and test them out?*

She was a brazen harlot…an archaic terminology, but she preferred it to dirty whore. She needed to get out of this situation as soon as possible.

He was walking toward her again, a glass full of amber liquid in his hand. "Drink, Ms. Charles, and tell me about this girl fight of yours. I regret having missed it. Start from the beginning."

She took the glass, lifting it to her lips because, what the hell, she needed a drink. The whiskey burned her throat and sent a tingling warmth through her limbs. The good stuff. How could it be anything else? "I…it's not really an interesting story, Mr. Warren."

"Not to disagree, but I'm already fascinated. Indulge me, Sara. Why now? Why this week? What changed?"

She studied him over the rim of her glass. He was more than curious. What did he care about one accountant on one floor he'd rarely set foot in? And what reason could she give him when there were so many? Today was the last straw, but she'd been dreaming about leaving for a while.

"Nothing changed," she answered instead. "It was time for a new challenge."

"A challenge? Interesting choice of words." He licked his full lower lip and stepped closer, so close she could feel the heat coming off of his body. "You're not going to admit it easily, are you?"

She frowned at the way he'd worded that. "Admit what?"

Dean Warren sent her a look so heated that Sara felt like she might have a stroke, then he left her, walking around her and toward the hallway. She turned to watch him walk away, admiring his long stride and the lean muscles flexing beneath his gray pants.

He didn't have a body that belonged in an office. Though his suits had obviously been tailored to perfection, she never thought they were right for him. It was a tragedy to button and tie that much man. She'd seen a picture of him in the tabloids once, taken at a hotel pool as he was getting out after a morning swim in nothing but a pair of short, wet swim trunks. She'd felt dirty and cheap and a little disloyal as an employee when she purchased it in the checkout line, but she couldn't resist the impulse. She'd needed a longer look at those abs.

He raised his voice so she could hear him from wherever he'd disappeared to and she jumped guiltily. "Let me get you a shirt to change into. After your shower, you'll want to be comfortable."

Her shower? What? "Sir? I thought—"

He reappeared, a white t-shirt bunched in one hand, his other loosening his tie. "That you were going to wash up, slip into this while your clothes were being cleaned and eat the early dinner I'll be ordering for us to make up for the late lunch I wanted to skip anyway? I'm glad we're on the same page."

So he wasn't calling security and he wasn't upset that she was quitting… He was inviting her to eat with him and telling her to take off her clothes?

Maybe Terry Anne had knocked her unconscious and she was dreaming on her way to the hospital.

He took the glass out of her hand, setting it down on the table before wrapping his fingers around her wrist—gently but firmly—and guiding her to the bathroom door. This was no dream. Electric sparks of awareness were traveling from his hand up her arm and spreading throughout her body. The man packed a punch.

"Mr. Warren?"

"Dean." He pushed open a door in the hallway and handed her the shirt. "If I'm not your boss anymore, Sara, you can call me Dean."

She wasn't sure she could.

But her day *had* been horrible and now one of the hottest men she'd ever seen in real life was demanding she get naked…not in the way she would've liked him to, but it still counted as a highlight.

"Thank you…Dean."

He placed his palm on her lower back, gently nudging her inside the room. "The towels are on the top shelf and I'll be here if you need anything."

His words were completely innocent, but they made Sara's thighs tremble anyway. She could think of a million things she needed from him. None of them acceptable for polite conversation.

She stepped inside and he closed the door behind her with a silent groan. This was *not* how she'd expected the rest of her day to go. A long ride through afternoon traffic, her shirt sticky and clinging to her skin in a continuous reminder of the day's events, was more what she'd had in mind. Instead, she was standing in the lavish penthouse bathroom, gratefully wriggling out of her straight-off-the-sales-rack skirt and blouse to use his shower.

Dean Warren's shower.

Sara turned the faucet and dared a glance in the mirror while the water heated. She couldn't stop the momentary grimace. She looked exactly the way she felt—done to the point of overcooked. Her loud, curly red hair, usually restrained with pins in a professional chignon, was a mass of loose strands coiling damply around her flushed face. Her lipstick had been worried off hours ago and her body…well, it was still there in all its abundant glory.

On a good day she'd call herself lush. Large hipped and big breasted and…healthy. Nothing like any of the women she'd seen on the arm of McHotpants in the tabloids, but she had her moments.

Sara didn't hate her body. Far from it. She didn't starve

herself—if she had a craving she indulged it—but she also went to yoga twice a week and rode her bike in the park every weekend the weather allowed. She knew herself and had no illusions that she would ever be one of those airbrushed Vogue models. But she was aware that she could stand to lose a few pounds before she felt comfortable in a bikini. Or naked in front of a man like Dean.

It was temporary vanity or insanity that she was even thinking about her figure right now. He wasn't going to see her naked. He was a good man who didn't want someone leaving his building looking like this.

*He was ordering her dinner.*

She shook her head as she peeled off her damp bra. A *very* good, very thorough man who may or may not still suspect her of nefarious accounting activities. And she definitely needed to scrub her breasts. They were covered. "Lovely."

She dropped the sticky restraint in a heap on the tile floor and studied herself in the mirror. These, at least, she was proud of. They hadn't lost their fight with gravity, despite their impressive size. Had Dean noticed them when he studied her stained blouse?

He usually dated slender brunettes with decidedly smaller cup sizes. Would he enjoy the chance to fill his hands with more?

She cupped them and shivered, imagining his hot, large hands on her instead. Imagining that this was *exactly* what he wanted. Her fingers squeezed her nipples and Sara gasped, feeling the rise of her arousal and knowing it was his proximity that was turning her on. The idea that he could open the bathroom door at any time and see her standing naked in front of the mirror, touching herself.

A man like that would never apologize and close the door, swearing he hadn't seen anything. A man like that would come closer. Watch her. Join her.

It was her darkest fantasy. Being caught. Being seen. It

was too tempting a moment for her to resist. She'd already been thinking about him, and when would she ever be this close again? Get another chance to do something so erotic and forbidden right under his nose?

She squeezed one nipple hard, her other hand dropping between her legs to caress the wet lips of her sex. In her mind Dean Warren was behind her, unzipping his perfectly pressed pants and bending her over the sink as he watched her reaction in the mirror.

He was too far gone for foreplay, and he slipped two thick fingers inside her, readying her for more, for all of him. She moaned softly. *Yes. Yes, I'm ready now. I've been ready. Please, Mr. Warren, fu—*

"Sara?" His voice filtered through the door and her fingers stilled, her eyes opening wide to stare at her flushed face in the mirror. "I've set a pair of sweatpants outside the door and the food is on its way. Also, I realize that last drink might have been too strong for you to enjoy. What's your pleasure?"

*Your fingers inside me. Your tongue. Your...oh, yes. Yes, like that.* "Yes...umm, are you sure about dinner?" She knew she sounded out of breath, but she couldn't help it. His voice so close it was making her crazy. She started to touch herself again, leaning against the sink while she pressed and rubbed on her clit and bit back a groan, marveling at her shamelessness. "You don't have to go to any tro...oh...trouble."

He was silent for a few, desperate heartbeats. Oh God. Was it her imagination that made her think he knew what she was doing? Knew she was naked and touching herself?

"No trouble, Sara." Was his voice deeper now? "What can I get you?"

"I'm easy...I mean, whatever you're having is fine, thank you, sir. *Dean.*"

*Thank you, sir. Yes, sir. Fuck me, sir!*

She wanted him to see her. All she had to do was call out

to him and he would open the door to watch her as she touched herself, widening her stance and going deeper, faster, her fingers sending zaps of desire up her spine as she let the fantasy continue. His hazel eyes would demand she lift her breast to her mouth and lick her nipple while he watched. Demand she touch herself until she came.

*Now, Sara. Indulge me.*

She shuddered as a small ripple of pleasure swept through her body. *Not enough*, her greedy body whispered. *Not as good as it could be with him.*

The instant that thought began to fade, sanity crept in and she dropped her hands. What was she doing?

Diddling herself in a billionaire's bathroom.

She groaned, lowering her chin to her chest. He was being a gentleman and she was starring in her own private porno.

Granted, he seemed disturbed and overly interested in her choice to leave the company, but he'd still gone out of his way to help her in her distress. The last thing he needed was her throwing her sticky flesh against his expensive suit and demanding sex instead of a severance package.

Dinner in his penthouse wearing sweatpants. That would have to be good enough.

She stepped into the shower and turned off the hot water, gritting her teeth at the icy spray and trying to think about clowns.

Did men actually do this? It didn't help at all.

## CHAPTER TWO

He wanted her naked. Now.

As soon as she admitted the truth, Dean promised himself, he was going to get her undressed and see if he could work this sudden insanity out of his system. It was only fair since she had been the one to cause it. The way she looked in his shirt…

He barely managed to suppress an impatient growl as he watched her across the glass coffee table. He'd always believed he enjoyed a woman in sexy lingerie best—lace and ribbons he could tear with his teeth—but Sara Charles was fast changing his mind. The sexiest clothing on this woman was his.

His vee neck cotton shirt was long on her, but it strained against her heavy breasts, giving him shadowed glimpses of her lickable nipples when she brushed her long, glorious auburn curls back over her shoulders. His sweatpants were rolled up to her calves, drowning her in fabric, but there was no hiding her tempting body. Not from him.

It was hell not touching her when she was this close, so difficult resisting her when she looked so warm and approachable that he'd made sure to sit in the chair across from the couch she'd settled on after dinner. It wasn't helping to temper his desire. Neither was the several hours he'd spent plying her with small talk, his favorite Chinese takeout and whiskey.

After all this time, Sara was in his clothes, on his couch and—because of him—a quarter past tipsy. The sun had set and she hadn't noticed. Her box had been cleaned up and set into a sturdy bag by the door. He'd changed into a t-shirt and a pair of sweatpants as well, the only clothing he kept here for comfort's sake or when he needed to work out and work off some steam. Her clothes were dry, folded and waiting for her on his bed, and she could leave whenever she liked, but he wasn't going to be the one to remind her. Not when he finally had her where he wanted her.

It was the reason she was here that was eluding him and making him a little crazed. He'd phoned his secretary while Sara was in the shower to confirm her story. There were several witnesses to the altercation, too many for him to doubt. Mrs. Grandholm assured him that it was the other woman who'd gone around the bend about her clowns, and that Sara Charles had indeed quit without giving notice. So she was telling the truth about what happened. And the result—that she no longer worked for him.

The timing was beyond suspicious, there was no getting around that—the odds weren't something he could explain away—but that didn't stop Dean from enjoying her voice or the scene Sara was currently describing in humorous detail.

"You told her to get *laid*?"

She covered her mouth with her hand, her eyes bright with laughter. "I can't believe I'm admitting this, and I'm awful, I know. It just came out. And her hand just came up."

His knuckles tightened in reflex. "That was inexcusable."

"No it wasn't. No one responds well to that kind of insult, and to be honest I'm not even one to talk in that department. Lately I've only had enough energy to crawl back to my apartment and curl up with…" Her cheeks flushed. "Let's just say there's been a drought and I plan to enjoy my month off making it rain."

"I know exactly what you mean."

Sara sent him a disbelieving look. "I doubt that. I hear the weather is pretty active in Warrenland all year round."

"I meant about working too hard," he improvised quickly.

*She doesn't work for you anymore.*

It kept repeating in his head, taunting him, tempting him. She'd taken his only obstacle out of the way. And the way she was talking, almost flirtatiously, making it all seem so easy. Too easy. Damn it. "As to the other, you'd be surprised. As surprised as I am that this squabble made you decide to leave us when you don't seem that upset. Was that the only reason?"

*I plan to enjoy my month off.*

She took another sip of her whiskey and licked her lips, clearly savoring the flavor as she nodded. He could easily become obsessed with that mouth. Bow shaped lips that were more often smiling than not. He wanted to be the reason she smiled. Wanted to feel those lips on his skin.

"Why a month, specifically? Did you win the lottery, Ms. Charles? Are you selling secrets to my competition or going back to an old job?"

"My old job might have had a few more laughs, but it didn't have comprehensive insurance benefits...and you have no competition." She shook her head, her adorable smile making him shift in his chair to hide his reaction. . "Even if you did, I promise I would resist them to take this vacation. I've been putting together my fun fund for a while now and it is time to use it. Lately I've been spending my lunch breaks fantasizing about tropical islands and long, deep tissue massages."

"I've been told I'm something of an expert at deep tissue massage." Why had he said that?

*Don't let her distract you.*

"I've heard that about you too." Sara's green eyes

widened as if she'd surprised herself, but she didn't look away. "That is, I've heard you have a wide variety of unexpected skills. Hobbies. It's good to have hobbies. I'm a fan of yoga, myself. It's a good way to stay flexible when you spend so many hours behind a desk, though I wish they'd rename a few of the positions. Downward Facing Dog for example. Not the image you want in your head when your behind is pointing to the sky. Please say something, Mr. Warren, so I can stop digging this hole."

"Why, when I'm enjoying it so much?" Dean shook his head, unable to resist responding with a tight smile though adrenaline raced through his veins as he readied himself for the truth. "No reason for you to deny it, Sara. What people say about me. I imagine you've heard a lot. Anytime my assistant wants to know what my employees are talking about, he visits the twenty-third floor. Most of the rumors aren't true."

She pointed at him sternly. "Don't ruin the illusion, Mr. Warren. For some people in this building, your exploits—real or not—are the only light in their otherwise gloomy and boring existence."

"Dean, remember? What else have you heard about me, Sara? Anything recently? Perhaps something that helped you take that extra step during today's 'Clown Catastrophe'? Something that led you to believe you had other options?"

Sara set her drink down with a regretful smile. "And the fantasy ends," she muttered softly, before getting to her feet. "I really enjoyed the dinner, Mr. Warren, and your generosity."

Dean stood up quickly. "Surely you don't have to go yet."

She blinked. "I think it's possible whiskey isn't my drink after all, but I can pick up my car in the morning. It's time for me to call a cab, name it pumpkin and get myself home before midnight."

Before he knew what he was doing he was standing

beside her, his hands firmly on her shoulders. He didn't want her to leave. "Where's the fire, Cinderella? Don't want to answer my question?"

She lifted one slender reddish-brown eyebrow. "You haven't asked one. Not the one you want to. I don't do subtle, sir. You've obviously been waiting for something since I got here, and nothing I've said has satisfied you. I'm an open book, but you have to actually ask me. Otherwise, I'll say goodbye, no harm done."

This wasn't what he wanted. He hadn't thought about her leaving at all. He'd had a plan, damn it, or most of one. One he was certain he could have put in motion in a few weeks and he didn't like thinking she'd had help in making that plan moot.

"You don't do subtle? I can appreciate that, Ms. Charles, if *you* can accept that I don't do coincidence. In my experience it doesn't exist. Maybe I'm off base, but I find it odd that less than a week after a Ms. Anonymous article on fantasies leads me to share personal information with a small group of interfering friends, you show up happily unemployed, inviting and receptive and practically naked in my living room."

"*You* brought me here, and the only parts of me that are naked are my feet." Sara's expression conveyed utter confusion. "I guess I had more to drink than I thought because I have no idea what you just said. What information? What friends? What does it have to do with me?"

Dean could see her confusion, but he couldn't allow himself to trust it. And his frustration made it impossible for him to let it go. "You know what's funny? I'd already decided they might be right about my rules. Already decided to come after you on my own. But one of them must have gotten to you first and offered you something in exchange for fulfilling my fantasy. Because they're *worried about me* and God knows I'm not capable of getting what I want without their help."

"Hold the phone, buddy." She pushed away from him and crinkled her forehead in confused disbelief. "Am I hearing you right? You talked about me to your friends? *Me?* I would be flattered if it wasn't for the intimation that I agreed to quit my job so I could throw myself at you without company policy standing in my way. That you think I took something in exchange for... I never believed the bad press, but is that some kind of game the four of you play? Do you and your *friends* do that for each other a lot? Bribe women to date you? Procure each other's sex partners?"

Dean flinched. The way she'd laid it out sounded tawdry. Beneath her.

She had no idea what he was talking about.

"I apologize, Ms. Charles." His jaw was so tight it was difficult to get the words out. His mind was too busy racing to find a way to take his accusations back. "I haven't been the best judge of—I came to the wrong conclusions..."

"Oh, no." She scoffed at his choice of words. "You came to *epically* wrong conclusions, Mr. Warren and you are a *horrible* judge of character. Who even thinks like that? You've been dating the wrong kind of women, Bossy McHotpants, if you haven't been cold-cocked for talking that kind of trash."

He'd definitely been dating the wrong kind of women, but they'd been the ones who taught him not to trust what he saw.

Bossy McHotpants?

Did she think he was hot?

She turned away from him but stopped herself, whirling back around, her chin high. "And, by the way, if I *had* been coming up to your office to seduce you? I wouldn't have done it covered in soda and looking pathetic to get you to feel sorry for me. You would have known right away what I wanted and I doubt you'd have been able to refuse. I told you, I don't do subtle. Thank heaven I resisted the temptation."

"Were you tempted, Sara?" The question escaped before he had the chance to stop himself.

Sara looked at him sideways before turning around again and heading down the hall to the bedroom. "Like I'm going to tell you now."

"Shit," he hissed, following her because he couldn't help himself. She'd just been so... Close. Beautiful. Sexy. He swore again. "There's no excuse for my behavior or the way I spoke to you, but I can't let you call a cab. Please allow me to take you home, Ms. Charles. It's the least I can do."

For being such an arrogant prick.

She picked her bra up from the top of her pile of clothes, refusing to look into his eyes. "I'm perfectly capable of getting myself home. And making my own decisions. Also paying my own way and seducing my own sex partners, in case you were wondering. Now if you'll excuse me, I'm going to change."

He didn't leave. Couldn't. "Sara, I wish you would let me... What do you think you're doing?"

She'd lifted the shirt over her head and dropped it on the bed, giving him an unexpected view of her breasts. They were without question the most beautiful breasts he'd ever seen. Full and firm and flawless.

*Jesus Fucking Christ.*

They made his mouth water, made him weak in the knees. He could happily spend the rest of his life exploring every curve and slope and die a happy man buried between them.

She clasped the hooks of her bra, spun it around and slipped the straps over her shoulders, taking away his short glimpse of paradise.

"I think I'm getting dressed."

*Showing you what you can't have. Making all the blood rush to your cock so fast your head spins.*

She was right. She didn't do subtle. She was magnificent

and fearless when she was being righteous. Irresistible. God, he wanted those breasts in his mouth more than he wanted to breathe. Wanted to hold their weight in his hands and kiss her until she forgot the last five minutes completely. Would she show him everything, strip down completely so he'd know all he'd lost when she disappeared from his life?

"A month ago," he said, his throat raw with need as he watched her slowly buttoning up her blouse, hiding the creamy flesh completely. "It was a Monday, I think. It had rained and you came running into the elevator laughing at something a security guard had said, soaking wet because you hadn't brought a coat or umbrella."

Sara paused on the third button. "That would be Andrew. He's the funny one with the beard."

"Your hair was in a braid falling down your back," he continued softly. "And when you turned to make room for the other woman who followed you in, I could see those hard pink nipples through your clinging ivory blouse and bra."

She gasped, looking up at him, her green eyes darkening with surprise and desire.

Dean kept talking. "I spent the rest of the day reliving the morning. Changing how it ended it my mind. I'd be a gentleman and take off my jacket to cover you up. I'd come up with an excuse to get you in my office so I could seduce you and strip you and find out if you tasted as good as you looked. Then I imagined you on your knees in the elevator, your braid wrapped around my fist as I came."

"Stop." She didn't sound like she wanted him to.

"Why, Sara?" He shrugged, feeling frayed around the edges. "I thought I owed you some unsubtle honesty. I've already made a fool of myself. Already ruined whatever good impression you had of me. You no longer work for me, so why not go all the way and tell you what I think about whenever I see you? Why it's so hard for me to believe you could be here. Politically correct or not."

"What do you think about?"

Dean's smile was tight with restraint. "Sex. No matter what I'm doing or how bad my day has been, no matter how professional I need to be or how good the weather in *Warrenland* is, I see you and all of that falls away. I see you and every thought in my head centers on what I want to do to you. All the ways and positions and number of times I could have you until you'd had enough. It's not something I ever thought I'd admit to, I can't explain it and it damn sure isn't something I'm proud of, but I can't deny it's there."

"Ah… Oh."

"Yes," he answered wryly. "Oh. And in a weak fucking moment when Henry and the others asked me what I wanted, it slipped out. Despite my rules, despite my decision to focus on work, despite my knowledge that they would never let it lie…I described you."

She continued buttoning, biting her lip. "And you say you were planning on asking me out, but then you thought they'd—"

"Don't say it again," he interrupted, rubbing the back of his neck in frustration. "I hate myself enough as it is. I spent this week avoiding you in the elevator so I could be clear-headed enough to find the right way to approach you that didn't make me come off like a sexual predator."

She was watching him from under her thick lashes. "What did you decide on?"

"Does it matter?" Dean grimaced. "An early lunch to discuss the annual review was my best possibility, but I wasn't sure how much control I'd have if I got you alone."

He watched as she wriggled into her skirt, still wearing the sweatpants until she was covered and could drop them on the floor.

She was leaving.

He deserved it.

"Mr. Warren? Is the offer to drive me home still good?"

Anything if it meant more time to redeem himself. "Of course. Let me get my shoes and keys and I'll take you home."

She didn't say a word as they stood in the elevator, watching the numbers for each floor light up and disappear. Her arms were crossed over her chest almost protectively. Was she thinking about what he'd said? Was she afraid of him now?

With that thought, his arousal was replaced with pure regret. Other than the suspicion he'd been unable to shake all evening, he'd genuinely enjoyed her company. She was funny and smart and...Henry was right. He wasn't doing fine. He'd lost his ability to read people. To trust that someone could just want to spend time with him, want *him* and not what he was or had or could do for them.

When had that happened? When had he become that man?

They arrived in the parking garage and a driver who'd been leaning against a column talking to one of the night security guards straightened and stopped them. "Mr. Warren?"

"Yes?"

"Mr. Vincent wanted me to inform you that he's borrowed your car for some competition he's in with Mr. Faraday. He left me to take you wherever you want to go until he brings it back, sir."

Dean scowled. Damn it, he should never have given Henry a spare set of keys. "He did, huh?"

The man's pleasant smile disappeared. "He was sure you wouldn't mind."

"He was sure?" Dean didn't want to think about what Henry and Peter were up to. He had too much on his own plate at the moment. "That's fine..."

"Roy, sir."

"That's fine, Roy." He glanced at Sara when Roy disappeared to get Henry's ride. "How do you feel about Hummers?"

She looked away from him quickly and Dean saw the

restrained laughter in the young security guard's face as she met his gaze instead. "Don't get me in trouble, Ms. Charles," the man warned lightly.

"Sorry, Bruce," was her muffled response.

The guard sent a respectful nod to Dean before he started walking down the rows, obviously eager to be out of the owner's sight.

"Are you and *Bruce* laughing at me, Sara?" Dean murmured, marveling at the interaction. She knew the people who worked in his building better than he did. "Why, I wonder?"

Her shoulders were shaking. "I can't. If you don't…no, I can't."

The amusement was infectious. "I suppose it isn't a question you hear every day."

She turned her head to glance at him quickly, then watched as the long, Hummer limousine pulled up in front of them. "Not once since high school, no."

Dean bit the inside of his cheek as Roy opened the door and helped Sara inside. "Henry has a thing for Hummers, doesn't he, Roy? He gets one in every city. Likes the feel of them. Says he couldn't live without them."

Roy closed the door and Sara started laughing uncontrollably, tears running down her cheeks. "I know," she gasped, wiping her face. "Juvenile, I know. I just can't help myself."

Dean smiled at her. "I'm glad. You have a beautiful laugh, Sara."

Roy rolled down the smoky dividing glass enough to ask where they were going and Sara gave him her address. Then they were alone again and Dean glanced around Henry's ride. His old friend had learned to embrace the clichés.

This limo could fit half a nightclub. When the neon blue lights that lined the ceiling turned on as the car began to move and the music started pounding through the speakers, Dean thought maybe it *was* a damn nightclub. The idiot could have gotten his own car, he grumbled to himself. He just wanted to mess with Dean and force him to ride home in this strip club on wheels.

He leaned toward Sara. "I'm sorry, this is a little over the top, even for Henry. Hang on, I'll turn it down."

Sara placed her hand on his knee stopping him cold. She shook her head. "I like it."

He tried not to show his disappointment. He'd been hoping to use the drive home to convince her to have lunch tomorrow in a public place where he couldn't say anything offensive. That couldn't happen with this thrumming drumbeat. Damn Henry.

Sara pressed her lips against his ear and he closed his eyes in surprised pleasure. "I appreciated your honesty upstairs, Mr. Warren. I want you to know I wasn't lying about my fun fund. I've been saving it since I was sixteen. Set a little bit aside, even when I was paying for college, because I knew there would be a time when I wanted something frivolous, like a pair of designer shoes or a cruise to Hawaii, and I wanted to be able to give it to myself."

Dean nodded his understanding. There weren't enough synonyms for asshole as far as he was concerned. Or enough ways to express his regret.

"Also," she continued, leaning into him so Dean could feel her breasts against his arm. "You should know that if someone had tried to bribe or cajole me into quitting my job, even if it were Henry Vincent himself—or that handsome Mr. Reyes—I would have either reported them or cut off something they would need at a later date. It would be wrong, whether they were doing it with the best intentions or not. Even if it was something I desperately wanted."

She was fantastic. Sexy and honest, full of fire and laughter and...Lord help him but her body felt good against his. "You think Tracy's handsome?"

"Every woman with a pulse thinks he's handsome." She hesitated before raising her voice enough to be heard. "I was insulted that you doubted my character, but you don't know me that well. To be fair, since it would be hypocritical of me not to be as honest as you were—what you said you think about? What you imagined doing with me? You could have been describing my fantasies."

Dean pulled back to look at her, needing to make certain there were no more misunderstandings. That she was saying what he thought she was.

Sara got up on her knees and started lifting her snug skirt. "You hid it well, so well that to say I'm surprised would be an understatement. But I was hiding something to. When I said you'd know right away if I wanted to seduce you, it's because I've imagined doing it before. *Many* times."

He didn't move. Didn't dare. This was one fantasy that could slip away at any moment. One he could ruin with a word. He bared his teeth, hissing out a breath when she straddled his hips on the long leather seat and lowered herself onto his lap. He couldn't hold back the groan when she leaned into him, her cheek pressed against his.

"Do you mind?"

"God, no."

"Good. Don't think I'm letting you get off easy." She laughed and he felt the joy in it on his skin. "I might be, but I don't want you to think I'm a pushover, and I'm still not sure if I'm more insulted or intrigued to know you thought someone giftwrapped me and sent me up for you to play with."

*Jesus.* The visual of her in nothing but red ribbon binding her hands and feet made his cock pulse, and he knew she could feel it against her blue silk panties, the same pair he'd smoothed his fingers over while folding them.

He wanted to touch them now. "Sara."

"You're a very confusing man, Mr. Warren," she sighed, her fingers curling into his shoulders and her hips beginning to rock against his lightly. Teasing him. "Kind one minute, rude the next, and then you say something like…*mmm*…like that, and it's all I can think about. I can't believe I'm doing it, but it feels so much better than I imagined it would. Which is saying a lot."

God help him it did.

"What can I do to make it up to you?" he rasped, his whole body focused on the motion of her hips. "Tell me and it's yours."

"I need more," she mumbled as though she were talking to herself. "I want to feel more of you."

"So torture then." Dean unclenched the fists that he'd been holding at his sides and reached for the elastic of his sweatpants, lifting them both up as he pushed the fabric down to his thighs.

Sara stiffened and he gripped her hips with his hands. "Nothing else. Just this. Just what you asked for." He guided her against his erection, grunting as the hot, wet silk slid across his shaft. "Do you feel me now, Sara? Is this what you need?"

She looked down at him, her breath coming in soft pants against his lips. She nodded and her thighs tightened around him. "And this."

It didn't feel like a first kiss. Maybe because of how often he'd thought about her lips. There was no hesitation or tentative tastes from her. Just bold curiosity and raw, pure need. He knew her. Knew she would love it when he bit her lower lip and tugged it in gentle warning. That she would taste like his favorite whiskey and remind him of strawberries. Knew she would shiver when his tongue slid against hers.

Dean tilted his head, exploring her lips with his as he rocked her more firmly against his erection. He was desperate to get inside, but he knew that wouldn't happen tonight. Couldn't. She was giving him this and he had to take it. He needed it. Needed to hear the sounds she made when she came.

He lifted his mouth and bit down on the bare lobe of her

ear. "I think I need more of that honesty, Sara. I'm craving it. I told you, in detail, a few of the things I imagined doing with you. Tell me. What did you fantasize about when you thought of us together?"

God, she was so fucking wet. He lifted his hips and rocked her more firmly against him, his erection painfully hard.

"The last time?" She bit her lip, taking one hand from his shoulder and running it over her breast unconsciously. "I was in your bathroom. You came in to bring me something to wear and saw me touching myself. Then you bent me over the sink and—*oh, God.*"

He'd slipped one hand between them, his fingers finding their way beneath the fabric and touching her...*fuck, yes.* She loved it. She threw her head back with a loud moan, her hand still caressing her breast. She was already wild in his arms and they'd just started. She was so damn responsive.

"Is that what you were doing on the other side of the door, Sara? Were you thinking of me doing this?"

Dean pushed one finger inside her, growling at the tight heat. "Did you come without me while I was driving myself crazy imagining you naked?"

"Yes!" she cried. "But it was nothing like this. It's never been this. Do that again. Please."

"Never?" He wasn't sure what madness came over him— her admission that she'd wanted him as much as he'd wanted her, was aroused by his sexual fantasies about her, her erotic confession... Whatever it was, it had him sliding off the seat and whirling her around until her beautiful luscious ass was turned in his direction and her breasts were pressed against the leather.

He pushed her skirt up to her waist and groaned at the sight revealed to him. "So beautiful, Sara. Such a luscious fucking handful." He tugged the silk roughly to the side and cupped her sex, bending over her to murmur in her ear. "You've never imagined this?"

He thrust one finger, then two, back into her wet pussy, pushing his thumb between the cheeks of her ass as he reveled in her moans. His finesse had disappeared. His mind was lost. But he could tell she liked it. Could feel how hot it was making her. "Have I taken you from behind? In any of your fantasies did I fill this ass with my cock? Did you like it?"

"Yes." She was sobbing, tilting her hips higher and spreading her legs helplessly, begging for more. "Yes, I liked it. *God*, yes."

He watched her reaction with a male satisfaction that should have shamed him. He could take her now, do anything he wanted to her willing body and she would ask for more. "I like *this*, Sara. How ready you are for me. How sweet and greedy your pussy is around my fingers. You like hearing that, don't you, Sara? You're getting wetter."

He swore when he felt her hand grip his shaft.

"Yes. I want…" She pressed her cheek against the seat and licked her lips. "I want you to come with me."

He was right. She wanted to kill him. And he obviously wanted to die. "It wouldn't be the first time, sweet Sara. I've come for you before. On your back, in your pussy, your sweet mouth and between those beautiful breasts."

She groaned, her grip tightening on him as her sex clenched down on his fingers. "But this time is for you." He quickened his thrusts, pushing his fingers deep, stretching her as he thought about how good she would feel around his cock. How addictive. "Before I let you go and you slip into your bed without me, I want to hear you scream my name."

"Oh God. *Oh God.*" Sara's hand released him and clawed at the seat as he fucked her with his fingers. The music beat around them, matching the pace of the blood pounding in his ears. The desire pumping through his veins as he watched his fingers disappear inside her tight sex, watched her delicious ass jiggle as she pumped her hips helplessly.

His mouth watered.

"Dean, Sara. Say it."

"Dean, I'm...*Dean!*" she screamed. "*Yes. Oh God, Dean I'm coming!*"

He could feel it, the powerful contractions around his fingers as she found her orgasm. He pulled out, gripping her hips and lifting her easily until she was kneeling on the seat again. Then he spread her legs and lowered his head.

"What are you—Oh my God!"

He felt her trembling in his grasp and knew she was calling out to him, but once he'd gotten his taste he couldn't stop. Sweet and rich and *Sara* on his tongue. She instantly became his new drug and he knew he would never get enough. He pressed his open lips against her and licked her clit, loving how she instinctively opened for him. No holding back.

He'd always enjoyed the taste and feel of a woman's pussy. Loved the delicate folds and the heat, the feel of silken thighs against his cheek and the sounds a woman only made when she came in his mouth. But Sara's taste? Sara's sounds? Sara's pink lips and red, tender clit... He growled and thrust his tongue deeper, wanting inside. More. He wanted more.

"Oh my fucking...*oh God!* Where did you learn—*Yes.* Please, Dean, don't stop. Like...yes, like that. Oh God, I'm going to come again!"

*Yes. In his mouth. Down his fucking throat. Again and again.*

*Come for me*, he pleaded silently, his hands between her thighs and lifting her knees off the seat so she couldn't escape when she seemed to be trying to move away.

More.

She reached back, tugging hard on his hair.

*No.* He didn't want to stop. Couldn't stop. Not when he was finally here. Not now that he knew.

"Dean, wait, we've stopped."

He lifted his mouth and licked his lips, already impatient

for another taste. "I'm just getting started, Sara. You're so wet and you taste so fucking good. You don't want me to stop. I can tell. You want more."

She tugged again, moaning at the expression on his face. "I mean the car. The car stopped. Roy could open the door any minute. See us like this. See you...down there."

Dean heard something in her voice, felt her reaction, and his erection jerked in response. Jesus, she might be as bad as he was. As hungry. "You like the idea of being caught, Sara? Do you want me to stop or shall we let him find us?"

She blushed. "Not tonight."

He gave himself a mental gut check, reminding his dick that this night was for her. He'd fucked up, and giving her the lead was the only way it would ever get what it needed. He nodded roughly. "Not tonight."

With regret and as much restraint as he could manage, he pulled down her skirt and lifted his sweatpants, watching her struggle to calm her breathing as he chose one of the seats that lined the side to pull himself together. "Sara?"

He heard Roy opening the driver's door, whistling under his breath.

"Yes?"

"Not tonight." He tilted his head, his heart still thundering in his chest. "Tomorrow?"

"How do you feel about breakfast?" She smiled shyly, her face still pink from their ride and Dean felt something inside him crack open.

He hoped he could wait that long.

# CHAPTER THREE

Someone was flinging rocks at her bedroom window. Sara sat up quickly, throwing the covers back and grabbing her head at the same time.

"No more whiskey," she moaned softly. "I promise."

Whiskey.

Warren.

Dean Warren with his face buried between her thighs.

"Holy shit."

She couldn't blame that on the alcohol. She'd had enough to give her a headache, not enough to take away what few inhibitions she had around him. Dean had been the one to do that.

*After* thoroughly putting his foot in it and making her second-guess her attraction to him, no less. The man was talented.

She stopped in the middle of her room and sighed, remembering everything he'd done. So very talented.

His initial suspicions about her motives had kept her up for hours after he walked her to her door. She'd let herself fantasize about him, heard every detail of his dating life from the gossip mill in her office, but she'd never stopped to think about what it was like for him. To be the one everyone talked about. The one who couldn't make a move without drawing attention.

She knew about his father. That, when he was alive, he'd made work a nightmare for any woman who caught his eye. That he'd had more mistresses than houses and hadn't tried to hide any of them from his wife and son.

Dean's personal life was constantly being held up for comparison. Did the apple fall far from the tree? Was he going to backslide into his wicked college habits? Would he ever marry—and if he did, would it last?

She hadn't deserved his doubt, but objectively, she understood it.

*Was that because of his apology?*

Sara shivered, thinking again about the things he'd done with his tongue. It had been one hell of an apology.

*Ping!*

Another small rock hit the glass, making her jump. "What the hell?"

She lifted the window and leaned out, her legs bent as she carefully kept her bare breasts out of view. What she saw made her wonder if she was still dreaming.

"Are you awake?"

"Are you kidding?"

Dean smiled as if he weren't standing a few feet away from her first floor apartment with three men in white chef coats holding silver trays. As if he weren't out of uniform again, in jeans and a faded black t-shirt with Henry's band logo stretched across his broad chest this time. "Good morning, Ms. Charles. It *is* morning now, right? I sent Roy home a few hours ago so he could get some sleep, but these guys were kind enough to give me a ride. Hungry?"

She ducked lower. "I'm not sure yet. I'm not even *dressed* yet. I don't think you and I have the same definition of morning." She looked over her shoulder and sighed. "And I don't think there's enough room in my apartment for a party."

Sara turned back in time to see Dean's smile change. He licked his lips. "This isn't formal, Sara. No need to get dressed on my account. Not for the breakfast I have in mind. Anyway, they're just here to set the table. This will be a party of two."

She shook her head and started to close the window. "I can't believe I'm doing this. You should come in before my landlord sees you and notifies the Times."

A look in the mirror above her dresser had her groaning. Her face was flushed but devoid of makeup and a wrinkle from her pillow had ironed its way onto her cheek. She wasn't wearing a stitch of clothing and her hair was a bird's nest. She started to put it in a bun then paused, thinking of what he'd said last night.

She settled for a loose, sloppy braid instead.

Racing into the tiny bathroom, she threw some water on her face and brushed her teeth, grabbing her bathrobe and wishing she had something sexier than purple and white floral print cotton.

He knocked and she took a calming breath before opening the door. It wouldn't do to look too eager. "When I said breakfast, I didn't mean you had to go to all this trouble. I was thinking coffee and maybe a croissant. An orange if I was feeling sassy."

Dean opened his mouth, then closed it again as he studied her. "You *are* sassy. If I'd known how good you look in the morning, I wouldn't have brought company."

She held the front of her robe together and stepped back, allowing him and his entourage into her small one-bedroom apartment. "The kitchen's right through...well you can see it, can't you? Sorry about the tight fit." She laughed.

One of the men smiled back and nodded and she asked his name. His eyes widened.

Dean came up behind her and placed his hand on her back. "These are my friend Franco's sous-chefs, Sara. He's militant when it comes to silence and discretion. They don't usually talk to their patrons."

She tilted her chin, but kept her smile in place. "I'm militant about not letting strangers in my kitchen." She turned to the man again. "My name is Sara."

"Javier," the man offered solemnly. "I think you will be pleased you let us in after you taste what Franco has prepared for you."

"I'm sure it's wonderful," she assured him, leaning against Dean's warm hand, every inch of her aware of him.

He bent down to whisper in her ear. "Good morning, Sara."

She turned, her hand lifting to his chest, unable to stop herself from touching him. If only to make sure he was real. "Good morning, Mr. Warren."

"You have a cozy apartment."

"I told you it was too small for a party, but thank you. I like it." She did. It was about the size of a closet with a bedroom, but she didn't need much space to make a home. She'd made her own coffee table out of an old door, and covered her secondhand couch in soft, sky-blue fabric, adding enough stuffing to the cushions to make it decadent. She was still hunting for the right bookshelves, so her books were in neat, decorative piles on the floor. It *was* cozy and the rent made it possible for her to add to her fun fund each month. "You haven't even seen the bedroom."

Sara knew the men were whirring around her kitchen, setting her small table and rifling through her silverware drawer...and she didn't care. She was too focused on Dean, already aroused as she thought about everything they'd done. Everything she still wanted to do.

"Stop looking at me like that or I'm going to open that robe and have you for breakfast in front of Javier," he murmured softly. "I'm too hungry to be teased."

Her lips parted on a gasp. She could picture that too easily. Poor Javier and the men with him frozen by their training, forced to watch in silence as Dean laid her on the table and buried his tongue deep inside her until they were both completely satisfied and Franco's meal was cold and forgotten.

His fingers traced the neckline of her robe, slipping beneath it to caress the slope of her breast. "Do you think I won't do it? Believe I'm too civilized? Or are you daring me to try? Franco has entertainment at his restaurant that's made these men difficult to shock, but I'm more than willing to take on the challenge."

Sara lowered her head, her heart racing and her curiosity getting the better of her. "What kind of entertainment?"

Dean removed his hand abruptly, swearing under his breath. "Tell Franco I owe him one," he said to the men in a brusque, authoritative voice that gave her chills and they immediately stopped what they were doing, nodded and walked out of the kitchen.

Javier smiled at her again then disappeared, closing the door behind him. The instant it shut, Dean pulled her back into his arms and lowered his head to kiss her.

She wrapped her arms around his neck and held on as his wicked tongue scrambled her brains and made her thighs shake. His hand was already inside her robe, cupping her breast, thumb scraping across her nipple as his tongue sparred with hers.

She wasn't prepared for this, already close to begging and he'd just started touching her. They would never have the conversation she wanted to at this rate.

Why did she care again?

"Dean," she breathed as she pulled away from his lips. "Breakfast."

"Yes," he groaned. "I'm starving."

He placed his hands under her arms and lifted her off her feet, carrying her to the table. With one leg he dragged out a chair, sitting in it and pulling Sara down to straddle his lap the way she had last night.

She'd at least been partially clothed then.

A deep sexy rumble came out of Dean's chest as the robe splayed open above and below the knotted belt and he looked down at what was revealed. "Damn, you are gorgeous. Look at you. I can't decide what I want first. These breasts I've been dreaming of or the honey between your thighs. I need a taste before breakfast, Sara," he growled. "Only a snack. Say yes and I'll tell you about the entertainment at Franco's."

She could get into so much trouble with this man. "Yes."

He closed his eyes in relief and lowered his head to her breast, sucking and licking and nibbling her flesh while his palm flattened against her stomach and slid down. His fingers pushed past her damp curls and inside her sex, making her arch her back and groan.

"They do *this* at Franco's?" She felt his mouth all the way to her toes. And his touch was... "Lucky Javier."

He lifted fingers glistening with her arousal and stroked her other breast, dampening her nipple until it hardened. Then he turned his head and covered it with his mouth, sucking roughly, greedily, his hoarse needy growls vibrating against her skin.

Sara whimpered. She was just as greedy. She wanted to finish what they'd started last night, what they'd started here as soon as they got their hands on each other. She was lowering her hands to his jeans when he lifted his head.

"Breakfast," he ordered raggedly, lifting her off his lap and setting her in the chair beside him. "You said breakfast. And no, they don't do that at Franco's, but I don't think I can tell you more just yet. I only have so much willpower, Sara."

He served them from the silver trays, putting food on her plate and filling her glass with mimosas Javier had left in a glass pitcher on the table, and Sara couldn't stop staring at him. Dean had more willpower than she did. The fact that he'd stopped was proof of that. She'd felt his erection, could see that his eyes were glittering with need and his movements were tense. Restrained. Why?

He was used to restraining himself, she answered her own question. Buttoned up in a suit with his nose to the company grindstone. She might have decided to take a vacation but Dean had the look of a man who needed one. Despite his wealth and status, despite the gossip about his conquests, she'd gotten a firsthand glimpse of all the bottled-up passion he was holding onto so tightly. She shivered, already knowing after last night and this morning what it would be like if he popped the cork.

Dean Warren needed the prescription she'd already given to herself—uncomplicated X-rated fun. And God knew she needed more of what he did to her. As much of it and as often as she could get it. She wanted to be the one to help him find his release. The thought was beyond tempting. Beyond arousing. And there were so many reasons why it was a bad idea.

Late last night she'd thought it was a brilliant plan, but she'd decided it wouldn't work. The main sticking points were that they hardly knew each other and he might not agree. The first she could get around. The second she didn't want to think about, which was why she had definitely decided not to bring it up.

The tic along his temple and his controlled movements made her change her mind again. "I've been thinking about skipping the tropical island for my month off."

He paused as he was ladling some delicious-looking sauce over her eggs. "Oh?"

"Mmm-hmm. Of course, the other vacation option involves you, so I thought we should discuss it to see if you were interested before I made my final decision." She glanced down at her plate. "Strawberries and cinnamon? How did you know?"

His hazel eyes remained focused on her intently. "Discuss what?"

"My new vacation plan," she reminded him patiently, her

heart pounding in her ears. "After my first Hummer experience last night, I realized there are several things I've never done before that I'd love to try a heck of a lot more than windsurfing."

"What kind of things, Sara?" His voice had that sexy rasp she was starting to love.

"Sexual things." She popped a strawberry into her mouth and groaned, feeling hopeful when he didn't look away. "Fantasies. As in fulfilling them, preferably with an open-minded and energetic partner. You brought up the article that made me think of it, and you also mentioned you were good at deep tissue massage, so of course you were the first person that came to mind. Are you?" She swallowed again, reaching for her mimosa. "Interested?"

"Am I a man? Am I breathing?" he responded so quickly she smiled.

"Let's find out." She set her glass down again and shrugged off her robe so it pooled at her waist before reaching for another strawberry. Dean swore. Loudly. "Yes. You appear to be breathing in a very manly fashion."

It was never a bad idea to promote your positive assets, her inner devil insisted. Put your best foot—or breast, in this case—forward before negotiations begin. "Let me tell you about my rules before you decide."

Dean groaned, his attention firmly focused on her assets. "Rules? You want to talk to me about rules with that kind of distraction?"

"You'll like them, I think."

"I love them."

"The rules, Mr. Warren," she chided playfully. "For one month, instead of me vacationing on a sandy beach and downing umbrella drinks until I fall for the first Casanova in a Speedo with a good line, I stay here at home. We share our sexual fantasies with each other the way we did last night, no holding back, and we take turns making them a reality."

He didn't respond right away so she kept talking. "Before

you start to worry about the fine print, I don't want anything but your body." She winced. "That came out wrong. I *mean* there's no need for getting-to-know-you dates or wooing. I have no desire to go to any red carpet premieres, charity balls or fancy cocktail parties—unless you have a fantasy related to that. And, though it's delicious, I don't expect breakfast ala Franco every day, trips to Venice or diamonds. I'm more a pizza and beer at the park kind of girl. And when the month is over, I won't even expect a thank-you card, so you don't have to be concerned about unwelcome attachments."

Sara had to admit to a certain amount of trepidation. He wanted her—after last night and this morning there was no way she could doubt it. It was a wonderful adrenaline rush, a dream come miraculously true, but did he want her enough to give her a whole month? What if her bold proposal sent him running in the opposite direction instead of seeing it the way she'd thought he might last night—like a welcome relief from constant expectations?

She had to try. She could always go to the Caribbean. How many opportunities did a girl have to live out every naughty daydream she'd ever had with the starring attraction himself?

"Just to be clear..." Dean lifted his coffee cup to his lips and took a drink before continuing, "You don't want me to take you out or buy you things. You don't want romance or commitment. You want to spend your fun-fund vacation fulfilling *my* every debauched, depraved fantasy, in between you using my body like your own personal ride at Warrenland. Have I got that right, Ms. Charles?"

She tried to hide her smile. "That about sums it up, Mr. Warren."

"You're doing it again you know."

Her eyes widened. "What?"

"Saying exactly what I want to hear," he said softly, his gaze rising to her lips. "What are your limits?"

Her smiled disappeared. "What do you mean?"

Dean leaned back in his chair, breakfast forgotten. "I'll give you a few examples. If my fantasy involved tying your wrists to my bed so I could enjoy your body without distraction, or taking you to one of those premiers you say we don't have to go to and ordering you not to make a sound while I touched you in the dark. If I craved sex in public, having you ride me in the dark corner of a crowded nightclub, or taking you home and spanking your ass and pussy until you came, etcetera. Do you want to set limits? Are there things you have no desire to do?"

Sara bit her lip, feeling the air conditioning brush against her sensitive nipples. All of those sounded...

Exciting. Arousing. Forbidden.

She aimed for nonchalant, even though she was squirming in her seat a little impatiently. "We'll add a rule that if either one of us has a fantasy we don't want to fulfill, we can say no and move on to the next one."

Dean grinned. "Don't want to or can't feasibly do without endangering ourselves. For example, I would say my first fantasy is that you go topless for every meal, but we'd both die of hunger and you'd never get any dessert."

"Do you want me to cover up?"

"Now?" He lowered his gaze to her nipples again. "Don't you dare. You've definitely aroused my interest. Your offer is generous and sounds too good to be true. Something I believe in as much as I do coincidence."

She shook her head, not trying to hide her disappointment as she reached for her robe. "That's too bad. In my experience, occasionally those things can be better than you ever imagined."

Dean's hand shot out and stopped her from dragging the fabric over her shoulder. "I'm willing to test your theory. I accept. However, I do have one condition before I agree to your erotic vacation plan and we start sharing our secret desires."

She held her breath. "What is it?"

"I need something from you." He stood up and started to unbuckle his belt, watching her reaction carefully. "I haven't been able to sleep or think about anything but getting inside you since our ride home last night. I can still taste you in my mouth. Still feel you. I don't think I can start this project of ours until we deal with the problem at hand."

That was his condition? All he wanted before he agreed to spend the month with her was…her?

She stood and her robe dropped unnoticed at her feet. "Deal."

He moaned and reached for her, pulling her into his arms to kiss her. Sara unbuttoned his pants frantically, desperate to touch him. To feel his thick, hard—

"Fuck," he rasped against her lips. "I wanted to take my time. I imagined it for hours—my tongue fucking that sweet pussy again and again until you were sobbing for more. I was coming up with ways to keep you naked for the rest of the weekend, and then you offer me this." He lifted her up again, spinning them both around to press her back against the door. "Wrap your legs around me, Sara."

She did, surprised and thrilled at how easily he controlled her. She couldn't remember the last time anyone had made her feel this sexy. This powerful. He swore, shifting her in his grip as he searched his pocket and pulled out a condom, ripping the wrapper open with his teeth.

"Hang on," he muttered as he rolled it on before gripping her thighs in his wide hands. "Hang on tight."

Sara opened her mouth on a soundless moan when he started to fill her. Oh God, he felt good. Her body was stretching around his thick cock, welcoming him with a new flood of arousal as he thrust inside.

"Jesus, Sara…baby you're…."

He pulled back slowly, making both of them groan before he pressed his hips forward again. A little harder this time, and she shivered, grabbing his t-shirt and tugging on it until he pulled it over his head with one hand.

She dug her nails into his shoulders and he reacted with a rough stroke, his cock filling her completely. "Yes," she gasped. "Like that."

Dean's laugh was rough and dirty. "Like that, Sara?" He pumped against her, his flesh smacking against hers and shaking the door. So deep. God, he was so deep. "It's the first time I've gotten inside you and I was trying to be gentle. Trying to take it slow. But this is what you want, isn't it?"

She dug her nails in deeper and looked into his eyes when he hissed. "I don't need gentle."

He swore and slung his hips against her so forcefully the door shook again and made a banging sound. Again. *Yes.* Again. Faster and harder. Each thrust as deep as he could go, making Sarah cry out with the intensity.

"That's good," he groaned. "Because this is what I've wanted since I had you bent over that damn seat. What this body was made for." He snarled when she clenched her muscles around his shaft. "I knew you would feel good, but you're killing me, baby. Talk to me, Sara. Tell me you love me fucking you like this. Let me hear you say it."

At first she couldn't catch her breath enough to respond. Could only listen to him and gasp as her body opened up to his, giving him everything. No one had ever brought her to the edge so quickly. Given her the kind of wild passion she'd dreamt about. Said the sexy, delicious things he said. His hips were bruising in their force and she loved it. Craved it. Wanted to beg him for more.

He wanted her to say it.

"I love it," she cried, letting go of the last of her inhibitions. "Fucking me *so hard.* Love... Oh, *oh yes* like that. Fuck me harder. Make me come. *Dean!*"

"Hell yes." Dean lowered his head and bit the curve of her breast, his thrusts so fast now her body began to vibrate. She could see stars.

And then she was flying. "Dean!"

He shouted against her skin, his fingers digging into her thighs as he came with her. The door was banging so loudly now she breathlessly wondered if it would come off its hinges. If someone would call the police to report the disturbance.

She didn't care. Didn't care about anything but what she was feeling right now. Every inch of her skin was tingling with electricity, her blood was humming, heart racing and she wanted to laugh and cry at the same time.

She wanted to do it again.

Dean knew he was in trouble as he reclined at the bottom of her bed, watching her bend her spread legs and slip her hand down her stomach toward the patch of damp, auburn curls he wanted to touch again. How was he supposed to run his company, think about the upcoming vote, or fulfill his end of this fantasy bargain when he couldn't stay away from her body long enough to begin?

But it had already started the minute he saw her on her knees in the elevator.

She was his fantasy and she'd blown his mind.

He was willing to admit he'd had a few years of bad luck in the satisfaction department, but he'd had great sex before. More than most got in a lifetime. Hot sex. Angry sex. Kinky sex. Hell, he'd been a part of more than a few three-ways in his day, experiences he'd never expected to top.

Sara made them all disappear. She was uninhibited. Sensual. Playful.

Obedient. But only when she wanted to drive him wild.

He groaned when her fingers caressed the lips of her sex. "Are you ready, Sara?"

"Yes, Mr. Warren."

He growled. "Turn them on."

"All of them, sir?"

It had been a mistake for her to tell him what she used when she fantasized about him. He had to see them, and when she admitted what she used to do for a living, he'd needed to hear her describe what each one of them did. Then he'd convinced her to use them.

He'd watched without helping as she got on her knees and inserted a small, vibrating butt plug. Watched as she gently thrust her purple vibrator inside her sex and showed him the circular oral stimulator that had more speeds and motions than humanly possible, though she swore it wasn't as satisfying as his tongue had been.

"Do it, Sara."

She turned them on, one hand pressing the round device to her clit as she shuddered on her queen size bed in reaction to the others. It was a beautiful sight.

Dean had promised to watch. Only watch. But he was doing it through the camera on his phone.

It was a fantasy he'd never dared indulge, a dangerous one that he'd always declined to participate in when it was offered—despite his curiosity. Scrutinized CEOs did not make sex tapes or take photographs of naked women.

But he used to. He wanted to with Sara.

And the irresistible fucking woman had bitten her lip for a single uncertain moment before agreeing to let him hit record.

"Keep your legs spread so I can see everything," he growled. "Tell me how it feels."

"Too much." She shook her head against the pillow, her eyes closed. "I can't describe it. I can't even…"

"Do you like it?"

"*Mmm-hmm.*"

"Do you like knowing I'm watching?"

"Yes, sir."

"And this is what you'd do at night when you imagined me fucking you?"

Her small smile was siren-like, her lips trembling. "Not only at night. And usually just one at a time…sir."

He kept the camera on her while lowering his free hand

to his erection, unable to stop himself. "I'll tell you a secret, Sara. I'm starting to like the sound of that word on your lips. More than I thought I would. When you say it. I can see you on your knees in my office or over my lap with your skirt up as I spank you."

He'd broken her rhythm. She liked the sound of that. Good. Because he was definitely going to spank her. "Now you tell me a secret for the camera. I can see how much you're enjoying your toys. Have you ever fantasized about two men at the same time?"

"Oh God."

"Sara?"

She moaned. "Yes, sir."

*Yes, sir.*

"And if I told you one of *my* fantasies was to make that happen, hypothetically of course, would you agree to it?"

"Dean—"

"*Ms. Charles?* Would you agree to my fantasy?"

"I'll do whatever you want, Dean. Anything."

He threw his cell phone on the floor and climbed over her trembling body. "That's a dangerous thing to say, Sara. Whatever I want."

He reached for one of the condoms on her nightstand and opened it swiftly, sliding it on, pulling her vibrator out and thrusting inside her before the buzzing toy landed on the bed.

"Tight," he hissed. "I can feel it. Fuck, I might never want you to take that damn plug out again. It's so fucking good."

She cried out, lifting her legs until her knees were digging into his sides. "*Dean.*"

"I'm here," he groaned, pressing her breasts together so he could lick and bite her nipples as he took her.

"We might have a problem, Sara." He scraped his teeth along the curve of her breast, groaning every time he felt her tighten around him. "If you'll do whatever I want and I can't think of anything I don't want to do to you... God, this is too good."

"Dean," she cried. "Don't stop. *Please.*"

"I don't want to stop but you...I can't... I want you to come, Sara. Now. Come for me."

"*Oh! Oh God. Yes!*"

*Whatever he wanted.*

He felt her shatter around him, her nails scratching his skin, her thighs tightening as she found her release. Fire and lightning ripped up his spine and he lifted his head from her breasts, his back arching with the force of it.

"Sara!" He was crashing, tumbling hard into the most blinding orgasm of his life.

The best he'd ever had.

When he had some control over his senses again, he kissed her and rolled to her side, reaching out with one hand for the phone that had dropped on the floor. Sara put her head on his shoulder and kissed his chest. "What are you doing?"

"Deleting," he responded gruffly, not willing to think about how right she felt cuddled against him. How soft.

She laughed, still a little breathless from her orgasm. "You wanted to film me so you could delete it?"

He pushed another button to empty the trash, erasing the video completely while pulling her closer with his other arm. "I wanted you to *let* me film you. I don't need anything on my phone to remember that, Sara. Trust me."

"I did trust you. Hours ago when you said we'd talk about our fantasies after one—"

"I remember that too," he interrupted wryly. "You might have a few minutes while I recover if you want to make your list. You start. I'll tell you one of mine if you tell me one of yours."

She buried her face in his neck. "I was hoping you'd be the one to start. Fantasies are usually things you imagine doing, not things you've already experienced. Your reputation combined with your stamina? Odds are my to-do list is embarrassingly longer than yours."

He reached over, lifting her chin until she was looking into his eyes. "If you think I won't be dreaming of what you just did for me even when I'm too old to do anything about it, you're wrong. But we agreed not to hold back, so if you want to ask me about my history, I'll answer."

She lifted up on her elbow to look down at him. "You'll be completely honest?"

"I'll say yes, though in my experience most women don't usually mean the 'completely' part."

"In my experience I'm not like most women, and I do." She lifted her chin. "First question. Have you ever had sex on a boat?"

"*That's* your first question?" He laughed, surprised again. "What kind of boat?"

"Raft, gondola, canoe, yacht. Pick your flotation device."

He wanted to kiss her again. "Yes."

"What about an airplane? Have you done that?"

"Are you sure you don't want to tell me about one of *your* fantasies?"

She traced his stomach with the tips of her fingers. "I'm simply establishing a jumping off point based on your previous experiences."

He reminded himself she wanted honesty. "Yes."

She sucked on her lower lip and he groaned. She was imagining it. He could see it in her expression. Imagining what it would be like. With him? "What about you, Sara? Planes, trains, gondola?"

"Automobile. A Suburban on a back road in the middle of nowhere." She made a face. "That wasn't my fantasy though, it was his, and I was seventeen and terribly insecure so I don't think it counts. An airplane, on the other hand, that sounds exciting."

*Because you could get caught.* She hadn't said it, but Dean could hear it all the same. He started to caress her hip, unable to stop touching her. "What's next? A mountain bike?"

Sara chuckled. "Let's skip transportation copulation because after the Hummer and the airplane, I can see that's a regular thing for you." He laughed in surprise while she continued, "Workplace sex. Anyone ever joined you in the office for a little afternoon delight?"

*Sweet heaven.* "No one. You know that. I tend to keep business and pleasure in their separate corners."

"Because of your..." She bit her lip, but for the first time in years Dean didn't feel defensive. How could he when she was soft and warm against him?

"My father. Yes."

Sara's eyes darkened. "But you wanted to with me."

With her. In the atrium. His office. He clenched his jaw. "Yes."

"What was your hottest office fantasy?"

He bit out the first thing that came to mind. "Blow job. You're under the desk, wearing nothing but white lace panties. My pants are open and my office door is closed but unlocked."

She shivered. Good. He didn't want to be the only one affected by this conversation.

"Any nooks or hideaways you've fantasized about sneaking away to?"

"The elevator," she whispered. "I've imagined the elevator a lot."

So had he.

"Someone could see us." He hadn't meant for his voice to sound that guttural. That needy. He slipped his hand between her thighs, already hard again.

"Mmm, I know." She closed her eyes, letting her thighs shift so he could explore her. "But we're alone and you can't help yourself. You push me against the wall and kiss me while you hike up my skirt and undo your pants. You're so impatient you rip my stockings and underwear and groan when you realize I'm already wet for you. That I want it as much as you do."

"Sara," he rasped, rolling with her onto his back and reaching for another condom. "What happens next?"

"I'll show you."

# CHAPTER FOUR

It had been twelve days since Sara had entered the Warren building. Since she'd sat across from Terry Anne and hoped to see Bossy McHotpants in the elevator. She nodded at Andrew and stepped into the lift as the doors opened.

Things had changed. She'd changed.

Dean.

He'd called to invite her to his office for lunch. Told her he hadn't been able to stop thinking about her and he was fantasizing about seeing her at work again.

She could never deny him a fantasy. He knew that. They'd spent nearly every waking moment together, neither able to keep their hands off the other, and she hadn't turned him down yet. Not when he whisked her away in his private jet to take her to dinner in a nearby city and show her how exciting the mile high club really was. She'd never forget the expression the steward was wearing when they reappeared from the tiny bathroom, thoroughly mussed and smiling. Flying would never be the same.

She hadn't turned him down when he called Roy to take them out in the Hummer again—Henry Vincent still hadn't returned Dean's car—and made sure the driver found his way into a traffic jam.

Sara shivered and leaned back against the railing of the elevator, feeling wanton as she lowered her hand between her legs beneath her short trench coat. She wasn't wearing anything but a pair of panties underneath.

She hadn't been wearing anything that day either. Not for long. He'd opened the skylight so they could hear the hum of the engines outside and had her take off all her clothes. Then he pointed through the dark window at the bored young man in the car idling on their right and told her to watch him.

Dean made her kneel on the seat and placed his hand on her back, applying pressure until her breasts were mashed deliciously against the glass.

"He can't see us. What shall we do to get his attention, Sara?" he whispered in her ear before he dripped lube between the cheeks of her ass and slowly inserted the plug he'd had her bring from her apartment.

*Twenty-four.* She watched the number light up in the elevator as she pushed aside her panties and thrust a finger inside her wet sex, remembering what he'd said next.

"I know your fantasies, Sara. And it's your turn. Let's make one of his come true at the same time. Don't take your eyes off him, baby. Let him hear you."

The palm of his hand landed hard on her pussy and she cried out in pleasure at the sting. "Yes!"

The man flinched in surprise, looking over at the limousine. He'd heard her.

"Yes, what?" Dean murmured hotly. "Tell him what I'm doing. How much you like it."

He spanked her sex again. And again. She'd never imagined it would feel that good. Or make her feel that bad. She wanted to turn that stranger on. Never wanted Dean to stop.

"Yes, spank me!" She raised her voice, aroused beyond caring. "Spank my pussy. Oh God, I've been a bad girl and I need to be punished. It's making me so wet!"

She watched as the man, who didn't look old enough to be out of college, bit his lip and gripped his steering wheel with white knuckles. She'd definitely gotten his attention. She wanted to laugh as adrenaline made her reckless. Greedy for more.

Dean's own laugh was ragged. "You *are* a bad girl, Sara." He spanked her harder, making her clit swell with each successive smack. "And better at this than I was ready for. Tell him what bad girls want after they've been spanked. What you want from me."

She couldn't believe how turned on she was. "I want your big, hard cock inside me," she begged, raising her voice so the man beside them could hear her. "In my mouth, in my ass, in my pussy. I need you to fuck me so bad!"

Sara gasped when the man looked around surreptitiously and unzipped his jeans, reaching in to pull out his erection. He started to stroke himself and Sara licked her lips, fascinated. High on the knowledge that she'd done this to him. High on Dean.

"Don't leave us hanging now, baby." Dean gripped her hips hard and knelt on the seat behind her. "I know how much you like to scream. Give him what he needs. What *I* need."

He filled her with one long thrust and she cried out, loving how wild she'd made him. How crazed she felt. Her hands pounded on the glass. "*Yes. Yes!* It's so big. Make me take it. Don't stop. Oh God, yes, fuck my pussy with your big, hard cock!"

The man stroked his shaft faster, his hips lifting out of his seat as he listened to her shouts. He was going to come right there in his car where anyone could see. He wasn't going to stop.

"That's enough to keep his hands busy for a year, Sara," Dean snarled, dragging her onto the lush carpet of the limo and lifting her legs over his shoulders. "Now forget about him. I'll make you come so hard you can't think of anything else but me."

It was one of her strongest orgasms yet.

*Thirty-nine.*

Sara took her hand from between her legs and put it in her pocket, shuddering as she got closer to him. She'd always known she had a kinky side, an inner exhibitionist...but until that moment, until the last week or so, she'd never been sure how far she would go.

With Dean, there didn't seem to be a limit.

It would be dangerous in the long term—it was dangerous now. The chemistry between them was intense. So strong it couldn't be questioned or denied, and he never gave her time to doubt it. He found a way every day to show her how well their bodies fit together. How it only got better, wilder, more dangerous every time.

She'd expected the sex to be good, but she'd never expected his generosity, or how much she'd enjoy making him laugh and having him around. The minutes or hours between their sexual feeding frenzies, when they'd lie in bed—hers or the king-sized playground he had in his townhouse—and talk about movies and life and whatever came to mind.

It couldn't last. There were only a few more weeks to fulfill every whim and fantasy she'd ever had before this vacation from reality was over. That was the limit. The rule she couldn't break unless she wanted to prove him right about things being too good to be true.

Unless she wanted to get hurt.

Mrs. Grandholm was standing by her desk shoving things into her purse when the elevator doors opened and Sara stepped out. The older woman studied her over her glasses. "Good afternoon, Ms. Charles. Mr. Warren is expecting you."

Sara smiled politely, pushing a curl that had escaped from her braid behind her ear. "Going to lunch, Mrs.

Grandholm?"

The woman's lips twitched. "Apparently I am. Mr. Warren sent his assistant off on a wild goose chase to discover the whereabouts of his vehicle, and my daughter just phoned me from the lobby to inform me she was taking me to lunch at my favorite restaurant on his tab. Apparently he thinks I need to relax before the annual parade of ridicule begins."

The review for the board. Nobody seemed to enjoy it, but from what she understood, it was the way things had always been done. She felt a twinge of guilt at the dread on the secretary's face. "I know I don't work here anymore, but if you want to get the accounting over with as swiftly and efficiently as possible, you'll want Handler or Bends up here with you. They're quick studies and the best you've got in that department."

She was talking to the dragon lady about work wearing nothing underneath her jacket after fondling herself in the elevator. She sighed. But it was her fault since she didn't seem to be able to mind her own business.

"Your supervisor says *you* were the best. He's rather desperate to get you back, you know." Mrs. Grandholm adjusted her purse on her shoulder and smiled. "He wanted permission to pull you in for the review, with an offer to pay you double what you were making before."

"He did?" Sara laughed politely, feeling moderately vindicated that he'd finally realized her worth and rude for wishing the secretary would speed things up. "He can't be too serious about it since he hasn't called me."

"No, I don't imagine he has." The secretary hesitated then shook her head. "But for what it's worth, that mad woman is gone and I believe you could get your job back if that's what you wanted." She stepped into the elevator. "I shouldn't keep my daughter waiting. Have a good afternoon, Ms. Charles."

She could come back. The way Mrs. Grandholm told it,

she would be given a raise to boot. A small part of her was flattered, but even that part knew what it would be giving up in return. Her sexy vacation with Bossy McHotpants.

The twenty-third floor wasn't remotely tempting in comparison. Sara shook her head and turned toward Dean's office.

She had a fantasy to fulfill.

Her heart rate started to speed up when she turned the doorknob and opened the door. This office was just as impressive as she remembered. Behind the formidable-looking desk, there was another wall of windows like the ones in the penthouse. On the other side of the room, chairs and a couch surrounded a gas fireplace that was framed by enchantingly crowded bookshelves. This room was nearly as big as her apartment.

Dean was at his desk, his chair turned toward the window as he spoke in a low, threatening voice into his cell phone. "Don't test my patience. You'll get all the information you need when—"

She closed the door harder than she'd meant to, causing him to spin around in his chair.

"I'm done talking about this." He turned off his phone and stood, shaking his head. "Sara, I'm sorry. I didn't hear you come in. Lunch hasn't arrived yet."

Sara bit her lip. "Is this a bad time?"

"For you? Never. I shouldn't have answered the phone." He sent her a charming, if puzzled smile when he noticed her coat. "Did I miss the rainstorm?"

Maybe this was a bad idea.

*Or the perfect one*, her inner devil/nympho whispered. *Look how tense he is. Think of how much better he'll feel afterwards.*

She was already dressed for it, she thought, slowly untying the belt of her trench coat. "You aren't missing anything," she assured him, undoing the buttons before shrugging off the jacket and letting it drop at her feet. "I, however, couldn't find anything to wear for lunch."

Dean's knees seemed to give out as he sat down abruptly in his chair. "Fuck me, Sara…"

She cupped her breasts playfully and slipped out of her heels before walking toward his desk. "I'm game if you are, but that wasn't your fantasy. Under your desk in nothing but white lace panties, door closed but unlocked. Am I remembering correctly, Mr. Warren, sir?"

His cheeks were flushed, the muscle in his jaw twitching. "You are. I wasn't expecting you to— Oh baby you have no idea what you're doing to me right now. What you're starting."

She'd pushed back his chair while he was talking, just enough to drop to her knees in front of him. Her hand slid up his thigh and caressed the hard length of his erection through the fabric. "I think I might, sir."

Dean's hand went to her braid, gently dragging it over her shoulder. "No, you don't, but you will. And when you do I hope you'll remember who began this game." He bent down to kiss her lips softly, wrapping her hair around his fist to tug her head back when he was done. "Are you going to suck my cock now, baby?"

She swallowed a moan and nodded, her nipples beading and sex tingling as she reached for the button on his suit pants, sliding the zipper down slowly. He used his free hand to push down his boxer briefs, freeing his erection for her touch.

It was a beautiful cock. Thick and hard, ridged with slender veins and satin covered steel to the touch. She licked her lips. She couldn't believe they'd gone this long without her getting to taste him. They hadn't stopped making love long enough to enjoy the other pleasures.

At least, she hadn't. Dean couldn't go more than a few hours without spreading her legs and thrusting his tongue inside her.

Now it was her turn. She lifted her breasts and leaned

forward, slipping his hot shaft between them and squeezing them together while she looked up at him with sparkling eyes. "I think you mentioned *this* fantasy the other night."

He growled. "Trying to kill me again, Sara? When did you become such a tease?" His grip tightened on her braid. "Open that beautiful mouth for me and give me what you promised."

She loved it when he got like this. When he dropped the civilized façade and let the wild man take over. She craved it as much as she craved his touch. It made her feel feminine. Desired.

She placed her hands on his thighs and her lips parted over the head of his shaft, flicking her tongue out to lick him lightly. Man. Sex and salt and man and him. Dean. Her mouth widened and she lowered her head, taking more. Good. More than that. Addictive. Arousal drenched the white lace of her underwear as she gently sucked his shaft, feeling an answering tug in her sex.

"Fuck you *are* a tease," he groaned, his other hand cupping the back of her head. "A sexy, wicked goddamn tease. Are you trying to make me beg?"

Maybe she was. She moaned against his erection when he started guiding her, pushing her head downward in desperation. "Like that. I've wanted to fuck this sweet mouth for so long. Wanted you on your knees like this. Suck me, Sara. *Yes*. Fuck, baby that's it. So good."

It was. Sara pressed her fingers to her clit with one hand, the other gripping the base of his shaft as she gave them both what they needed. She'd never felt more desirable as he caressed her head, whispering sweet and dirty nothings as he got closer to climax.

"Your mouth was made for my cock, baby. Made to suck it. After I come down your throat I'm going to get you on this desk and bury my tongue in your pussy. When I get enough I'll flip you over and fuck your ass until you want to scream but you can't because we don't want anyone to know what we're doing in he— *Ah!* Sara, yes baby. Your tongue..."

A quick knock on the door and the sound of it opening made Sara freeze and Dean groan in denial. His hand tightened on her head warningly. *Do not stop*, it demanded.

"Dean?" The voice was male, but not familiar. Sara wondered how well she was hidden behind his desk. From the doorway, whoever it was might not be able to see her. "There's a cart out here with our lunch on it. Should I bring it in or are we waiting for your mysterious lady friend?"

"Bring it in, Tracy," Dean snarled. "And make sure to close and lock the door behind you. I'm...don't stop, baby, please...I'm in the middle of something."

The man hesitated while Dean kept her exactly where she was. "Should I come back another time, Dean?"

"I think...*mmmm*...I think she'd like it if you stayed."

She was so aroused she almost climaxed at Dean's words. He wanted his friend to know she was here. To know what she was doing. Oh God, it was wrong, wasn't it? Why did that turn her on? Make her so hot her hips started rocking impatiently against her fingers, desperate to come.

Dean knew it would. He knew her darkest fantasies. To be watched. To be seen. That the idea of being caught aroused her, but the idea of being seen on purpose...of performing turned her on more than anything else. He hissed when her tongue pressed against his sensitive flesh and chuckled breathlessly. "Yes, I think I'm right. He doesn't have to leave, does he, Sara?"

She groaned and shook her head, sucking him harder, feeling wilder than she had only moments before. Greedier.

"Christ, I'm coming, baby." He sat up straighter, one hand bracing himself on the desk while the other still clutched her head. He pumped his hips against her. "I can't....*fuck*...Sara!"

She closed her eyes when the taste of him filled her mouth. *Dean.*

A few thoughts started competing with each other for level of importance. Tracy Reyes was in the room with them. She was naked. She still hadn't come and the new arrival hadn't lessened her need at all.

*Hussy.*

She looked up at Dean to find his hazel gaze fixed on her. "Thank you."

Her lips quivered. "Anytime."

He smiled back. "If I'd known this was your plan when I asked you to lunch, I wouldn't have let Tracy invite himself."

"I know."

Dean reached up to shrug off his jacket, loosening his tie and pulling it over his head before he reached for his shirt buttons.

Sara felt like her eyes would pop out of her head. Now? Was he still going to do what he promised? With Tracy Reyes watching? "Dean?"

"We have a very strict dress code for lunch, Ms. Charles," he murmured. "Remember? Those breasts must be covered if anyone is going to be fed."

He handed her his shirt and she slipped it on gratefully, wondering how she was going to get off her knees and meet the gentleman cowboy when he'd seen… How much had he seen? And how did she get herself in this situation?

Dean pushed back his chair and stood, holding out his hand. "Tracy's a friend, Sara. You can trust him."

She let him help her up, tugging his expensive shirt down to cover up her lace undies and squaring her shoulders before turning around to face Tracy Reyes.

He was gorgeous. Dark eyes, dark wavy hair beneath a worn cowboy hat and skin golden-brown from his time in the sun. A giant, he had at least three inches of height on Dean and his biceps were so impressive they threatened his tailored blue shirt as he lifted an appetizer from the tray in front of him and popped it into his mouth.

"Good afternoon, Mr. Reyes," she said with as much calm as she could muster. "I've heard a lot about you."

He smiled politely at her, as if there was nothing unusual about their meeting. Or perhaps he was attempting to put her at ease. "Good afternoon to you to, ma'am. Sara, is it? It is definitely a pleasure to meet you."

He held out his hand as Dean guided her across the room, and she shook it, trying to pretend she wasn't naked beneath Dean's shirt and she hadn't just been under the desk giving him a blowjob while she touched herself.

"Sara," Dean turned her to face him and lowered his voice. "Are you okay?"

"Sure." She nodded, still shaky and definitely a little out of sorts, but she wasn't sure if it was embarrassment or sexual frustration. "I'm fine. This is all perfectly normal."

He squeezed her shoulders and chuckled, guiding her down to the couch while gesturing Tracy to the chair across from her. "Sit down, Reyes, while I get Sara something to eat. You sounded strange when you called. Anything wrong?"

"Other than the fact that none of you have been answering the phone lately and you told me Henry disappeared with your car?" he glanced over at Sara with an apologetic smile before continuing. "It wasn't that important, Dean. Just wanted some advice on a project. It'll keep. Have you heard from anyone?"

Dean set several plates on the table and sat down beside her. When she saw what he'd served her, she couldn't help smiling. He'd ordered from the tapas restaurant they'd gone to last week. She'd loved it…and he remembered all her favorites. There was also a plate of strawberries, which didn't surprise her. Dean was obsessed with feeding her strawberries. Or covering her body with strawberry slices that he insisted on eating off of her while he brought her to orgasm with her vibrator.

She reached for a napkin and an *empanada*, listening to

them discuss their friends' strange behavior and trying not to think about sex.

"I did get ahold of Peter. Once," Dean sighed. "We were talking about the new business venture, but as soon as I told him about Henry and the car, he made some excuse and hung up. Still hasn't called me back."

"I have a feeling about that." Tracy's voice was wry. "The competition must be on again."

"What competition?" Sara licked her lips and wiped off her mouth, wishing she'd stayed silent when both men focused on her with sexy bedroom eyes. She tugged on the shirt again. "I'm sorry, it's none of my business."

"They've both been after the same woman since college." Dean dropped his hand to her knee, pushing up the hem of her borrowed shirt as he traced a path to her thigh. "Well, they chased her in college, caught her for a minute, and now they might be chasing her again. We can't be sure."

Tracy sounded surprised. "Did I miss the catching her part? Where the hell was I?"

Dean laughed. "Christmas break. That time they both stayed at the house instead of their usual trips abroad?"

Both. Sara was too fascinated to hold her tongue. "They both caught her? At the same time?" And they wanted to do it again?

"She never could choose between them," Tracy answered. "I suppose it was bound the happen. Might explain why she ran scared, though."

Sara was dubious. Peter Faraday and Henry Vincent were—individually—practically irresistible. A woman with men like that, two of them, both focused on her pleasure? She pressed her thighs together, swallowed hard and spoke without thinking. "Who would run away from that?"

Tracy chuckled. "Good question."

"Fascinating question." Dean's fingers tightened on her thigh. "Sara. I think it's your turn."

Oh God. They'd just been talking about two men and one

woman having... "Maybe we should wait until after lunch?"

"I'm not talking about that...yet." Then he chuckled. "But after your reaction to the Hummer, I think it's time we graduated and got rid of the tinted windows."

Tracy took his hat off and ran his hand through his hair, studying them intently. "Care to let me in on this conversation, Dean?"

She started to tremble.

"It's the same conversation we've been having since Franco's, Tracy. Fantasies. As fate would have it, Sara has an interest in them as well. When we discovered we had a shared obsession, we began taking turns checking off each other's forbidden wish lists. She just fulfilled one of mine and, coincidentally, she has one or two that I'd only trust with you."

"I see."

She couldn't stop the blushing. Even after all they'd done. What she was tempted to do. "Mr. Reyes, ignore him. He doesn't even believe in coincidence. And you don't need to do any—"

"For this conversation you should call me Tracy, Sara." His smile was gentle but his eyes were darker than they'd been before. Narrowed. "Believe me, I never do anything I don't want to do. And I'm intrigued. What's this fantasy of yours he thinks I can help with?"

She turned to look at Dean, her heart racing so fast she was worried she might pass out. Up until now it had just been talk. Just the two of them, skirting the edge of the forbidden.

Dean wrapped his arm around her. "Tell me something, Sara. Did the rumor mill in accounting ever talk about Tracy? Ever mention anything about his predilections?"

She shook her head. Everyone on the twenty-third floor was in love with Tracy Reyes, and dumbfounded that such a decent, family-loving man spent his free time socializing with sexual deviants.

When she told him Dean's expression was humorously resigned. "He really is the Teflon Cowboy, isn't he? He's also a rope top, among other things, who's in fairly high demand when he's in town. That man knows his way around kinks you and I haven't scratched the surface of discussing, and he has some serious control issues."

The cowboy billionaire was a *rope* top? She bit her lip to keep her mouth from dropping open. She had a sudden graphic image in her head of what that might look like, an image that changed Tracy Reyes forever from handsome to *hot*.

Tracy nodded. "We're sharing, I take it. Good. I've got nothing to hide. I do crave control. But what about you? Does Sara know you were the one that introduced me to that world? That you used to take photographs of the naked women I tied up and call it art?"

"He did?" She turned to Dean and licked her lower lip, dying of curiosity. "Do you still have them?"

He inhaled sharply. "Yes, Sara. I'll show them to you if you'd like. But none of them compare to the look on your face when I'm inside you. Or when you're doing something you know you shouldn't. I wouldn't mind capturing that for posterity."

Dean wanted to take photographs of her? "Oh."

He laughed. "So much curiosity and excitement packed into one little word. You asked what her fantasy was, Tracy? *One* of them is to be thoroughly taken and made to come while someone is watching. And it is a beautiful thing to watch her fall apart, my friend. Sara is the sexiest, most openly passionate woman I've ever known."

Sara melted at Dean's words and glanced at Tracy, noticing his fingers had curled into fists on his legs. Was he interested?

"I'm more a director than observer, Dean. You know that. But you were right, she is a luscious beauty and the offer is too generous to resist. I'd be honored."

Oh God, just hearing him say that made Sara's breath catch with excitement. Dean, too, seemed primed for what was about to happen.

"I think we can accommodate everyone's needs, Reyes. We should take this up to the penthouse in case the first fantasy leads us to another. Now, before my secretary gets back from lunch."

In the elevator, wearing nothing but lace panties and Dean's shirt and standing between two aroused, sexy men who were on their way to make her fantasy come true, Sara couldn't help but think that no one got everything they wanted without a price.

Whatever it was, she'd find a way to pay.

# CHAPTER FIVE

She was standing beside the bed, Dean staring down at her and Tracy in a chair in the corner of the room, before she remembered to breathe. Were they really going to do this? Maybe it was something that happened to men like them every day, but for Sara it was a once-in-a-lifetime event.

Once again she gave into vanity, momentarily worried that Tracy wouldn't like what he saw.

*Dean does.*

That reminder was all it took. When she looked into his eyes, all she saw was admiration and lust. Awe and affection. Desire. She loved the way he looked at her. He was better than any dream doppelganger. Better than she wanted to admit.

He undid the buttons on her shirt slowly, as if savoring his prize. "I haven't forgotten what I promised in the office, Sara. Do you remember what I said I was going to do to you?"

Make her come with his mouth, then turn her over and... She shivered. They hadn't done that yet, either. "I remember."

"It's a good thing you love your toys," he muttered

roughly as he parted the fabric and slid it off her shoulders. "I don't think I have the restraint I'd need otherwise."

Tracy swore softly when Dean stepped to the side and he saw her breasts. "I no longer blame you for ignoring my calls, Dean. I'm not sure how you made it to the office at all."

She smiled shyly and Dean groaned. "Neither am I." He slipped his fingers inside her underwear then dropped to his knees, pulling them down her legs until she had to place her hand on his broad shoulder to step out of them.

She wasn't sure how she ever *let* him leave for the office. Dean's back rippled with lean muscle when he moved, his sandy hair tousled and begging for her hands. He was no longer the forbidden and unobtainable boss. He was her lover and with each new experience she only wanted him more.

She was his.

Dean straightened, picking her up unexpectedly and tossing her backwards onto the bed.

She laughed. "Showing off?"

"That wasn't showing off," he corrected her darkly. "This is."

Dean crawled up on the edge of the bed, placing her legs over his shoulders. "Got a good seat, Tracy?"

"Not as good as yours."

Dean looked into her eyes, something a little primal and thrilling in his expression. "If I were showing off, I'd respond to that. I hope you have something to hang onto, Sara." He lowered his head with a wicked grin and then his face disappeared between her thighs.

"Oh God."

He was more aggressive in his movements, his hands spreading her pussy lips wide as his tongue thrust deep. He moaned the way he always did when he tasted her, and the vibration made Sara buck against his mouth.

She could feel Tracy's eyes on them. On her. It

heightened every sensation. Dean's teeth biting down gently on her lips, her clit. His hair brushing against her sensitive thighs.

Her breasts ached and she reached up to squeeze them, pinching her nipples hard and gasping at the sting.

"Beautiful," Tracy whispered from the other side of the room.

He liked that.

Dean slipped a finger through her arousal and then pressed it between the cheeks of her ass, seeking entrance. A small taste of what was coming, she knew. What would happen when he could no longer wait to get inside.

His tongue was going so deep, in and out at a pace she could hardly keep up with. "Dean! Yes, that feels..."

Forbidden. Knowing they were being watched. Knowing what he was going to do.

She dug her heels into his back and lifted her hips for more, rocking against his face shamelessly. He pushed another finger in her ass and she shouted out at the pinch and stretch.

Dean lifted his mouth. "I know you love your little plug, but are you ready for more? Ready for me to fuck that sweet ass?"

"Yes!"

"Beg me."

What? She was close. Teetering on the edge. Why was he stopping? "Dean, please."

"Please what?"

Tracy was listening. Watching. Wanting? And Dean was going to make her beg. "Please. Please, I need to come."

"Not yet. Not until you say it. You know how I love it when you're bad."

She bit her lip so hard she tasted blood. "I want it," she whispered. "I want you to roll me over and fuck my ass. I used to put the plug in and imagine you. No one else...I've never let anyone else take me there. But I'm begging you to do it. *Please, sir.*"

"Hell." She barely heard Tracy swear, she was too busy studying the look in Dean's eyes.

"Is that true?"

She nodded. "Please, Dean. I'm so close…"

He lowered his head with a growl and started sucking on her clit. "Oh God. Yes, Dean, *oh, suck it, please. Please, I…Oh my God!*"

She was soaring with her orgasm while Dean reared back and repositioned her on the bed. She could hardly catch her breath. He dragged her up onto all fours and she lifted her head and saw Tracy watching her quivering body. The chair was closer, his shirt was unbuttoned and his jeans were open, his hand stroking his erection while Dean reached into his nightstand.

"Words can't describe what a gift it is to watch your pleasure," Tracy murmured. "You're just as passionate as he said."

She lowered her eyes, unsure of how to respond and struggling to catch her breath.

"Don't get shy on me now, Sara." Dean kissed her shoulder before opening a bottle and dripping several drops of thick liquid between the cheeks of her ass, rubbing her there and making her shudder. "You're *not* shy. You're wild. You are sex incarnate. Passion in the lush, soft flesh sent to tempt me. You were made for this."

She turned to look over her shoulder and Dean was there, kissing her with carnal intent before lowering his head to bite her neck. "My fantasy."

The first push of his erection through the tight muscles made her gasp and hiss at the sting. Dean cupped her shoulder with one hand and her hip with the other. "Breathe, baby," he soothed. "Breathe for me."

She breathed out and he pressed forward, pushing through the resistance with a pop and then… "So much. Too much, Dean. It's too much."

Her hands dug into the bed cover, her mind unable to take it all in. The intensity of feeling. The sensation that was both breath-stealing pain and earth-shattering pleasure. Her toy hadn't prepared her for this. For him. She looked up wildly, her gaze slamming into Tracy's.

"Do you want me to stop?" Dean's voice was gravel rough.

Tracy shook his head subtly.

"No. Don't stop." *Never stop.* She lowered her forehead to the bed and cried out when he thrust deeper.

"Good girl." She heard Tracy's praise and shivered.

"Fuck, you're tight. You can take me, baby." He rocked against her, shallow at first until she instinctively pushed back against him, wanting him to fill her completely. "Jesus, just look at you. Greedy Sara. You don't want to stop, do you? You want it all. You want more."

She did. More of him. More of this feeling. *More...*

He slung his hips forward until she could feel them slap against her ass and she shouted his name, hoping the mattress would muffle the volume.

"I want to see her face." Tracy sounded as aroused as she was. Commanding.

Dean only groaned in response, but the hand on her shoulder moved to her neck, his fingers on her chin. She gasped when he applied pressure and lifted her until her back was pressed to his chest, revealing her completely to Tracy's gaze. His fingers stretched to her mouth and she opened her lips to suck them in, tasting the salt on his skin and making both men moan.

The hand on her hip moved between her thighs to caress her clit while he rocked gently from behind. "So sexy," he muttered. "Fuck, Sara, you're driving me crazy."

Tracy was standing a few steps away from the bed now, his eyes black with desire as he stared down at her breasts with a hunger that made her feel helpless. Her hands came up to cover them instinctively.

"Oh no, luscious." Tracy reached down and slid his unbuckled belt out of the loops of his jeans. "This is your fantasy, remember? How can I watch you if you cover yourself? Do you want me to leave?"

Dean bit down on her shoulder with a groan. "She just squeezed my cock and my hand is soaked. I think she wants you here."

Tracy made a snapping noise with the folded leather belt in his hands and she started to shake. "I could bind you. Or you can lower your hands for me."

Dean pinched her clit between his fingers and she cried out in surprise and need, lowering her hands. "*Dean.*"

"I'm right here, baby. Right here and thinking Tracy wants to do more than watch now. Are you ready for me to give you the rest of your fantasy?"

It took a few minutes to process what Dean was saying. Sara's gaze was hazy with pleasure when she looked up at Tracy Reyes again.

Dangerous. The gentleman cowboy had changed dramatically since they came into the bedroom. This man knew what he wanted, knew what she could take and how to control a woman's pleasure. Masterful.

And he wanted to join them.

"Limits, Dean?"

Sara moaned when he slowed his thrusts, the sensations intensifying. "She doesn't seem to have any. But mine are anything but everything," he responded.

Sara frowned in confusion and Tracy reached out to trace her lips, to touch her for the first time. "He's saying I can take your mouth, your breasts and I can taste you, but I can't come inside. I agree to his conditions. Do you?"

*OhGodohgodohgod...* "*Oh God.*"

"Is that a yes?" Dean's laugh was a rasp in his throat.

"Y-yes."

He groaned softly in her ear. "I'll hold out as long as I can while you give him a taste."

THE CEO'S FANTASY

Tracy's shirt disappeared and Sara had a hard time looking away from all that muscle. Her gaze lowered to his open jeans. And big. Intimidating. Mouth-watering. He knelt on the bed in front of them, his large rough hands cupping her breasts.

"Thank you, Sara," he murmured. "I've been wanting to make my mark on these exquisite breasts from the second I saw them."

His mark? He lowered his head opened his mouth wide over her nipple, sucking hard.

*Fuck.* She reached back to grip Dean's hip, needing something to hold onto. Needing him. It felt good. Should it feel good? This was Dean's friend. A stranger who was now biting her breast and licking the pain away.

Was it wrong that she liked it?

"I'm here, Sara." Dean pressed his lips against her hair. "Let go and let me feel you fall apart around me. Give him a glimpse of how lucky I am."

"Showoff," she gasped again, her other hand landing on Tracy's shoulder when his fingers slid past Dean's hand and dipped inside her sex. "Ah!"

Tracy lifted his mouth and snared her gaze. "It's a good thing we're friends, Dean, or I'd steal this one. She has all the instincts of a perfect submissive. I could easily imagine tying her up and carrying her back to my bed." He raised his fingers to his mouth and moaned. "She's delicious."

"Get your own fantasy, Reyes. This is hers."

Tracy laughed at the possessiveness they both heard in Dean's voice. "And she's yours, I know. Let's make it memorable, shall we, Sara?"

He got onto his back and shifted until his head was between her thighs, his impressive erection all she could see. He moved Dean's hand away from her sex and gripped her free hip, tugging her toward his mouth.

Sara knew what he was doing. What he wanted. So did Dean. "Oh you bastard," he growled, his hips picking up their pace when she leaned forward on her hands and knees again.

She gripped the covers on either side of Tracy's body and cried out at the dueling sensations. Dean's deep strokes in her ass. Tracy's teeth and tongue, and the way he tugged the lips of her sex and sucked. Two of them. Both of them focused on her. Only on her.

It was intoxicating. Insane.

She lowered her head and took Tracy's erection deep into her mouth. She could feel the head of his shaft touching the back of her throat and she knew she wouldn't be able to take all of him in, not unless she could swallow.

Different from Dean, but still salt and male. Just as dangerous. His hips jerked and he made a sound of approval against her clit, his tongue teasing and dominating in turns.

A sudden urge to take away his control seized Sara. She wasn't entirely submissive. She and Dean were lost to their passions, lost in the fantasy. If this man was going to join them, she needed to make sure he was just as far gone.

She reached into the opening of his jeans and caressed him—the tight sac at the base of his erection, the sensitive skin beyond. She licked and sucked his shaft as hard as he'd sucked her nipples, knowing now what he liked.

A warning rumble came from his chest and he bit her thigh. Sara answered by swallowing against his cock, taking more of him while she pressed one finger between the cheeks of his ass.

"Sara!" he shouted, his hand lightning fast as it reached down to grip her wrist. "Don't challenge me, sweetheart," he warned. "You couldn't handle what comes after."

He caught her braid in his fingers and wrapped it around his hand, pulling her head down while his hips pumped upward, filling her mouth.

She gasped, her eyes watering when her throat tightened around his thick shaft. The thrill of arousal she got when she realized she'd shaken him made her press her needy sex against his lips, pleading.

"Hell yeah," he moaned. "Good girl. Let's go for a ride."

Dean's palm was hot between her shoulder blades, his hips slapping against hers as Tracy did things with his tongue that made her scream. Sara closed her eyes and gave herself up to it. Blinded to everything but sensation.

*Yes, fuck me. Everywhere. Inside me everywhere. Love it, Dean. Love everything. Love you...*

Tracy shouted and pulled his cock out of her mouth, rolling away from them, his own hand stroking himself to climax.

"Thank fucking God," Dean swore, curving his body over hers and moving them both forward with the force of his thrusts. "*Thank God*," he repeated. "Need to come. Gonna come so hard inside you. Sara! *Now*."

"Dean!" Her orgasm slammed into her with the force of a train, meeting his in a collision of shouts and trembling muscles. Her body shuddered against his and she covered the hand still gripping her neck, feeling like she was shattering. Ripping apart and there was nothing to put her back together. Nothing left.

She wasn't sure how much time passed. She only realized she was crying when Tracy, mostly dressed now and sitting beside her broken body, wiped the tears from her cheeks tenderly. "Thank you, Sara. I can see now why he was tempted to break his sacred rules for you. And from the look on your man's face, I get a feeling this is the last time I'll be invited to witness your pleasure. But I'll never forget it."

"He's not mine." She wouldn't forget either.

Tracy narrowed his eyes. "Sure about that, are you?"

Then Dean was there, a warm washcloth caressing her body, soothing her. She sensed more than saw Tracy leave the bedroom as Dean began placing tender kisses on her thighs, her sex. His tongue flicked her clit lightly and she released a shuddering sigh, her drained body coming back to life the way it did every time he touched her. He groaned and she knew he wasn't done yet. He wanted more.

Before she was swept away by sensation she thought a few more weeks of this might kill her. She would die happy and with more memories of pleasure than one girl probably deserved, but still. Where did she go from here? How would she go back to normal after this? It was already changing everything. Affecting everything.

When it was over, what would it do to her heart?

# CHAPTER SIX

Dean was in a foul fucking mood and he was holding the reason why in his hands.

Do you have your seatbelts securely fastened? You'll be glad you did when I deliver the latest dish on one of our favorite billionaires.

The word is out and it's spreading like wildfire that the reformed rogue might be reverting to his former bad boy status. Over the last three weeks he's been spotted all over town in dark restaurants, crowded nightclubs and—though this can't be confirmed—in a limousine during rush hour traffic, getting cozy a new partner in crime. Let's just say that particular report made Ms. Anonymous blush. And you know that takes creativity and effort.

The woman who has brought out our rogue's inner devil, however, isn't his usual type. I haven't been able to get her name, but I hear she and her nonstop curves stand out in a crowd. Unfortunately their escapades might add up to trouble for our handsome young tycoon.

An unimpeachable source has informed me that his

lack of discretion has concerned the board at Warren Industries. The annual vote on whether our rogue can keep a hold of the reins has been moved up and could happen as soon as this week. What do you think, readers? Should a wild and kinky summer fling result in a slap on the wrist, or a permanent boot in the behind? Our billionaire's bank account won't suffer, but his reputation will definitely need more polishing. I'm sure his new lady friend will be more than willing to help.

You'll know more as soon as I do.

"You're responsible for this aren't you?" Dean glared at his uncle while the older man sat in his chair, looking smug and victorious. "You can't give up your crusade and enjoy retirement, I know, but this is low even for you."

"I'll disappear to an island as soon as I get this albatross off our family's neck," he replied. "Stop trying to make me the bad guy. I'm not hiding my involvement in the article, Dean. Nor that I've kept an eye on you. Why would I? You obviously don't want the responsibility or you wouldn't have chosen this time of year to lose control of your baser urges. When your parents died, the will clearly stated—"

"That you and an appointed board of trustees would retain the ability to offer a vote of no confidence once a year until you were satisfied with my commitment. If a no vote was cast, you would instantly retake controlling interest and be able to sell off the company as you saw fit." Dean finished for him. "That will was written when my father thought I had no desire to take over for him and you thought you did. How you've managed to convince them to continue this farce and make it about my personal life instead of my job performance is beyond me, but I want you to know it's over now."

It should have been over years ago, but Dean had been so busy trying to prove he could run the company better than his father had. His uncle had only added fuel to that fire with his constant comparisons, but he'd stepped over the line with

Ms. Anonymous.

With Sara.

"Of course you're not the bad guy. It's normal for relatives to hire people to spy on each other. It just shows affection, right? But why would you give this gossip ammunition about my private life if you care so much about the family name?"

Sara had seen it. She must have. She hadn't answered his calls or responded to his messages all morning.

She'd already been pulling away without telling him why. For days she'd been finding reasons why they couldn't get together. Why she couldn't stay the night. Would this article, which had thankfully stopped short of naming her, end their fantasy vacation for good?

The knot in his stomach hardened. He wasn't ready for that to happen.

He studied his uncle, needing to ask. "Why won't you let me buy you out? My offers have been more than generous."

"Spite, of course." His uncle shook his head almost regretfully. "Or good sense. Dean, your father was a spoiled idiot who got away with everything and had no concern for who he left drowning in his wake. I watched you grow up, and for the most part, I can't see the difference between you. The more you've tried to pretend you're not like him, the stronger the resemblance grows. I knew you wouldn't be able to settle down. Knew you'd slip." He paused. "I also know exactly who you slipped with. You were clever enough to compile a whole file on the woman who was technically still on the books as an employee when you started up with her. No doubt you convinced the poor thing to quit her job so you could pat yourself on the back for not breaking your own rules."

"You don't know me at all." Dean realized it was true. He'd wasted the last five years trying to gain the approval of a stranger.

"No? I don't know that her supervisor put in a

recommendation to hire her back that has conveniently been ignored? You didn't have a hand in keeping a valued employee from earning you a profit so you could bang her in a public restroom?" He shook his head again, getting to his feet. "If I can find that out, Ms. Anonymous can too. You don't want that, which is why you'll let this vote happen next Tuesday and have it play out the way it needs to. And when the trustees perform their final function, you can breathe a sigh of relief, and I'll treat them all to a European vacation before I sell lock, stock and barrel to a buyer who has already offered me three times the annual revenue. I hear he wants to build a multi-level parking garage."

He knew about Sara. Had her file. Knew what Dean hadn't told her about her job being available or the supervisor's requests.

But Dean knew things too. His uncle might believe he'd won, and he'd let him go on thinking it while he could.

He'd find out soon enough.

*If I can find that out, Ms. Anonymous can too.*

He needed to talk to Sara.

Once his uncle left, Dean made a few phone calls then found himself in the parking garage. His car had shown up in his driveway last week with a smiley-faced Post-It taped to his windshield and no clues as to where it had been.

At least Henry hadn't crashed the damn thing.

Before he could get take three steps, he ran into a familiar security guard who glared at him as if he'd kicked his puppy.

"Bruce, right?" Dean nodded at the man. "Nice to see you again."

If the look on Bruce's face was any indication, the feeling was not mutual. Great. Twenty-third floor gossip had struck again, and he didn't have the time or patience to deal with anyone's judgment. Sara's was the only one that mattered.

"Mr. Warren, sir?" Bruce was following him. Dean stopped, turning around with an impatient frown. "I have something for you."

He reached into his pocket and pulled out an envelope. "Ms. Charles is a nice girl."

"I'm sure she is." Dean sighed apathetically, knowing the only way to protect her was to deny their relationship. "I appreciate the character reference, but since all I did was drive her home, I'm not entirely certain why you felt the need to share that with me."

"You know why," Bruce muttered as he turned and walked away.

He did. Nice girls didn't end up linked to billionaires in tabloids. Nice girls didn't have summer flings that eyewitnesses felt the need to observe and report. He should have been more careful. Should have known his uncle would hire people to watch him, but even if he hadn't, he should have been more careful. Someone was always watching. His desire for Sara had blinded him to his reality.

What was he going to say to her when he found her? *I'm sorry* wasn't enough. Being more careful with her wasn't something he could guarantee, not with the way he reacted every time he touched her. The more he had her, the more he wanted. He hadn't felt so alive, hadn't laughed or played so hard, in years. He didn't want it to end yet.

He didn't want it to end period.

The square note card in the envelope had an address on it. Below were the initials *SC*. Sara. Dean didn't hesitate. He got into his car and started to drive.

The phone rang almost immediately and he pushed a button on his steering wheel. "What?"

"I always feel like the voice of God on your damn car speaker. Hello, Dean. This is God calling. I can see you. *Stop touching that!*"

Dean rolled his eyes. "Funny. You sound a lot like that bastard Henry. You can't be, though, because he went missing a few weeks ago after stealing my car and turning off his phone. If you find him, let him know I'd really like to kick his ass."

Henry laughed. "Don't pretend you didn't enjoy the Hummer. A little bird told me you got more use out of it than I ever have. I'm guessing that means you took my advice then? Broke your rules with the curvy redhead at work?"

"She quit before I got the chance to *bend* the rules. And what little bird? Because someone's been talking to my uncle and Ms. Anonymous, and what she wrote not only pushed the board vote up to next Tuesday, but it might..." Destroy my chances with Sara. End the best month of my life. "It might ruin everything."

Static filled the silence when Henry paused. "She quit? What are the odds?"

One in a million. Like Sara. "Where the hell are you, Henry? Did Peter find you? Or did you hit the road again without telling anyone?"

"It's a long, fascinating story and I'll tell you about it soon, I promise. But first, what are you going to do about your redhead?"

"Sara?" Dean clenched his jaw so tight he could hear the grinding of teeth and bone. "I'll do what any man in my position does in these kinds of situations."

"Handcuff her to the bed until she forgives you?"

He pulled into the driveway the address specified and parked. "That isn't the worst idea I've ever heard. But then, I'm not exactly myself lately. For example, I usually disagree with your ideas."

"I hear you," Henry muttered. "I'll call you back after the vote. I want details."

"And where will you be?"

Henry hesitated. "Buying handcuffs."

Dean heard the phone disconnect and grimaced. He wanted details too. But not until he discovered where Sara had brought him. And why.

It was a quiet street in a tree-lined neighborhood dotted with townhomes and security fences, not unlike his own. The gate wasn't locked. Dean walked up the steps, wondering what she was getting him into when the door swung open, revealing a familiar face.

"Tracy?"

The man looked pleased with himself. "Dean. I thought that was you. Come on in, we just finished your surprise and I don't want to keep her waiting."

Dean's hands curled into fists at his sides as he followed Tracy into a large, empty entryway. "*We*? What are you doing here, Reyes?"

Tracy smiled. "You want to hit me, don't you? I know that look and it's a good sign, but I swear I was just helping out a lady. She needed to talk."

Seeing red, Dean stepped closer to his large friend. "I didn't know you'd gotten friendly."

Tracy crossed his arms over his chest, lifting one dark eyebrow. "It was cute once, but don't insult me, Dean. Anyway, blame your secretary for giving her my number. Sara was worried her vacation could destroy the damn company you love so much. Guess who gave her that idea? She thought if she stopped seeing you it would help."

*No.* That was exactly what he'd been afraid of. He had to talk to her. Reason with her. Handcuff and beg her if he had to. "Why are we standing in a vacant house, Reyes? Where the hell is Sara?"

Tracy moved closer to the door. "I did a little impulse shopping after convincing her to indulge you in one last fantasy where no one will think to look for you. She's upstairs and a bit…tied up at the moment, and she shouldn't be left alone. Get to it."

Dean swore as Tracy disappeared out the door, closing and locking it behind him. "Tied up?" he muttered, turning and taking the stairs two at a time. "Sara? Sara where are you?"

He opened the door to the impressively large master bedroom and froze, his mind needing a moment to register what his eyes were seeing.

Sara Charles was a goddess.

She was kneeling on a featherbed that had been draped with throw pillows and white sheets. Her gold-streaked auburn hair curled over her shoulders, caressing her flawless bare skin and reminding him of a Renaissance painting. The eyes studying him as he stood like a statue in the doorway were glittering green perfection. Vulnerable. Aroused. Determined. Despite her strength, he could see the fine tremor in her limbs. He didn't have to wonder at the cause.

"Tracy did this?"

She nodded and he stepped closer to study his friend's handiwork. Sara was well and truly bound. Thick white rope had been knotted expertly to form a harness framing her large breasts, tying her arms—wrist to shoulder—behind her back.

The rope was wrapped around her thighs and calves beautifully as well, spreading her knees wide. Dean knew she wouldn't be able to move. Knew how much trust was required to allow this kind of bondage.

Trust in him, or Tracy?

"You are..." His throat was tight and he swallowed. "I don't think I've ever seen anything so breathtaking in my life. But whose fantasy is this, Sara? I don't remember this on my list."

She licked her lips and gestured toward the end of the bed. "It's your fantasy, Mr. Warren. Your turn."

He forced himself to follow her gaze and started swearing. She was right, this was his fantasy. A camera identical to his stood on a tripod facing the bed. After Tracy had left that afternoon he'd shared Sara, Dean had taken her home and let her look through his old photographs. Particularly the series he'd done of bound submissives pleasuring their Doms. At the time he had been obsessed with capturing their expressions at the moment of realization. The ecstasy and revelation when they embraced their desires and understood their power.

Every inch of Sara's skin had been flushed as she looked through them. It had turned him on so much he hadn't been able to resist taking her right there on the floor. He held her arms above her head, telling her how he wanted to pose her, what he would do to her body to ensure he got the perfect photograph.

She'd remembered and recreated it perfectly. With Tracy's help. "Sara, this is more than I could have asked for. More than I deserve. I wanted to find you. To tell you—"

"Dean?" she interrupted shakily. "I can't think like this. Not about that. You're too far away and there's rope between my thighs and Tracy told me how it would feel when you... Please, Dean. I need you."

*Jesus.* "Damn, I'm coming, baby. Hold on." He started to strip out of his clothing, hearing a button fall to the ground and roll away as he walked to the camera. His hands were practically shaking as he checked the roll of film and ensured the shutter speed and auto timer were set correctly, then finished undressing and joined her with the control in his hand.

He saw a bottle of lube, nipple clamps and a small hill of condoms on the floor beside the bed and chuckled roughly, climbing onto his knees behind her and stroking the skin of her back. "I hope we have enough."

Sara shivered. "So do I."

Dean reached for her chin and turned her face toward him, kissing her with everything he had inside. Things he hadn't said yet. Things he wasn't sure he could. She responded just as passionately, leaning into him.

"I want to touch you," she moaned when he lifted his lips.

He shook his head. "Not this time, Sara. This time you have no choice but to let me do whatever I want to this body. When you let him—"

"Wrap me up like a present for you?" she interrupted,

reminding him of their first conversation.

"Yes. When you did that, you gave me permission."

"For what?"

"Everything."

She shivered. "Whatever you want."

"God, Sara." He didn't know where to begin. All the blood rushed away from his brain as he studied her body. Her full breasts were pushed together, perfect for his cock. Her soft lips parted and ready, her legs spread wide. Her ass. Jesus, her sweet, round ass.

His. She was his.

He gripped the ropes that crisscrossed her back, binding her arms, and tugged. "How does this feel, Sara?"

"Constricting," she answered breathlessly. "Revealing. Dangerous and safe at the same time."

He let her go, reaching down for the clamps before shifting himself to her side so he could see everything.

"Don't feel too safe," he murmured, lowering his head and sucking one nipple into his mouth for a hot moment that had her moaning. "You're lucky Tracy didn't give you a taste of what he does to women once he has them bound. Lucky I don't have that kind of patience around you."

Tracy was the lucky one. Dean didn't want to think about what he would have done if he'd found them together. Which didn't make a damn bit of sense since he'd invited the man into their fantasy game in the first place.

Dean closed one clamp on her nipple and she gave a shout of surprise. "Oh!"

"Yes, *oh*. Get ready to say that again, baby." He sucked the other nipple, closing his eyes as her sweet scent surrounded him, before repeating the process. "You like that?"

"I don't know." Her eyes were wide and dilated, her breasts rising and falling swiftly, making him painfully hard. "It hurt when you put the first one on but now…it feels like you're still sucking them."

He groaned, lowering one hand between her thighs and tugging at the ropes so they rubbed against her sex. "And this? Do you like this too, Sara?"

Her "Yes" was a nearly unintelligible moan.

"Everything," he growled, pulling the rope aside and pushing two fingers into her pussy, his other hand lowering without warning to spank the cheeks of her ass for taking away his control so easily. "I'll never get over how perfectly you respond. How greedy you are. The way you need as much as I do."

"*Yes.*"

His palm tingled as it connected with her soft flesh again. And again. She threw her head back, shouting in surprise. "And I'll never get enough of this sweet ass, Sara. How it feels against my thighs, under my hands. How delicious it looks when it's spread for my cock."

"Oh God, Dean."

He caressed the pink cheeks softly, marveling at their heat before he started to spank her again, the fingers in her pussy giving her just enough to keep her on the edge. "When it was just a fantasy, I could resist you. I could put it out of my mind for hours, even days at a time. But now I know. Now I've been inside and I know how you feel around me and it's all I can think about. Getting inside again."

*You're all I can think about.*

"Dean, *yes*. Please, I want you inside me. I need it." Sara's pleas had him blindly reaching for a condom as he clicked the camera's control and tossed it on the bed.

He pushed her hair to the side and kissed her neck, shifting her body until it was at an angle to the camera and he was behind her again. "Let me have this. Show me how much you want me, Sara. Cameras can't lie."

He gripped the bonds on her back again to hold her up with one hand, the other holding back the rope long enough to guide his cock inside. "You're so wet, baby. Let me…"

Her back bowed, his hold on her the only thing keeping

her grounded as he sunk deep. "Dean," she whimpered. "Dean, it's—I don't know how, *oh*, how to explain it."

"You're out of control. Completely. Your body is in my hands and you can't move." He reached around her and caressed her clit, pressing her back against him. "The whole world is just this. Me inside you. Touching you. All you can do is let me make you come. Let me take you."

"*Yes.*"

He looked down at her body, watching the bounce and sway with every thrust of his hips, and swallowed a groan. "You may feel out of control but you're not, baby. I'm the one in knots." He pushed her forward and raised himself over her, using her arousal to coat the tender skin between her cheeks before pushing inside her ass.

"Dean!"

"Tell me you want this," his voice was garbled with need. "Tell me again that this is mine, that no one else has ever gotten this close to heaven."

She was moaning almost continuously, her body shaking in his hold. "I want this, Dean. God, I love it."

"Love what, bad girl?" He wanted to hear her say it. Loved hearing the words coming out of her sweet, bow shaped mouth.

"Love your cock," she sobbed. "Love it when you fuck my ass. Love everything you do. Love... Harder. *Fuck me harder.*"

"Damn it, Sara!" He was completely out of control, his muscles trembling as he bowed his body over hers and shafted her with the long, hard strokes she'd begged for. "Like this? Is this what you want, baby? Is this how crazy you want to make me? I... Fuck, Sara, I'm too close. I have to slow down."

"No! Don't stop, Dean."

He couldn't resist her. Couldn't stop the powerful climax from throwing him off the edge of the world. He shouted her name, shocks of electricity blasting up his spine as she devastated him.

How did it get better every damn time?

She was still moaning. Still clinging to the edge when Dean pulled out of her with a shudder and fell onto his back, lifting her bound leg until his face was between her thighs.

"Come for me," he muttered, raising his head and plunging his tongue inside her dripping sex. Yes. Her taste. He'd never get enough. Never stop. Never. Fucking. Stop.

He heard her find her climax, felt the flood against his lips and growled greedily. More. Again. Had to have more. He never wanted stop.

He didn't want it to end.

# CHAPTER SEVEN

Sara stared at herself in the bathroom mirror. She'd stood under the shower until the water turned ice-cold. Her lips were too pale, her eyes were too wide and her body...

Her body was the same one she'd seen nearly a month and a half before. Healthy. Ordinary. Nothing to show for all the passion she'd known. No rope marks or bite marks from the last wild session of fantasy fulfillment. No whisker burn on her thighs, just the memory of her begging and crying out for mercy when his voracious mouth refused to stop until she'd lost track of her orgasms. Until she'd been sure she would black out from pleasure.

She sighed and walked naked to the closet, staring at her clothes without seeing them. Her vacation had been over for two weeks. She got up, went to work, came home and cried herself to sleep. Monday to Friday, rinse and repeat.

She'd been impulsive again. And not in a good way.

The Ms. Anonymous article had been the catalyst, but not because she cared what anyone wrote about her. She wasn't ashamed of the time she'd spent with Dean and no one could cheapen it, no matter what they said.

But she hadn't realized how tenuous Dean's standing as

CEO was or that his uncle was quite so rabid about selling the company. Tracy Reyes had told her the situation was so ludicrous anyone would be surprised, but she should have known better. She'd helped during the last review. Where had the office gossip been for her then? How could she have missed that vital bit of information?

Because she'd wanted him. She hadn't been thinking about anyone but herself.

Until she'd had to.

Mindy, Bruce, Andrew and the others didn't deserve to be voted out of a job so she could play spin the bottle with their boss.

She'd called her supervisor before Dean's last fantasy and listened to his pleas. He was in over his head and he needed her back, regardless of the current rumors. He'd offered her a raise and said all the right things. Water under the bridge. These things happened. And despite the fact that she hadn't had a single regret about leaving the stuffy twenty-third floor and had never planned on returning, he'd been so pathetic that she agreed to come back. *Temporarily.*

*Why?* she wondered as she buttoned her blouse and slipped into her low-heeled shoes. Since when had she become such a masochist? Why would she volunteer to be in the same building as Dean every day again, the one decision about her future that would ensure they could no longer continue seeing each other?

She hadn't told him it was a two-week deal. That she was training someone of her choosing to take over for her. That she was ensuring she wasn't to blame for the board's vote of no confidence.

"Good jobs are hard to find," she'd reasoned carefully, avoiding his gaze. "I can't turn down a raise like this for a sexual fantasy, no matter how amazing it is. I'm just glad Mrs. Grandholm told me my supervisor wanted me back."

He'd looked like he was going to argue, but something stopped him. He'd taken her home, walked her to her door and bent down to kiss her. So softly she'd almost started to cry.

She hadn't seen him since. Not in the elevator. Not in the lobby. She had to be thankful for that, at least. There was no guarantee she wouldn't embarrass herself by grabbing onto him and never letting go. By telling him something she'd known even before he got into his car and disappeared.

She'd made a mistake.

She locked the door of her apartment, turned around and nearly ran into the man standing there.

"Roy?"

"Ms. Charles."

"Are you kidding?"

Roy adjusted his driver's cap and smiled as he stood by the gratuitously oversized limousine. "I don't think so, Ms. Charles. I rarely kid this early in the morning."

When the back door of the Hummer opened, the broad-shouldered Tracy Reyes stepped out, holding his hat in his hands. "Good morning, Sara. I think you should let us give you a ride to work."

In *that*? After she and Dean had... "I have my own car, but thank you."

"*The* Sara Charles? Is this her?"

Sara's eyes widened when the stunning Peter Faraday popped his head out of the limousine and sent her the dazzling grin that was famous for getting him into—and out of—trouble.

"It's a pleasure to meet you, Sara," he told her. "Though redhead isn't an adequate descriptor, is it, Tracy? Titianesque, I'd say."

"You'd say that if your name was Dick," she heard Tracy mutter.

Peter's smile dimmed. "Sara, I'd wager you're an understanding and kind soul. We would much rather you ride with us. Tracy, Henry and I have situations to get back to that require all of our attention, and it would save Roy here from a drawn-out car chase and Dean from the unwanted attention that occurs when we descend on him en masse."

All three of them were in the limo? Tracy Reyes, Peter Faraday and Henry Vincent had all come to give her a ride to work?

She glanced at Roy, who sent her a look of encouragement. "Please, Ms. Charles. It would be my pleasure."

There was no way to get out of this gracefully. Not without Dean knowing about it. She walked toward Tracy, her movements stiff and tense as she was reminded of all the things she'd done with him. And Dean.

*Dean.*

Shit.

Tracy helped her step up into the limousine, and after giving her eyes a few minutes to adjust, she still wanted to pinch herself as she viewed her carnal carpool. The Billionaire Bachelors should be called the Pantheon of Porn instead. They were gods, all of them. Gorgeous sex gods who proved the Rod Stewart lyric true—some guys did have all the luck. Four of them, anyway.

Henry Vincent, the bearded guitar player, who lounged against the leather like the god of wine, rock and sin. Peter Faraday, the beautiful sun god with rakish golden curls, disarming smile and unusually piercing blue eyes that seemed to read her too easily. And Tracy... Sara bit her lip. The gentleman god of rope and kink.

The only one missing was Dean.

She missed him. So badly it made her ache.

She clenched her hands together over the purse in her lap. Gods or not, she didn't appreciate the reminder. Or the staring. It made it easy to forget her awe and hang on to her pique. "The building isn't that far away, fellas, and you have things—or people—to do, so unless you're trying to intimidate me with the silent treatment, you should tell me why you're here."

Henry laughed. "She's got fire."

Sara lifted one eyebrow. "I've got all my teeth too. I'm a catch. Tracy? What's going on?"

"You tell us, Sara." Tracy, looking entirely too long-legged to be comfortable, leaned forward. "What have you done to Dean? And when were you planning on fixing it?"

She frowned. "Has something happened? I thought last week's dissolution of the board had solved his problems."

"So you don't know what happened? You haven't heard anything about what happened with the vote?"

Impatient, Sara reached out and whacked Tracy's knee. When his eyes narrowed in warning, she closed her eyes and took a calming breath. She really hadn't meant to do that. "I'm sorry. But do I look like I know? I thought his uncle had second thoughts and decided to give up his bid to sell the company."

Peter chuckled, his arm wrapped around one bent knee as he studied her. "Fire and innocence. The board voted against Dean and Uncle Warren sold the company, but that was exactly what we wanted. I created a bidder he couldn't resist, with just the right amounts of greed and callousness to tempt him, then we pooled our resources for the purchase and promptly sold enough shares back to Dean that he retained the controlling interest. It was the perfect plan."

"Not to toot your own horn," Henry added dryly.

Sara's shoulders started to relax in relief. "Thank God."

"You're welcome."

"Dick..."

Peter glared at Tracy. "He's got Holly doing it now, you know. I hope you're happy."

Holly?

"Oh, you found her?" She blushed. "I mean, never mind."

The privacy window lowered enough for Roy to say, "Sirs? We're nearly there. If you're going to ask her..."

He disappeared again without finishing his sentence and

Sara wrinkled her nose in confusion. "Ask me what? And how does Roy know what you're going to ask me?"

Henry winked. "He's the one who gave us our intel. His sister is dating Bruce, the security guard, and when he heard your friend Andrew telling him that today was officially your last day and that you were talking about taking a job on the other side of the country, he thought I might like to know. He was right."

"Remind me to thank Roy personally." Sara's smile was tight. "But why would you want to know? Why do any of you care?"

Tracy answered her. "Dean is free, Sara. He has what he's wanted after five long years, though I can't tell you why he didn't let us do this sooner. Some people can take pride a little too far. Anyway, he can have a life now without worrying about his father's will or his uncle's meddling."

"And?"

"And he doesn't care."

"He's an ass," Peter offered. "More than he was before his recent vacation, and that's saying something."

Sara held her tongue. He wasn't hers to defend. And did they all know what she and Dean had done? Did they tell each other everything? "What does that have to do with me?"

"Sara," Tracy chided softly. "I know how clever you are. I've also seen the chemistry between the two of you firsthand. It doesn't take a genius to see that your leaving and his mood are connected. And I'd have to have been blind not to know why you were really crying that night. How you feel about him."

She shook her head, focusing on breathing. He couldn't know. She hadn't even realized it until last week. Not consciously.

She'd made a mistake thinking she could live out her fantasies and walk away unscathed. If she were honest, she'd begun to realize it was more than that after Tracy left the penthouse. Wasn't that why she'd made the effort to slow down and back away—because reality was turning out to be better than her wildest dreams? It was always going to be temporary. She'd known it, but like a fool she'd fallen in love with Dean anyway.

"We had an agreement. One month without complications or commitment. When I came back to work for the company, however temporarily, that ended it. I'm following the rules."

Henry made a sound of disgust. "Your rules, his rules, Peter's damn rules—I am so sick of everyone talking about Goddamn rules!"

Peter sighed. "You're a real rock and roll rebel, Henry. If you had your guitar right now, you could smash it to emphasize your point."

"Rules are walls for you to hide behind." He was looking at Peter but he gestured to Sara. "Look at those two. They both wanted each other, but despite his plans, it was only after she quit that they got together. And when it got too scary? When she felt too much? She actually got herself rehired again. *Bam.* Up went the wall. And Dean? Even after he found out, and he must have, that she's a temp who's on her way out the door again, he's still holding back. How the hell do babies get made if relationships are this complicated?"

Sara leaned back in her seat, feeling hopeless. "Maybe he doesn't feel the same," she whispered.

He'd mentioned before that he'd planned to ask her out anyway, despite his policy. If he'd really wanted her again, then after his coup against the board, he could have let her know.

Henry crowed. "Ding, ding, ding! We have our answer. She loves him."

"Henry, don't put words in her mouth," Tracy warned carefully. "Is he right, Sara? Would you stay if he asked?"

A tear slipped out before she could stop it and she angrily

rubbed it away. "It's nice the way you all look out for each other, it really is, but this is too much. Do you know that first night we were almost over before we began because he thought I was a present from you? That's one of the reasons I made my rules in the first place, so he wouldn't feel like I was trying to trap him or trick him. And now, *what* is it you want to know? If I'm in love with him? Why? So you can add another name to your roster of broken hearts? So you can stop me from leaving? He's the only one who can, and the only one who should decide whether or not he wants to."

The limousine slowed to a stop and she reached for the handle, brushing Tracy's hand away. "I'm sorry. I just can't…"

"I'm the one who should apologize, Sara. We were wrong to gang up on you this way."

"Yes, you were." She stood beside the car and turned to face the three chagrined, still devastatingly handsome faces. "Thank you for the ride, but you all have situations that require your attention. I'm sure Dean Warren will manage without you." She straightened her shoulders as a piercing pain struck her heart. "Without any of us."

When she finally made it to the elevator, she leaned against the wall and buried her face in her hands. Eight more hours. She could survive anything for eight hours. Even a breaking heart.

***

"Did you get all that, God?"

Dean was pacing the floor of his office when he stopped and slammed his hands on the desk. "No one asked you to do that. Damn it, Henry."

"Are you kidding? You've been begging for an intervention for days." Peter's voice sounded distant and tinny through the Hummer's speakerphone, which Henry had called him with during their conversation with Sara.

Thank God they'd had him on mute. He hadn't been able to stop swearing.

"Yell at us later, Dean," Tracy urged. "But you had a question and now you have your answer. As your new partners, we give the CEO permission to terminate the non-fraternization policy and grab the girl before she can leave."

He hung up on them and kept pacing, going back over the conversation in his head. She hadn't admitted to being in love with him.

She hadn't denied it either.

That night when she'd told him she'd found out about the job still being available, when she couldn't look him in the eye, it had thrown him into a tailspin he hadn't gotten out of in time to argue. He told himself it was for the best. That something as combustible and limitless and fantastic as this thing that was between them could never last. She was just smart enough to see it first.

Sara Charles had kept her word. She hadn't asked for anything more than his body and his pleasure. She'd been honest...until their last conversation. But now it seemed even that white lie had been mostly for his benefit. To release him from any feelings of obligation. To protect him from Ms. Anonymous and the now defunct board.

*Maybe he doesn't feel the same.*

He went to his desk, opened a drawer and pulled out a large envelope. As he walked by his secretary's desk to the elevator, informing her he would be unavailable for the rest of the day, he swore he heard Mrs. Grandholm sigh in relief.

Dean had been a lion with a thorn in his paw. An ass. He was not fit to live with—not since he'd gotten a close up look at something he'd always wanted and had it snatched away.

When the elevator doors opened on the twenty-third floor he made a beeline for the supervisor's office and sent the kowtowing man out of the room with specific instructions. Then he stood beside the man's desk. Waiting.

"You wanted to speak to me, sir?"

Dean's hands tightened on the envelope and his throat went dry. He was hanging by a thread. "Ms. Charles, please sit down. There's something I need you to see."

She sat down in the small chair in front of the desk and Dean stood over her, unceremoniously dumping out the contents of the envelope on top of it.

Sara gasped and Dean was riveted once again to the photographs he'd developed of them together. The black-and-white images were profoundly intimate and erotic. Her bound body was perfectly framed, her face lit by the sunlight coming through the window and locked in an expression of passion so beautiful it took his breath away.

"Why are you showing me these?" she whispered. "Why here?"

*Why now?* The unspoken question lingered in the air.

"I told you the camera didn't lie." He sifted through the pictures, forcing himself to look away from Sara's form and study his own. The mortal man who'd captured and seduced a goddess. "Look at him, Sara. Look at his face."

Dean could see it clearly. The man in the photograph was looking at his lover with need and desire and admiration. Even as he took her his expression was almost one of disbelief, as if she would disappear at any moment. As if she were a dream.

He was in love.

Sara shook her head and stood abruptly. "If that's all, sir, I should get back to work."

"I have a fantasy," he started softly, his words stopping her stumbled flight to the door. "I've had it for a while, but you ended our month before we could fulfill it."

She didn't turn around. "Dean…"

"Don't you want to know what it is? It involves you, and it would require both of us to break a few of our rules to make it happen. Indulge me, Sara."

*Say yes.*

"What is it?"

Dean walked over to her, cupping her shoulders with his hands and moaning softly at the contact. It felt like forever since he'd touched her. "In my fantasy, I ask you to extend our relationship to include deep tissue massages, boring charity balls and long, sex-filled flights to Venice...potentially some jewelry that you'll be too nice to turn down...definitely beer and pizza in the park."

She stiffened at that, but Dean couldn't stop. "In my fantasy you're there in the morning when I wake up, and you're curling up against my side after hours of lovemaking before I fall asleep... And occasionally you show up wearing nothing but white lace panties in my office when one of us has to work late."

Her laugh sounded a little like a sob and she covered her mouth with her hand. Dean whirled her around to face him. "Sara? Is this too much? Have we finally found your limit? The one thing you don't want to do with me?"

She dropped her hand, worry evident in her eyes. "For how long?"

"How long have you got?" he joked with a rasp in his throat. She took a step back and his grip tightened. "No amount of time with you will make up for these last two weeks without you, Sara—they were fucking miserable. I know it's not my turn, but give me this fantasy. Say yes."

Her shimmering green eyes were dark as she studied him. And then he saw it. A spark of excitement. A smile. "I have one condition."

He held back his victorious shout. Barely. "I'm listening."

"We need to start this fantasy of yours as soon as possible. And you're never allowed to show those pictures to anyone but me. Okay, two conditions."

Dean kissed her with all the relief and need and pain that had been locked up inside him since she'd walked away. She loved him. He could feel it. And before this night was over he was going to get her to admit it.

He pulled back. "Technically you still work for Warren Industries."

She moaned and dropped her forehead on his chest. "Damn it. Yes. For seven hours and forty-five minutes."

If he had his way, it would be much, much longer. But only if it was what she wanted. They could talk about it later.

Sara shrieked when he bent down, gripped her hips and threw her over his shoulder. "We should hurry then. I plan on breaking company policy at least seven times by then. Eight if I'm being honest—which I know you love—because the first time might not last that long."

He gathered the pictures back in the envelope and handed it her, his arm tightening on her wriggling thighs. "Hang on to something, Sara."

The walk to the elevator was swift and so silent Dean could hear the clocks ticking. When the elevator door opened he stepped inside, disappointed. "No clapping? Cell phone cameras? Nothing?"

Sara chuckled against his back breathlessly. "Accountants are boring. Didn't you get the memo?"

He lowered her to her feet and opened the panel to enter his security code. Then he dropped to his knees in front of her. "I beg to differ, Ms. Charles. Grab onto the railing and allow me to show you how wrong you are. It *is* your turn."

Dean pushed up her skirt when she obeyed and, with a growl, tore her stockings and red lace underwear. "Someone could see us," he looked up at her, challenge in his eyes.

Sara slid her fingers through his hair. "Let them see. I can't wait, Dean. I've missed you. I want you to."

"Are you sure?" He watched her closely, asking for more than this ride. Asking for everything.

He could see it in her eyes. Awareness. Passion. Love. "Yes, Dean. I'm sure."

"Say it again."

"Yes...*oh, yes*, Mr. Warren!" She groaned when he

spread the tattered fabric and traced her sex with his tongue. "Oh God, yes."

"Whatever you want, Sara Charles," he rasped. "Anything."

# THE COWBOY'S KINK

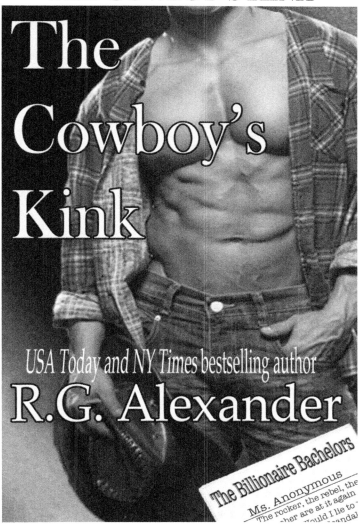

124

# Chapter One

I don't have to tell you what the topic is today. Why?

Because if I suddenly decided to wax rhapsodic about my love of pickle chips or pounce on the latest political outrage, you would set me aside without hesitation and find another columnist to give you all the juicy details on your favorite topic: the Billionaire Bachelors.

Ms. Anonymous isn't that stupid.

What I *am* is well connected enough to tell you everything you want to know about the rocker, rebel, rancher and reformed rogue.

Speaking of the latter, I'm sure by now you've gotten the news that the CEO of Warren Industries is still standing, despite his early summer scandal. He's also—brace yourselves—off the market for the foreseeable future. His paramour du jour is none other than the curvaceous temptress who got him into trouble in the first place.

Since I've discovered that the mysterious redhead is a genuine Cinderella, a regular girl punching the clock in the big city, I'm more intrigued than ever.

Can this be true love?

As you know I've been cynical on this topic for a while. Our bad boys have the resources and seduction skills to woo the unwary and willing alike, but they don't usually stick around long enough for things to get serious. In fact, I have a running bet with myself that none of them could last three months in a row with the same woman. And I always win. Still, there is no denying this change in the CEO's status. Our tantalizing tycoon has been seen with his ladylove every night this week, and he's looking anything but grim.

But don't let that news depress you. There are still three princes standing. Correction—one prince and two men who could buy a small country and a crown if they so desired.

Our royal rocker and his lewd playboy pal have been staying frustratingly under the radar, so no news on them just yet. But the rancher—known to journalists far and wide as the Teflon Cowboy—has been in meetings with his lawyers and financial advisors for days. And more interestingly, he was spotted at lunch with a certain billionaire matchmaker.

It could be a coincidence. She could be a friend of the family, or in the market for a special kind of saddle. Or could it be that our gentleman rancher has finally decided to settle down and rope himself a filly?

Give Ms. Anonymous a break, I couldn't resist.

If he *is* hunting for his very own Mrs., it looks like he doesn't care who knows it. Color me impressed at the size of his...spurs.

Get in line, ladies, wear your best riding boots and show us why you should be the one.

The Bride Wars are on and this is turning out to be one hot summer.

"You get that rope around her good and tight. Then take her down and make sure she's securely tied. That way you and the boys can get your business done and she won't be able to do anything about it."

The older woman drinking a martini beside him in the airport's VIP lounge turned around to eye him warily, her hand fluttering up to grip her pearls as if they were a protective talisman.

"Cow," he mouthed. When she gasped at the perceived insult, looking around as if to gather witnesses to his verbal abuse, he resisted the urge to roll his eyes and raised his voice so she could hear him over her outrage. "I'm talking about branding a cow."

If anything, she looked even more offended. Great. A vegetarian.

"Hold on a second, Miguel." Tracy sighed and got to his feet, setting a wad of cash on the bar for his unfinished drink and hers by way of apology. "Pardon me, ma'am."

He should have agreed to let Roy wait with him and stayed in that beast of a limousine while they refueled his plane instead of wandering into the bar. His phone was on and that usually meant it would be ringing. Though it was usually with business, not bullshit.

"Miguel," he muttered into the phone as he headed for the exit, "there are at least ten men in shouting distance who know how to do this blindfolded. Why didn't you ask them what it entailed before volunteering?"

And why the hell was Miguel calling *him*?

But Tracy knew why. His cousin appeared to have all the Reyes pride and none of the natural aptitude or common sense. The others would have given Miguel hell before teaching him the ropes, and he was obviously trying to avoid that. Tracy would have been tempted to fire the boy already, or at least find something less challenging for him to do, but his mother was a favorite aunt who'd never asked for anything until now. Not even when her husband left her and the boy in the Big Apple after cleaning out her bank account. That woman had spent years juggling two jobs and raising her troubled child without any help before she finally decided to come home.

Reyes pride.

Unfortunately, her city-born son wasn't faring well, despite being given a job on the small, original homestead in Colorado near his mother. And while Miguel, like his mother, rarely asked for help, according to the foreman he had no trouble coming up with excuses when something went wrong.

He was asking now, but Tracy was the wrong person, and frankly, in the wrong mood to give a shit.

"But Patricio, you're the—"

"Shut it, Miguel. I'll have Frank give you a hand. Do everything he says and you'll still have a job and the use of all your limbs when branding is done. Now I have a plane to catch and actual business to attend to. I'm looking forward to not hearing from you again unless someone is in the hospital."

Tracy ended the call without waiting for a reply and turned off his phone before shoving it into his computer bag with a heavy sigh. There was always a plane to catch. Always business to attend to. Four ranches, two of them the largest producers of beef in the country. One famous for breeding thoroughbred horses. Add those to the land they leased for oil and mineral rights, and the small towns in Texas and Colorado they owned most of the deeds to, and Tracy rarely found himself at loose ends.

There were managers and foremen and extended family he trusted to handle the majority of the day-to-day business, but he'd never been able to let go of the reins. He supposed he was too much like the grandfather who'd raised him. He liked to be in control and he wasn't overly fond of change.

But things *were* changing. His friends were the most recent example of that. These few weeks he'd spent in the city had proven it. He'd had to do most of his work via laptop and cell phone, but it was worth the inconvenience. Peter, Henry and Dean had accepted him for who he was—

all that he was—since college. They were the only people he truly trusted outside of his family. Hell, they *were* family. So when Henry claimed there was something wrong with Dean and he needed their help after Warren's annual charity gala, Tracy hadn't hesitated.

The royal pain in the ass had been right. Something had been wrong, and it wasn't simply business related. The man who'd taught him the value of accepting who he was and going after what he wanted was denying himself the freedom to do the same. In business and pleasure, Dean had been hedging his bets and playing it safe. By trying to prove to the bastards in the press and his interfering uncle that he wasn't his father, his old friend had gotten mired down in his own rules.

Tracy wasn't sure if it was because of their presence or in spite of it, but shortly after their arrival his friend had done a one-eighty. When they'd met for lunch a few weeks later, Dean was back to his old, wicked ways. The appearance of a suddenly-unemployed Sara Charles—in Dean's bed and under his desk—probably had more to do with the transformation than anything else.

Watching Dean and Sara together had been more satisfying than any of Tracy's recent sessions at the club. They had something special. The electricity they generated shot out between them like sparks, something they couldn't hide. That kind of connection couldn't be faked or denied. To Tracy, it looked a hell of a lot like love.

Sara had managed to turn his friend upside down with her honesty and passion. She was a refreshingly sexual, smart and goodhearted woman, and he'd name Dean for the fool he was if he didn't convince her to stick around for good.

Henry and Peter agreed, which was a rare occurrence since their college days. They were also now after the same thing Dean had found. With the same woman, it turned out—again—which Tracy doubted could end well. But at least they knew who they wanted. It was more than he could say for himself.

Peter's advice—that Tracy stop bitching and go after the family he'd always claimed he desired—brought him to the realization that, for all the noise he made about settling down, he'd never actually set himself the goal of finding a woman he could trust, who he wanted to marry. Never thought about what he would want from her other than children. What he had to give her other than his name.

Now he couldn't think about anything else.

He made his way to the tarmac, nodding at men giving his ride a once-over. The jet was his main mode of transportation these days and he'd definitely put it to good use. It was—as the sales rep had claimed—a luxurious hotel room with wings, filled with every bell and whistle currently available for the wealthy man on the go.

Comfortable, he supposed, but it wasn't home. In the last few years, Tracy had been in the air more than he'd been in his saddle, and the people who maintained his property and cleaned his pool got to spend more time there than he did. It was a fact that didn't sit well with him. Still, it couldn't be helped.

Or maybe it could.

The current plan was for him to make a stop at each Reyes' holding, put out any fires that had sparked in his absence and catch up on the work he'd let slide while he sorted Dean out. Being summer, by the time he got to his last stop he'd no doubt be called to do it all again. This was his life. He worked hard, when he had a chance he played hard, and for the most part he'd always been satisfied with that. Focused on that.

Right now work was the last thing he could focus on, and he blamed Henry Vincent. All that bullshit about fantasies and going after what they desired regardless of the consequences. It might not have bothered him so much if he hadn't seen the success Dean had when he'd followed the guitar player's advice.

Regardless of the consequences, at the moment all *he* wanted was to sleep in his own bed, look out of his own windows and keep both his feet on the ground. He wanted to be home.

Tracy ducked his head into the cockpit as soon as he boarded the plane, greeted his pilot and informed him of the change in plans. He wasn't given to impulsive decisions, but damn it if these last few weeks hadn't been full of them. After talking to his lawyers and financial managers, he had helped Peter create a fictional buyer as a smokescreen and now had shared interest in Dean's company. He'd participated in an erotic lunchtime threesome with his best friend to fulfill a fantasy. He'd bought a house for the sole purpose of bringing Dean and Sara together and participated in an intervention.

He'd also hired a goddamn matchmaker. Something he'd sworn never to do because it felt too arranged and forced. But he'd made his decision, and he'd be the one who had the final say on who he married. It was done, and Ms. Anonymous had already reported on it this morning.

He wasn't used to being the subject of one of her articles, but he supposed he'd been asking for it. That woman got information faster than his second cousin, the detective. Maybe he should hire her. If he had control of her paycheck she'd stop digging up dirt on his friends fast enough.

The matchmaker he'd hired was a professional and known for her discretion, so he was confident she hadn't revealed their meeting. From the sparkle in her eyes, having one of "The Billionaire Bachelors" as a satisfied client would be a feather in her cap in the industry, so he knew she wouldn't do anything to chase him away.

That initial interview had turned out to be a gentle, if awkward, inquisition. She'd asked the right questions, and listened as Tracy explained his busy lifestyle and loyalty to family. He'd told her he wanted a confident, smart and open-minded partner. Someone adaptable, who could be comfortable with both city and country living. A self-sufficient woman who wouldn't resent his regular business trips and the time he spent with his friends.

"And what about in the sex department?" she'd asked bluntly. "Any hang-ups or turn-offs I should know about while I'm finding your Mrs. Reyes? Are you looking for blonde or brunette? Experienced or virginal?"

Tracy had stared her down without blinking. "I believe I can handle *that* department without your help, ma'am. But I am an average red-blooded man who wants children, so if you're asking about sex, my answer is yes."

The matchmaker looked away first. "Of course, and I apologize, sir. But I wouldn't call you average. You'd be surprised how many clients require specific physical attributes—down to the measurements—as well as particular sexual types. Your reputation as a gentleman, I see, is well deserved."

He hadn't responded, though he realized his omissions wouldn't aid her in narrowing the search for his future bride. He *was* a gentleman, damn it. And because he was, he didn't advertise his particular sexual type, or say or do anything that could place his previous play partners in compromising situations with the press.

His experience as a rope top and Dom wasn't something the matchmaker needed to know. If she found someone who fit most of his requirements, he would be able to discover easily enough how adventurous the woman would be in the bedroom. If she'd be up for his brand of rough play or if he would need to find another outlet to fulfill those needs.

Another outlet. The idea didn't ease his mind, but it was one that had to be considered. When Dean had taken him to his first club in college and introduced him to kink, Tracy had been hesitant. He was a big man with big appetites that sometimes got the better of him. But the club had been a transformational and educational experience, giving him the skills he needed to control his strength, restrain his passions and ensure his partners' pleasure while enhancing his own. It wasn't something he was willing to give up. Not completely.

When the plane was in the air, a tall blonde stewardess dressed in the small, snug outfit he'd personally selected approached his seat. "Can I get you anything, Sir?"

Tracy studied her, wondering how the session could have slipped his mind. Speaking of outlets... He may be looking for a bride, but while he did, he had no intention of denying himself. He'd had scenes with the lovely young Janice at the club for several weeks before she told him about this particular desire. A skilled lifestyler and stewardess by trade, she'd always wanted to serve and be dominated by a handsome passenger.

Sexualizing the mundane wasn't an unusual fantasy, and it was a scene he was more than happy to indulge her in. Better to see to her pleasure than spend the hours it would take to get him home thinking about the kind of woman his matchmaker would find. And whether or not she would be open to his special cravings.

"Sir?"

"Not in that position, princess. Get on your knees and ask me again."

His erection stirred when she obeyed without hesitation, hiking her short skirt up to her waist to reveal her thong and lean, strong, perfectly tanned thighs, her eyes respectfully downcast.

"Can I get you anything, Sir?" she repeated softly.

Tracy undid his buckle and slid it out of the loops in his jeans. Slowly. "I'm not sure, princess. Why don't you show me what's on the menu?"

She lifted her hands to the buttons of her shirt and slipped them out of their holes until she could part the fabric, revealing small breasts with long nipples that he knew were particularly sensitive.

"Nice," he murmured. "You certainly know how to please your passengers."

She licked her lips, betraying her excitement. "I try, Sir."

"You succeed. Now clasp your hands in front of you without covering your breasts." She obeyed and Tracy swiveled his chair toward her, leaning forward to easily loop his thin leather belt around her wrists and knot the ends. It wasn't as versatile as his rope would have been, but after his experience with Sara Charles he had the desire to use it. His partner gasped in surprise.

"Too tight?"

"No, Sir."

"That's good." His hands caressed her arms before tracing their way to her nipples. When he pinched them between his thumbs and forefingers, she arched her back obligingly but her moan was too distracted...more about sensation and less about him. Tracy increased the pressure until her breathing grew ragged and she was watching him for his next command. That was more like it. "Very good. Are you wearing what I sent you underneath your uniform?"

She nodded. "And I've left what you asked for under your seat, Sir."

He caressed her lightly with his fingertips before letting go and reaching under the seat, finding the small remote device that went with the dual bullet vibrator he'd given her for the flight.

"Convenient." He turned it on the lowest setting, watching her lashes flutter in response. "As to what I want, I think I'm in the mood for something stronger than beer today. My time in the city has spoiled me. Whiskey on the rocks should suffice."

She didn't move and he smiled. "You may stand now."

"Yes, Sir." She got to her feet, wrists still bound in front of her, and hesitated. "Should I serve the pilot as well?"

Tracy hit a button on the device, pausing the vibration, and she made a low sound of regret. "Don't be greedy. I'm a first class passenger and I require all your attention. And since I'd like to arrive at our destination in one piece, the answer to that is no."

"Of course, Sir. I'll do anything to make sure you fly with us again."

She walked away to fix his drink and Tracy sighed, turning his chair toward the window. Maybe he shouldn't have invited her onto his plane. She was a beautiful woman and a truly proficient submissive, but he was too distracted to pay her the kind of attention she deserved. He'd have her taken back home as soon as he landed.

He hit the button again and saw her stumble as he gave her what he knew she wanted.

What in the hell did *he* want?

The question told him his instincts were right. He needed to go home and get his head on straight. Somewhere he could think. He'd make some calls and see what loosening his vise-like grip on the family's holdings would result in while he rode his neglected but loyal American Paint through the mountainside trails he loved. Maybe a few weeks alone would help prepare him for what came next. Namely, the files of women the matchmaker assured him would be in his email within days.

A wife and family of his own. It was time to put the past behind him and make it happen.

Tracy caught a glimpse of his bound stewardess, her walk slow and shaky as she tried to perform her duties with her hands tied and the vibrating bullets inside her as an added distraction. His erection hardened once more. He was going to spend the rest of this flight fulfilling her needs as he'd promised to do.

Would a woman he could see spending the rest of his life with want anything to do with this? With his brand of kink? Would she think he was a monster?

*You could make her like it.*

God, he fucking hoped so, because he was a beast, but in some ways he was also a traditionalist. Just like this grandfather before him.

Marriage was forever.

## CHAPTER TWO

Alicia was in the bathroom with a towel wrapped around her body and another around her hair when she heard the front door rattle.

"Jinny, is that you?" she called through the open door. "I thought I told you to go to bed."

Her sister didn't answer. A few minutes later she heard the front door slam open and a male voice swearing.

Alicia froze, holding her breath. Her reflection in the mirror showed wide eyes in a face that had gone pale with shock. That wasn't Miguel.

"Whoever the hell is in my house better show themselves by the time I count to ten, or I'll have to decide whether to tow your car and throw your ass in jail or just shoot you for trespassing."

Alicia hesitated for a split second, thinking about where they were—small town in the mountains, ranchers who lived as if they were still in the Wild West—before she bolted, sprinting down the stairs and through the long hall that led to the front entrance.

"Don't shoot!" she called out before she rounded the corner. "We were invited, don't shoot!"

She clutched her towel and skidded to a stop when she saw him. Looking up, she swallowed a surprised gasp. The stranger was a giant of a man. Big and muscular and...angry. He was definitely angry. And just as surprised to see her as she was to see him. He didn't appear to be armed but that didn't ease her mind. He was huge and he could no doubt snap her like a twig if she didn't tread carefully.

"What are you doing in my house?" he repeated softly. Dangerously.

Alicia couldn't hide her disbelief, despite her nerves. "This is *your* house? I thought it belonged to Mr. Patricio Reyes."

Old Mr. Reyes, the often-absent cowboy cousin of Miguel's who'd given him a ranching job at the bottom of the mountain.

He set down his bag and leaned against the closed door, crossing his arms. "That's what I said. My house. My land." He looked down at her with narrowed eyes. "My towels. I didn't send out for company, naked or otherwise. I'm not in the mood. Tell me who did or tell the sheriff when he takes you back to town."

*Old, my bare ass.*

Oh shit, her ass was bare.

She should have known. Should have expected this. "Miguel. Miguel Reyes-Faris? He had a key and he said he had permission for us to stay here until he made other arrangements."

"Miguel told you..." The man stalked toward her, making her stumble backward and hold her towel more tightly to her chest. "We? Is he here shacking up with you when he's supposed to be in the bunkhouse?"

He headed toward the stairs and she instinctively reached out to grab his arm. There was no give. He felt like hard iron under her hand. If she survived this, Miguel was in so much trouble. "He's not...I mean *we're* not...look, just let me get dressed and I'll explain."

He gripped her wrist and took her hand off his arm, not letting go. "You've got nothing I haven't seen before, little girl. I'm tired. I'm pissed. And I'm not letting you out of my sight until I know what's going on. Explain now."

"Alicia?" Jinny's voice wavered down to her from the stairs. "Is Miguel here?"

Her fear disappeared. She didn't care how intimidating this man was, her sister needed her protection.

Alicia struggled against his hold and glared at him when he didn't release her "Take your hand off me," she whispered angrily. "If you're actually Mr. Reyes, then I'll tell you your cousin brought us here when I refused to leave the ranch until he explained why he wasn't taking care of his wife and unborn child."

The forbidding man released her wrist abruptly and stepped back, studying her body in silence.

Alicia sighed. Now he thought she was pregnant. At least he'd stopped touching her. Her wrist was still tingling from the contact. She raised her voice. "Jinny, come on out honey. Miguel forgot to tell the giant, scary owner of the house that he had company."

"Oh no. He couldn't have." Her sister appeared, walking around the corner toward them with one hand protectively cupping her rounded belly through her pink tank top.

Alicia looked at her through the stranger's eyes and knew what he saw. Very pregnant. Too young. Pale and far too slender for her condition, with shadows under her eyes and her beautiful golden curls mussed from a restless sleep.

She wanted to kill Miguel all over again, the same way she had when she'd answered Jinny's call and driven to Colorado after the last day of the June session and found her like this.

Jinny's gray eyes were wide as she looked up at their new arrival. "The owner? *You're* old Mr. Reyes?"

Exactly.

"I'm the owner, anyway. But I wish you ladies would

stop with the flowery descriptions before I get a big head." His expression changed in an instant from hard to handsome. Kind. He smiled and Alicia's breath caught in her throat. "My name is Tracy. Jinny, is it? Miguel never told me he had such a lovely bride. And my aunt didn't tell me she was going to be a grandmother, which I would imagine she would want to shout from the rooftops."

Jinny sent a guilty glance toward Alicia. "She doesn't know yet. Miguel said we needed to wait until he could afford a place for us before he told her he was married with a baby coming."

"Son of a bitch, Jinny," Alicia exploded, forgetting about their witness or the tenuous situation. "He hasn't even told his mother you're *married*? It's been nearly two years, what the hell is he waiting for—your fiftieth anniversary? And why are we still here, again? Let me take you back home. You can start taking college courses and I'll find you a good obstetrician. You don't deserve this kind of abuse."

"I'm here because *my husband* is here." Jinny's chin jutted out defensively. She looked the same way she had when she was twelve and seventeen-year-old Alicia had refused to let her get her ears pierced. "Miguel loves us and he's doing the best he can. No one ever gave him a chance until now. He brought us here to start a new life, thanks to Mr. Reyes, but a bunkhouse full of men is no place to have a pregnant wife."

When Alicia looked down in frustration, the towel on her head unraveled and fell to the floor, covering her face with long, wet hair. She swept it back with an impatient hand. "Well, neither is that rat trap I found you in."

"It was all we could afford."

Alicia noticed the man watching her and flinched. "Pardon my language, Mr. Reyes. I am truly sorry for invading your home like this and bothering you with our problems. I assure you there is no need to call the Sheriff. Let us get dressed and packed and we'll be out of your way within the hour."

He tilted his head, studying her. "I don't think dragging a pregnant woman around town looking for a hotel at ten o'clock at night is the best idea, do you?" He smiled in Jinny's direction. "We aren't city folk, and most places are shut down by now anyway. If Jinny is Miguel's wife, she's my family. I don't turn family out on the streets."

She shook her head. "I appreciate that, sir, but it isn't—"

"Why don't we let her get back to sleeping for two, and you dress in something besides that towel?" He interrupted softly, the smile he'd had for Jinny dimming slightly. "I'll be in my office making a few calls. When you're ready, I would appreciate you coming down to continue this conversation."

He wanted more information. It was beyond uncomfortable, and she'd rather just leave and endure her embarrassment in a hotel room far away from here, but since the poor man hadn't expected to come home to an episode of *General Hospital* and he was related to Jinny's husband, she knew he deserved answers. She nodded and turned back toward her sister, who really did look like she needed some sleep.

"Alicia what?" His question stopped her and she glanced over her shoulder to meet his dark, penetrating stare. He must have heard Jinny say her name.

"Bell. Alicia Bell."

She felt his gaze on her even after she'd disappeared from his view. Tracy Reyes was a striking man, and nothing at all what she'd expected.

He wanted to talk to her alone.

She took a steadying breath. She'd faced down enough raging parents and stubborn students. She could handle one angry rancher, no matter how overwhelming his presence was. Jinny, on the other hand… "We need to get you to bed, baby girl."

Jinny chewed on her lower lip. "I'm sorry I didn't tell you about his mother. She's had it rough until recently and she always taught Miguel to keep his business to himself. He's a little overprotective of her. Of both of us. I knew you'd be upset if I mentioned it, and I didn't want to ruin our week." She smiled. "It's been perfect, hasn't it? Like when we were kids."

She was still a kid. A twenty-one-year-old, married and eight-months-pregnant child who didn't seem to know what she was getting herself into. Alicia forced herself to smile in return. "When we were kids we lived in an apartment the size of a closet and you hated my guts. I know because you told me every day."

Jinny waited until they were standing beside the bed and turned to hug Alicia, a task made more difficult by her bulging middle. "I was a brat, I know. And I was lying because I love your guts. I always have. Thank you for coming when I called, Al. I missed you. I feel better every day and so does the baby."

"I love your guts too."

Her sister lowered herself onto the mattress and frowned. "He must have forgotten. Mr. Reyes, I mean. Miguel swore he told him we were here."

Alicia snorted. "Old, forgetful Mr. Reyes?"

Jinny's eyes sparkled. "I did have an entirely different picture of him in my head. That man obviously ate his spinach as a child. He's definitely related to my Miguel, though. Did you see how handsome he was? That family is blessed in the gene department. My baby is going to be gorgeous."

"And stubborn," Alicia added. "There'll be a few of your genes in there as well. You just wait and see."

"I'm sorry about this mix-up, Al."

Alicia shook her head. "Look, don't worry about it now. The baby needs you rested. I'll take care of it and I'll see you in the morning. Try to go back to sleep."

She turned out the light and went across the hall to the bedroom she'd been using. Jinny's was obviously the master suite. His room. She would have to let Mr. Reyes know before he got another surprise when he tried to go to bed.

She closed the door, dropping her towel and reaching for her underwear. The thin white-cotton pajama bottoms dotted with apples, which were lying at the foot of the bed beside them, were not going to cut it. Apples. Jinny was always getting her teaching-related presents. Her birthday. Christmas. Alicia didn't have the heart to tell her to stop, even though she had enough apple-scented shampoo to get her through the apocalypse.

She rifled through the drawer and pulled out a long-sleeved shirt and a pair of jeans. Showing up in pajamas didn't make the right kind of statement when you were planning to apologize for squatting. She needed armor to face this dragon in its lair.

Absently staring at her reflection in the mirror, she brushed and braided her damp hair. Dragon wasn't really the best comparison. Maybe it was the Colorado mountains or the way he walked, but Tracy Reyes reminded her more of an oversized mountain lion. Or maybe a panther, with those waves of dark hair and rich brown eyes.

Either way, he struck her as predatory. Dangerous. Territorial.

*Sexy.*

Despite Jinny's blessed genes comment, Alicia had a hard time believing the bumbling Miguel was related to someone who exuded authority the way the man downstairs seemed to. It wasn't just his size or his height—though he must be at least six foot six and wide as a wall. Tracy Reyes wore his confidence more comfortably than most men wore clothes. His reactions—from enraged and suspicious to kind and solicitous of Jinny—didn't distract from her awareness of his masculine charms. Or the unnerving effect they had on her as she stood beside him, practically naked.

She puffed her cheeks and blew out a forceful breath. That train of thought led to a town called Trouble, and she'd be smart to avoid it entirely. Mr. Reyes actually seemed to care about family, unlike Miguel, and she couldn't repay his compassionate hospitality for Jinny with coherent conversation if she was drooling over the rich-toffee goodness of his massive biceps.

She finished her braid and let it hang instead of wrapping it in a bun the way she always did for work. It swayed saucily against her behind as she walked down the stairs again and toward the office she'd explored days before, after they first arrived, because she was curious about this family member who had "saved" Miguel.

Alicia's search for clues during Jinny's naps hadn't yielded as much information as admiration. The large, high-ceilinged room was filled with an impressive selection of books and warm, masculine furnishings. There were antiques on the wall that shouted cowboy, in case anyone had missed the stable a few yards away from the two-story house and the private road that ended at a cattle ranch. An iron horse bit, an old rusting spur, a faded photograph of the Reyes ranch and its original owners. There was also a long, worn rope hanging from a brass hook.

From his literary collection, she could tell he was educated, and from his knick-knacks, his computer and wall-length flat screen television, she could see that he had a healthy respect for history while still enjoying the comforts of the present.

It was the same in his living room and master bath, as well as the large wrap-around deck that had stairs leading down to the most decadent hot tub she'd ever experienced and an infinity edge pool with a breathtaking view of the mountains beyond.

No one with this kind of mountain hideaway—the kind that cost more than she'd make in her lifetime—would trust a man like Miguel with its upkeep. Or welcome strangers without any supervision. In the back of her mind, Alicia had known that as soon as Miguel brought them here, but the

THE COWBOY'S KINK

relief and awe in Jinny's expression had made her hold her tongue. Even if it was only for a few days, her sister deserved to be spoiled. Miguel owed her that much.

Now Alicia just had to explain that to the owner.

Mr. Reyes was speaking on his cell phone in rapid Spanish but he stopped the moment she stepped through the door. She sent him an apologetic look and started to back out, but he lifted one hand to stop her.

"I will talk to you in the morning, yes? Get some rest." He disconnected the call without taking his eyes off of her. "Come in, please. Can I get you something to drink?"

She folded her hands in front of her and stood, feeling like she was being called on the carpet by her school's principal. "No, thank you."

He walked over to the small bar, pouring himself a glass while he took in her clothing. "You don't look old enough, anyway. Are you cold?"

She sucked in her cheeks and nodded, not really lying. "It does get chillier here at night than I expected. And I'm old enough. I'm also a lightweight, and I believe you wanted to find out more about why there are strange women in your house instead of how badly off key I'll sing when I'm tipsy."

"I do. How old *are* you, Goldilocks?" he murmured over his glass. "And who's been sleeping in my bed?"

Her hands tightened at the unexpected wave of heat his words sent through her. "Kind of a personal question and not very original, but I'll answer it regardless. I'll be twenty-seven next month. And my younger sister has been sleeping in your bed, because it has a mattress that doesn't hurt her back and its own master bathroom with a strong bench in the shower."

He nodded, downing his drink and setting the glass on the bar. "She's Miguel's age, yes? Twenty-one? I suppose she's right then. Old Mr. Reyes." He shook his head. "A few hours ago I wasn't quite forty and still in my prime. Time flies."

Alicia took a step further into the room. "I wanted to tell

you again how sorry I am about this."

He waved her words away with one large hand. "It's not you who needs to apologize. But I would like to know about the events that led to this temporary living situation. In detail, if you would, Ms. Bell."

She ignored the small shiver that rippled through her at his commanding tone. She had no problem remembering the details. In fact, it was just the distraction she needed. "I arrived in town last week and discovered my pregnant sister living in one of those week-to-week furnished apartments, the kind that should have been torn down in the seventies. She looked a little worse than she does now because she's had a rough pregnancy—her morning sickness apparently just ended a few weeks ago—and she only saw her husband for lunch and on his days off, and I...frankly, I was mad as hell. Looking back, I think Miguel convinced us we could stay here until he found them a new apartment because I scared him and he knew I wanted to take her away."

He frowned. "I'm not surprised at your anger. He has family here, family who would have made sure your sister had all of her needs met. If he had told me he was married with a child I would have made the appropriate living arrangements. We do have couples on the ranch and housing specifically for families. I'll make sure he understands my feelings on the matter tomorrow. Trust me, Ms. Bell, things are going to change."

"I appreciate the thought." She didn't realize she was shaking her head doubtfully until he commented.

"But...? Do you doubt my intentions?"

"Not at all. Honestly? I have no desire to insult a member of your family, but I'm thinking I've seen boys like Miguel a thousand times in my classroom. I'm thinking talking won't change anything and the best thing I can do to protect *my* family, my sister, is find a way to convince her to drive back to New York with me."

His chuckle was sinful and rich as he walked toward her,

approval in his gaze. "It's hard to argue with that logic. Hard not to admire your determination to protect young Jinny." He stopped a few feet in front of her, forcing her to look up again. "Are you her only family?"

Her eyes narrowed suspiciously. "How could you possibly know that?"

He shrugged one shoulder in a lazy motion that belied his intent expression. "For a scary giant, I'm remarkably observant. You protect her like a mother would. As if you're the only one who can. And she argues and, it seems, hides things from you like a rebellious daughter."

That was a little too observant for her comfort, but she couldn't deny the truth. "We lost our parents when I was seventeen."

"And you took care of her by yourself? Went to school and worked to feed and clothe your sister without anyone to help you?"

Had he moved closer? She could feel the heat coming off him in waves, but she didn't back away. She didn't want him to see how his insight threw her off balance. "We made do. And there was a neighbor who watched Jinny when I had to work."

"What about Alicia Bell?" He said her name as if it were poetry. "Did she find time to do anything other than work and study and raise her sister? To make mistakes with the wrong boy? Did she sneak out of the house to meet him, knowing she shouldn't?"

Her shoulders tensed. What did that have to do with anything? "*She* did most of her sneaking out when she was sixteen. Then she grew up, became a teacher and made sure her sister graduated high school at the top of her class."

Alicia hadn't had time for relationship mistakes. A few safe, consensual one-night stands through the years. A few sexless dates with friends of friends. One casual boyfriend who lasted nearly a year before they both decided they were better off as friends.

Not the most impressive dating résumé for single city girl, but with her body type and freckles, she was more likely to be asked to the junior prom by one of her students than approached by a man in a bar.

She'd never experienced the kind of wicked passion she read about by the light of her e-reader before bed. The kind she'd barely scratched the surface of when she was rebelling before her parents' accident. Looking back, none of her intimate relationships had ever given her as much pleasure as she gave herself.

It was a pathetic thought, but it was the truth.

Even worse was the feeling that Mr. Observant knew it. Knew how lacking her sex life was, realized how obviously lacking her parenting skills had been and recognized her for the future spinster schoolmarm she was already becoming.

She stepped away from him. "I should let you get some rest. Miguel told us you were traveling on business. Jinny and I will leave first thing in the morning."

"Don't." The command was subtle, but she could hear it. "I apologize for offending you, Alicia, but after tonight's revelations I could use the company. Don't go just yet. Please, sit down and talk to me."

He gestured to the long rawhide couch that lined the far wall of his office. "For my aunt's sake, I'd like to know more about his life in New York. Tell me how he and Jinny met."

She was walking toward the sofa before she could think of a way to reject his suggestion. But then it wasn't a suggestion. Nothing he said seemed to be. As a rule she hated men who were too sure of themselves, too bossy and used to getting their way. But he wasn't like that at all. He was...

An irresistible force. Irresistible. That was the right word.

Alicia sat down and reached up to rub her shoulder absently, feeling the pinch the shower hadn't quite worked out.

He paused in the act of pouring more amber liquid into his glass. "Are you hurt? I grabbed your wrist before...did I injure you?"

"Not at all." She smiled ruefully as he sat down beside her. "I came back from the store yesterday with a flat tire. I think this happened when I was tightening the lug nuts back into place. It's fine."

"What's a tiny thing like you doing changing a tire alone?"

Alicia rolled her eyes. "What is that kind of question doing out of the nineteen-fifties?"

Tracy held out his glass with a chuckle, raising one eyebrow when she hesitated. "My way of apologizing to the women of the world, particularly all those in my family who would have me tarred and feathered if they heard me say it. Lightweight or not, a taste of this will help relax your muscles. Drink."

Alicia took it, unable to look away from him as she took a sip of the strong whiskey. When she coughed in reaction, he took it from her and set it on the table, patting her back lightly before taking her shoulders in his hands and turning her to face away from him.

"Mr. Reyes, what are you doing?"

She bit back a moan when his strong fingers pressed into her sore muscles. "I'm ensuring the comfort of my guests, Ms. Bell. You are the aunt of my future cousin. I wouldn't want it said I didn't do everything I could to make you feel better. While I do have a hot tub outside that would do the trick, you will have to be satisfied with this. I'm not willing to wait for the story of Jinny and Miguel." Her chin dropped to her chest and she gasped when he rubbed the exact spot that was causing her pain. "Do you want me to stop?"

She should. She didn't know him. It was strange and totally inappropriate and it felt absolutely wonderful.

*Did she* want him to stop? God, no. She shook her head mutely, unable to react normally with his hot, rough hands sending electric zings and shivers through her melting body.

"You could do this for a living." She couldn't remember the last time anyone who wasn't being paid by the hour had given her a massage.

"Thank you. Now tell me how they met."

How could she think? It felt so amazing she couldn't bring herself to care that a stranger was touching her with more intimacy and skill than she should be allowing. He was that good.

He was also, it turned out, an amazing listener.

She found herself telling him more than she meant to. That Miguel was Jinny's boyfriend in high school, one Alicia had tried to dissuade her sister from dating since he'd just gotten out of a short stay in juvenile detention and his friends were all troublemakers and criminals. She knew from Jinny that his father had abandoned him and his mother was always working, but feeling sorry for him didn't mean she was okay with his sneaking into her sister's bedroom or following her home from school. They'd broken up for a few years, but on Jinny's nineteenth birthday he'd shown up with flowers, a full-time job and an apology for his past misdeeds. Her sister had fallen all over again.

A few months later Jinny had dropped out of her first semester of college. A few months after that, Alicia had received a phone call telling her Jinny and Miguel had eloped. Four months ago her pregnant sister had left her with a tearful goodbye before getting into her husband's beat-up truck and moving to Colorado, where Miguel had been offered a better job outside of the city and away from their crime-ridden neighborhood. Despite all Alicia's efforts to stay in touch, she'd hardly heard from Jinny again until last week.

His hands stilled on her back and she sighed in disappointment and relief. She hadn't wanted it to end, but he was making it very difficult for her to concentrate.

"I think, Alicia Bell, that I am destined to offend you

again."

Only because he'd stopped massaging her. "Why do you say that?"

She started to turn back around but froze when she felt his fingers playing lightly with her long braid. "I'm thinking of the best way to put it. You're a teacher. Do you like Shakespeare?"

"Of course." She closed her eyes, focusing on the sensation. Why did that feel so good?

His voice was low. Hypnotic. "For never was a story of more woe…"

A giant quoting Shakespeare. This had to be a dream. "Romeo and Juliet?"

His knuckles brushed the nape of her neck when he gently gripped her braid. "From your story, they fell for each other in high school," he murmured. "All teenagers in love cast themselves as star-crossed lovers with the world against them. One word of caution, even with the best intentions, proves the illusion true."

Her head tilted back instinctively, as if giving him permission to continue. "I'll concede the point in general, because I'm faced with that truth every day at school. But Jinny is an adult now. A married adult with a baby on the way."

"So it's a habit—you obviously trying to protect her from making a mistake, and Jinny pulling away each time you try."

There was something seductive in his voice that didn't match his words and she had the disconcerting feeling that there were two conversations happening simultaneously. One about her sister…and one that was entirely unspoken.

The unspoken chat was sending heat through her body and making her tingle. She focused on talking instead. "You're saying I should stop telling her to leave, even though she's obviously unhappy and she deserves better."

His fingers were still curled around her thick braid. Just

that. No stroking or pulling. Just the warmth of his hand on her hair. The weight of it. "I'm suggesting a temporary cessation. Let me have my talk with Miguel. Let Jinny go to our doctor, who has delivered a whole generation of Reyes with great success. Let my aunt meet her daughter-in-law and pamper her as I know she will. Stay and watch and offer your support, at least until the baby arrives. I have a feeling, close as you are to your only sister, that you would never forgive yourself if you missed it. And who knows? Without the habit of fighting you to lean on, Jinny might decide to return with you on her own. At the very least, she will receive better treatment than she has since she arrived and you'll be able to enjoy each other's company."

It was a crazy conversation to be having with a stranger, but still it all made perfect sense. Reverse psychology. Alicia laughed softly, turning her head to look at him over her shoulder and swallowing hard when his hand tightened on her hair. "Shakespeare. I can't believe I let a Colorado cowboy win an argument with a sneaky massage and Shakespeare. I don't even like Romeo and Juliet. I'm a Puck fan."

"Did I win the argument?" His smile was a study in sensuality. "I hadn't noticed. And it's not my favorite either."

"No?" It was getting hard to focus on the words when all her attention was centered on that strong grip. Wondering what he would do next. "I bet I can guess which one is."

His gaze was fixed firmly on her lips. "Please do."

Her chuckle was breathless. "You're a guy. If it's not Julius Caesar it has to be Taming of the Shrew. What's not to like about a man driving a woman so insane she's willing to kneel at his feet?"

He tugged on her braid, making her gasp before letting it go. "You read my mind."

# CHAPTER THREE

Alicia Antonia Bell. Teacher at an underfunded and overpopulated middle school in New York City. No parents. One sibling. No priors. Single.

Tracy leaned back in his desk chair and studied the report his efficient relative had sent him an hour after he'd put in the request. It included a copy of Miguel and Jinny's marriage certificate, and the obituaries of Mr. and Mrs. Bell, dated nearly ten years before.

But it was Alicia's name he kept returning to.

She was the kind of woman who wouldn't appreciate his prying, but he made no apologies for being thorough. Every woman and business associate in his life was given the same treatment to protect his family from the grifters of the world. The ones he knew from experience were out there. The Teflon Cowboy moniker had been earned by having the sense to look before he leaped. A lesson he'd had to learn at great cost to his pride and his family's fortune. A lesson the brilliant Peter Faraday could learn if he cared to.

Two beautiful blondes in distress showing up in his house, with a sad tale and an unborn Reyes, was suspicious. He'd be an idiot if he hadn't looked into it.

On the other hand, he'd be an ass if he requested more information on her now that he'd verified her story. He would rather take the direct approach and discover all her secrets on his own.

*Slow down.*

He was trying. But he'd be damned if he could recall the last time he'd had to try this hard. It was why he'd said goodnight more firmly than he intended a few hours ago. He knew it had seemed abrupt to her but he'd had to put on the brakes before he scared her. And he could have scared her. He hadn't wanted to stop touching her, hadn't been able to stop thinking about her wrapped in nothing but a towel. About seeing her wrapped in rope or, better yet, nothing at all.

He'd taken one look at her big, deep-set blue-gray eyes, the freckles scattered across her cheeks and her lush pink lips, and felt like he'd been kicked in the gut. The attraction was instantaneous. When her long hair—so pale it was more the color of moonlight than the sun—had spilled out of the towel and touched the floor? He'd wanted to tie her up with it and fuck her, right there in the living room.

It was a stronger reaction than any he could have prepared for, but he'd managed to keep his distance—until Alicia had come down with her delicate skin all covered up and her pale hair braided in a winding rope down her back.

It wasn't an exaggeration to say she reminded him of an angel. A good girl that might be shocked if she knew what he wanted to do to her. The kind of woman he usually resisted. The kind he avoided. But resistance had been impossible from the moment he walked in the door. He would have to make an exception.

Would she really be shocked by his desires? Surprised, maybe, but shocked? He'd tried to read her, but about this, he wasn't sure. All kinds of people enjoyed all kinds of kinks without anyone being the wiser. But he'd touched her with purpose, and he couldn't have asked for better responses to his casual commands, his massage. There was no practiced air to her reaction, no awareness of the game in her expression, just instinct.

She *was* attracted to him. He could feel it. It had thrown her off at first, and she didn't quite know what to do about it, but it was there. And it hadn't been easy for him to pretend he hadn't seen it. To soothe her with harmless conversation when he wanted to kiss her instead.

She was a natural submissive, though obviously one without much experience. If she had more, she would have recognized his actions for what they were. Alicia Bell was what she appeared to be—a strong, responsible, beautiful woman who would look perfect bound on her knees or bent over his lap.

He wanted to see that. Despite the voice is in head telling him to stay away, he wanted to know what it felt like to have her give herself over to him. He wanted to have her in a hundred different ways, but getting her to stay long enough to discover what she wanted would be a challenge with the current situation. She was focused on her sister, the baby, and his cousin's epic fuck-up.

Tracy would deal with that, because he wasn't lying— family was important to him. He would solve that problem and find a way to negotiate the other obstacle. Seducing Alicia.

All thoughts of time alone and preparing for his future were pushed aside by the overwhelming desire to hear her cries of frustration and pleasure. To get wrapped up in all that glorious hair and feel her bare skin beneath him.

Tracy growled and pushed away from the desk, shutting off the screen and heading toward the back door. It was close to two in the morning, but he needed a long cold swim to clear his head and break this fever.

He undid buttons as he walked barefoot on the deck, loving the feel of the cool wood beneath his feet, the smell of the mountain air he'd missed more than he realized. Home.

It always centered him, and it would help him hold on to his control now. He hoped.

He dropped the shirt behind him and was reaching for his buckle when he stilled at the sound of rushing water. The hot tub was on. He moved closer to the railing slowly, allowing his eyes time to adjust to the darkness.

God, give him strength.

His sexy little angel had been transformed into a siren by the water. Dressed in a white tank top and white cotton panties, she may as well have been naked. The thin fabric clung to her wetly as she leaned her head against the rim with her braid laid out behind her and floated, revealing the tempting handful of her breasts, the tight nipples that topped them and lower, the pale blonde curls between her slender legs. He bit his lip hard enough to draw blood, trying to distract himself from the painfully swift arousal just seeing her like this had caused.

If he was the gentleman everyone believe he was, he would leave—her shoulder was probably still hurting her enough that she'd decided to take advantage of his custom-made hot tub, and a gentleman wouldn't take advantage of her injury this way—but he couldn't make himself move. He'd come across a water nymph, pale and ethereal and looking like she would break or disappear completely if he touched her. How could he resist the chance to watch her unseen?

He grimaced. Fuck poetry. He wasn't any good at it. He was good at taking charge. He should announce his presence and claim her before she had a chance to get away. He should chain her to the wall in his bedroom and bury his face between her legs until she was willing to agree to anything.

*Slow down.*

What the hell was she doing to him?

She reached up with her eyes still closed for something on the edge near her towel. Music drifted softly up to him…an mp3 player? Her phone? Wherever it was coming from, the beat and the bluesy melody sounded like slow, satisfying sex to his ears. As the song washed over her along with the churning water, Tracy couldn't help but grip the wooden railing so hard he thought it might splinter in his hands.

He listened while memorizing every inch of her body he could see. The freckles on her shoulders. The hollow at the base of her neck. The gentle curve of her small hips. He could see what he'd felt when he was touching her. She was more petite and slender than the women he usually enjoyed. Not since he was too young and stupid to know better had he gotten involved with someone he could carry in his pocket. Someone he could hurt.

But there was no going back now. He was just going to have to be patient to get what he wanted. To make sure she could take all of him, that she wanted to take all of him, and everything he planned to do to her.

Until tonight, he was actually known for his patience. Loved and hated for it by the women who frequented the same clubs. Alicia Bell was the first one to truly test him and she hadn't even had to try.

She dragged her body onto the corner seat of the hot tub and lifted her legs until they were bent over the rounded rim. One hand reached back behind her head and the other lowered between her legs.

*Fuck me.*

Sweet Jesus, he knew exactly what she was about to do. Knew before she slid her soaking panties to one side and pressed closer to the large jet that was powerful enough to ease his stubborn back aches. Powerful enough to make her feel as if she were being well and truly fucked.

In hotel Jacuzzis, with water toys and showerheads, he'd done this to women—guided a hard stream of pulsing water between their legs and brought them to climax without actually touching them. But he'd never seen anything as erotic as Alicia doing it to herself by moonlight.

*Good girl*, he thought, as heartened by her actions as he was turned on. She *was* a natural. Passionate. She wanted and needed release, enough to risk a late-night encounter to seek it out. There was at least a slender thread of wild rebellion inside her, begging to be released.

He could do things with that slender thread that would make her scream.

It would be easy to let himself imagine she knew he was there. That this was an invitation, an opening for him to take what he wanted. To join her in the water and enjoy exploring his brand new obsession. But she wasn't that manipulative, and he wasn't that lucky. Not tonight.

She moaned softly, so softly it almost merged with the music, and he knew that was what she intended. Clever. The muscles in her legs worked as she rocked back and forth against the massaging jet, her fingers spreading the lips of her sex...for him. Begging him to come closer and taste.

His jeans were tight against his cock and he hissed, swiftly undoing the buckle and sliding the zipper carefully down over his shaft. He gripped his erection tight as she pressed her sex on top of the jet's short nozzle and pumped her hips against it, riding it, her mouth opening on a silent cry as she closed in on her climax.

She *was* ready...but not for him. Not yet.

Tracy stroked himself in time to her thrusts, thinking about what he would do to get her ready. It wasn't ego to think she would need to be prepared before he could take her. He would stretch her sweet little ass with a smaller plug at first, and bind her wrists and ankles to get her used to being restrained while he filled the pussy he couldn't take his eyes off of. He would see how much she could take. What she liked. He would have her begging for his cock by the time he was through. Just thinking about how good she'd feel around him brought him to the brink of orgasm in a shamefully short amount of time.

When he thought he couldn't take it anymore, her softly

gasped, "*Tracy*" sent him over the edge.

He backed away from the railing, his teeth bared as he came in his own hand. He shuddered at the intensity of it. Too hot. Too fast. Too out of control.

Taking a deep breath, he turned, scooping up his shirt to wipe himself off as he went back inside and headed for the empty guest room upstairs.

It had been unexpected—*she* had been unexpected—but he was going to need a hell of a lot more restraint than that over the next few weeks. He was a grown man, for God sake, not an adolescent with his first hard-on. Alicia was a sweet temptation, but he knew that regaining his control would be the only way to guarantee her pleasure.

She'd said his name.

He wanted to hear it again. As he stripped and threw off the covers he knew he wouldn't need, he made a promise to himself. Before Alicia Antonia Bell got in her car and went back to her life in the city, she would know what it was like to scream his name while he was inside her. She would learn to crave his touch and know what it meant to submit to him completely.

He would give the freckle-faced teacher a lesson she would never forget and himself the satisfaction he knew he would find in her body. When she left, he would turn his mind back to the task of settling down. But tonight *she* was all he could think about.

The morning was too far away.

"Oh, God." Alicia muttered raggedly, letting the waves of a magnificent orgasm ripple through her even as the need for another built inside her. What was wrong with her?

Tracy Reyes.

The answer was immediate and set off a new rush of shivering sensation. She'd tried to sleep, tossing and turning for two hours before she'd decided a relaxing soak in the hot tub might help relieve her tension.

All of her tension.

It wouldn't be the first time. A few days ago she'd discovered, almost by accident, another use for the massaging jets that covered the heated pool. It had been exciting and a little taboo then, experimenting with the different sizes and power levels, but tonight? It was mandatory. She' desperately needed relief and her hand wasn't enough.

His hands... She could still feel his strong fingers on her back and the weight of his hand on her braid. Still smell his clean spice-and-leather scent all around her. When she wasn't thinking about what would have happened if he hadn't said goodnight when he did, she was thinking about the way she'd reacted to him.

Alicia could have been sixteen again, letting her boyfriend stick his hand inside her panties as they made out against the lockers at a school dance. She hadn't been able to say no to Robbie, despite the danger of being caught or her mother's lectures about self-respect. There'd been something about him that made her want to be bad. Made her want for the first time.

Tracy Reyes made her want, too, but there was no comparison—the chemistry she'd experienced in his office crushed the memory of her innocent high school rebellion. It wasn't just sex, though she couldn't help but wonder what it would feel like to be with someone that big and muscular. He really was a beautiful beast of a man. But there was something else that drew her to him.

It was the way she'd responded when he took control, massaging her without asking permission, because she needed it. It hadn't felt invasive or aggressive to Alicia. She'd felt pampered. Cared for. The way he could read her... She had a feeling he would be the same in the bedroom. Devastating. Her previous lovers were considerate, gentle, even skilled, but they didn't know what she craved.

Would Tracy? Would he be rough in his passion?

Forgetting to treat her like a breakable doll and making her feel like a woman instead? Would he grip her wrists the way he had in the living room and hold them over her head so she couldn't push him away?

Alicia moaned and started to rock against the powerful jet again, feeling the pounding pressure on her clit. She knew he would. A man like that would know exactly what he was doing. Would know what she needed before she did. Would make her do things she never would have dared to before. Make her come so hard…

"*Ahh.*" She ducked her head under the water to muffle her cries as her second climax hit her. It had never happened that fast. Never without a detailed fantasy and a long, slow build. Never twice in a row.

If just the thought of him could get to her like this, how would she survive the real thing?

She lifted her head, gasping for breath as she dropped her shaking legs back down into the water. "Enough."

Tomorrow when the sun came up and sanity prevailed, she would remember that she hadn't known him a few hours ago. That she was here for her sister and the baby. That she didn't lose her head like this for anyone, but especially not for a man who'd done nothing more than rub a kink out of her neck. She was too smart for that.

Alicia pulled her body out of the water and reached for her towel, drying herself off with shaky hands, turning off the music on her iPod and slipping on her pajama bottoms before walking back toward the house.

When she reached the top of the stairs, she opened the door to the master bedroom quietly, checking on her sister and reminding herself about her priorities. Jinny had thrown off the covers and was curled up tight with the body pillow Alicia had bought for her on the trip here. She looked so young and peaceful, reminding Alicia of the months after their mother had brought her home from the hospital. They used to lie on the floor beside her crib, talking softly and watching little Jinny sleep, planning all the tea parties they would have and games they would play when she was older.

A baby. Jinny was having a baby. Alicia closed the door and turned toward her room with tears in her eyes. Mom would have been so excited at the prospect of being a grandmother, but Alicia had only been able to focus on protecting Jinny. Keeping her safe. She'd been doing it for so long, worrying and trying to make up for their parents' absence by being the voice of reason, that she wasn't sure she remembered how to be anything else for Jinny. How to be a sister. But she had to try.

Mr. Reyes was right about that. She needed to be here for Jinny without pressuring her. She wouldn't say another word about leaving or getting a divorce, no matter how much Miguel's behavior tempted her. Jinny didn't need the extra stress so close to her pregnancy and Alicia didn't want to chase her away again.

She missed her family. She just had to trust that Jinny would make the right decisions on her own.

Damn it.

Alicia stripped naked and fell into the bed with a sigh. Tomorrow she would find a nearby bed-and-breakfast for them to stay at until the baby came. She would miss the hot tub, but the mountain getaway was no longer a place of serenity.

Tracy Reyes and his larger-than-life presence had taken over and changed everything.

## CHAPTER FOUR

Her sister was gone.

Alicia had gone into Jinny's bedroom—a little late, since she'd showered, primped and put on her favorite sundress due to last night's new arrival—to see what she wanted for breakfast. It was the same thing she'd done every morning since they arrived, only today, her bed was stripped and her body pillow was gone. Jinny wasn't there.

She ran down the stairs, calling her name and opening every closed door in the house. Had she gone into labor? Had she been taken? Had the sexually charismatic man claiming to be Mr. Reyes actually—

She couldn't finish the thought, feeling sick to her stomach and imagining the worst. Flinging open the front door, she barreled down the steps and straight into an old man with a thick mustache and a wide grin.

"Are you the sister?" he asked.

*The sister.*

"Yes?" She gripped his arms. "Jinny is my sister. Do you know where she is? Is she in the hospital?"

He nodded, his smile turning to a concerned frown. "No, no. And of course I know where she is. Are you okay,

Miss?"

"She's from the city, Luca." Tracy's amused voice made her turn her head toward the barn to see him walking slowly in their direction. "They're a skittish people and notoriously late risers. She slept the morning away and missed all the excitement. Good morning, Alicia Bell. Don't you look pretty?"

The man nodded in understanding and Alicia let him go, putting her hands on her hips as she turned to her host with a glare. Slept the morning away? It was only nine o'clock. "Where is Jinny?"

Tracy pushed his hat back, his smile still firmly in place. "She went down a few hours ago with her mother-in-law and Miguel. I gave him the day off so they could pay a visit to the doc, but by now they're at the main house for the small baby shower being thrown in your sister's honor."

Luca chuckled. "Small, he says. I can't believe how many Reyes have already descended on the ranch and it's not even noon. Your aunt sent me with a list of supplies to get in town after I dropped off Old Man. She also wants to make sure you and Miss Bell will be there so Jinny won't feel overwhelmed by her new family."

"We'll be there eventually," Tracy affirmed. "I have some business to attend to."

Alicia stood frozen, eyes wide, when Luca nodded respectfully and walked to his truck without another word. Jinny was safe and the baby wasn't coming early. Tracy wasn't a murderer. Instead, he'd introduced her sister to her husband's mother, gotten her a doctor appointment and put together a party for her in less than twelve hours. And Jinny had let him, instead of brushing his ideas off the way she did Alicia's.

The truck disappeared and she still hadn't moved. It wasn't until Tracy put his hands on her shoulders that she started to shake. "What's this? Why are you trembling, Alicia? What is it?"

She shook her head and pulled away from him, walking blindly. "I'm fine. I was just surprised."

Tracy was following her. "If you're fine, why are you about to walk into the barn wall?"

She stopped and looked up in surprise at the wooden slats in front of her. Shit. She turned to find him closer than she'd expected. "She's never up before I am. And she's had a rough time with the baby. When she was gone and the bed was stripped I thought..." *Horrible things.* She shrugged. "I was worried."

Tracy swore again, dragging her close and wrapping his arms around her shivering body. "Jesus, I'm a thoughtless bastard. The last thing I wanted to do was scare you. My intention was an intimate welcome to the family for your sister, but once the aunts found out about her, it took on a life of its own."

He was rocking slightly on his heels, soothing her. He really smelled fantastic. She sniffled and buried her face in his white short-sleeved shirt. "That was very nice of you. I wish she'd woken me up to let me know."

She felt his sigh on the top of her head. "She planned to. I suggested letting you sleep and bringing you down myself when you were ready. She was so excited to be meeting Miguel's mother I think she might have agreed to anything."

Alicia could imagine. She lifted her head and took a step back. She really needed some distance from this man. "Thank you, Mr. Reyes. You didn't have to go to so much trouble but I know Jinny is over the moon. The least I can do is give you back your privacy. I'll just throw my bags in the trunk of my car and go see if they need any help putting the party together."

He stared at her with something in his eyes that made her heart start racing again. "What? Did she take my car?"

She started to look but he shook his head. "She didn't take it. But I just got off the phone with a mechanic who's on the way to pick it up. I poked around under the hood and kicked the tires this morning, and frankly I'm not sure how you got here in one piece. I'm tempted to take it out back and shoot it."

Alicia frowned in consternation. "How long have you been awake? Because *I'm* not sure I've ever met anyone who could get into so much business that wasn't his this early in the morning. Thank you for helping Jinny out, but I'm fine. My car is *fine*."

Tracy crossed his arms across his broad chest, his biceps doing their best to distract her. "Your car is a fifteen-year-old heap of junk on wheels. The windows don't work, you have one taillight, you may have fixed one tire but two others are bald and you're leaking oil all over my driveway. Doesn't sound like you know what 'fine' means."

Before she could respond he turned and headed into the barn.

"Wait a second," she called as she followed him in, fuming. "I may have given you the wrong impression last night. Just because I listened to your advice about Jinny and accepted your invitation to stay until morning doesn't mean I enjoy being bossed around."

"Too bad."

His back was to her and he was in hidden in the shadows of the dimly lit barn. She moved closer. "Excuse me?"

He turned, gripping her hips and lifting her until her back was against a wooden stall before she had time to do more than gasp her surprise.

"I said, that's too bad," he murmured close enough that she could feel his breath against her cheek. "Because I think you need a little bossing around. In fact, just between you and me, I think you'd love it."

"Wh-what?" His words sank in and she felt something wholly feminine flutter inside her stomach. "You're not talking about the car anymore."

"No, I'm not."

"Are all cowboys this forward, Mr. Reyes?" If they were,

she was moving here immediately, but she wasn't going to say that out loud.

"Not if they're gentlemen." He pressed his forehead to hers, his grip tightening on her hips. "I didn't mean to scare you, and I was planning on approaching you differently, but you kept me up all night, Alicia Bell. The least you can do is call me Tracy."

"I did?" Alicia sounded breathless because she was. He was so close it was hard to think. "You didn't scare me."

"Yes, I did." He nodded against her head, splaying his hands so his thumbs pressed against her lower belly over her green sundress. "But I kept you up too, and there's no use denying it. For the same reason, I'm guessing. I usually have more patience than this, but I'm not a man who likes to waste time, Alicia. When I see something I want, I go after it. And I see something I want."

He looked into her eyes for one tense heartbeat. Then another. Waiting. Flexing the hands she'd placed on his hard, warm chest she licked her lips.

Tracy groaned. "I think I'm going to take that as a yes."

The first brush of his lips against hers was light. Teasing. He waited until she moved closer before deepening the kiss. Alicia's bones turned to butter and she melted into him, loving how his body felt against hers.

He pulled back, just enough so their lips were barely touching as he spoke. "You haven't asked me what I want. Wouldn't you like to know? I do have something specific in mind."

"What, specifically, do you want?" Other than to kiss her brainless.

His fingers tightened in reaction. "You're in town until the baby is born, right? Well, as long as you are, I want you to stay here, in my house. With me."

She whimpered when he pressed one thickly muscled thigh between her legs, rocking her sex against the rough fabric of his jeans. He bit her lower lip gently. "Your body is already agreeing to it and you wouldn't even have to unpack, so this is where you say 'Yes, Tracy.'"

"I don't want to cause any trouble," she moaned, moving her hips instinctively against him, unable to help herself. "We shouldn't have been here in the first place."

"Stay with me."

"Yes," she gasped, unable to deny the command.

He stopped her movements with a bruising grip. "Yes, Tracy," he repeated in that voice that made her start to tremble.

This wasn't fair. It was coercion. But she couldn't find a single reason to deny him. What harm would staying at his house do? Especially if he was going to keep doing what he was doing. "Yes, Tracy."

He kissed her in approval, the passionate kiss she'd been longing for, his tongue stroking hers as one hand left her hip and slipped beneath her dress. His knuckles pressed against her clit through her panties and she moaned into his mouth.

*Yes. Touch me.*

He lifted his mouth again. "Good girl. But I want more. I want you to give me permission to do whatever I want to this body..." He paused and did something to her clit with his fingers that made her jerk against him and gasp. "Whenever I want it, as long as you like it and don't tell me to stop."

"Don't stop," she whispered, more turned on than she'd ever been before. Ready to burst. Ready to come right now. She lowered her hand to cover his and pressed it harder against her. "Please."

"I like that word," he growled. "But that isn't what I need to hear. Say it."

When he stopped his caresses and lowered his thigh, she groaned, raising her hand and letting it land with a frustrated thud on his chest. "We hardly know each other. I can't just— Why are you playing with me like this?"

Tracy released her and stepped back, his expression enigmatic, his bronze cheeks flushed with the same need she was feeling. "I do want to play with you, Alicia Bell. But it isn't a game. So let's get to know each other. I'll tell you a little bit about me. I suppose you could call me a kinky bastard. I spent the night imagining you tied to my bed while I spanked your pussy until you came for me. I lay there for hours picturing you on your knees, letting me have you in ways that you never dreamed were possible. That's who I am. What I want."

Holy— She took a shaky breath and lifted her chin, knowing he was expecting to shock her and succeeding a little more than she wanted him to know. "You mean like BDSM?"

He reached out with one hand and hooked his fingers around her bodice, tugging her closer. "An apple for the teacher. What do you know about this subject, Ms. Bell?"

She licked her lips, amazed she was having this conversation at all. It was surreal. Unexpected. Exciting. "I've read about it."

"Textbooks? Psychology papers?" His knuckles were brushing against her skin.

She shook her head, swallowing. "Erotic fiction. There's one author whose books are very detailed named Eden Brad—"

"Did you like it?" he interrupted softly. "The details? Did they make you wet?"

Oh God. "Yes."

She'd loved it. It was her guilty secret. While other teachers at her school were reading young adult books to connect with their students or sweet romance to escape them, Alicia was reading about dungeons and dominant men who craved submission and love.

"Tell me your favorite—" Tracy's jaw clenched and he inhaled sharply. "Damn it." He let her go and lifted his hat long enough to run a hand through his hair. "There's a truck coming up the drive. Probably for your car. Stay here and I'll deal with it."

*Oh my God.*

Alicia covered her face with shaking hands. Was this actually happening? Making out in a barn with a man she hardly knew? Having a conversation with him about kinky sex?

She wanted to say yes. It was almost frightening how badly she wanted to agree to this proposition from a man she hardly knew. She'd never felt anything like this—like they were two magnets drawing closer together. She could feel the pull in her stomach. In her sex.

As long as she was in town, he'd said.

There were rules to this kind of thing, she knew. Safe words and limits. She would have to let him know if she wasn't okay with any of the things he mentioned. Being tied up. Being spanked. Being taken whenever and wherever he wanted her. Her rule would be that her sister could never find out what was going on, which wouldn't be easy when they were all under the same roof.

Or that would be her rule...if she were saying yes. Which she would only do if the idea of Tracy spanking her until she came turned her on.

*Which would be crazy.*

Alicia jumped when she heard a whinny in the stall beside her. "Oh lord, when did you get here?"

A horse. A large white-and-brown speckled horse was eyeing her with a resigned air. She laughed. "So what do you think I should do?"

Tracy's chuckle made her close her eyes in embarrassment without turning around. "I see you met Old Man. He's going to be our transportation for the day."

That got her attention. She whirled around. "He's going to what? I'm skittish city folk, remember? I've never been on a horse in my life. If my car were still here I'd just meet you and save Old Man the aggravation. It isn't that far, right? I could probably walk."

Tracy was leaning against the door, his lips tilted in a

slight smile. "Your car is still here, Alicia Bell. You told me to stop sticking my nose in where it doesn't belong, but your car is a death trap so I'm compromising. I asked my guy to come back in a few days and do any work that needs to be done in my driveway instead of towing it out of your sight."

"You did?" Her voice rose in genuine shock.

He nodded. "I want to control your pleasure, Alicia, not your life. Despite evidence to contrary, I'm not an asshole."

*I want to control your pleasure.*

Oh God.

"Tracy I think—"

He held up his hand. "We should hold off on making any firm decisions for the moment. You know what I want and you've admitted to more than a passing interest in the topic. Neither one of us can deny our mutual attraction without lying. Do you agree?"

"Yes, Tracy." It slipped out and his eyes narrowed.

"Good," he responded with a rasp. "That's good. Then let's do an experiment. While you're thinking, you're going to ride down to the party with me. It will take a little time, and we'll be all alone on a private road. Until we reach the front gates of Reyes ranch, you'll do what I ask and let me do what I want to your body. Just a taste of what's coming, to see if you want the main course."

She bit her lip, wondering how they could do anything but cling for dear life to the big animal's back. "Okay."

He raised one eyebrow and she corrected herself. "I mean, yes, Tracy."

He strode toward her and kissed her forehead before pushing her toward the door. "Let me get him saddled while you go inside and take off your underwear."

She laughed. "What?" He stared at her. He wasn't kidding. "But I'm going to meet your family. Jinny's in-laws. I can't do that in a skirt with no…"

He'd already started the experiment, she realized. If she wanted this, wanted to see what it was like, she had to follow

171

his instructions. Going commando would be embarrassing, but only for her, as long as she was careful and there were no sudden breezes.

Did she really want to do this? A little experiment? A little excitement?

Yes, she *really* did.

It only took her fifteen minutes to freshen up, make sure her braided bun was secure and slip off her underwear before returning to the patio. Tracy was waiting beside the giant but thankfully serene-looking animal, a thoughtful expression on his face.

"Are you ready, Alicia Bell?"

She nodded and started down the steps, loving the way he said her name.

"Show me."

She froze, her cheeks heating. "Now?"

"Now."

God, he had a sexy voice. She reached for the knee-length hem of her sundress and pulled it up slowly, her heart pounding in her ears when it finally revealed her bare sex to his gaze.

She heard him growl. "You're a beautiful woman. I could look at you for hours, but then we'd never make it to the party. Are you ready to go for a ride?"

Yes. But not the kind he was referring to. "I'm ready."

"You can drop your skirt now and come down."

*Shit.* She let go of her skirt, still blushing. When she reached him he picked her up with one arm and got up on the horse in a move so smooth she had to smile. Such a cowboy. There was only one problem.

"I think I'm facing the wrong way," she said with a laugh.

He reached around her and took the reins, looping them on the saddle horn. "No, you're not. Put your legs over my thighs and hold onto me."

"Oh God." She obeyed nervously as the horse began to

stroll in an unhurried gait down the driveway. Her hands tightened on his shoulders. She was so close she could see every long, dark lash that framed his eyes and the small, barely visible scar on his strong jaw. "Are you sure this is safe? Shouldn't you be steering?"

"Old Man knows where to go. You need to trust me, Alicia. You'll have to if we're both going to get what we want. I won't let any harm come to you."

"Okay." Some part of her already trusted him to a certain extent. It must. Why else would she be in this situation, waiting for his next command? *Wanting* it? "What now?"

His smile was wicked. "Eager to start this experiment, are you? Now we get to know each other." He reached up and undid the buttons on the bodice of her sundress, sighing in satisfaction when he spread the fabric and saw her breasts. "And I find out how sensitive you are."

He cupped her breasts with his large, rough hands and she shivered. When it came to him, she was apparently very sensitive. Every squeeze, every scrape of his thumbs across her nipples made her ache.

"Do you like this, Alicia?"

Did he have to ask? "I do."

"Take off my hat and hold it for me." He waited until she complied then lowered his head. "Let's see how you like this."

"Oh!" He sucked one nipple hard against the roof of his mouth, and she could feel each tug of his teeth all the way to her sex. She was wet. Empty. Her position didn't even allow her to press against him or feel the hard leather of the saddle as they rocked to the rhythm of the horse's stride. She needed more. "Tracy, please. *Please*."

He raised his head, his eyes nearly black. "Please what?"

She dropped one hand from his shoulder and tugged at the hem of her dress. "Touch me."

The hands on her breasts slid up to her neck, his fingers tracing her jaw, thumb pressing against her lip. "I am touching you, Alicia." He glanced up at her hair. "And suddenly realizing I might have a Lady Godiva fetish. I want to see you naked astride a saddle, your hair flowing down around you, your wrists bound as you hold the reins."

She made a fist around the green fabric between her thighs. "Tracy, don't tease me."

He lowered his hands to her breasts again, caressing her nipples then pinching them firmly. Alicia moaned. "Baby, if you can't take this tiny tease, the experiment might be over before it's even begun. Put your hand back on my shoulder."

Damn it. She bit her lip at the pressure of his pinch before obeying, studying his shirt so he wouldn't see the frustration in her eyes.

"Look at me, Alicia."

When she did, his dark eyes snared her. "I *will* touch you. I'll tangle my fingers in those tight blonde curls and feel how wet you are for me. I'll suck on your clit the way I sucked on your nipple and taste you on my tongue."

"*Yes.*" He was tugging on her nipples now, punctuating his words with small twists and squeezes, and Alicia could almost feel what he was saying. Feel his hands and his mouth between her thighs.

"I will know every inch of your sweet pussy, better than anyone ever has. I'll make you come harder than you thought you could, and I'll do it again and again. With my hands, with my mouth, with whatever pervertible toy I have at my disposal. And then, Alicia...? Then I'll make you come on my cock."

"Oh God." She was panting. Needy. Ready to do whatever he asked as long as she got to come.

His next words were like a splash of cold water on her head. "But not yet."

She tensed and he released her nipples, stroking the undersides of her breasts lightly with his knuckles. "I hope those books you read talked about patience. How much better it can be when the heroine gives her body's pleasure over to her lover."

They did, but she was having a hard time remembering the details. If he was feeling even half of what she was right now, she wasn't sure how he could form coherent sentences. "But aren't you...?" She looked down at his jeans and he laughed roughly, his hand coming up to grip her wrist and drag it down his broad chest and into his lap.

"Tempted? Turned on? Hard as fucking stone?" he replied. "Just so we're clear and there's no misunderstandings between us, you can feel for yourself."

Jesus he was... Her fingers gripped the thick, steel-hard erection and, with his direction, traced its length until his belt halted her progress. He was *big*. Alicia shivered and her eyes met his again, uncertain but undeniably aroused.

His expression was one of grim restraint. "You will take me, Alicia Bell, and sooner than you're ready for if you don't stop looking at me like that." He took her hand off him and raised it to his lips. "I know exactly what to do to make sure you're ready for me. Trust me to take care of your body and your pleasure. Stay with me and be mine until you leave. You can complain and cuss and tempt me all you like, and we can stop whenever you give the word, but if you give yourself to me...I'll make sure you won't regret it."

She opened her mouth and he shook his head. "Don't answer yet unless it's a yes without hesitation." He smiled tightly and started to button her sundress again. "We're nearly there. We better cover you up so those ranch hands and my single cousins don't get any ideas."

Alicia held her tongue while he straightened out her top.

They reached the gate and he swung off the saddle, reaching up to wrap his hands around her waist. She'd lifted her leg and was facing him, ready to be lowered down when he groaned. "Wait. Show me again."

Her heart fluttered in her chest and she lifted her skirt, spreading her legs just enough to give him what he wanted. She could feel her arousal on her thighs, knew he would be able to see how much she wanted him.

She gasped and jerked in his grip when he lowered his head and flicked her wet sex with his tongue. She could feel his groan against her clit and arched her neck, so sensitive and aroused now it felt like she was one touch away from finding her climax.

He raised his head and she blew out a shaky breath. Torture. If she agreed to his proposal, this would happen again. He would take her to the edge and leave her there until she was desperate. And then he would do it again. She lifted the hat still dangling from her hand and placed it back on his head, adjusting it until it looked right and she got her breathing under control.

He chuckled roughly. "Thank you kindly, ma'am. I wouldn't be much of a cowboy without that."

He lowered her slowly to the ground, looking into her eyes with a fire that gave her a small amount of comfort. She wasn't alone in her need. He was right there with her. He just liked to be in control.

When they reached the gate, Tracy released her hands and the reins to open it for them. Alicia could hear children laughing and screaming and music drifting toward them, though the long driveway and tree line made it impossible for her to see anyone yet.

She started walking and then stopped, turning to watch him close the gate and guide Old Man in her direction. When he noticed her staring, he smiled.

"Yes, Tracy." She said the words and waited for them to sink in, for his smile to disappear and his jaw to tighten. She saw the tic of his pulse at his temple and it was her turn to grin.

Alicia whirled around and walked swiftly up the driveway ahead of him, reveling in her small but glorious victory. She'd surprised him, she knew. Put a dent in his control.

*He'll make you pay for that.*

She knew it. And for whatever crazy irresponsible not-like-her-at-all reason, she didn't care. He was offering her something she'd always fantasized about, and Tracy was the kind of man who could deliver. It was thrilling and a little scary, but those feelings—while new and disconcerting—were better than the regret she knew she'd feel if she turned him down.

Now she just had to get through this party without thinking about all the things he was going to do to her tonight, without imagining all the wicked, delicious things he'd described on the way over, while she was meeting her sister's new family and making a good first impression.

Alicia tugged on her sundress, feeling naked without her underwear. She wouldn't think about that either.

*Good luck with that.*

## CHAPTER FIVE

"You did a good thing today, Tracy. It was just what the doctor ordered."

Tracy finished his beer and glanced over at the ranch foreman. "Sorry to interrupt the schedule for this, Frank. I know you're busy."

The older man laughed. "Are you kidding? We got more work done today than I expected. The Reyes men needed something to do while their wives cooed over Miguel's pretty little bride." He shook his head. "I don't know why I didn't think of this sooner. He's like a new man."

"Who?" Tracy frowned. "Frank, did you know Miguel was married?"

"Hell no. No one did. I meant bringing in the family. He didn't know half of them yet, and with his father being a no-account and all, I guess he wasn't looking to. But now look at him. He refused to take the entire day off, helping us with his first branding, and I can't remember if he's ever been this relaxed."

Neither could Tracy. He watched Miguel laugh at something one of his uncles had said, his arms full with a wriggling two-year-old and his young wife by his side. He

178

looked different. Happy. More so then he'd looked this morning when Tracy had pulled him aside and given him a harsh talking-to about his wife's health and happiness. About responsibility to family. Even as he berated the boy, he'd taken responsibility for his own mistakes—he knew his aunt had a difficult time asking for help and he should have been more observant with them. Should have welcomed Miguel with a gathering like this instead of tossing him a job and leaving him to sink or swim on his own. He should have known about Jinny and made sure she was taken care of.

Frank patted his shoulder. "Son, I've known you since you were shorter and skinnier than I am, which is a damn long time. You have enough on your plate without adding a helping of guilt. The Reyes haven't been so flush and happy since your grandfather was young and feisty, so you're doing fine." He chuckled. "Better than fine, if the way you and the lovely Ms. Bell have been eyeing each other across the yard all day is any indication."

Tracy turned toward the cooler behind him and reached for another bottle. "You're getting old, Frank. Seeing things."

"Sure I am." Frank grabbed the bottle out of his hand and toasted him jauntily. "I'm old, boy, but I'm not dead yet. Or deaf. I heard Luca say something about Jinny and Miguel moving into the main house tonight while we build them a little lean-to of their own on the property."

Tracy narrowed his eyes dangerously. "That's right."

The old man was undeterred. "I also heard her sister will be staying up the mountain with you until the baby is born."

"Is this a question?"

"Not at all. Just hoping you think about the fact that you two will be connected by blood when the little one arrives. And Miguel's wife only has the one sister as her kin. She'd definitely miss her if Ms. Bell wasn't around on special occasions."

*Hell.*

"Damn it, Frank." He put down his beer and started walking to the stable. All damn day, all he'd been able to think about was getting Alicia back to his house. Hours of the women in his family wondering when he was going to get married and the men congratulating him for holding out. Hours of celebration and family togetherness and it felt like torture, because he wanted to be with her. Only her.

She'd said yes.

And he hadn't given a single goddamned thought to what might come after. Hadn't thought about Alicia being alone at Christmas because she regretted or was ashamed of what they'd done together and she didn't want to take the chance of running into him. Hadn't thought about the baby's birthdays or graduation or wedding. Not until Frank had to go and open up his damn mouth.

He'd fire the bastard if he weren't like a second father to him. If he didn't care so much about his opinion.

He swore when he reached the stable and made a beeline for Old Man. He'd leave. He'd get back on that damn plane again tomorrow and do his business and his thinking on the fly. Alicia deserved to have this time with her sister. To see her niece or nephew come into the world.

She didn't need him or his desire for her to do that.

He'd just gotten the horse saddled when he heard her voice. "Are we leaving now?"

Tracy tightened the cinch without looking at her. "I am. You can stay as long as you like."

"I can?"

He nodded, spending more time then he needed to gathering up the reins. "You might need a ride up tomorrow if you decide to stay the night. I'll be in the air on my way to Texas for business. Not sure if I'll be back in time for the baby, but I'd still like it if you stayed at my place for the duration."

"Wow."

The way she said it made him turn his head. Her arms

were crossed and she was studying him as if he'd just sprouted an extra head. "Wow, what?"

She shrugged. "Nothing. Fine. Thank you for the offer and I hope you have a successful business trip. Before you leave, maybe you can get me a list of men in the area who might be willing to take over our experiment for you. I'd really appreciate it, because I hate leaving things unfinished."

Tracy's muscles tightened to stone. She did *not* just say that.

Glancing around to make sure they were alone in the stable, he pulled her into the stall with him and pressed her against the wood. "Out, Old Man."

The horse walked out of the stall and stood like a sentinel, his ears twitching as he listened to the laughter outside. Then Tracy turned his attention to Alicia. "A list? That won't be happening."

She lifted her chin and glared up at him. "You think so? You wanted to control my body, not my life, remember? And now it looks like you changed your mind. Which is fine, except that I haven't. You've piqued my curiosity, Mr. Reyes. Now I'll just have to find a substitute to fill in the blanks. If not here then when I get back to New—"

He kissed her. He hadn't planned on it but he was sure that if she kept talking, he'd have her bound and gagged and thrown over his horse for his whole family to see. Whatever it took so he would stop thinking about another man giving her what *he* wanted to. Another man touching her without his permission.

Her mouth opened for him greedily, but her hands were pushing him away. He understood the conflict. Still, he couldn't let her go.

He forced his thigh between hers to spread her legs in the confined space, his hand seeking and finding what he hadn't been able to get out of his mind. One taste and he'd known he wanted more. One touch and he groaned against her lips, unable to resist filling her slowly with a single finger. He shuddered. She was so damn tight.

Alicia wasn't motionless in his embrace. Her hands had reached down and had his jeans unbuckled and unzipped before he could stop her. He tore his mouth away and struggled for breath when her fingers wrapped around his erection. "Alicia, don't."

"You broke our deal," she whispered, her hips moving against his hand, forcing his finger deeper inside her while she stroked him. "Which means you're not the boss of me."

Oh yes, he fucking was. He let her go, gripping her wrists and tugging her away from him, trapping her arms behind her back. "I was trying to be a gentleman, Alicia Bell. Trying to make sure you didn't have any regrets that would keep you away from your sister. This would be temporary, but family isn't."

She struggled a little against his grip, but he could see it in her eyes. She liked it. "You really are a control freak, aren't you? But I can make my own decisions. I've been doing it for a while and I've had a lot of practice. Especially when it comes to sex."

He lowered his head and pressed his lips to her cheek. "What I want from you is more intimate than sex. I know that, and you don't. Which is why I was trying to be smart about it."

"I know what I want, Tracy. I wouldn't have agreed to this if I didn't. If you don't, that's okay. Just let me go."

"Too late for that, baby." He let her go and grimaced as he zipped himself back into his pants before picking her up and getting on his horse. He guided her body until she was behind him and made sure her arms were wrapped around his waist. "Hold on. There's no backing out now."

\*\*\*

Alicia felt like she'd been on a roller coaster. For the

most part, the day had been full of joyful revelations and laughter. She'd focused on her sister, since Tracy—who was apparently the most popular member of the family—was instantly surrounded and on the other side of the party from her for most of the visit.

Jinny had bloomed for the Reyes family and been so grateful for Alicia's new attitude toward Miguel that she practically glowed. It made Alicia happy and sad at the same time. Happy for Jinny, and sad that she'd been the cause of any stress or drama in her sister's life. And Miguel, for the first time, had come to Alicia and apologized for allowing his pride to get in the way of Jinny's comfort and wellbeing. He'd admitted to being afraid he'd screw it all up. Being a father. Working on his family's ranch. Everything. He said after his talk with Tracy, he'd realized what was most important—making Jinny happy. It had given her hope that things would be better for her sister. A hope that turned to slightly selfish excitement when Jinny told her she and Miguel would be staying at the ranch with her mother-in-law until the baby was born.

She and Tracy would have his whole house to themselves to continue their experiment.

When she saw him disappear into the stable she'd been relieved, until she realized what he was doing. She wasn't sure what made her so bold, her anger or her desire…but whatever it was, she'd won. She'd gotten him right where she wanted him.

Naked in his living room.

*Smack!*

"Oh, Jesus!" She tried to move, but her wrists were bound behind her back with nylon rope. Her bare body was draped over his lap as he sat on the big leather couch. Her legs were stretched out behind her on the cushions as he pinned her with one firm hand, while the other spanked the cheeks of her ass with merciless and arousing intent.

*Smack! Smack!*

"Tracy!"

Her skin was on fire. Stinging and tingling and hot. Her breath coming in gasps as she lay over his muscular thighs, the ridge of his cock pressing into her side. She never knew where his palm would land next. If it would be hard or soft, fast or painfully slow. She'd had no idea spanking would feel so good. Or make her want him more than she already did. "Tracy, please."

"Please what, baby? Spank you harder? Don't tempt me, I know how much you can take." His voice was gritty with lust and restraint. His hand landed on her left cheek and she shouted at the sharp sensation. "Should I stop? Have you learned your lesson about tempting me to lose my control in public, when I can't do anything about it?"

Not if this was the result. "Yes!" she promised. "Oh God, yes."

"I think you're lying," he rasped, but she could hear the smile in his voice. "Spread your legs."

Alicia whimpered and turned to look back at him, but did as he asked, gasping when she felt his fingers sliding through the arousal between her thighs.

"So wet," he groaned. "Your ass is bright red and you are soaking fucking wet. You like this, Alicia?"

"Yes!" She felt him drag his wet fingers over her ass gently, tracing designs on her heated skin. "Mmmm."

"I like it too," he confided softly. "Seeing my marks on you. Watching the way you respond. It's the sexiest thing I've ever seen."

He gripped her under her hips with his big hands and lifted, bringing her to her knees with her ass in the air. Her sensitive breasts pushed against his firm thigh as his tongue lightly followed the path his fingers had taken over her tender cheeks, tasting her arousal and making her shiver. She moaned and pressed her forehead into the couch helplessly.

His fingers slid between her thighs again. "You're making me hungry, Alicia. Too hungry. I'm going to need more." He pushed one finger into her sex and she tilted her hips back invitingly. "Good girl."

She felt the second, thick finger and she gasped. "*Yes*. Oh that feels..."

"Tight." She felt his erection press harder against her side as he started to thrust in and out with his fingers. Stretching her. Pressing against a spot inside her that made her moan. He swore. "You have no idea how badly I want to fuck you."

"I do," she gasped. "I want you too. Tracy, I'm— Yes, *God*. I'm ready."

"No, you're not. What did I say I would do first? Before you could come on my cock?"

"Your fingers. Your mouth..." She moaned when his fingers pushed deeper, curving inside her and making her restless, breathless.

"Among other things," he agreed darkly. She felt his strong arm reach under her shoulders, lifting her head off the couch. "Kiss me, Alicia Bell."

He held her as her head turned blindly toward his, groaning at the carnal kiss that seemed to mimic the thrusts of his fingers. Her tongue tangled with his and she used the arm holding her up as leverage so she could pump her hips more forcefully back against his hand. She felt dirty. Sexy. Wanton.

When he bit her lower lip and tugged, she opened her eyes to see his glittering with need. He slowly released her then shifted on the long couch and flipped her over so she was on her back. Her hands, still bound behind her, pressed into her spine as he positioned himself between her thighs and draped her legs over his broad shoulders.

"Damn, you are a tempting sight. Too fucking tempting." He lifted her hips off the couch with his free hand, bringing her closer to him. Then with his other hand, still damp with her arousal, slipped two fingers back inside her sex, filling her again. She impatiently tilted her hips down to get more of his thick fingers inside her, needing more.

"Tracy!"

He paused. "Do you want to use your safe word already, Alicia?"

"No." She shook her head, licking her lips as she looked into his eyes. "I want you."

He groaned raggedly and lowered his mouth, spreading her swollen lips apart with his thick tongue and sucking on her clit as he fucked her with his fingers.

"Oh God," she cried. "Oh Tracy, that's..." She tightened her legs on his shoulders, not sure whether she wanted to push away or pull him closer. Too many sensations. Every inch of her tingling and sparking with need and pleasure.

Tracy curled his tongue around her clit as he thrust his fingers deep into her pussy. He lifted her hips higher with his other hand, pressing her sex into his hungry mouth. He was everywhere. Stretching inside her. Filling her everywhere.

Alicia instinctively pulled him into her with her legs as she came with a scream, and he slid out his fingers and thrust his tongue deep inside her sex, moaning as he drank in her arousal. When she pumped her hips against his mouth, he used both hands to grip her sensitive ass cheeks and drove his tongue deeper as she came for him.

The waves were crashing in on her and they wouldn't stop. *He* wouldn't stop until she was crying out again with another climax, this orgasm stronger than the first. "Oh my God! Tracy!"

As her thighs finally relaxed on his shoulders, he slid her legs down his sides and let her catch her breath for a moment. She opened her eyes, dazed and smiling weakly.

"*Yes.*" Tracy got off the couch, scooped her small body into his arms and carried her up the stairs to his bedroom, not stopping until they were in the master bath. He set her down long enough to remove the rope from her wrists and turn on the water then pulled her quivering body inside the large shower. Letting her feel the pounding heat on her shoulders, he held her against his huge frame and rubbed her arms and hands, making them tingle with renewed circulation.

He kissed her and she lost herself in the mixture of her arousal and his taste in her mouth. His gentle nips on her lips and playful tongue continued to tease her while he washed her body. As awareness came back to her, she took the soap from his hands and started to pay him back in kind. He shuddered when she pressed her soapy body against his, reaching around him to wash his back. Sliding her tummy against his thick, hard cock.

She wanted him.

"Alicia," he sighed, cupping her shoulders and stepping away from her. "Let's rinse you off."

She frowned. "Why won't you let me touch you? When do I get to drive *you* crazy?"

"You already drive me crazy, Alicia Bell. I'm hanging on by a thread here. What is it you want?"

She let him guide the shower's wand over her body before lowering her hand to his erection. "This."

His laugh was raw. "Jesus. And I was worried you'd be shy."

"I thought you were Mr. Observant."

"Look at that devilish smile." He kissed her softly. "You want my cock? I'd like to see those lips wrapped around it."

Her heart started racing again. "Yes, Tracy. Right here?"

"No," he muttered. "I want you in my bed."

He turned off the water and reached for a towel, wiping himself off briskly before grabbing another and turning his attention to her.

Alicia watched him through her lashes as he caressed her body with the soft white towel. He was thorough, tender, paying special care to the still-sensitive cheeks he'd spanked so wickedly not an hour ago. Seeing this big, confident man on his knees as he rubbed the cloth along her damp calves tugged at something inside her.

She could get used to this.

Her hand went to his head and she ran her fingers through

the thick, dark waves, smiling. "I think I'm dry."

He dropped the towel and looked up at her with a grin. "Wanna bet?"

She gasped and reached for the bathroom counter with the hand that wasn't tangled in his hair. He'd lifted one of her legs and placed it over his shoulder, kissing her again, his tongue filling her sex. "Tracy. *Oh*."

It felt deeper in this position. She had more control. She tightened her hand in his hair and started to move against him. God, it felt good. He growled, but he didn't stop, his fingers tightening on her thigh while he let her set the rhythm.

"That's so good," she moaned, amazed at how swiftly her arousal had spiked again. Her body was reaching for it greedily, wanting to come. "*Like that*. I'm close. Don't stop. Oh!"

Tracy had stopped long enough to place her clit between his teeth and slap a warning hand firmly on her ass, pulling her abruptly out of her sensual haze. She looked down at him in shock. "Tracy?"

He lifted his mouth. "Don't come."

*Don't come?*

He saw the question in her eyes. "Trust me." He set her leg down and stood, his broad chest heaving as he sought to slow his breathing. "I need you to let me stay in control, Alicia. I need… Take your hair down for me."

She tilted her head, sensing his tension. She raised her arms and made short work of the pins before loosening her braid.

He watched as she ran her hands through it and let it fall to her waist. "I've been dreaming about getting this in my hands. Silvery blonde and soft as satin." He moved closer and one of his hands slipped around the back of her neck, gripping the hair at the base of her skull and pulling in a way that made her knees turn to Jell-O. "I'm in love with this hair."

Tracy smiled when he pulled again and she gasped. "You like that."

She did. She liked everything he'd done to her. Everything he said he wanted to do. Even the frustration she was feeling because he wouldn't let her come was exciting...which didn't make any sense. But she didn't want him to hold back because she wasn't experienced enough. Because he thought she wasn't ready. She had to find a way to show him she was.

"Will you do that when I'm...sucking your cock?"

She blushed and his hand tightened in her hair. "Trying to see how far you can push me? Let's find out. Go into the bedroom and wait for me."

She had a feeling he was done holding back. She could only be so lucky. "Yes, Tracy."

# CHAPTER SIX

He was not in control.

Tracy stared at himself in the mirror, hardly recognizing the dark-eyed man who struggled with labored breaths to push down the need for the woman in his bedroom. The woman who trusted him to guide her through her first experience with domination and submission outside of a romance novel, who had already been spanked and restrained and was still trying to test him with her roving hands and sassy responses.

This should have been a night for conversations about limits and discovering what pushed her over the edge while he earned her trust and learned her body. While he taught her what he expected and found out what she needed in return.

Her body. All he could think about was getting inside. From the second she'd challenged him in the stable, he'd been one raw nerve. One wrong move away from spreading her legs and losing himself completely.

He hadn't been careful enough, and worse than that, he didn't want to be. Years of restraint, decades of skill, and in twenty-four hours she'd nearly wiped it all away. Why?

Because her eyes were haunting as a storm in a summer sky and her hair smelled like apples? Because the fear in her expression when she'd first seen him had vanished and she'd turned into a spitfire to protect her sister from him? Because she tasted like every good dream and the best sex he'd ever had?

He set his hands on the bathroom counter and bent his head, focusing on slowing his pounding heart. There was no way he was going to allow himself to hurt her, really hurt her, and that was what could happen if he didn't regain some semblance of control. This was a test, but it was one he wouldn't fail. Not tonight. He would give Alicia what she needed, and he would control himself.

He knew what he had to do. And what he couldn't.

Tracy forced himself not to do more than glance at the bed when he walked out of the bedroom, but one look was enough. She was kneeling at the edge, her back to him as she looked over her shoulder at the mirror above the dresser.

She was trying to see the marks he'd made when he spanked her. For some reason that innocent curiosity made him harder. He ground his teeth together, heading toward her and the narrow chest at the foot of the bed.

He opened it without a word and started to gather the things he would need, tossing them on the cover beside her. A length of blue nylon rope. Nipple clamps connected by a silver chain. A strip of black silk. A small bottle of lube. He saw one package that he'd forgotten was there and felt a small sense of satisfaction as he set it down beside her as well.

"You're like a BDSM Boy Scout," she breathed, turning on her knees to face him. "I had no idea that bag of tricks was in there. What are we going to do?"

He closed the lid and used his leg to slide it out of the way before he looked at her. "As long as you don't say the word and stop me, *I'm* going to do whatever I want. And you're going to let me."

She was watching him closely, seeing something in his expression that made her pause and lick her lips. "I thought you wanted me to su—"

He leaned close and pressed two fingers to her lips, reaching for the strip of silk and caressing her cheek with it. "I'll admit it's sexy as hell to hear the word cock come out of your mouth, baby, but I'm going to add a rule to tonight's play. If you want more, want to find out how good I can make you feel with my bag of tricks? You'll stop trying to make me lose control. In this bed, right now, I want you to do what I say. And unless you want to have this tied and put in your mouth, you won't try to say, kiss or lick anything without my permission."

Her eyes were wide as she listened to his words. He saw hesitation...and excitement. Good. "You can agree with me, Alicia."

"Yes, Tracy."

Fuck, maybe he *should* turn the silk into a gag. Just hearing her say his name made him want to forget his plans and push her back onto the bed. "I want to see you in my rope, Alicia Bell. I want you to give yourself to me, the way you said you would. Will you trust me?"

She nodded, her glance dropping to the rope beside her. Tracy saw her swallow and his lips quirked. "You liked having your wrists bound. I think you'll like this even better. And I know you'll love having your nipples pinched."

She opened her mouth and paused, as if remembering his warning.

"What is it?"

"What are you going to do with the other things?"

His smile was genuine, though it still felt strained. "I'll show you. We'll have to put this first one in before I can secure the rope. Put your hands on the bed, baby, and let me get you ready."

He guided her until she was on her hands and knees, turned to the side so he could reach every part of her. He skimmed the palm of his hand over her ass. "This will be sensitive, I know. I'll be gentle with you. Careful."

He reached down and opened up the wrapped butt plug. It was a starter, smaller than the one he'd been thinking of for her, but maybe that was a good thing. It would remind him that he needed to go slow. If he saw her take anything bigger...

"You have such a sweet ass, Alicia." He set the plug down between her hands where she could study it while he prepared her. He reached for the bottle of lube and flipped up the cap, hearing her whimpers when he squeezed out the liquid and let it glide down between her cheeks. His finger followed, rubbing the tight ring of muscles soothingly, hissing when she pushed back against him, as if she couldn't help herself.

He picked up the plug and used one hand to gently spread her while the other guided the narrow black toy into her ass.

"Oh!"

"Breathe, Alicia. Breathe out slowly and relax your muscles. It will feel full, it will pinch at first, and it will intensify everything we do for the rest of the night."

God, she was taking it. He watched the small cone-shaped plug disappear inside her and he swallowed a sound of agonized need. "Good girl," he rasped. "Keep breathing."

She was gasping and he could see the fine tremor that went up her spine. "Do you like it, Alicia?"

"I think so," she whispered. "I don't know. I..."

"Are you ready for more?"

She lowered her head and blew out a long, shaky breath. "Yes, Tracy."

"Then get up on your knees again and wait for me."

He turned and went back to the bathroom to wash the lube off his hands and give her a minute to experience the new sensation before he started to bind her. He grabbed her pins with a regretful sigh and strode back to the bed. "I hate to do this, but we're going to have to put that beautiful hair of yours up again so it won't get caught up in the rope."

She held her hand out but he ignored it, filling his hand with her hair and twisting it into a loose knot on top of her head before sliding the pins in to hold it up.

"You're awfully good at that, cowboy," she said softly, forgetting his rule for a minute.

He shrugged, putting the last pin in and letting it pass. "My cousins have a lot of children."

"I noticed."

Tracy couldn't help but wonder if she wanted children. She'd raised her sister. Was that enough for her? He looked down and saw her take another shaky breath, her nipples tight and her knees slightly spread, and all other thoughts left his mind.

"Put your arms behind your back...that's right. Trust me, Alicia?" She nodded. "That's good, baby."

As he picked up the rope and began to design the harness on her body, the world fell away. He knew how tightly to bind her arms and how the rope would frame her breasts and make them more sensitive. He knew how to snugly encase her hips, and the size and placement of the knot against her clit before he slipped the rope between the cheeks of her ass and over the plug.

He always made sure he took care with his partners, but Alicia was different. He lingered tenderly on her bare skin, tracing every freckle on her shoulders. He kissed her neck gently as he tied the final knot behind her and she tilted her neck with a shivering sigh.

He reached for the nipple clamps and opened his mouth over each of her breasts in turn before he put them on her. Her moan was soft and breathless, and it was nearly impossible for him to look away.

He forced himself to step back to study his work and he could see it in her expression. He'd been right. A natural. She was already there, in that blissful space, her eyes dilated and her cheeks flushed. "Alicia Bell, you are a vision."

She was. From the diamond design of the rope down her sides, to the blue that made him think of her eyes and the way she'd tilted her hips forward just slightly against the knot between her legs.

He wrapped his fingers around it. "Do you like that, baby?" He wiggled it and she moaned. "You do. I think one day soon I'm going to take you out to dinner, let you get all dressed up but make sure I bind you like this, just here. No one will know. You'll have to wait until we get home to come. Wait until I cut you loose and get inside you."

He couldn't look away from his hand between her legs. Could feel her arousal on his fingers, on the rope, and he had to resist the desire to fall to his knees and taste her again.

Not yet.

His hand went to his erection and gripped it at the base. "Are you ready, Alicia?" he growled. "I'm going to hold onto you while you suck my cock, and whenever you move you'll feel the rope rubbing between your legs and the plug filling your ass. You'll feel the weight of the chain pulling on your pinched nipples. You're going to want to come but you'll wait for me. Do you understand?"

She made a soft sound and nodded. "Yes, Tracy."

He reached behind her to grip the back of her harness while his other hand guided the already damp head of his shaft to her mouth. "I'll be careful, Alicia Bell. I just need to be inside you."

She leaned forward and moaned when her lips opened over the tip of his cock. Jesus. "That's good, baby." She took more and he shuddered, holding his hips still and watching her mouth stretch wide around him. "So fucking good."

He tugged the harness, knowing the move would tighten the rope between her legs even more. She sucked harder and he couldn't contain his hoarse sounds of approval. Couldn't stop the slight rock of his hips. He'd been hard and ready since she cornered him in the stable. Too primed, he knew, to last long. "Alicia, fuck, I love your mouth. Can you take a little more, baby?"

*Please God, take more.* She groaned and opened her mouth wider, taking more and making him feel like he was about to explode when the tip of his shaft hit the back of her throat.

He pumped against her a little faster, too close to coming to resist the temptation. "Alicia. Fuck, Alicia you have to stop or I'm going to—"

She pressed on the underside of his shaft with her tongue and a bolt of energy shot up his spine and set him on fire. "*Jesus.* Come Alicia. Come now."

Alicia cried out against his erection and he knew she was with him. *Yes.* He let go of the harness and held her head with both hands, thrusting into her mouth as he came so hard he saw stars.

He was fucking flying. She hadn't said a word, hadn't touched him, had let him do whatever he wanted to her, and he'd still lost control. He'd come in her mouth. He didn't do that. Most of the women he'd dated didn't enjoy it and he always had a harder time controlling his thrusts during climax. She'd felt so good. Too good.

He didn't know there was such a thing until now.

He looked down and saw tears in her eyes and pulled out with a curse, cupping her face with shaking hands. "Baby? Are you with me? Are you okay?"

"I'm okay." She nodded, staring at him with eyes hazy and glistening from their play. "I think I like the rope."

His chuckle sounded raw. Jesus, her innocent admission was making him hard again. "I do too. And your mouth. A little too much, I think. Seeing you tied up, feeling you...you are a small package of dynamite, Alicia Bell. I need to be more careful around you."

She smiled as if proud of herself, and Tracy couldn't help it. He kissed her.

He needed to be a lot more careful.

# CHAPTER SEVEN

"Earth to Aunt Alicia. Come in, Al."

Alicia jumped then made a face at her sister. "I'm here. And I'm not an aunt quite yet, which is a shame because I've been ready both times you've had these Braxton Hicks contractions. You faker."

Jinny grimaced and leaned back against the headboard of her bed. "I'm ready too, believe me. Poor Miguel. Maybe the baby is just helping me by making sure my husband doesn't turn white as a sheet and nearly pass out when it's finally time." She squeezed Alicia's hand. "Thank you for staying over last night and spending the day with me. Everyone's been wonderful, but it's weird having so many people hovering. And I miss my sister. I've been at the ranch for three weeks and it feels like I've hardly seen you."

Alicia's cheeks flushed and she got up to find something to fold. "You've been busy getting to know everyone and bonding with Miguel's mother. I think she's warming up to me. I think Mom would like her too."

"So do I, but you can't distract me by making me cry. You've been living up on the mountain with old Mr. Reyes, and I'm about to have a baby so I deserve details."

197

Alicia rolled her eyes. "What kind of details do you want, Jinny? You already know what his house looks like."

Jinny threw a pillow at her. "I'm not asking about the house, Al, and you know it. He's big and gorgeous and single and I've heard things about him that make me worry about you spending all that time alone with him."

"You're worried about *me*? I might faint from shock. But there's no reason to be, Jinny. He's really very boring. A good host, but boring. He's usually in his office working."

Alicia was a liar. Over the last three weeks she'd learned that Tracy was many things—a control freak, a creative and kinky lover and a man who put too many jalapenos in everything he cooked—but he was never boring. He did go into his office for a few hours every day to make calls and answer emails. That, at least, was true. And sometimes he would have her join him. She bit her lip. She wasn't sure how he was able to concentrate on work and playing her at the same time. He was a multitasking and talented bastard.

Jinny sounded thoughtful. "Really? He seems so…I would say sexy, but I'm as big as one of those cows out there and I don't remember what that word means."

"Funny," Alicia snorted. "Pregnancy has made you funny."

"Something must be wrong with him. No man should look like that and not have a line of women out the door. Do you know he's *never* had a girlfriend? Not since his senior year in high school, and he's practically forty, isn't he?"

Alicia folded another towel and frowned. "That can't be true. Trust me. He's boring but I wouldn't put money on him never having a date. Where are you hearing this?"

"I didn't say he didn't date, I said he'd never had a girlfriend." Jinny gestured toward the window. "And everyone. Well, not everyone. They really love him and respect his privacy, but they worry about him. His family? The people who have worked here since he was a teenager? They said he was engaged to his high school sweetheart, but then something bad happened and he changed."

"Something bad? That's frustratingly vague for gossip." She felt a pinch of pain in her heart at the idea that he'd been engaged to someone, even if it was twenty years ago. For someone like Tracy, that kind of commitment would mean something. He was old fashioned like that. "Maybe Mr. Reyes just likes his privacy. Maybe he doesn't want his family to know about his girlfriends so they won't pester him about getting married and having kids. I was at your baby shower, you know. I must have heard them mention it a dozen times."

Jinny giggled. "A billion. But you're right, it's probably just gossip. Miguel's mother said he told her on the phone last month that he'd be settling down soon. That it was time. Now everyone is speculating, and I'm learning all sorts of things about him. Like his nickname in the papers. Apparently they call him the Teflon Cowboy because nothing bad ever sticks to him and no one's even been able to get an interview with him. Ever."

"Now that, I can believe," Alicia responded absently. Tracy was settling down? It didn't look that way to her. Didn't feel that way either.

"I can't," Jinny argued. "He's young, but he's been the head of the Reyes empire for the last twelve years. Young and a *billionaire*. Patricio Reyes is the kind of guy you expect to see splashed all over the tabloids, or at those Hollywood parties with a runway model on his arm. Or a princess. But there's never been anything. No scandals. No pregnancy scares. And no interviews, not even about his business dealings. He has people to do that for him, apparently."

Alicia waggled her eyebrows playfully, ignoring the visual. "He sounds important. Who knew my sister was marrying into an empire?"

"Not me. Miguel never told me anything. Until Mr. Reyes threw that party, I thought they had one ranch, which was impressive enough. I didn't know they were all like landed, secret gazillionaires. Even Miguel's mother. Her husband stole her trust fund, but she had stocks in her name that she found out about when she came home. She's already talking about paying for the baby's college."

Alicia didn't want to think about it. Not now. "It's going to be a challenge at Christmas. I'll have to get really creative if I want to be known as the cool New York City aunt."

Jinny stopped smiling and fiddled with her blankets nervously. "You could stay."

"*What?*"

"There are teaching positions available in this district, Al. You could move here. Be near me and the baby."

Alicia came over to the bed and sat down beside her sister, reaching for her hand. "Not that I'm not thrilled that you actually want me around, sweetheart, but what brought this on?"

Tears spilled down Jinny's cheeks and she brushed them away impatiently. "Miguel and I have been talking about family. He didn't really get that he had one for a long time, other than his mother, and now that he's here and he's getting to know them? He says he can't imagine being without them. Without having people he can trust to have his back." She looked at Alicia, her heart in her eyes. "I had you, Al. You always had my back, even when you didn't agree with me. I know I didn't appreciate it until now. Until the baby. Whoever he's going to be, I want him to grow up having you around."

Alicia was crying too. She had to remember to thank Tracy for giving her such good advice. She hadn't felt this close to Jinny in a long time. They were a family again. "How do you know it's going to be a he?"

"He's being a pain."

She laughed and wiped her damp face. "Jinny? Thank you. I mean it. You don't know how wonderful it is to hear you say that. But whether I stay or go, this baby is blessed, because he has you. You are going to be a phenomenal mother."

Jinny took Alicia's hand and placed it on her stomach in time for her to feel a kick. "I should be. I had a good teacher."

They forgot about everything else and talked about baby names and childhood traditions Jinny wanted to pass on until Miguel had come to the room to bring his wife to dinner. Alicia made her excuses and left before they could ask her to stay another night, needing to process what her sister had said.

Missing Tracy.

She started her car and began the drive up the mountain back to the main house, lost in thought. Jinny wanted her to stay after the baby came.

It was hard to believe that three weeks had gone by so fast. Every day she grew closer to the woman Jinny was becoming and every night she discovered something new about herself in Tracy's arms.

He was still an exciting, frustrating mystery. He'd had her car fixed, he'd given her presents—most of which she would never be able to show anyone or wear in public—and he'd shown her more about her desires and fantasies, more about her body, than she could have imagined.

The things they'd done together, that he'd done *to* her… Just thinking about them made her tighten her hands on the wheel and drive faster.

The first week she thought she'd die of frustration. Not because he wasn't letting her come. She'd had more orgasms in those seven days than she'd had in her entire adult life.

It was because he wouldn't have sex with her.

They'd done everything else. And everything else in Tracy's world was more sexually stimulating and satisfying than most women dreamed about. Once he'd tied her up in the loft of the barn, with that damned delicious knot between her legs, and given her an orgasm without touching her—just by reading one of her erotic stories out loud. Once he'd taken her to the hot tub to reenact the scene he admitted to witnessing the first night he'd arrived—with his own unique twist. Once...

She felt her face heat and shook her head. Some of his ideas should be illegal, but none of them could put the fact that they hadn't actually done the deed out of her head. When she'd finally asked him if that was ever going to happen, it seemed to be the question he was waiting for. He'd spent hours playing her that night without letting her come, hours exploring her body until she was begging for release.

And then it happened. She was on top but he still had all the power, lowering her so slowly she wanted to scream as he filled her inch by thick, delicious inch. He was a big man, but he'd been thorough in his desire to make sure she was ready for him. She was so aroused by that point that all she felt was passion and need and a connection that was beyond intimate. Even the fullness that brought a momentary pain only made it better. They'd been so close, staring into each other's eyes as she came, that it felt like they were coming together in every way.

That was something she wasn't sure either one of them had been prepared for. That perfect first time. For Alicia it had been earth shattering. One of those rare moments you actually recognize as it's happening and know what it means. That you'll never be able to look at things the same way you did before.

She'd known—lying across his broad chest as he stroked her hair after it was over—that anything less than this wouldn't do. Would never satisfy her. She'd also known it was going to end. That however perfect this interlude had been, Tracy wouldn't ask her to stay.

His walls had gotten higher after that. He seemed more determined to hang on to his control. He never left her wanting—if anything he was more insatiable and passionate with each day that passed. But he was holding something back.

Maybe it had to do with Jinny's gossip. His high school sweetheart. Had she died? Did he love her so much that he'd vowed never to give his heart again? She knew firsthand that he hadn't been a monk. He was too experienced. Too skilled. Too up front about his sexual history.

That, she sometimes wished he held back more, but she was curious and, she had to admit, titillated by his descriptions of the things he'd done. He'd participated in several ménages, but usually only if he was the one in charge. He'd been to an orgy once, and she'd been unable to keep herself from laughing at his description of the oily, confusing mass of bodies.

And a few days after he'd tied up his best friend's girlfriend to help her enact a fantasy, he'd even played with a woman on his personal jet on the way home, though they hadn't had sex. The same day Alicia had met him and he'd decided he wanted her.

The opposite of a monk.

From what she'd learned about BDSM so far, sexual honesty was one of their Boy Scout badges. He hadn't been trying to make her jealous. He'd been forthcoming. That was how it worked. She gave herself into his care and he hadn't given her any reason to believe it was a mistake.

He'd also told her this was the first time he'd had this kind of "relationship". He'd had weekends with a single partner in the Bahamas and Las Vegas, but he'd never had a sexual playmate living in his house.

Sexual playmate. He hadn't meant those words to be hurtful, she knew. But they painted a picture she couldn't mistake. They defined what it was they were doing in a way that left no wiggle room for more.

If Miguel's mother was right and he was planning on settling down, it wouldn't be with her.

She refused to regret the decision she'd made to say yes

to his proposal. Making love, swimming naked in the mornings and going for rides together on Old Man at sunset...trying to cook in the kitchen without it turning into a sexual food fight.

Alicia had never had this before. She'd been forced to grow up overnight and had to focus on being responsible. Reliable. She'd never even had a real vacation, telling herself that New York had all she needed and summer school was relaxing.

This wasn't real, but it was the best time she'd ever had, something just for her that she couldn't feel bad about even if she wanted to.

She was a realistic woman. Even if he weren't a controlling cowboy who didn't know how to express his feelings, he'd be an impossibility. Jinny hadn't had to tell her how often he traveled and how much he had on his plate. She'd heard enough of his phone calls to know people were surprised that he'd taken any time off at all. Being the head of a billion-dollar family didn't leave a lot of time to start a life with someone. Certainly not a teacher with a junk heap of a car and a lifetime of paying off student loans to look forward to.

She turned into the driveway and her throat closed when she saw the outline of Tracy's roof. It felt like home. Which was why she couldn't do what Jinny wanted. She couldn't move to Colorado.

No matter how much she would miss seeing the baby grow up, she knew herself well enough to realize she wouldn't be happy here. Not when this was over. Not when he'd moved on and settled down with someone else.

Against her better judgment, his honesty and all her sound, logical reasoning, she was in love with Tracy Reyes.

The long, ostentatious Hummer limousine in the driveway pulled her abruptly out of her thoughts and she blinked away her tears with a frown. Someone was here.

Alicia couldn't stem the initial flood of resentment for the stranger. She'd been looking forward to making up for the night she'd spent away from her lover, for making as many memories as possible before Jinny had her baby.

Guests were not in her plans.

There was a man leaning against the car and talking on his cell phone. When he saw her he hung up swiftly and smiled. "Good evening, Miss."

She drew her long braid over her shoulder and tugged self-consciously on her t-shirt. "Hello."

Alicia moved closer to him on her way to the door and he held out his hand. "My name is Roy."

She shook his hand and smiled politely. "Alicia. It's nice to meet you, Roy." She looked around, dying of curiosity. "How long have you been standing out here? Would you like something to drink? Some water or something?"

He laughed, delighted. "That's nice of you, Miss Alicia, but I've got everything I need in a cooler on the passenger seat. I've never been to Colorado before. It's beautiful and I was just admiring the view."

"It is, isn't it?" Alicia's gaze drifted to the mountains she could see beyond the house. "They don't have views like this in New York."

"Nowhere," he agreed companionably. "When Mr. Warren told Mr. Henry Vincent he wanted me to join them on their road trip, I wasn't expecting this kind of scenery. The city will never hold the same appeal."

She knew she looked surprised. "Wait, Henry Vincent, the guitar player for Shattered Pieces? *The* Henry Vincent?"

She loved that band.

Roy was beaming with pride. "The very same. He, Mr. Reyes, Faraday and Warren have been friends since college."

Warren. Dean Warren, his best friend he was just visiting with the sexy new girlfriend? "So Mr. Warren is here?"

"He is."

And he'd taken a road trip from the city...in a Hummer?

She stepped back uncertainly, sticking her hand in her

jeans pocket to grip her keys. "I should let you get back to your view, Roy. I think I'm going to spend the night at the ranch. If Mr. Reyes asks, let him know I'm with my sister."

Roy frowned slightly, nodding at her as she turned and walked back to her car. She should have called first, or Tracy should have let her know he'd be entertaining. It wasn't exactly something he needed a sexual playmate for.

She grimaced and opened the car door.

"Alicia Bell? What in the hell took you so long?"

She looked up to see Tracy striding down the steps and past Roy with a nod. He didn't have his hat on, and his thick hair looked disarmingly tousled. He was also wearing the blue button-down shirt she loved.

When he reached her, he cupped her shoulders and bent his head, kissing her with a carnality that made the keys drop from her limp fingers.

He pulled away with a growl. "You are in trouble, you know that, right? When you drove away last night you didn't mention anything about being gone for eighteen hours."

"She was having contractions," Alicia gasped, leaning helplessly against him. Damn, he was one hell of a good kisser. "She's frustrated it's taking so long."

"I'm frustrated too," he muttered. "And I'm planning on making up for lost time as soon as possible."

Alicia bit her lip and placed her hands on his chest, resisting when he would have kissed her again. "You have company."

"I do."

"I'm going back to the ranch with Jinny so you can visit."

His grip on her tightened. "No you're not."

She patted his chest gently. "It's okay, Tracy. I don't mind at all. This *is* your house, and I'm just visiting. Enjoy your friends. I'll see you when they're gone."

His eyes narrowed. "Are you still wearing your plug?"

She gasped and glanced around him to see if Roy had heard him. He was on the phone again. Alicia swallowed. Of course she was. He'd gotten her a set of different sizes. He'd wanted her to wear one for a few hours every day and threatened to withhold her orgasms unless she obeyed him. "Yes, Tracy."

"Good. I wouldn't want to think you'd forgotten about me. Now unless you want me to bend you over the hood of your car and spank you in front of Roy until you're begging, you'll give me your car keys and get your ass in the house. Now."

She handed him her keys but she couldn't soothe her nerves. How was she supposed to behave around these people? What did he expect from her? "Are you sure?"

Tracy's expression was enigmatic. "Am I sure I'm going to spank you if you don't do what I say? Yes." He hesitated. "Dean and Sara already know about you, Alicia. I'd like it if you joined us."

She melted a little. He'd told them about her. What and how much she wasn't sure, but it was something. "Okay."

"Inside. Now."

She smiled and blushed when Roy caught her eye. Tracy noticed and stopped beside him abruptly. "They're staying for the night, Roy. I got you a room at the B&B in town. It's a nice place and the owner is a fantastic cook. Tell her to make you my favorite."

"Thank you, sir."

Alicia laughed. "Be careful, Roy. His favorites usually burn the taste buds off your tongue."

Tracy smacked her behind in warning and she jumped. "Think you know me, Alicia Bell?"

She did. Not as much as she would like to, but as much as he would let her.

It would have to be enough.

## CHAPTER EIGHT

She'd done this to him. Close to a month of Alicia Bell in his bed, in his ropes and in his life and Tracy was an addict. So strung out that he couldn't stop touching her during dinner. Even now, as they sat on the deck watching the stars come out, his arm was around her shoulder, his fingers tangled in her long braid.

This morning had been his own special version of hell. He'd wanted to join her at the ranch, to call her to hear her voice. Instead he'd been reduced to computer porn.

He must have watched that video she'd let him take of her three times. He couldn't believe he'd gotten her to do it. Let him put her in that position. Hell, he couldn't believe he'd given in to the impulse to purchase that "gift" in the first place. Tracy had seen the machine at the club once or twice, but he'd never been tempted to use it on anyone.

Until Alicia.

Did he think seeing her on her knees, handcuffed to a rack with a motorized dildo filling her from behind, would help him keep his distance? Would allow him to see to her pleasure without losing control?

He hadn't started filming her until the fourth orgasm,

when he'd turned the machine to its highest speed. By her sixth climax he was jealous of the damned fucking machine and he'd dropped the camera, kneeling in front of her to thrust his way to heaven in her mouth, cursing his lack of control.

The next day he'd shoved that monstrosity in the barn loft so she wouldn't be tempted to use it, and he wouldn't be tempted by the memory of how much she loved the hard, fast pounding. The kind he still didn't feel she could take from him without getting hurt.

He shifted in his seat and tried to focus on the lively conversation around him. Sara and Alicia had instantly taken to each other, and he wasn't surprised. Sara Charles was outgoing, open and full of life—and she'd had Alicia relaxed and laughing within minutes of their introduction.

Tracy had wondered if she would feel awkward around someone he'd been with, even as a tertiary player. He'd harnessed the curvy redhead. Tasted her while she sucked him and Dean took her from behind. He wouldn't have been surprised if there'd been at least a moment of discomfort. Particularly from someone who hadn't had that much previous experience with kink.

But if it was there, he hadn't seen it. Which should have been a relief.

He didn't want to think about why it wasn't. Or why the idea of her being jealous didn't sound that bad.

"That sounds like a great idea."

"I'm game."

Tracy scowled at Dean when the women stood and slipped off their shoes. "What the hell did I miss?"

His friend chuckled. "Bored, Reyes? Sweet Sara and the lovely Alicia have decided we should go for a moonlight swim." He stood up and Tracy watched him remove his frayed t-shirt. "Wake up or you'll miss all the fun."

He stood, towering over his friend and shaking his head. "You are not the same grim bastard I had dinner with at

Franco's last month."

Dean was watching Sara strip off her dress. "No, I'm not. And I'm praying she'll make sure I never turn into him again."

Tracy stilled in the middle of unbuttoning his shirt. "That sounds like you have a plan."

The CEO of Warren Industries lowered his voice. "This road trip isn't just to see you, Reyes. Though I do have a few things I need to talk to you about." He took a breath. "Somewhere between her fantasy to make out in a Rocky Mountain truck stop and our trip back home, I'm going to convince that woman to marry me."

That explained Roy and the Hummer. Tracy knew it was in the back of Henry Vincent's limo where they'd first started their fantasy fulfillment adventure. Where his friend had fallen in love. "Good man. She's a keeper."

The sounds of splashing had both men turning to see the women entering the pool in nothing but their bras and underwear. Dean groaned. "She is something." He elbowed Tracy as he moved toward the stairs. "Alicia isn't your usual style, other than her hair color. She's cute as a button and smart too. She's staying here? In your house? A big step for Mr. Private and Discreet."

"She's a guest. Her sister is pregnant and married to my cousin."

"Sounds complicated."

He had no idea. Changing the subject, he motioned toward the girls. "They're waiting for us."

Dean shook his head. "Okay, Reyes. I hope you know what you're doing."

He didn't. He followed Dean down the steps, peeling off his shirt and watching the women swimming in his pool, talking and laughing like it was any other day. Two couples enjoying a summer evening together.

Couple. Was this what it felt like to be with someone in an actual relationship? His lips tilted when he saw Alicia cover her eyes and stick out her tongue at Dean when he jumped in beside them with a splash. It filled him with a strange sense of pride to see how well she got along with them. To show her off.

He took off his boots and unbuckled his pants, frowning when she chuckled at something Dean said and looked over at Tracy. On the other hand, showing her off meant not being able to pay her back for the sleepless night and all the frustrating hours before Dean had called from the road to tell him they were nearby.

He reached into his pocket and pulled out a condom before dropping his pants. He wasn't sure he could wait for them to leave.

Alicia gasped and Dean groaned when Tracy walked into the water without a stitch on.

"Jesus, Reyes," Dean complained. "Put that thing away before you scare the women. Wear boxers like a normal man."

Sara swam to him with a smile. "No one is scared, Mr. Warren, sir. Why don't you let me make you more comfortable?"

She ducked under the water and Dean made a sound of approval before she reappeared with his wet boxers in her hand. "Ta-da!"

Tracy glanced over at Alicia, who'd blushed and was looking down self-consciously. He reached her side and pulled her into his arms. "Look at me."

Her blue-grey eyes were wide when they met his. Not afraid or disgusted or prudish, just unsure of where the night would take her. She knew Tracy had participated in threesomes before. "You're with me, Alicia Bell. I've got no plans to share you."

She nodded and he leaned down to kiss her, tensing when he felt Sara tap her finger on his shoulder. He stepped aside to look down at her. "Yes, Ms. Charles?"

But she was studying Alicia. "I can tell by your

expression that you know about us, don't you? The fantasy thing?"

Alicia smiled shyly. "Tracy told me."

Sara moved closer, her breasts above the water completely visible through her wet bra. "I'm glad. I'm not ashamed of it. I thought I would be, but I'm not."

"I understand exactly what you mean. And I don't think you should be. It sounds exciting."

Tracy heard a tone in her voice that Sara responded to and he knew they were speaking in a language not usually meant for mortal man. "I had a feeling you would think so. Which is why I wanted you to help me with something."

"Sara," Tracy warned. "Dean, what the hell?"

Dean just smiled and shrugged from the other side of the pool.

"Of course. What is it?" Alicia's curious question had him whipping his head back around to stare at her. She didn't look unsure any more. She looked fascinated. Hell.

Sara took her hand and pulled her away from Tracy and closer to the shallow end of the pool. He kept himself from following.

"We take turns," Sara began. "Fulfilling each other's fantasies? And Dean's had one for weeks that I haven't been able to satisfy. I just never found another woman I was comfortable enough with to kiss."

He saw Alicia tense and he clenched his fists, one hand still holding the condom. He wasn't able to stop the rush of desire that hardened his cock at the idea of the two women together, but he knew it might be too much for Alicia to handle. "No one will be offended if you say no, baby. Believe me."

Sara reached up to caress Alicia's arms. "Of course not! I can see that you're his." She looked down at the bite marks on Alicia's bare side and the fading rope lines she still had on her wrists. Her skin was so damn pale. "I trust Tracy. That's why I knew I could ask you for a kiss. And Dean and

I both think you're beautiful."

Tracy held his breath when Alicia reached out to touch one of Sara's auburn curls. "*You're* beautiful. I wish I had your hair," Alicia laughed. "And other things."

"Tracy?" Dean's voice was restrained, but careful. "Does Sara have your permission?"

Fuck. "If she has Alicia's, she has mine."

Sara took Alicia's hands and placed them on her breasts, causing both men to groan. "These other things?"

Alicia nodded, her lips parting as she explored Sara's curves. *Goddamn.* Tracy felt his knees start to buckle. He couldn't take his eyes off her. She was his water nymph again, unashamed and wild.

Sara moaned, reaching out to pay Alicia back in kind as she moved closer and pressed their lips together.

"Fuck," Tracy muttered, reaching beneath the water to grip the base of his shaft. Sara was gently caressing Alicia's lips with her own, but her fingers were pinching and tugging on her nipples in a way he knew Alicia loved. The way he touched her.

He heard her whimper into Sara's mouth and move closer, their tongues tangling experimentally as their hips met beneath the clear water.

"That's beautiful, Sara," Dean rasped. "She likes it. Squeeze her nipples, baby. Jesus, I love you. You are so fucking sexy."

Tracy was frozen by his lust. Hard and crazed as he watched Alicia respond to Sara's attention. The redhead tugged down Alicia's bra, revealing one bare breast to Tracy's gaze before covering it again with her hand. Alicia tilted her head, lost in the kiss as her hands slid down Sara's luscious body and reached behind her to cup her ass, pulling her closer.

She liked it. She fucking *loved* it. Having two men watch her as she rocked her hips against Sara's pussy, arching her back as the other women plucked at her tight nipple until it was pink and begging to be sucked.

Dean was growling his encouragement, and Tracy had a sudden desire to punch the man's lights out. He didn't want anyone to see Alicia like this. How stunning she was in her need. The sexy siren hidden beneath that innocent façade.

He knew it wasn't fucking fair after the way Dean had shared Sara. Knew it didn't make any sense. He forced himself to stay where he was. To watch the fantasy unfold.

And then Sara let go of Alicia's nipple and her hand slid down into the water, beneath her simple, white panties to disappear between her legs.

Alicia cried out in surprise against Sara's lips but she didn't stop her. Tracy knew she would be wet. Knew Sara's talented fingers would slip inside that tight warm heaven that was his. His to fuck. His to taste. His to pleasure.

"Enough," his command was a garbled growl as he strode through the water and tore Alicia away from his friend's lover. He tossed her over his shoulder and glared at Sara, but Dean had already pulled her toward him while he worked to get her out of her bra.

His best idea of the night.

Alicia was quiet as he carried her up the stairs and into the house. It was a damn good thing. If she'd argued or said a word about him stopping her, he wasn't sure he could be held responsible for his actions.

The dam had fucking broken. That kiss had pushed him over the edge and it wasn't in him to care. He just had to get inside her and remind her who she belonged to.

He made it to his bedroom and managed to close the door before tossing her on the bed. She was struggling to sit up as he was ripping open the condom still clutched in his damn hand and rolling it onto his cock.

She was flushed. Aroused. "Tracy?"

He growled, grabbing her ankles and dragging her until her ass was on the edge of the bed. His big hands tore her clinging panties off her slender hips like wet paper. He spread her legs wide and high around him, and filled her without a word, forcing her to gasp in surprise.

"Oh, Tracy. *Yes.*"

*Mine*, he thought as he powered inside her until his hips were pressed against her wet skin. He leaned forward, pushing her legs to her shoulders and placing his hands on either side of her head.

Mine.

He didn't go slow. He didn't make sure she was begging for it before he started his deep, brutal rhythm. Fucking her so hard. So good. She was tight and wet around him and he shouted as he claimed her.

"Oh God," she cried.

He bent his head to bite her breast. "Do you like it, baby? Like what you get when you make me lose control?"

"Yes!" she moaned. "God, Tracy I love it. *Fuck me.*"

Jesus Christ, she didn't know what she was asking for, but he was going to give it to her anyway. "More," he moaned. "Roll over."

He pulled his hips back long enough to flip her over and grip her braid, tugging it roughly until she got on her knees. One hand closed over her hip and he entered her again in a long hard thrust that had her screaming.

It wouldn't be for the last time.

She was so tight. So small. She gripped him like a strong fist, bruising his cock. "You've been begging for this. Leaving me alone all night, coming back to let someone else touch what's mine. And you liked it, didn't you? Sara has a talented mouth. Talented hands. Did you like her fingers in this pussy, baby?"

"Yes!" She lifted her hips higher, taking more of him, taking everything as his thrusts jarred her body and left her clinging to the covers for purchase. "Yes, Tracy. I liked it. Liked you watching me. I was begging for this. Please don't stop... Oh, God. *Oh God.* I love it."

Some part of him was trying to hold back, trying to slow

down, but her pleas and his own desires refused to listen to caution. He'd wanted this for so long. Wanted every part of her.

He released her braid and lowered his hand to the plug still nestled between her cheeks. He gripped it, pulling it out two inches before pushing it inside her again. Alicia's moaned was ragged and broken.

He did it again. "This is all you'll get, Alicia Bell," he swore, his thrusts shaking the bed. "The closest you'll ever fucking get to knowing what it's like to have two men inside you."

He matched the rhythm of his hand and hips until she was sobbing. "I don't care if it's your fantasy or theirs, I'm not sharing this."

"I'm coming," she shouted. "Tracy!"

Her muscles tightened so hard around his cock he was helpless to do anything but join her.

He couldn't see. Could hardly breathe. All he could do was let the explosions go off, shattering everything around him. Inside him. He shouted her name over and over again as he came against her until it was the only thing left he could hang onto.

"Alicia," he rasped against her back, his hand still on the plug between her thighs. "Did I hurt you?"

She moaned, still trembling, and shook her head. "I'm wonderful. As soon as I can feel my legs I'll be perfect."

He frowned, lifting himself off the bed and picking her up in his arms. "Don't joke about that."

She smiled up at him. "I'm not that easy to break, Tracy Reyes."

"We'll see," he mumbled, carrying her into the bathroom. "I'm not finished with you yet."

He set her down and took off her bra, making sure she could stand before he turned on the shower. He pulled her back into his arms and walked beneath the spray with his lips on hers. She wrapped her arms around him and melted into his kiss. He loved the way she responded to him. Loved how willing she was to let him have his way, with her body if nothing else.

His cock started hardening again as he thought about what he wanted now. What he'd been denying himself. The one part of her he hadn't claimed as his own. He lifted his lips. "Alicia Bell. I want you to face away from me, bend over and put your hands on the bench."

She looked into his eyes and her lips parted. "Yes, Tracy."

He would never get tired of hearing that. He waited until she was in position and slowly pulled out the plug, setting it down behind him and reaching for the lube he'd left on the shelf. She hissed at the sensation and looked back at him over her shoulder, her pleasure and anticipation was clear in expression.

He could hear her shaky breaths as he rubbed the thick liquid on his cock, then between the cheeks of her ass. "Breathe, baby," he growled. "You can take me."

Fuck, he prayed she could, because he needed this more than he'd thought possible. Needed to have all of her. For her to be his in every way.

He held onto her hip as he guided his cock inside her, shuddering hard when the head of his shaft pushed through the tight muscles in her ass. "Fuck."

She was panting, moaning as he continued to press forward. He gritted his teeth and forced himself to go slow even though it felt like torture. He was halfway in when she started shaking.

"Oh God," she moaned. "Tracy, it's too much. It's so…"

"Breathe, Alicia. Baby, please. I need you to let me—" He swore, stopping himself before he begged. "Do you want me to stop?"

She lifted her head and looked back at him again, her eyes dilated as she focused on him. "No," she whispered. "Don't stop. I want you inside me."

He inhaled sharply. "Are you sure?"

She nodded, struggling for breath. "Fuck me, Tracy. Please."

He slid his hand around until he was gripping her wet sex, his fingers pressing her clit as he slung his hips forward, filling her ass.

"Oh God!" she screamed. "Oh God, Tracy."

He started to move inside her, unable to help himself. He curved his body over her and his free arm wrapped around her to grip her shoulder, holding her in place.

All he could hear were her moans and the sound of his heart pounding. All he could feel was her sex soaking his hand and her tight ass around his cock. His. She was his. No one else knew what this felt like. No one else knew how sweetly she took him inside.

The sounds she was making started to change. Surprised pleasure. Need. "Tracy. Oh, do that again." He circled his hips and she moaned. "Yes. That's so good. Deep."

He swore and held her tighter against him, rubbing her clit with his fingers the way he knew she loved. "You like that, baby? Can you come for me like this?"

She moaned and nodded, reaching down to cover his hand between her legs as she sought her climax. He needed her to come. Needed to come. Fuck, he was close. "Come for me, Alicia. Come for me, baby. Now."

Her cry was low and shaken, and when he heard it Tracy couldn't hold himself back. His hips slammed against her ass once. Again. By the third deep thrust he was coming inside her. "Alicia! Jesus."

He wasn't sure how long they wrapped around each other, both of them shaking and clinging to each other like survivors after a storm. It had never been like that. He'd never been like that. Vulnerable. Out of control. Desperate.

When he pulled out, she whimpered and he winced. He'd hurt her. Taken her twice, both times without enough care. "Alicia?"

She turned in his arms and buried her face in his chest, still crying from her release. Tracy held her, washing her body with gentle, soothing strokes of his hand. Kissing her forehead. Her neck. Trying to show her without words how sorry he was for his earlier carelessness.

He liked to be in control. It was who he was, who he'd worked hard to become. Alicia would always push his buttons. Always have him struggling to keep a handle on his desire for her. And the longer he was with her, the harder it was to think about being without her.

How was he going to let her go?

## CHAPTER NINE

"Old Man is a beauty," Sara walked beside Alicia, an arm laced through hers as they strolled slowly out of the barn. "Thank you for letting me see him before we left."

"I owe you." Alicia blushed when Sara's smile grew.

"Yes, for that."

"Right back at you, Ms. Bell. You are a great kisser, and Dean's reaction was even better than I imagined. From the way your caveman carried you off, I'm betting we both had a night to remember."

"God, yes." She was still tender in the best way possible. She loved it when Tracy controlled her and tempted her and took her slowly. But he'd destroyed her for any other man forever after last night.

If he hadn't gotten distant this morning, she would be blissfully happy right now and ready for more. She'd known from the moment she opened her eyes and saw him already dressed and watching her with an enigmatic expression that he was pulling back. Her unintended wince when she sat up and only made things worse.

Sara had released her and was rubbing her hands together in delight, still enjoying last night's memory. "Now I need to think of something spectacularly shocking since it's my turn." Her smile turned soft around the edges. "A fantasy he'll have to make come true if he wants to keep me in sickness and health."

Alicia stopped and lowered her voice. "Are you going to propose to Dean Warren?"

"That's the plan. When he told me about this road trip I thought it was the perfect time to present my case." She chuckled. "The man can't resist me in a Hummer."

Alicia knew from dinner last night that she and Sara had similar backgrounds. Penny-pinching city girls who'd had to struggle on their own to get through school and make a life for themselves. "And they lived happily ever after?"

Sara made a face. "I know, right? I've already been labeled Cinderella by the gossips, but I don't care. Dean isn't a prince. He's a sexy, stubborn, flawed and wonderful man. Do you know when we first got together he accused me of being a present from your cowboy and his pals? Not exactly a glass slipper and violins...but he made up for it later."

"Dean is a lucky man."

Sara winked. "I know. So is Tracy. You're exactly what he needs."

Alicia stepped back. "Oh no, we're not... I'm just here until my sister has her baby. That's the deal."

"Whatever deal you made, I can tell there's more going on, Alicia. So can Dean. He said he's never seen Tracy like this before with any woman. And they've known each other a long time."

She pushed down the hope those words created. "He's never given me any reason to think there's more. Tracy is very up front about our relationship."

"Men can be stubborn," Sara sighed. "I'm surprised about Tracy, though. He's the one that got Dean and me together. I had him pegged for a true romantic. A rooms-full-of-roses-and-candles romantic."

Alicia sighed, shaking her head. She'd never met that

Tracy. And she hated the expression that crossed her new friend's face in that moment. It looked too much like pity.

"I have to get something inside," she mumbled. "I'll be back out in time to say goodbye."

"Alicia, wait."

She didn't turn around. Sara might be living a fantasy, but Alicia was just on a temporary vacation. One that was nearly over.

"Viral what?"

Dean laughed as he sat at Tracy's desk typing something into the computer. "Videos. Women have been making videos about why you should marry them and posting them online when the matchmaker turns them away. They're calling it The Bride Wars. Mrs. Grandholm sent me some of the links. It's crazy."

"The Bride Wars? Why does that sound familiar?"

"Why do you think?"

Ms. Anonymous. Her last article where she mentioned him looking for a goddamned "filly". "That is it. I am shutting her down. One article in one paper is fine, but this? This is embarrassing."

His friend pushed play and Tracy leaned over the desk to see a stunning young woman in a white corset appear on the screen.

*"Cowboy, take me away,"* she gushed. *"I have a PhD in psychology, a medal in gymnastics and I practically live at the rodeo. I love horses, babies and—if you'll let me—I'll love you with all my heart. I should win the Bride Wars. Marry me!"*

"Son of a bitch," Tracy muttered.

Dean leaned back with a smile. "Welcome to my world, Teflon. At least they're not talking about ropes and chains. We'd have a whole different batch of videos for that, and Ms. Anonymous could write a bestselling book if they knew about you."

THE COWBOY'S KINK

Tracy glared down at his friend. "Thanks for the support."

"Hey, at least I told you before you had a bus full of women in white arrive at the ranch, which is where this seems to be heading. Now you can make an official announcement that you're off the market, fire the matchmaker and call it a day. See? I'm helping."

Tracy looked down and shifted from one foot to the other. "Tracy?" Dean lowered his voice. "What's the problem?"

"I'm not off the market until I have a wife." It felt wrong as he was saying it, but he and Alicia hadn't made any promises. She had a life in New York. "I didn't hire that woman lightly. I made a decision to follow Peter's advice and find a suitable woman to marry and raise a child with. She's sent me enough files in the last three weeks—there's bound to be someone in there that fits the bill."

"Fits the bill? You aren't getting groceries, Tracy, you're looking for love. After last night, I just assumed—"

"We're having sex, Dean. That's all we agreed to."

He heard the sound of someone inhaling sharply and turned to find Alicia standing in the doorway, her knuckles white on the knob. Shit. "Alicia?"

She shook her head, backing away and disappearing. He heard the front door slam and Dean swore behind him. "Man, you are an idiot, Reyes. I thought you were the one with all the sense."

Tracy was already in motion. He caught up with her and gripped her arm before she could get in the car. "Where the hell are you going?"

"Are you serious?" She struggled against his hold, but he refused to let her go. "Damn it, Tracy, I can't do this anymore."

"Let me explain." He knew Sara and Roy were standing by the car. That they could hear every word. He didn't care. He knew it wasn't fair but he didn't want her to leave.

"Explain what? That we weren't serious? I know that. That we were just kinky playmates? You made that clear. That we only agreed to sex? I heard you the first time."

"You jumped in the middle of a conversation. You don't know what—"

"Don't." She'd stopped struggling and started crying and his gut was twisting into knots, knowing he'd caused it. "You asked for my trust, Tracy Reyes, not my fucking dignity. You don't get to corner the market on pride, you know. I'm not going to be some toy you pass the time with while you're actively looking for a *suitable* bride and starting your own bachelor reality show."

He winced. "I haven't been. I mean, she sent the files, but I haven't even opened them yet. And I had nothing to do with those videos."

She stared at him until he looked away, knowing it was a bullshit response. He let her go.

"You know what?" she laughed darkly. "This might be a good thing. Here I was, ready to throw myself on my sword and ignore my sister's request to move here and watch the baby grow up. All so my heart wouldn't break every time I saw *you*."

She got into her car and put on her seatbelt with angry, jerking motions. "But fuck you, Mr. Reyes. Fuck you and your control and your shut-down heart and that whole lonely kinky cowboy routine. I'm not going anywhere. I hope you find a suitable baby machine who won't make you feel anything too taxing so you can run your family empire in peace. I wish her lots of luck."

She started the car, slammed the door and drove away without another word. She was gone and Tracy couldn't move. Couldn't believe that had really just happened. That he hadn't been able to talk to her, reason with her. That he'd been such an ass.

"Sara, don't." He glanced up in time to see Dean gripping Sara's wrist to stop her from clapping. "He knows. He's too smart not to."

Tracy wasn't so sure about that. He'd been behaving like a first rate jackass. Last night he'd lost control with her. He'd lost himself to his own selfish desires and hurt her. She hadn't been able to hide it. This morning he'd known it was time to pull back. To try and pretend what they had together was less than it was, that he would be fine when she left.

Only he would know it was a lie.

He could have fought harder. Could have told her everything he was thinking and feeling, but he hadn't. He'd been closed off and shut down too long to realize the problem until it was too late.

He wasn't fighting to keep control, he was trying to protect himself from getting his heart broken. From being a fool for love. He was a coward and he didn't deserve her.

But he needed her. Seeing her leave made him realize he couldn't live without her.

He was in love with Alicia Bell, and she never wanted to see him again.

"Son of a bitch."

What was he going to do now?

*** 

*4 months later…*

Alicia made a face at herself in the mirror. "I really don't think this is a good idea, Jinny."

Her sister responded from her new living room. "It's a great idea. Motherhood has made me brilliant *and* funny. You tell me so all the time."

Alicia joined her and held out her arms for the baby. "Let me hold her. Just for a minute. It's been two days since I've seen her and I want to make sure I haven't missed anything."

Jinny held little Antonia closer, shaking her head. "She'll spit up on you and you do not have anything else in your closet that looks half as decent on you as that dress. I checked. Which reminds me, we should go shopping soon. New York teacher and Colorado teacher? Not the same thing."

Alicia laughed and looked down at her blue cap-sleeved dress. "Are we sure this isn't too short? I don't want to give him the wrong idea."

"It's dinner and you're too skinny. He'll think he needs to feed you."

"I'm *too* skinny? I should cancel and we can order a pizza."

Jinny sighed. "Stop it, Al. Miguel and I both think you need to go out. And before you ask, I didn't tell him anything. He knows you haven't been happy and he wants us to do something about it. Now that he's moved from ranching to real estate, he's a lot bossier."

"It suits him," Alicia smiled sadly, hating the fact that they were worried about her. "I'm actually doing okay, you know. It's not like I had an exciting dating life in New York."

Jinny set the baby down in the crib Alicia had gotten for when her niece came over. She turned back and took Alicia's hands. "No you're not. You've never been in love before, not really, so you may not recognize what a broken heart looks like. I do."

Hell. "Don't set me up with some stranger and then make me cry. He'll run screaming in the other direction."

Jinny bit her lip, her expression hesitant. "He's not a stranger, Al. I never said he was. I said there was someone we wanted you to have dinner with."

"You didn't." Alicia pulled away from her sister and crossed her arms protectively. "Tell me you didn't."

Jinny pushed her blonde curls behind her ears, a sure sign of guilt.

"Damn it, Jinny, I could kill you!"

"Don't swear in front of the baby," Jinny responded, an

apology in her eyes. "And think of little Antonia. You can't kill me because she needs her mother. She'd also like a happy aunt who doesn't spend her nights alone crying into her pillow. It's been four months, Alicia. I was on your side until I realized it wasn't getting better."

"You shouldn't use the baby you named after me to win an argument. It isn't fair."

The knock on the door made Alicia jump and start to panic. She couldn't do it. She didn't want to see him. At first she'd been a masochist, poring over articles about him and his obsession with privacy. All the columns from Ms. Anonymous that she'd never seen before about the Billionaire Bachelors. Jinny was right, he went out of his way and used all of his influence to make sure people didn't talk about him. And they seemed to respect the Teflon Cowboy for his efforts.

When it got to painful, she'd done everything she could to stop thinking about him. Ignoring the Internet and every article that started out with Bride or Cowboy. When he'd started sending letters and trying to call a week later, she'd returned them all unopened and blocked his number on her phone. She'd even refused to see Sara when the poor woman called to see if she would meet her for lunch.

The fact that he was still trying to communicate with her didn't mean he cared, she told herself a million times. It just meant he had a hard time not being in charge. And he wasn't in charge of this. She was. She'd ended it and he didn't like the feeling. That was all. "I can't, Jinny. You don't understand."

"Was I wrong?" Jinny asked softly. "I thought you were still in love with him but…was I wrong?"

She wasn't. And that was the worst part of the whole ridiculous situation. She still dreamt about him at night, still woke up expecting him to be there. She missed being with him, even after she realized how little she meant to him. Which wasn't submissive, just pathetic and sad.

"No. You weren't wrong," she responded to her sister's question. "But if I was smart you would be."

Another knock rattled the door and Jinny took a step toward it. "I'm your sister, Alicia. I will be on your side no matter what. If, after tonight, you decide you never want to see him again? I will support you one hundred percent. I just thought—Miguel and I got a second chance, and you and I got a second chance—maybe Mr. Reyes deserves one too."

"Now I can't be mad at you," Alicia sighed. "But this isn't going to end well."

Jinny opened the door and frowned. "Who are *you*?"

"Roy," Alicia responded before he could. "I thought you were back in the city."

Roy smiled kindly at her, reminding her that he'd been a witness to her less-than-finest hour. "I'm here on special assignment for Mr. Vincent and the future Mrs. Warren."

Sara had proposed. Another fantasy came true. "You really deserve a raise."

He laughed. "My bonus package is more than satisfactory, but thank you for your concern. Shall we?"

She picked up her purse and held it liked a shield in front of her. "Where exactly are we going?"

"Not too far."

Alicia wanted to be thankful for small favors. The first favor? She didn't have to face him yet. The second? She didn't have to face him in front of her attentive sister. The third? She might be able to talk Roy into making a run for it.

He opened the door to the monster and she made a face. "Really?"

Roy grinned. "It's lucky. You'll get used to it."

"Not on a teacher's salary." She let him help her inside and groaned when he closed the door.

Why was she doing this? What would it accomplish other than reminding her what an idiot she'd been?

And how lonely her life was now that she knew what she was missing?

Roy rolled down the glass partition. "There's something recorded for you to watch while we get where we're going."

The panel beneath the partition opened automatically, revealing a large, flat-screened television. "O-kay."

It turned on and Roy disappeared from view again as Alicia leaned forward. It was one of those entertainment channels that interviewed or gossiped about the lifestyles of the rich and famous. Someone recorded this? On purpose?

*"He said he'd never do it, but in a first for this or any channel, we have an exclusive interview with the most reclusive member of the Billionaire Bachelors, the Teflon Cowboy himself, Mr. Tracy Reyes. Mr. Reyes, a few months ago there was a lot of talk about you, and a lot of women who seemed to think they were in the running to be Mrs. Reyes. Were the Bride Wars a media hoax or were you really in the market to marry?"*

Tracy's face appeared on the screen and Alicia's eyes widened. He'd done an interview? When? Why did he want her to see this?

*"Well, ma'am, I'll be honest. I did hire a discreet matchmaking business to aid me in my search for a bride. I haven't had much luck in that department, despite what you might have heard."*

*"You've never come close to walking down the aisle? I find that hard to believe, Mr. Reyes, a handsome man like you."*

Alicia glared at the flirting interviewer.

*"I'll admit, I almost married my high school sweetheart until I found out she only wanted me for my last name and what came with it. Now? When you work as much as I do and your social life is under the kind of scrutiny my friends and I have become accustomed to, there aren't as many viable avenues for finding the right girl."* She saw him send the woman a chagrined smile, but her heart was still twisting from his admission. *"The videos and The Bride Wars were the apparently unintended product of a gossip columnist who*

*likes to remain anonymous. I didn't even realize it was happening until a friend pointed it out. I was too busy falling in love."*

Alicia covered her mouth with her hand as the interviewer smiled in delight. *"Falling in love? Was this one of the women your matchmaker found? Tell us all about her."*

Tracy's expression warmed and he looked directly at the camera. *"She and I were thrown together by circumstance, and she didn't know anything about my search and I didn't have it in me to tell her. The second I saw her—well, I think I lost my heart that first night. Somewhere between Romeo and Juliet and Taming of the Shrew. I was too stubborn to admit it, of course, and by the time I realized I couldn't live without her—that she was the only woman I would ever want to marry—she was gone."*

*"That's so sad,"* the interviewer cooed. *"Is it really over? Are you back on the market now? Answer carefully, we don't want to start another Internet sensation."*

*"Well now, that's entirely up to her. As far as I'm concerned, my bachelor days are over. She's it for me. The last and only woman I'll ever love. But she's the one with all the control. The one who holds my heart. My only hope is that she'll see this and know how sorry I am for not telling her until now."*

She was crying damn it. She got off her seat and knocked on the partition, waiting for Roy to roll it down. "Is this real, Roy? Did he really do this?"

"He did," Roy confirmed somberly. "And to hear Mr. Vincent, it's a bigger deal than you or I would imagine. Mr. Reyes is a very private man."

She knew. "Why? I'm not a grand gestures sort of girl, you know. I don't need sky writers or billboards. He could have just told me himself."

"Mr. Vincent mentioned something about you not answering your phone and your sister threatening him with a restraining order unless he gave you time?"

She pressed her forehead onto the seat and let out a shaky breath. He'd said he loved her. He'd told her she had all the control. He'd said it to the world on cable television.

*She's it for me.*

Roy stopped the car and she looked over his shoulder and out the window.

Tracy's house.

Home.

"He said you should go inside."

Alicia put her hand on his shoulder and squeezed. "Thank you, Roy."

"Just doing my job, ma'am."

She opened the door to the limousine and hopped down, trying to focus on her breathing as she climbed the familiar steps and opened the door.

The entryway was full of roses. Large vases of them blocked her way to the living room and his office. On the floor, there was a trail of petals. She couldn't help but smile as she followed them up the stairs toward the bedrooms. It made her think about what Sara had called him. A roses and candles romantic.

The door to the master bedroom was shut, and she frowned in confusion when she saw the trail leading to the room across the hall. Her room. She stepped inside and covered her mouth. "What are you doing in here?"

Tracy was handcuffed to the bed, wearing nothing but a towel around his waist. It looked like the same towel she'd been wearing when they met. His smile was subdued. "I didn't want to presume. Not until we talked."

He didn't want to presume, so he was naked in a bed? But she knew. This was him, totally giving up control. Being vulnerable.

So much better than a billboard.

She set down her purse and crossed her arms, walking slowly toward him. He looked tired. Tense. "Roy showed me the recording."

"Good." He tried to sit up but the cuffs were obviously an obstacle. He grimaced. "There were things I couldn't say on television. About my past."

"Your high school sweetheart."

He nodded. "I want you to know everything."

"Now?"

"I need you to know why I...why I behaved the way I did. She was pushed into dating me by her parents. They were after the Reyes money and were willing to do whatever it took. She was a tiny little thing, and I fell in love. Or thought I did."

Alicia moved closer, wanting to comfort him, needing to hold back. "How did you find out it wasn't true?"

"My grandfather warned me about the family, and I thought he would stop the engagement unless we made it impossible. He was pretty old fashioned, so I convinced her to have sex with me."

"Of course you did. You were a teenage boy."

His jaw tensed. "She was willing, probably because her parents told her to be, but a virgin. I was young and uncontrolled and I didn't know. Imagine an eighteen-year-old with my size. I didn't do it on purpose, but I wasn't as careful as I should have been and I hurt her. The next day her parents attempted to have me tried for assault. It wasn't pretty, but in the end the truth came out and I discovered that they didn't care about their daughter at all, just the money they got in the settlement. The last time I saw her she told me I was a monster."

So many things started clicking into place. How careful he was with her. How worried that he was going to hurt her. His obsession with control. "My giant, scary, Shakespeare-quoting cowboy. Why didn't you tell me about the matchmaker? The files?"

"To be honest, I wasn't thinking about it at all. Until Dean mentioned it, you were the only thing on my mind. The only woman I wanted to know."

Good answer. "Tell me, why exactly are you wearing handcuffs?"

He narrowed his dark eyes on her. "I'm making a gesture."

She bit her lip. "This wasn't your idea was it?"

"Hell, no," he growled.

She smiled. "And the roses don't seem like your style either. Sara?"

His eyes started to sparkle with something. Hope? "And Henry. Fool apparently thinks he wrote the book on love now, though why I ever listen to that royal pain in the ass I'll never kn—"

Alicia found the small key on the bedside table and held it in front of him, stopping him mid-sentence. "You hate being out of control. You've probably never been voluntarily handcuffed or tied down in your life. If you had your way you would have shown up at my place, thrown me over Old Man and tied *me* to the bed until I agreed to anything."

"You think you know me, Alicia Bell?"

She nodded. "I know I do. But you did this for me. All of it."

She watched him as he studied her face, lingering on her lips. "I think I'd do just about anything for you."

Her heart full and feeling like it was going to beat out of her chest, she lifted her skirt, climbed up on the bed and straddled his lap. "I usually have more patience than this, but I'm not a woman who likes to waste time, Tracy Reyes. When I see something I want, I go after it. And I see something I want."

She could see the recognition in his eyes as she repeated his words back to him. Then she kissed him, melting the instant his tongue started dueling with hers, her body coming back to life after months of neglect and heartache.

His kiss grew wilder, his growls making her crazy. She wanted him. Needed him. "I love you, Tracy."

He leaned away from her lips and looked into her eyes. "Say it again."

"I love you. I lost my heart that first night. Somewhere between you calling my car a heap of junk and that massage."

"Take off the handcuffs."

Her thighs actually started to tremble. "Are you sure? This could be fun."

"Alicia Bell."

She looked down at him, her body reacting to the command in his voice and she knew nothing would ever be the same again.

"Yes, Tracy."

# THE PLAYBOY'S MÉNAGE

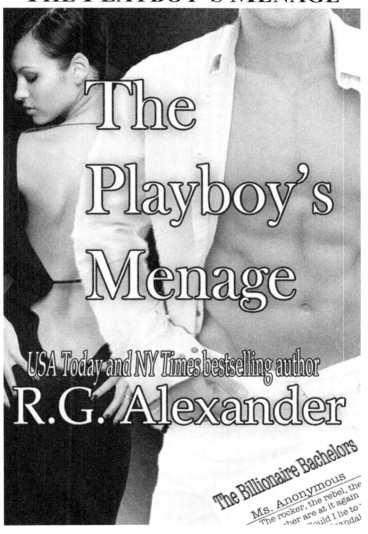

236

# Chapter One

*I'm with Holly. She says hi. Want to join us?*

Peter sat in front of his laptop inside his latest acquisition—an abandoned warehouse on the edge of the city—and ground his teeth together as he read the text.

Asshole.

According to his recent phone call with Dean, Henry had left his own Hummer and driver behind so he could take Dean's car without asking and wasn't answering his cell. Curious, since he'd gotten a message from him this morning, Peter sent Henry a text asking what the hell was going on... Why he'd expected an actual answer, when he'd gotten nothing but *this* all week, he'd never know.

*Fuck you.* He responded to the smartass text. *Dean wants his car back.*

He dropped his phone on the rusting worktable and stared blankly at his computer screen. Henry Vincent had a twisted sense of humor and a talent for ticking him off, but his bullshit was no longer remotely amusing. The man must be bored, and as restless as Peter was from staying in one place too long. Henry needed to give up his early retirement idea and get busy making music with his band again. Soon, before Peter found a creative way to get even with him for this aggravation.

It had started at last week's dinner, meant to be an intervention and a strategy meeting to get Dean out from under his uncle's thumb. That was why Peter was still in town instead of on his way to Italy and the energetic twin swimsuit models who'd left him an open invitation to join them for the summer. It was also why he'd purchased this vacant edifice of rust and steel—to create a physical address for the "mystery buyer" the older Mr. Warren couldn't resist.

Dean was a good friend and he needed Peter's special brand of help. The twins could wait.

A few simple keystrokes, an open back door or two on certain so-called secure servers and a bank account with funds from himself, Henry and Tracy Reyes, and the four of them would soon be the majority stockholders of Warren Industries. If all went according to plan, it would end the annual review game the board of halfwits was playing with Dean for good.

When it was done, the CEO of Warren Industries could stop being such a grim, sexless jackass and they could all go back to business as usual. Tracy to his cattle empire and his overabundance of cousins. Dean to his company and possibly the redhead he'd mentioned at dinner. Henry to his music, his traveling and the epic spoiling of his older brother's children and Peter to…wherever his life took him, as long as it was exciting enough to distract him from what he didn't have.

That was the plan, until Henry started going off about the latest Ms. Anonymous column, fantasies and wish fulfillment. About Holly. And he hadn't stopped after they'd left Franco's that night. Henry now sent him an email or text every day intimating that he knew where she was or that he was talking to her. Suggesting they all get together.

Like old times.

Four years. Until now, that's how long it had been since

they'd mentioned her name in each other's presence. Four years, five months, two days and six and a half hours since they'd gotten drunk in the red light district of Amsterdam and admitted that—despite the depths of debauchery they'd both unapologetically striven to reach over the years—the days they'd shared with Holly Ruskin were still unmatched.

But though that was the only time they'd talked about her, it was clear neither one of them had forgotten their first love. A year ago, after the last Warren charity gala, Henry had come to the Faraday estate and seen a few of the sculptures and paintings in his private collection—the ones Peter created whenever he needed to think or take his mind off a problem. He never meant to show them to anyone, particularly his best friend. They were too revealing and always depicted the same subject. The same woman who was the inspiration for the song on Henry's latest album, *Broken Heart Baby*.

It was her. As Henry had insisted at Franco's, she was their fantasy. Holly had left her mark on both their hearts. Which was why he couldn't understand Henry's recent behavior.

Peter had known Henry most of his life. Since his third birthday party, in fact, when the tiny terror had shown up with a pirate patch and a small but deadly sword that he'd used to annihilate the expensive four-tiered cake covered in ivory fondant after it made him sick to his stomach. Peter's mother had nearly fainted following the carnage, vowing to ban the toddler from all upcoming celebrations, so it was no surprise that the boys had instantly become inseparable.

Henry was the confident and troublemaking brother he'd needed to pull him out of his isolation—he'd taught Peter to swear and sneak out, and taken him on adventures with his older brothers that had sent Peter home with scraped knees, muddy shoes and the occasional broken limb. Shockingly normal stuff anywhere else, but unheard of at the Faraday estate.

Peter had been raised by servants who were paid to see to his care and feeding, since the older Faradays had no desire to deal with the terrible twos or the headaches of adolescence. His father spent most of his son's formative years across the ocean at the manor in England, and his mother was forever encircled by a small group of friends who filled their days planning charity events for other people's children.

It wasn't until his father was in the last stages of his quiet battle with cancer that he'd requested sixteen-year-old Peter's presence. He'd talked to him about his upcoming responsibilities to the employees of the estates, introduced him to the family's lawyers and financial advisors, and even said he was proud of Peter's scholastic accomplishments and heartened that his legacy would continue after death. But by then it was too late— a stranger's praise meant nothing to Peter. His mother's passing two years later had been harder to accept. She, at least, had remembered his birthdays.

Without Henry and his boisterous family to drag Peter away from the ancient estate where children weren't allowed to breathe for fear of breaking something priceless, he didn't want to imagine what he would have become. One of those eccentric, reclusive billionaires who lived in his perfectly pressed pajamas, Henry often assured him. Or a mad scientist who grew out his fingernails and couldn't get a date unless he built one from scratch in the lab.

He would always owe Henry for that. He'd owe Dean and Tracy as well. They'd introduced him to life and all its pleasures, and he'd made the ride his own. He traveled extensively, slept with as many women as he liked and took physical gambles whenever the opportunity arose. His parents had been hothouse flowers with more money than they could ever spend. They'd lived narrow, insulated lives that barely made a ripple in the world, and he refused to live by their example.

*And what ripples have you made, playboy?*

He lived. Peter supposed he could have channeled his energies and worked at one of the businesses he'd created over the years. The latest handful still held some of his attention—the private space and exploration company, the alternative energy research center and the educational app business he'd started during a long, dull flight to Hong Kong all showed promise. The reasons he gave for staying away were sound—he didn't want his reputation muddying the waters or in any way hurting a potentially profitable and beneficial endeavor.

But the truth was far less noble. Once a challenge was met, Peter inevitably grew bored and restless, and it was better for everyone involved—particularly the men and women he left at the helm—to take his ideas and money and allow him to remain as he was. A deviant who had embraced risk and excitement, experience and excess as if it were a career for so long that now it was all he was known for. The playboy. The lewd Billionaire Bachelor.

That moniker couldn't be entirely blamed on Ms. Anonymous. Henry had put him on that road long before the gossip column was created. He supposed it was a side effect of knowing him so well. Their friendship had no doubt lasted this long because it was based as much on rivalry and one-upmanship as mutual admiration. Everything was a competition. A new challenge.

When Henry won an award for his poetry, Peter became one of the youngest authors to have an essay published in an esteemed scientific journal. When Peter led their school basketball team to victory after Henry convinced him to leave the math lab and join the team, it was his friend who managed to celebrate with the cheerleaders. All of them, much to the dismay of Peter's teammates.

And their game was still going strong, Peter couldn't stop his lips from twitching in amusement when he thought about the night he'd celebrated Henry's Grammy win a few years ago. His evening with both an Olympic gymnast and an

Academy Award nominee in Paris had been scandalous enough to steal all the headlines away from his best friend's morning show victory lap. Henry had shrugged it off the way he always did, but he'd yet to top it.

Back in college, they'd both gone after Holly Ruskin with that same spirit of competition. At first. They'd each taken her out twice, doing their best to charm her out of those vintage dresses that hugged her hourglass figure before the other had a chance. How she'd managed to hold their interest while skillfully keeping her clothes on and not letting either get past first base, Peter would never know. It was a talent he hadn't encountered in a woman before or since.

By the end of his second date, after she laughed at something he'd been taking seriously and kissed him senseless in front of the bookstore, Peter had stopped thinking of her as a challenge to be met. He'd begun to want something different. Something new.

The kiss had changed everything. It tasted like the sweet mint tea she'd had at the restaurant and red cherry lip gloss. Like raw, carnal sex that lasted all night and a thousand lazy morning-afters. Like falling in love for the first time in his life.

The more he learned the more he wanted to know. Everything about her fascinated him. From her raven-black hair to the broken heart tattoo on her ankle, and every mouth-watering inch in between. The way she argued passionately with her professors in class and laughed in delight whenever anyone attempted to put her down because she worked in a diner instead of living off her stepfather's wealth. Holly was down to earth and fearless. Different. Sexy, funny, and completely unimpressed with his pedigree. She saw him, who he was beneath the surface, and she wanted to know more.

He'd been planning to talk to Henry about backing off when Holly turned the tables on him by inviting them both out to dinner. During appetizers she'd let them know she was aware of their competition. By dessert she'd made it clear that she wouldn't mind letting it continue.

His phone vibrated against the table and he sighed disagreeably, knowing who it would be.

Henry again.

*She still wants you. I can tell. You should join us before I forget we're friends.*

There was an attachment. When Peter clicked on it an image popped up, and he almost crushed the phone in his hand. "Oh, you lying, underhanded—"

He could only see an ankle. One sexy feminine ankle with a slightly faded tattoo of a broken heart.

Henry was with Holly. Their Holly. He hadn't been lying, just allowing Peter to think he was, to believe it was another prank designed to piss him off. But this was evidence he couldn't refute. He knew that ankle. They were together, damn it, and he was here. Alone.

Six minutes. That was how long it took for him to track Henry's location through the GPS on his phone. He recognized the address and swore again at the confirmation. Holly's house. He shut his laptop and tossed it into his case, grabbing his keys and heading out the door without hesitation.

It wouldn't take him long to get to the small, unassuming cottage-style bungalow she'd lived in for five and a half years. If he were blindfolded he would still be able to find it, since he'd driven down her street each time he came into the city. To test his resolve.

Knowing where she was and not knocking on her door was torture, but it was better than the alternative. They may have all moved on, but not knowing where Holly was in the world was simply unacceptable. He didn't linger on the reasons why.

That was where he'd drawn the line. He'd purposefully stopped himself from satisfying his curiosity and discovering any details other than her location. He could have easily sought her out on social media or hacked his way into her personal or professional life, but he didn't. He didn't know how she spent her free time, what she did for a living or how many lovers she'd had. He'd been respecting her privacy for years with herculean restraint, but now he wondered if he'd made a mistake. Clearly Henry hadn't felt compelled to do the same.

He started the car and forced himself not to think about what she and Henry had been doing together, how long they'd been doing it, or how he'd found her in the first place. Instead, because nostalgia was preferable to rage at the moment, he let his mind to wander back to the last time they'd all been together.

Neither he nor Henry had been able to deny Holly's intriguing request. By the end of that dinner, they were both wrapped around her finger, and they'd stayed that way for the better part of two semesters. They'd haunted the diner during her late night shifts to walk her home and brought her to the house they shared with Dean and Tracy so often she may as well have lived there.

In return for more of her kisses, more of her, Peter had been forced to watch Henry make her laugh with his bawdy humor and share a few passionate kisses of his own. The only thing that saved his friend from some variation of pistols at dawn was the knowledge that neither of them had gotten much more than that from Holly—which was unprecedented. For the first time since puberty had knocked them upside the head and introduced them to their new favorite pastime, they'd both been content to wait faithfully until Holly was ready to choose.

Maybe content wasn't the right word. He shifted in his seat, his foot heavy on the gas pedal as he thought about the months of sexual frustration. The number of times he'd taken himself in hand, wishing he were inside her. Wishing Henry would lose the battle of wills, or his patience, and move on, leaving Holly to him.

He'd been young and jealous, but even then his need had overpowered his envy. He hadn't wanted to take the chance of losing her. Had wanted her too much to risk it—so much that when she came to their house looking like she'd been crying and asked to stay over the holidays instead of going home, Peter immediately canceled his plans. He even called Henry, who'd been on the way to the airport for his winter break, because he knew it would make her feel better.

She hadn't wanted to talk about what was wrong, so he hadn't pushed. Whatever the reason, he'd been grateful for it if it meant they would be together.

He'd been a fool for her.

He and Henry had distracted her with picnics in the living room, tree-trimming, mulled wine and kisses under the ever-present mistletoe they'd started to carry with them around the house. Soon enough Peter could see it working. She'd relaxed and bloomed under their undivided attention. Her touches began to linger. Her kisses had grown more intimate. The second night they were all tangled together by the fire, talking softly about nothing, she'd been the one to bring it up. The subject that had been on Peter's mind every waking second since he'd laid eyes on her.

Sex.

She'd admitted to wanting Peter *and* Henry equally, and told them how hard it was to resist their advances. Her desire for both of them was the only thing stopping her from being with either of them. Holly didn't want to do anything to mess up their lifetime of friendship, or the relationship the three of them had been developing. She didn't want anyone getting hurt.

"I guess that's it," she'd said softly as she stared into the flames. "Saying it out loud—I know it's crazy. I know there's no solution. But you deserved to know I didn't mean to lead you on. Either of you. You've both been patient and perfect and...I was just being selfish. Greedy. I think it's genetic."

Henry wasn't able to leave it at that, though his tone was partially teasing, allowing her to laugh off his suggestion. "You've got a problem? Professor Henry has the solution. Allow me to educate you on what my book from psych class calls polyamory. Informally it's known as a threesome, but in France?" He offered up his abysmal attempt at an accent. "They call it ménage a trois. Problem solved."

Holly bit her lip. "I was trying to be serious, Henry."

"So am I," he insisted, his attention entirely on her. "I'm always trying. It makes perfect sense, and I think Peter would agree it's the only logical thing to do. We both want you and you want the both of us. Think about it, Holly. Two willing men focused on pleasing you. Two mouths kissing. Two pairs of hands. Two men giving you exactly what you want without making you choose between them. Best of all, you'll be naked. Sounds like a Christmas miracle to me." He paused, looking between them. "Or we could skip it and play Scrabble."

Peter had a difficult time reconciling his instant arousal at Henry's suggestion with his worry that she would say yes. He shared everything with his best friend, but could he share Holly when he wanted her for himself?

All his concern disappeared when he saw the spark of excitement and longing in her warm brown eyes. She wanted to say yes, wanted to give herself to them. And Peter wanted to be the one to give Holly whatever she desired. In that instant he'd taken the decision out of their hands.

Every moment that followed was burned into his memory. Peter took charge, needing to control every aspect of their lovemaking. Henry, for once, seemed more than content to follow his lead, particularly when he saw how perfectly Holly responded.

She was as real in her passion as she was in every other aspect of her life. There was no playing coy or hesitating when she undressed in front of the fire. No timidity in the way she reacted to the sight of their bare skin. Her sensual curiosity and desire to explore their bodies tested Peter's control, but he managed to hold back long enough to watch her face as they made her come that first time.

Everything about her was a revelation. Her full breasts in his mouth and narrow waist in his hands. The paradise between her thighs and the sounds of her moans echoing in every room of the house. When Peter couldn't wait any longer, he lowered her onto Henry and took her from behind. She didn't hesitate then either. She was so vocal with her surprise and approval, it was a struggle not to come the instant he felt her tight muscles around him.

He and Henry had come to a silent understanding, working together as if they always had, both knowing instinctively that this wasn't a competition. It was Holly. She was all that mattered. Her satisfaction. Her pleasure.

They indulged in those pleasures until none of them had the energy to move. And each time they woke up, it started all over again. Peter remembered wondering if he would ever get enough.

He wished that pleasure was his only memory. That she hadn't tried to sneak out of their bed without saying goodbye a few days later. That he hadn't been awake to try and stop her and said the things he'd said. Most of all he wished he hadn't promised to leave her alone. To let her walk away while there were good memories to hold onto, before time and reality destroyed what they'd found together. Her words.

Henry hadn't made that promise, Peter realized. He'd agreed to stop mentioning her name, but that was all. And now...what exactly was he on his way to find? Would they reminisce about old times and laugh at how dramatic first love could be and how insane it all seemed now? Would she look at him without interest, telling him over drinks about the man in her life who'd made her realize what love was all about? Would he find out Holly had finally made her choice, and it wasn't him?

Either way his friend was destined for a black eye or

something equally painful for springing this reunion on him without talking to him first. Just to fulfill a fantasy, just because of that damn gossip column...or was something else involved?

With Henry, there was always something else.

Holly. Jesus. Something switched on inside him as he turned the corner onto her street, knowing this time he wouldn't be leaving without hearing her voice. Seeing her. Sharing her again, if that was indeed Henry's plan.

He couldn't remember the last time he'd felt like this.

*Liar.*

Seventeen years, five months and fifteen days, give or take a few hours.

Too damn long.

## Chapter Two

"Should I be offended? I have this hazy memory of you being relaxed when you saw me again. What did Peter do to deserve all this pacing?"

Holly stopped long enough to stick out her tongue at the musician on her couch. "He didn't wear me down with emails. You'd been writing to me for months and I was, I believe, drunk off my ass, thanks to your drummer's girlfriend. This is different and you know it."

Henry was stroking his beard—a sexy addition she was still getting used to—and watching her with sparkling brown eyes. "She *was* under strict instructions not to let you get away until our set was over. But you hid your tipsy well. If I'd known you were drunk I might have taken advantage while I had the chance instead of pretending to be a gentleman."

"Romantic."

"I have my moments."

Holly studied him as if seeing him again for the first time. He was more muscular now, and his forearms were sleeved with tattoos she wouldn't mind studying up close. His black T-shirt and jeans looked comfortable and lived in and his black boots were scuffed by life, not design. She shouldn't be surprised. He'd never given off the rich boy vibe and nothing about him hinted at his mother's aristocratic lineage. Henry Vincent was his father's son. A rock and roll legacy from a loving family, he always knew who he was and where he belonged. It was a self-confidence Holly had found irresistible in college, and it was still difficult to ignore.

None of the things that drew her to him had changed. He still moved like a lazy lion that hadn't decided whether to cuddle or pounce. Still wore an expression of sensual mischief mixed with tenderness when he looked at her. Still had a voice with that hint of gravel that made her shiver and tempted her with an ease that shouldn't be possible after all this time.

Henry was—in a word—sex. Great sex. The kind that took hours and tangled sheets and made you laugh at the shameless, satisfying joy of it all. Everything about him, from his scent to his smile, reminded Holly of that word. No wonder his fans went crazy every time he got on stage.

He was also determined, something she never would have used to describe him until recently.

When he sent her that first email a year ago, she hadn't been sure what to expect. She'd read it more than once, memorizing each line but forcing herself not to respond. She'd wondered why he'd decided to become her pen pal after all these years, and it had given her weeks of tension headaches, anxiety and more sexual frustration than the situation warranted. Was it because of one of her work projects? Had he found out she was the ghostwriter for the model who'd written an autobiography with an entire chapter dedicated to her "disappointing fling" with his friend Dean Warren? Or was it not related to her work? Maybe he was going through a mid-life crisis and revisiting his youthful sexual encounters.

That was a reason she might have been able to get behind.

It wasn't until the third letter came, filled not with accusations or come-ons but humor and poetry and everything Henry, that she'd realized his emails were exactly what they appeared to be. An open door. And they weren't going to stop until she hit reply.

They still hadn't. Once a month without fail she would get another entry in what he laughingly called The Holly Report. He would tell her about the cities he was in, or the video game his lead singer was addicted to. He shared some of his erotic poetry, describing his more debauched experiences with other women in a way that stole her breath. He wrote about his family and sent her pictures of his oldest brother's children. He talked about his friends Dean and Tracy, and his worry that they were both too wrapped up in the responsibilities that came with their names to enjoy life. And once in a while, so sparingly it was almost like a tease, he would talk about Peter. Most of the time it had to do with a prank he was thinking of playing or what country Peter was currently causing trouble in. Sometimes it was more.

She'd become so used to hearing about them that she was still in an understandable amount of shock when she found out yesterday that Peter didn't know about any of it. The emails. The occasional phone calls. Their get-together at one of the smaller venues where Shattered Pieces got its start. Nothing.

Henry, apparently, hadn't said a word about her to his best friend.

"I'm still not sure why you didn't tell him," she muttered, starting to pace again. "It's not like we're doing anything wrong, or even anything close to the kind of wrong you two are capable of, according to the gossips."

Henry sent her a speaking look. "You know better than to believe everything you read, Holly. The truth is infinitely more complex and thankfully a bit more X-rated. And I already told you why yesterday. I made him a promise years ago, and for the most part I kept it. Until last week. His reaction told me all I needed to know—namely, that until he sees proof, he rarely takes me seriously, and that it's doubtful I'll get away with my sin of omission without some physical pain and a shitload of payback."

She tried to laugh. "You two and your paybacks. But I doubt he'll care enough to be that upset. He hasn't seen me since college."

"If you were that naïve you wouldn't be pacing." He tilted his head, his dark, mussed hair brushing against his shoulders. "Your reaction is telling as well, but far more promising. I knew it would be, which is why I'll promise to try not to be offended that you're so comfortable around me. Now sit down and have a drink. We don't want you nervous when he gets here, which should be any minute."

Holly bit her tongue before she admitted how *not* comfortable she was around him. How hard it was to remember that too much time had passed for it to be acceptable to climb into his lap and nibble on his neck. "I'm not nervous, I'm wisely cautious and not looking forward to feeling awkward when the happy reunion you're expecting doesn't happen. Anyway I'm sure he'll call first. You didn't even tell him where you were. That picture of my ankle could have been taken in Morocco for all he knows."

Henry held up his phone. "He knows. Have you forgotten how smart our Mr. Faraday is? He hasn't. Peter could take over the world if he wanted to, probably via cell phone while playing Sudoku and single-handedly solving the problem of global warming. How he didn't find you first is a mystery to me. But then, so many things are. Not this, though. I'm right about this. I think."

"Comforting." And she hadn't forgotten how smart Peter was. How could she? She'd been in awe of him in college when she found out he was more than he seemed. More than filthy rich and handsome and too charming to hate. Peter was a genuine genius. Her favorite professor called him a polymath. He had an eidetic memory, could rebuild an engine, paint and play piano like a savant, take eight finals in one day and still have the time and brain power to stay up all night talking to her about the stars, about history and art and life, without making her feel like an idiot.

The way he used to touch her... The man excelled at everything.

But what had he done with all those skills? She walked over to the couch, sat down and accepted the drink from Henry. Everyone with a television or an Internet connection knew how the globetrotting Peter Faraday spent his time. The man with degrees in chemistry, physics, art history and computer science was his own after-hours cable show, entertaining the masses with his special brand of kinky experimentation.

"He doesn't want to take over the world." She stared into the glass morosely, watching the ice cubes he'd added clink against each other and crack. "Neither do you. You want to shock it and strip it and make it do wicked things it will most likely regret in the morning."

The Peter from her memories was romantic. Sexy and capable of erotic feats that—combined with Henry's skills—were unrivaled, yes, but she didn't remember him being such a...

Playboy? Casanova? Man-whore?

Henry's laugh was loud and uninhibited. "We're men, babe. Spoiled men, as you were always so fond of pointing out. You don't point a hungry, spoiled man in the direction of a buffet if you don't want him to sample everything."

She rolled her eyes, but she couldn't help smiling. "I appreciate your honesty, if not your sexist food analogy. Anyway, it kind of goes with the territory for you, doesn't it? Women tear off their tops and throw themselves at you in every city in the world for the chance to touch some of that creativity."

Henry chuckled again. "I'm almost positive it's not my creativity they want to touch. At least, that isn't the first thing they reach for. But sure, I'll use the musician defense. Poor Peter doesn't get the same easy out, I'm guessing. If only he'd gone into underwear modeling or porn instead of living off his savvy investments and family fortunes, then you'd be able to understand his appetite. Too bad for him, huh?"

Holly frowned at him when her cheeks heated. "I didn't mean it like that. Not really. I suppose I wasn't expecting him to turn an extracurricular activity into a lifetime occupation, but who am I to judge? You know I haven't exactly done what was expected either."

Henry's smile widened and he licked his lips. "I only know enough to whet my appetite. All those jobs, all that research just to be a professional ghostwriter. I have to admit your life sounds more exciting than mine. I keep playing the same old songs, but you sing a new tune every few months."

She nodded, taking another sip of courage as she glanced at the door. "I do. And it *is* exciting for the most part, though not all of my research is that interesting, and it's rarely as glamorous as your career. Rodeo clown for example? Not my finest hour. And my roller derby debut was over before it started. I still can't believe I fell and broke my arm before completing my first lap. When I have time I'll try out again. I hate leaving a project unfinished."

"Roller derby? You're killing me, babe, I hope you know that. And I thought it would be hard to top dominatrix trainee and stripper on my erotic list of Holly's hobbies." He was enjoying this conversation a bit too much.

"Burlesque performer, Henry. Not stripper. Big difference."

He nodded. "You have no idea how long I'll kick myself for never getting to see you perform. With that Betty Page hair and those Betty Grable legs? I bet you were a hit. And now I'm going to start calling you Betty. Please tell me Betty Boom-Boom will be your next roller derby name so I can die a happy man."

She laughed, shaking her head as he tapped her glass with his. "What about the other? Did you enjoy bossing the weaker sex around for a change? Were all the power-suited men falling to their knees and begging you to crack your whip?"

"It was great therapy," she admitted with a shrug. "But it's not something I'd seek out for personal enjoyment. I was simply slipping into someone else's stilettos for a story."

Her personal cravings were something entirely different, in large part because of her experiences with Henry and Peter. She didn't want to be the one in control, not when it came to sex. She wanted to be overwhelmed and swept away. To be taken and ravished, which made her sound more like a romance heroine with a bodice in need of ripping and less like an independent woman, but there it was.

She'd checked off a few things on her sexual wish list over the years, though she'd never had any desire to be with two men at the same time again. That fantasy had very specific casting.

Since Henry and Peter, there'd been three or four steady boyfriends she genuinely cared about, despite the fact that the relationships had only lasted until they proposed or things got serious enough that she thought they might. It wasn't a character trait she was proud of. To avoid the guilt, she'd started confining her relationships to friends with benefits and short-term affairs.

In between those, she'd participated in a night of role-play with a married couple from one of her jobs when they were looking to spice up their relationship, and taken kinky photographs of her neighbors and closest friends—Bill and Chaz—that had turned into a voyeuristic night to remember. One of those pictures now hung over their bed, even though the image clearly revealed her reflection in the mirror zooming in on their intimate embrace.

She supposed she could give the Billionaire Bachelors a run for their money in the sexual experimentation department. Or at least make a decent showing. Luckily, no one was interested in recounting *her* exploits or exploring her fear of commitment for posterity. Unluckily, those exploits had a short shelf life in the satisfaction department. Soon enough, as regular as clockwork, she wound herself up thinking about Peter again. About Henry.

For years she'd tried to analyze it away and move beyond what had happened between them. She knew she'd romanticized it, put it on a pedestal in her memory. She knew that nothing was ever as good as it had seemed to be when you were looking back. A Christmas ménage with two men she thought she was in love with might sound perfect now, but she also had a vague recollection of being heartbroken and terrified of making the wrong decision in the harsh light of day. Of being as fickle as her mother.

So she'd made the choice *not* to make a choice, and that had its own set of consequences. The worst being that she knew exactly what it could be like. *Should* be like. Nothing else had ever come close, and nothing less was ever enough.

The knock at the door made her jump to her feet, adrenaline shaking her hand so hard her drink splashed onto her fingers. "Shit."

"Relax." Henry stood up with her, taking the glass away and distracting her by gripping her wrist and sucking her wet fingers into his mouth. Oh God. He watched her shiver as he let her go. "You should get that. We both know who it is, and that knock sounds serious."

It did?

Why had she agreed to this? Both men in her living room, in her life again after all these years, was a masochistic decision and a recipe for trouble. She should have remained a distant spectator, forcing herself to be thankful she hadn't stayed with them—especially when Bill and Chaz came over to gossip with her about the city's notorious homegrown billionaires. The orgies, and sex in public fountains, and hotel lobbies being overrun by young screaming female fans willing to do whatever it took to sleep with a member of the band.

Chaz was the only other person who knew about her youthful affair. The threesome, *not* the participants. He'd still thankfully kept it from Bill, who was the hairstylist city dwellers with money went to for salacious rumors as well as exquisite dye jobs. She couldn't let either of them know about her visitors. What if they were looking out their window right now? God, she should have thought this through.

*Why did you write Henry back at all? Why did you berate him for not telling Peter about you, practically demanding that he send that text? Why are you dying to open the door and let him in?*

All good questions she refused to answer on the grounds that they might incriminate her.

But the truth refused to be ignored. It hit her in the chest and stole her breath the instant she opened the door and looked into the beautiful, glowering face of Peter Faraday.

She still wanted them. More in this moment than she ever had. She'd gone to see Henry yesterday, invited him over and asked about Peter today *because* she wanted them. It wasn't to talk, or catch up, or even apologize and explain why she'd disappeared, changing schools rather than facing them again. It should have been, but it wasn't.

Her real reasons were simple and shameless. She wanted the chance to experience what they'd shared back then as a grown woman with no romantic illusions. Sex with Henry and Peter. They were here and she knew enough about herself to know she'd always regret it if she didn't get a chance to compare her memory with the real thing one more time.

He was staring at her and she realized she'd been ogling him for a good two minutes without saying a word. "Peter."

"Holly." Peter looked down at her, his piercing blue eyes like a physical caress as they slid down her body, taking all of her in. Holly suddenly wished she hadn't thrown her hair into a simple ponytail. That she'd worn heels and a dress for her afternoon meeting instead of the casual striped jersey that fell off one shoulder and her black mini-skort. Skorts didn't exactly scream sexy and irresistible.

She sighed, trying to curb her reaction to him long enough to say something other than his name.

"Are you going to let me in?" He stepped forward, towering over her and causing Holly to instinctively walk backwards until he'd closed the door behind them without releasing her from his mesmerizing stare.

"Of course. I'm sorry I…" Her words trailed off and she was fairly certain they weren't coming back any time soon. Peter packed a pheromone punch that would knock a nun to her knees.

If Henry was sex, Peter was sin disguised as an angel. Long lashes. Sensual lips. Eyes that impossible shade of blue she'd only seen in the waters off the Belize Barrier Reef, where she'd worked for a summer as a scuba instructor. Blond hair that would curl around her fingers if she touched it. He still had a heart-stopping face and a body that made her want things too dirty to even think about in public. The only thing saving him from Photoshopped perfection was the sexy scratch of stubble on his face, the smudge of grease on his white linen shirt and the flash of anger in his eyes.

The hardness in his expression was new. His social persona was that of a laid-back playboy and her memories of him were too soft around the edges to be entirely reliable, but the man she was looking at now was more dangerous than her Peter Faraday. Exciting…which was a thought that only reinforced her masochism theory.

Shit, she was still staring at him like a lovesick teenager. She needed to think of something witty to say. Something normal so he wouldn't know what he was doing to her.

She took a grateful breath when Henry spoke into the lengthening silence.

"So…this is awkward and uncomfortable. Aren't you going to say hello, Peter? Greet our old friend with a warm smile instead of that icy stare?"

She saw Peter's lips tighten at the sound of Henry's voice. He smiled, but it wasn't warm or relaxed. He leaned down until his lips were a breath away from hers.

"Hello, Peter," he mimicked obediently. "Has he kissed you yet?"

He used to ask her the same question every time he came back from class to find her at the house with Henry.

"On the cheek," she whispered, licking her lips in anticipation. She knew what came next. What always came next.

Peter's blue eyes darkened. "Shame on him. Do you remember, Holly? Shall we show him how it's done?"

Damn. She wasn't even aware she'd started nodding until his mouth was on hers. Holly moaned softly, forgetting how long it had been since they'd seen each other or how things had ended between them. His lips on hers sent her traveling through time. It was as if she'd been kissing him her whole life. As if they'd never stopped. Just this. His lips, the tug of his teeth and the skilled stroke of his tongue against hers were making her ache.

He hadn't even touched her yet.

Before she could wrap her arms around him, he was gone, his dark expression tinged with arousal. He turned to Henry, leaving her to recover in stunned silence. "Comfortable now? *That* is how you say hello to an old friend, your Highness."

Henry shook his head when he noticed her glazed expression. "I'll be damned. Wish I'd thought of it first. Consider me schooled, Dick." Peter growled and Henry held up his hands. "It slipped out. I know, I know, I'm lucky to be alive and you're surprised and I owe you an explanation, but you have to admit—it's a good surprise."

"I'll admit you're lucky."

Holly would smile if she could stop trembling. *Dick.* She seemed to remember the cowboy business major starting that particular running gag. Peter hated it, which only made all his friends pile on. Some things never changed.

"I'm glad you're here, Peter. It's great to see you again." *And kiss you again.* She took a deep breath. "Sit down, please. Can I get you something to drink?"

It was hard to appear sophisticated and composed when he'd nearly melted her damn skort off with that lip lock. She should be grateful she still remembered how to form a sentence that didn't start with "Please" and end with "Fuck me."

He was staring at her lips, only making things worse. "Thank you for letting me crash your party. You look good, Holly."

"I've got his drink, Betty." Henry grinned at the new nickname, sitting back down on the couch and reaching for the bottle on the coffee table. "You should come and finish yours so I have an excuse to pour you another. It feels like the start of one of those nights and we have a lot of catching up to do, now that the gang's all here."

Peter's expression changed and he moved into the living room, taking one of her armless chairs and twirling it around to straddle it. "I see you and your beard have made yourselves at home. I also noticed Dean's car parked down the street. Any reason you decided to play your own version of Grand Theft Auto to visit our old friend, *Betty?*"

Holly took the free chair and sat down, her arms crossed as she watched them eye-wrestle. This hadn't changed either. They loved their verbal sparring, no matter the topic, and while she didn't miss the jealous edge it could sometimes take on, she'd missed the exchanges.

Not as much as she'd missed the kissing. She was really ready for more of that.

Henry lifted one shoulder. "It's not stealing if you have a key and fill up the gas tank. I only *borrowed* it because I did some research and discovered Holly lives in a very anti-Hummer neighborhood. I didn't want to leave Roy alone and at the mercy of all these limo-hating, organic tomato-throwing hipsters, so I drove myself in that cramped, sexless tuna can of a vehicle. Because I care."

Holly couldn't hold back a soft sound of amusement. Her neighborhood was definitely a haven for hipsters and artisans. She liked it, but Henry was right—this was not limo country. "I have a feeling Roy would be fine."

Peter turned his attention to her and her throat closed. "Know him well, do you, Holly? Spend a lot of time with Roy? I have it on good authority that our boy Henry never goes out with the same girl twice, so you'll understand why I'm surprised to hear that. And I didn't think anything he did could surprise me anymore."

Henry swore. "Jesus, man, take a beat. Polite conversation usually precedes an inquisition." Peter didn't respond and Henry ran a hand through his hair and set his drink down. "She's met Roy twice. Once when she came to see the band perform and yesterday, when I took her out to lunch in a public place filled with witnesses who'll swear under oath that she wasn't under duress *or* under the table. Not that I have any obligation to spell it out for you, but this is the first time I've been here. And I had to text you to let you know. Because I care and I'm a moron."

Peter's hands clenched into tight fists on his thighs, and Holly swallowed. Now that she knew what she wanted, she was having a hard time thinking about anything else. The last thing she needed Peter and Henry to do was ruin the mood by fighting over her as if she were a hunk of meat.

"I think I'm ready for the pissing contest to end. I really like this carpet, and I wouldn't want to have it replaced. I know there are more interesting things I'd like to talk about, so let's get all our firsts out of the way."

Both men's attentions were now firmly fixed on her. God help her. "Peter? Henry emailed me a year ago, but before you get on his case about it, you should tell him *you've* known where I lived since the week I moved in." She pointed at him with one thankfully steady finger. "True or false?"

"True." He narrowed his blue eyes. "But how would you know that?"

She waved off the question as if it were obvious. "I trained with a private detective for a story and you always drive your canary yellow convertible when you're in town. It's not a subtle color, Peter. It's kind of a neon sign for criminals, if you want to know the truth, but that's not important."

"Sounds important," Henry muttered. "At least I waited until you gave me your address and didn't circle your block like a stalker."

Holly raised one eyebrow and continued, "You saw me first, Henry, talked to me on the phone first and had lunch with me first, but Peter was the first to kiss me, so as far as I'm concerned you're even." Peter looked like he was going to argue and Holly sent him a warning expression. "Can we pretend we're all grown up now or do I need to take your drinks away and send you home?"

Peter glanced at Henry, whose shoulders had started to shake with mirth. "What the hell are you laughing at?"

"The Dominatrix Detective. I can see it on the New York Times bestseller list already."

"Ha ha," Holly responded dryly. "So can I. Her first case will be the murder of the royal rocker, who so thoroughly put his foot in it that everyone he knew would have an understandable motive to commit the crime."

Peter sent her a surprised smile. "You're still writing? That professor called it, didn't he? You've given him a student to brag about at last."

He remembered what her professor said? Of course he did. He remembered everything. "Ghostwriting isn't what he imagined when he made his prediction, I'm sure. But if he ever picks up a celebrity autobiography or a work of women's fiction written by a reality show sensation? He'll most likely be reading me."

Peter's fascinated expression made her feel strangely relieved. As if she cared what he thought about the career she'd accidentally tripped into six years ago. Or careers, plural, if you counted all the side jobs this one had spawned.

"We're both writers," Henry sighed playfully. "Small world, right?"

"Dude, how many times do I have to tell you that dirty limericks set to music does not an author make?" Peter shook his head. "I might want to hire you to write Henry's life story, Holly. Ever authored a tragedy?"

She laughed and winked at Henry before responding to Peter. "I wouldn't take that on at any price. Besides, and don't take this the wrong way, but neither one of you would have as big a seller as you'd imagine. Everyone already knows all your dirty secrets."

Most of them. They didn't know about her.

Peter gripped the top of the chair and rested his chin on his hands. The casual pose belied his tension. Something primal below the surface was tensed and ready to strike. Her body heated in reaction and she crossed her legs.

He noticed. "We can talk about our secrets another time. Right now I'm more intrigued by yours. I'm beginning to think our meeting wasn't entirely Henry's plan after all."

"Of course it was," Henry scoffed. "Just because you're a genius doesn't mean other people can't come up with devious plans."

"Oh, I'm certain you had a plan, Henry," Peter assured him. "And I'm sure it was almost done baking under all that facial hair before she came up with hers. Why did you agree to invite this royal pain over in the first place, Holly? Why are we here? And what more interesting topic would you like to discuss?"

Years apart and he knew in five minutes what it had

taken her several days to figure out. What had been in the back of her mind since Henry invited her to lunch and told her he and Peter would be in town for at least a month.

"Are you sure you wouldn't rather talk about what you two are doing still in town after the annual Warren bash? The hot weather we're having? I could always give you the inside scoop on a certain basketball player's upcoming tell-all." They didn't respond and her mind raced as she searched for a way to broach the subject gracefully. When that didn't work, she lied. "Since you asked, something did just cross my mind. I've hit a research snag for a chapter in one of my current projects. Henry can tell you how seriously I take my research. Most of the time if I can't experience it, I don't feel like I can do it justice on the page. I was thinking the two of you might be able to help me out with the subject."

"Sounds like fun," Henry offered cautiously. "What's the subject?"

Holly blew her bangs away from her heated face and threw caution on the floor, stomped on it then tossed it out the window. "I'll give you a hint. The chapter's title is My Memorable Ménage."

"Fuck me."

Exactly, she nodded at Henry's response, holding her breath while she waited for Peter's.

"I might need that second drink after all."

# CHAPTER THREE

Holly didn't know it, but she'd just opened up a Pandora's Box that there was no way he was going to let her shut again.

Peter watched Henry fill her glass and bring it over to her, taking that time to process what was happening. They'd fallen back into their old rhythm without missing a beat, as if no time had passed and nothing had changed. He couldn't resist kissing her, Henry couldn't resist pushing their buttons, and Holly...she was exactly as he remembered. More than he remembered.

Peter hadn't wanted to stop kissing her. Everything in him was telling him to grab her and press her against the wall, remind her what they were like together. How much she loved it when he took charge. His ire at Henry and the surrealistic experience of being with her again had been the only thing that kept him in check.

It was clear he and his friend needed to have a talk. A year's worth of emails. How much had they shared that Peter had been excluded from? How many private jokes and intimate secrets and bad days had he missed because Henry hadn't had the balls to let him know he was back in touch with their old flame? He knew how upset Peter would be to find out after the fact, so why had he waited?

It left Peter feeling off balance. Unprepared. He'd just caught his breath when she pulled the rug out from under him again by asking for help with her "research."

*She still wants you. Both of you. She wants a repeat performance.*

And he wanted to give it to her more than she would ever know. If he were to calculate the percentage of time he'd spent in the last two years alone imagining a scenario almost identical to this one—including the Henry factor? He frowned. That equation he would take to his grave because the answer was too uncomfortable for him to admit to.

So why was he hesitating? Because of the slight sting of her subtle rejection? It was clear she'd developed a new bond with Henry. By the look on his face, he hadn't expected her request any more than Peter had. Hadn't expected the topic to turn to sex as soon as Peter walked through the door.

It wasn't a reaction he minded, as a rule, but with Holly it was different. Did she see him the same way everyone else did now? As the playboy?

He didn't care. There was no way he was leaving to prove he was more than a convenient research assistant. The will or pride or whatever the hell it was that he would need to walk out of the door after that kind of request? He didn't fucking have it.

Time had given him a certain amount of perspective and more experience, but it hadn't made him immune to Holly's charms. She crossed her bare legs again and he bit back a hungry moan. His pinup fantasy had only come into focus with age. Her breasts were still full and firm, her waist even smaller and her legs still endless. The shoulder revealed by her loose-fitting top was decorated with elegantly feminine flower tattoos that he wanted to lick. It made him curious, impatient to strip her down to discover what other additions she'd made to the body that he'd long ago memorized.

Her hair was different too. Shorter. She had sassy black bangs now that brought attention to the delicate silver studs piercing her left eyebrow, as well as her big doe eyes and thick lashes. They suited her, the changes. Gave her a bad girl edge that made her more alluring and him hard as a rock.

He was going to take her up on her offer. He wasn't an idiot. That didn't mean he would make it easy on her.

"You still have a talent for getting my attention, Ms. Ruskin. I'm sure you remember how much I enjoy research. And fucking," he added, feeling a hint of satisfaction when she swallowed too swiftly and gasped at the burn of the liquid. "Putting two of my favorite things together makes the offer practically irresistible, but I need more information. I appear to be at a slight disadvantage, thanks to our furry friend."

He met Henry's dark gaze, seeing his reaction to Holly's request beneath the apology. Like a kid at Christmas, Henry wanted to say yes and unwrap his present now. "She says you know about her style of research, Henry—should we expect her to conduct extensive interviews?"

Peter caressed the wooden arch of the chair he was straddling, already imagining her under his hands. "Do you think she'll have us recount our personal experiences in detail? Maybe we could start with the time I met you at your hotel room and found two naked women and four men sprawled across your bed? I spent hours trying to mentally rebuild *that* particular Jenga tower, I can tell you. And then, to be fair, we can recount my recent fetish for twins."

Holly surprised him by chuckling. "Are you trying to shock me, Peter Faraday? I told you neither one of you have many secrets left. My neighbor knows juicier tidbits about your sex lives. But if we're swapping stories, I have one of a beautiful Audrey Hepburn lookalike who did lovely things to me with her tongue while her husband watched. And no, I won't go into detail. Your turn."

Peter's fingers tightened on the chair until his knuckles went white and he felt all the blood rush to his cock. Audrey Hepburn and Holly. Now there was a fantasy that instantly went to the top of his list. She was good at this, knew just what to say to throw him off his game. Why was he surprised? "Did you know about that too, Henry?"

He saw his friend reach for the bottle and bring it to his lips. He'd obviously decided the glass wouldn't be enough. When he was done taking several long swallows, he lowered the bottle and shook his head. "Hell no, man, I swear. I don't think I could have kept that to myself without having a stroke." He wiped his mouth, watching Holly as if she'd suddenly turned into a cobra...or a porn star. Peter couldn't tell if he was shocked or impressed. He was betting on impressed. "But I do know she doesn't do interviews. Not in the traditional sense. She works for her intel. If she's writing about dog grooming, she grooms dogs, etcetera. And she's thorough. Three months per research project."

"Henry Vincent."

Peter smiled at the way Holly said Henry's name. "That *is* thorough."

Her fingers were tapping out a soft tune against the glass she was holding, signaling her discomfort to anyone paying attention. Were they making her nervous?

"Three months for a career project," she corrected. "For a single chapter? I rarely spend more than a few days. Otherwise I'd never get any actual writing done. It's nothing that would take too much time away from anyone's schedule."

Were her words meant to assuage their concerns or hers? It was a fabrication, her research request. Everyone in this room knew she had experienced at least one ménage. Knew she hadn't forgotten.

*Audrey Hepburn's tongue. Jesus.*

Peter was more than willing to go along with the charade, but she didn't get to set the terms. He would need more than a few days to get what he wanted.

"This isn't exactly a simple research request, Holly. Three months *might* be enough to cover the basics. We do all have previous experience with the topic, which is a plus, but if you want to be thorough—and I know you do—we'll need to put in the time." Her lips parted and he hid his pleasure at her reaction. "I'm sure Henry wouldn't mind using my place as home base for the duration. His city apartment is too small, and his family's home is far too crowded for what you have in mind."

"Sounds good to me," Henry agreed, wisely without any hesitation. "In fact, I could say you took the words right out of my mouth. I'm in."

"I had a feeling you would be." Peter tilted his head, as if considering. "I had a few projects of my own planned for the summer, but nothing that can't be rescheduled or worked around. When would you like to start?"

She frowned in confusion and Peter wanted to laugh. Her provocative offer had gotten away from her, the situation swiftly morphing into more than she'd expected.

"I think we got our wires crossed somewhere," she muttered.

He got up from his chair and walked over to hers, dropping to his knees and placing his hands on her calves to uncross her legs. "Not at all, Holly. We understand each other perfectly. You requested our services for your research, and you were right to do so. Not to brag, but I can't think of two men better qualified to give you exactly what you need."

She bit her lip when his hands reached her thighs, pulling her to the edge of her chair, closer to him. "I suppose we could drag you to the floor and take you right now. Henry and I could spend the rest of the evening refreshing your memory, making you scream so loudly you wake your neighbors." He tugged on her shorts. "I could have this off you in less than a minute and bury my face between your thighs until you forget all about Audrey. And I'm sure Henry would love to find out if you're still as talented with your mouth as we both remember."

Henry's groan merged with Holly's. Peter understood exactly what he was doing, how much harder he was making it—and himself—by continuing, but he couldn't back down now. He wouldn't. "There are so many things we could do to you, Holly, and if you'd just asked us for sex—for a walk down memory lane—that's what you would have gotten. But you didn't."

"She didn't?" Henry swore again from his perch on the couch.

"No. She didn't," Peter assured him with an undercurrent of warning. "Holly said it herself. We have well-deserved reputations. This is an opportunity to put all the knowledge we've accumulated to the best possible use. By the time the summer is over, Holly will have enough material to write a definitive work on the subject. Three months of graphic, hands-on empirical data she will never forget, as long as we do it right. We'll have to be discreet, in our pal Tracy's full meaning of the word, but I think it's the least we can do for our old friend from college, don't you?"

"The very fucking least."

Holly shifted in her seat at Henry's response, her hands clutching her drink to her chest as if it were a protective talisman. "Three months is kind of a big commitment for the two of you, isn't it?" she asked hesitantly, still unsure of his motives. "Considering those reputations, are you sure about that timeline?"

"Do you still want us, Holly?" She gasped and his grip tightened on her legs. "You said you wanted our help. If you truly do, this is one of my conditions."

He heard Henry get up off the couch and move toward them. "Not to barge into these fascinating negotiations, Peter, but I have a suggestion."

"Yes?"

"I think she needs a sample. It *has* been a while, and an

incentive might remind her how qualified we are."

Peter's smile was hard as he picked Holly up into his arms and followed Henry toward the only hallway in the house. "I'll give you that one. This plan I like."

Henry found her bedroom and Peter carried her through the door. He could feel her watching him and he forced himself to stay in control.

"Just a sample, Henry," he warned. "No one gets more than that until we've come to an agreement."

He set her on the bed, and when her head touched her pillow, she caught his eye. "You're bossier than I remembered. I like it."

"You have no idea." He gripped her wrists and took her arms off his shoulders, placing them above her head. "You are also entirely too relaxed. Don't lower your hands, Holly. Not unless you want us to stop."

Her eyes widened and she looked down toward the foot of the bed as Henry took off her flats, undid her shorts and dragged them down her legs. "Okay," she whispered. "You mentioned conditions. Plural. Other than the time limit, what are they?"

Peter wanted to respond but found himself distracted by the small skulls and hearts on her underwear. "Henry…"

"Her shirt. I'm on it." His friend's rasp was more pronounced and Peter knew the restraint was difficult for him. Henry wasn't used to delayed gratification. Not anymore.

"No," Peter replied softly. "Leave her shirt on this time. You haven't kissed her yet."

"I haven't, have I?" Henry tore off his own shirt, toed off his heavy boots and crawled onto the bed beside Holly with a playful, impatient smile. "I need to fix that. Hello again, Holly."

"Hello, Henry."

Peter watched Holly grip the base of her headboard when Henry lowered his mouth to hers. They both melted into the kiss and he clenched his fists, torn as he'd always been between satisfaction at their acquiescence and determination to ensure no one forgot his presence. He walked around to the end of the bed and lowered himself slowly between her legs.

This bed wasn't big enough for the three of them. One more excuse to get her back to his place as soon as possible. But first they had to convince her.

He looked down at her underwear, his lips quirking at the ridiculous design before he dipped his head, gripped the fabric in his teeth and tugged.

Holly's moan was muffled by Henry's kiss. Peter looked up and saw his friend's hand cupping her breast and, not to be outdone, Peter pushed the fabric to the side and traced the lips of her sex with his tongue.

She was sweeter than he remembered. So good he forgot about everything else and closed his eyes to savor the taste. Holly's taste. He reached up to spread her thighs wider, groaning while his tongue slowly thrust inside her tight heat. Jesus, he'd missed this. She was already so wet and he was hungrier than he'd thought possible. After all this time she still got to him more than any woman ever had. She only had to breathe to seduce him. Only had to gasp at the touch of his lips on her and he was ready to explode. He'd meant to tease, to play with her until she was desperate. He knew what she liked, remembered every climax and where she loved to be touched. But now all he could think of was getting deeper. Taking more.

He pressed his erection hard into the mattress and started to fuck her with his tongue. No gentle foreplay. No tender exploration. It had been too long and he wanted to hear her scream.

Her hips lifted against his mouth and he could taste her arousal on his tongue. He was forcing himself to remember the plan with every second that passed, knowing it was important. *The plan.* A sample and nothing more. Not until she agreed. Not until he had her where he wanted her. *Yes. More.*

Holly couldn't think. Could hardly breathe. Henry was making love to her mouth, his beard scratching her chin and cheeks in a way that only made her wonder how it would feel on her breasts and between her thighs. His fingers were caressing her breasts, teasing her by dragging the fabric of her shirt over her hard nipples.

And Peter. Oh God, Peter was doing things to her with his tongue that made her want to scream. They were here. Both of them touching her, giving her what she'd imagined so many times since they'd been together.

She wanted to lower her hands and grip Peter's hair until she came against his lips. Wanted to unzip Henry's jeans and wrap her fingers around the thick erection she could feel against her hip until he agreed to give her more than a sample, but she knew if she did they would stop. She needed them inside her with an urgency that was almost frightening. Needed it badly enough that she was close to agreeing to anything.

*Conditions.*

She groaned and turned her head, pulling away from Henry's kiss to gasp, "Peter. Oh fuck, Peter, that feels— What are the conditions?"

For a minute she wasn't sure he heard her, and the things he was doing didn't make her want to repeat the question. She was close. She could come like this, with Henry against her and Peter's tongue... "God, that's good. Don't stop. Peter, don't stop."

"Tell her the damn conditions, Dick." Henry's cheeks were flushed above his beard as he stared at his hand squeezing her breast. "Tell her before I forget why we started this and take matters into my own hands."

Peter's tongue stilled and Holly swore under her breath,

her body already begging for his return. *Don't stop, damn it.* He lifted his head and she could see the blue of his eyes burning up at her. He wanted this too. As much as she did. Why were they both being so damn stubborn?

He licked his lips and she shivered. "Conditions. Three months. You stay with us until our time is up and allow me to set the pace without argument. We need to relearn this body so we can give you the perfect ménage for your research. A *memorable* ménage."

She shook her head and lifted her hips again, silently begging. "You don't need to learn anything. Trust me, everything you're doing feels exactly right."

He narrowed his gaze. "I won't agree to anything less, Holly. Those are my rules."

There was a small but adamant voice in her head telling her to run away as fast as she could. Four nights with Peter and Henry in college had been unforgettable. Three months could ruin her forever.

She wanted him to stop talking and touch her again. Wanted to take back her request for research and beg them to fuck her. Wasn't that what she'd been going for in the first place, satisfying her curiosity and desire? They were grown, sexually active adults. There was no reason they couldn't scratch this one itch.

But she knew one time wouldn't be enough. Not for her.

But what he was suggesting might be. No landmine of choices to make, no fragile, youthful hearts that needed protecting—no chance of falling in love when you started with a time limit. Enough time that she might finally be able to get them out of her system. One summer with the two men she'd never forgotten sounded too good to be true.

How could she say no to that? Why would she want to? She looked away from Peter and up at Henry. In all the time they'd been talking to each other, he'd never asked for more. For anything like this. Not once. Had his feelings for her changed, or had it been about Peter? Had he been waiting for him, the same way she had? For their group to be complete? "Is this what you want?"

His smile made her heart flutter. Damn he was handsome. "How can you doubt it? I want you. I think you can feel how much. And you know we can give you what you need. Say yes, Holly."

She arched her back in reaction to his words, pressing her breast harder against Henry's hand, and his smile disappeared. "Peter? Can she come if she says yes?"

Peter pinched her clit with his fingers, just enough to make her inhale sharply in surprise and look back down at him. "No. She can come when she walks through my front door with her luggage and her answer."

Disbelief doused her in a shower of ice. "*Peter?* Damn it." She rolled away from both of them and got to her feet beside the bed, her knees like Jell-O. "I don't remember you being a tease."

He pushed himself off the bed and she could see how aroused he was, his erection—God, she still remembered how he felt inside her—pressing insistently against his pants.

"Funny," he responded darkly. "I remember quite clearly that you were."

Henry took her pillow and covered his face to muffle his scream of frustration. "You're tearing me apart," he shouted the iconic James Dean quote through the down and cotton pillowcase, making Holly smile. He lowered the pillow and blew her a kiss. "He's right though, Betty. You were an epic tease. The queen of the tease. Kept us dangling for months. Maybe that's why you were such a good stripper."

"Burlesque dancer."

"Don't spoil my dream."

Peter took her hand and she felt all her frustration start to fade. "Are you sure, Peter?"

He squeezed her fingers gently before letting her go. "I'm sure this is the only way it will happen. Think about it and we'll see you tomorrow. As soon as you come to us, you'll come for us. Henry?"

"Son of a bossy bitch," Henry grumbled, rolling off the bed and reaching for his shirt. "I guess we'll be going now that he's chosen his form of payback. I've got to tell you, this is not how I was expecting the evening to end."

Holly stood there in her shirt and underwear, crossing her arms over her chest to hold herself together until they left. "Me either."

She wasn't sure how she'd been expecting it to go, but this was not even close.

He pointed at her and wagged his finger. "I'm not so sure. I was settling in for an evening of banter and sexual innuendo that would eventually lead to the reveal of my master plan. You were the one who played the research card as soon as he walked through the door. I knew when you said it he wouldn't be able to resist. I think you did too."

He slid his finger under her chin and tilted her lips up to his for a soft, lingering kiss. "This is what you were waiting for, isn't it? What we were both waiting for. Now don't let me down. Pack your bikini and your Burlesque costume and join us at the Faraday estate tomorrow morning. If you don't show up by noon he might call out the National Guard. Or ninjas. You know he has the resources and he's in that kind of mood."

She laughed and closed her eyes when he pressed his lips to her forehead. "Goodnight, Henry."

*As soon as you come to us, you'll come for us.*

Holly definitely had a touch of masochism, but she wasn't an idiot. She'd needed to start packing.

Three months.

How much clothing would she really need?

## Chapter Four

Henry threw a balled up napkin at Peter's head as he finished his breakfast on the patio. "Are you done yet, 007? Satisfied?"

Peter glared up from his computer in irritation. He'd spent his morning shamelessly perusing Henry and Holly's email exchanges. Despite it being Henry's idea, he felt like a damn Peeping Tom reading her responses to the "Holly Report," but he wouldn't allow himself to be sorry. He'd been kept outside the loop for too long.

"Not even close, Vincent. But you didn't show me these to satisfy *me* as much as you did to ease your own guilt."

Henry rolled his eyes, grabbing his plate and getting to his feet. "Figure that out by yourself, genius? Look, forget it. You know just about everything now. We talked, we met for drinks, and we talked some more. Tame and boring stuff."

"I suppose you weren't trying to seduce her."

"I was taking my time, getting to know her again," Henry corrected. "Then you showed up and five minutes later, here we are. You get to run things for the next three months, we all get laid and I will do my damnedest to remember that I owe you and follow your lead. I have no problem with that role, as long as it gets me what I want. And just so you know, I've wanted to tell you about Holly for a while."

"Why didn't you?"

He paused, stopping beside Peter. "Honestly? I wasn't sure you'd forgiven her for leaving yet."

Peter scoffed. "After seventeen years you thought I hadn't...but you had?"

Henry nodded, his brown eyes sad and sincere. "I forgave her as soon as she walked out the door. You might have too, if I'd been a better friend and told you why, whether you were ready to hear it or not. Chalk it up to being young and dumb and too wrapped up in my own regrets to hold your poor little rich boy hand."

Peter slammed the computer closed and got out of his chair, following Henry inside to the cavernous kitchen where he used to chase the cooks around as a child. "You're telling me you knew why she left? That you always knew?"

"I'm telling you I respected your moratorium on all things Holly." Henry sighed. "I miss Martina. She made the best breakfast burritos. I know you have day crews still coming in, but are you sure we can't keep the permanent staff on for this project of ours? They've kept bigger secrets, and cooking might be the one skill you haven't mastered."

"Henry."

"Fine." He set his plate down and turned to lean against the counter, his large body tense. "Mom heard things back then. The world of the filthy rich is a small one, its own little cul-de-sac of sin where everybody knows everyone else's business. Mom hasn't got a judgmental bone in her body—I mean, look who she's married to—but when I told her I was dating Holly, she warned me to steer clear of meeting her mother. Said she was bad news, already on her third husband and looking to upgrade to a richer number four. From the implication, she wouldn't have been above seducing her daughter's young boyfriend if he fit the bill and she got a tiara out of it." He took a breath, shaking his head. "After

Holly left, I found out about the scandal that happened the day she showed up at our place. I guess her stepfather found her mother in bed with his married golfing buddy. There was a fight and the police were called. Everyone knew."

Peter ran a hand through his hair and tugged, feeling a headache coming on. "Bullshit. How did I not know this?"

Henry winced. "Because I didn't tell you. I thought if she hadn't said anything, had never mentioned her mother once since we started seeing her, it probably wasn't something she wanted to talk about." He shrugged. "I can't say that I blame her—you know how much flak she took at our school from those rich sorority bitches. Can you imagine how they would have reacted after finding out her mother was a bona fide gold digger?"

Had Holly thought Peter or Henry would judge her because of her mother's obvious ambitions? Had she made an assumption based on the kind of money they came from instead of who they were?

*I was just being selfish. Greedy. I think it's genetic.*

Her words came back to slap him in the face. And the emails—how many times had she mentioned to Henry the relationships she'd cut short because she didn't want things to get serious? She didn't want to hurt anyone when "reality" got in the way. Almost exactly what she'd said to Peter that last day.

Was that the reality she was talking about? Did she think she was anything like her mother? Or was she trying to make sure she wasn't by limiting her commitments? Hell, even the three-month project rule and her job writing other people's stories made more sense now.

She was still running.

It would be better for all of them if he kept that in mind for the next few months. Holly wasn't going to stay.

Peter crossed his arms. "No wonder you're being so agreeable, Henry. You haven't kept this many secrets from me since we were five and you thought you were a magician.

Is there any-*fucking*-thing else, Henry? Anything you didn't tell me that I should know about Holly?"

Henry's eyes shifted and Peter swore. "I'll be damned."

"It's a suspicion," his friend insisted. "Nothing concrete or anything."

"Tell me."

Henry shook his head. "If I do, you'll be pissed and this will be over before she gets here. You don't want that. I don't want that. Nobody wants that, man."

"Tell me anyway." He braced himself.

Henry looked down at his boots. "I think she might be Ms. Anonymous."

"What?" Peter shook his head adamantly, shock reverberating through his body at Henry's accusation. "That's insane. What would make you— No way."

Henry scratched his beard, his expression regretful. "You can see why I didn't mention it. But it adds up. She's a writer in communication with some fairly high rollers in Hollywood who've recruited her for her services. She has the connections. I looked into her professional bio. I know she wrote that book where Dean's lack of after-sex cuddling takes up an entire chapter. You remember that one. I know because you sent us all a copy for Christmas to get under his skin." Peter's head felt like it was going to explode. Henry saw his expression and took a step toward him. "On the other hand, how much harm has Ms. Anonymous actually done, other than irritating Dean? Tracy's the Teflon Cowboy and God knows you and I never gave a shit about being in the news. Sure, you don't want to believe the woman you're about to fuck five ways from Sunday thinks you're a lewd, heartbreaking playboy with a penchant for public indecency…but other than that, would it really matter?"

He refused to believe it. "Holly is *not* Ms. Anonymous. You just told me about her mother's scandal. Why would she become a gossip columnist after growing up around that?"

"I thought about that, I did, and I don't know the answer.

But if she isn't, then she knows the person who is." Henry was persistent. "You read my emails, man. You know for a fact I put in one or two stories that weren't true, just for shock value. Use that recording device you have for a brain and think about it. Did they sound familiar? Ms. Anonymous referred to them in her columns before I could tell Holly I was joking. That's when I started wondering."

Peter reached for one of the stools lining the kitchen island and sat down, floored. Henry was right about that. He had seen a familiar correlation. But there had to be another reason. "And *I'm* right back to wondering why you didn't tell me any of this until now. In fact, why are you telling me now? You're getting what you want. Why this confession?"

"Because I don't want any uncomfortable discoveries after she gets here. You'd poke and prod and end up pushing her away, and we need her." When Peter laughed, Henry scowled and slammed his hands on the counter. "Damn it, I'm serious. Call it closure, call it a satisfying form of payback, but don't deny that you want this chance with Holly. I've seen your gallery, pal—I know you haven't let it go. She might have been in a bad place back then but so were you. Before she came around, you were the fucking Batman origin story. The rich, genius orphan lurking in the shadows of his giant mansion. We got you into that house off campus after a hell of a lot of arm twisting, but secretly we were all waiting for the cheesy one-liners and the rubber-suited cry for help."

"Fuck. You."

"Until Holly," Henry continued, undaunted. "She changed you, changed us both, only I'm not denying it. But it was over too soon. Now we have a chance to taste that again, what it was like to be a part of that, and I don't fucking care if she *is* Ms. Anonymous. I don't care if she's as commitment-phobic as you are and only suggested this research as an excuse so she could write a tell-all book about us. I know she's more than that. *We* were more than that.

And whether you'll admit you do or not, *I* want her. Are you really going to mess this up for me by sending her away?"

Peter couldn't hold onto this anger, not when Henry was right. "No. I won't mess this up for you. I don't think I could send her away if I wanted to. What I have planned for the summer will be hard enough without you having to worry about that."

Henry looked up at the ceiling with a resigned laugh. "I had a feeling. Care to clue me in?"

"No." Peter turned to leave the room but stopped at the door, looking over his shoulder. "Henry, I need your word on a few things before she gets here."

"I'm not shaving."

He shook his head, hating the vulnerability that had crept into his heart. "No more secrets. And no sex or satisfaction unless we're all together. You can't take her unless I'm in the room. For now."

Henry held out his hands. "This is your show, boss. As long as Holly's here and we get to touch her, I'll read from your script."

His "show" was already being rewritten in his mind. He needed to think. To assimilate the new information he'd been hit with and alter his plans accordingly.

Was Holly Ms. Anonymous, the gossip columnist who'd coined their nickname, The Billionaire Bachelors, and hounded the missteps of his friends with her wit and judgment for years?

He'd find out before this was over, but right now Henry had said exactly what he was feeling—it didn't matter. Didn't change the plan or stop either one of them from wanting her. And whatever she truly thought about them, she still wanted them. Enough to spend the summer following Peter's lead, as long as she got her ménage.

He'd make sure the experience was one she'd never forget, but not before he added one or two more scandalous scenes to this play. Not until she was begging him for the

THE PLAYBOY'S MÉNAGE

final act. He had a lewd reputation to uphold, after all.

Peter heard the sound of a car coming up the drive and smiled. She came.

*Not yet. But she would soon enough.*

He was a man of his word.


Holly had obviously lost an important piece of her mind—the screw or bolt that kept her from doing things that weren't healthy for her, things that were dangerous to her physical and emotional wellbeing. Being an adrenaline junkie in the name of research was kind of her thing. She'd enjoyed cliff diving and bungee jumping. Even her experiences with cleanses had been moderately life threatening—or at least they'd caused some truly unfortunate hallucinations. But this? This was madness.

She hadn't told Chaz where she was going, despite his wide-eyed curiosity when the Hummer pulled up in front of her house at eleven-thirty in the morning.

Henry had warned her Peter might send ninjas…he hadn't mentioned the possibility of Roy.

She guessed she wouldn't be needing her car for this project.

"Nice to see you again, Holly Ruskin." He smiled as he helped her into the homage to indulgence. "I would ask what adventure you're off to this time, but I hear you're doing research on the old Faraday estate. I'm here to help if you need any details. It's the oldest mansion in the state, you know. I had a great-aunt who worked there years ago, said she needed a map just to find her way around the house."

Holly nodded weakly. "I've heard it's big."

"Big?" Roy lifted her luggage into the limo with her. "Big is a wee bit of an understatement. Can't imagine one man living there by himself, to be honest. I guess that's why Mr. Faraday is always traveling." He laughed at himself. "But if I ever stop talking and do my job instead, you'll see

283

it soon enough. Speaking of, I do need to hurry. This beauty is on loan to Mr. Warren for at least the next week or so, and me with it."

He closed the door, leaving her alone with her thoughts— the last place she wanted to be.

After they left her last night, Holly had gone through her closet with the ferocity of a tornado, packing and preparing, too excited to think about what the next day would bring. It was only when her head hit the pillow that her mind caught up with her. Thinking had swiftly led to panic when she realized how much could go wrong in three months.

If it really lasted that long.

None of them were models of commitment when it came to relationships with the opposite sex. As far as Holly knew, neither man had shown interest in a single woman long enough for her to be loosely dubbed by the press as a girlfriend. Not since college.

How had they not been taken off the market by an enterprising bride-to-be?

Henry was loving, thoughtful, affectionate and funny. He knew about the importance of family, and his parents had given him an unorthodox but positive example of marital longevity. He'd spent most of his adult life traveling with his band or hanging out with his friends, but it still didn't make sense that he would be alone.

Peter was brilliant and focused, intriguing and exciting— loving him would be a romantic adventure for the right woman. Holly knew his parents had died when he was a teenager and he didn't have any extended family. He was never lacking in temporary companionship, but she couldn't help but think he was lonely. It was a shame because if she remembered anything about their time together, other than the earth-shattering sex, it was his heart. He should be filling all those rooms with a family of his own by now, continuing the Faraday name and living happily ever after. Should be, but he wasn't.

*And you're glad.*

It was a selfish feeling, but that was nothing new when it came to these men. Even if she couldn't be what either of them deserved in the long term, she still wanted them too much to walk away from this chance. Not when the chemistry between them was as combustible as ever.

Greedy.

Holly leaned her head back against the leather seat and closed her eyes. They might act the part of perennial bachelors, but she was the real thing. She wasn't meant for a happy ending. She honestly wasn't sure if that kind of forever was meant for everyone, since she could count on one hand the couples she knew who'd managed to beat the odds and stay together.

Her mother used to tell her that an entire relationship could be experienced within the first three months of meeting. The honeymoon phase, a short period of intimacy and cohabitation, and the pressure and resentment that came from what she called the boring inevitable—all of it until two and a half months in, you could see your entire life with that person mapped out ahead of you. Each and every monotonous day until you finally reached the end, having no clue why you'd fallen for each other in the first place. She'd said in that moment you had to choose whether to accept that fate or reach for something new and shimmering. And she always chose the something new. Her mother loved falling in love even more than she loved the money her new husbands brought with them, and she *really* loved the money.

While Holly had long since parted ways with the woman she'd never been able to respect, the woman whose seventh husband had lost all his money in the stock market a few years ago, that nugget of information had remained lodged in the back of her mind, and so far it had proven true. She didn't need a psychiatrist to see the correlation between her work habits and her mother's advice. A shrink would have a field day with her three-month Mommy issues, but it was true in her personal life as well. None of her boyfriends after college had lasted more than a few weeks beyond that. She'd tried, if only to prove her mother wrong, to stick a relationship out for six months or a year, but in the end, the timing was always eerily similar. And she'd always ended up hurting someone she didn't mean to.

It wouldn't happen this time. They were all on the same deliciously dirty page, and all she had to do was relax and go with it.

So why couldn't she?

She fiddled with the pleats in her skirt. She'd worn one of her favorite sundresses, a white halter top with a flaring skirt and heart shaped bodice. It was covered in cherries that matched her red pumps and lip-gloss perfectly. The dress was her armor, making her feel sexy and confident and ready for whatever they wanted to throw at her.

*As soon as you come to us, you'll come for us.*

Holly was ready to come now. She hadn't given in last night. Hadn't used her vibrator and butt plug to ease the tension they'd left her with, though no one would ever know how badly she'd wanted to. So badly she'd woken in the middle of her restless night to find her pillow between her legs, her thighs squeezing it in desperation.

She glanced at the blackened window that kept Roy from seeing her and let her hand glide under her dress, remembering her dreams. Peter and Henry had her arms and legs spread and shackled, each of them taking turns bringing her a heartbeat away from climax, only to leave her unsatisfied. They'd been heartless, sexy machines, ignoring her pleas in order to punish her for walking away. The things they'd done to her body had her sobbing, begging for release.

She closed her thighs over her hand and rubbed her clit through her underwear. "Peter," she whispered. "Let me come."

*As soon as you come to us, you'll come for us.*

Not until then. Some part of her knew he wouldn't like it if she cheated by reaching her climax without them. Even this quick—*oh God*—moment of pleasure wouldn't be allowed. She stopped, her body shaking and her nerves frayed, and removed her hand. She'd wait. She didn't seem to have another choice.

The limo stopped and Holly didn't wait for the door to open before hopping out and reaching for one of her bags. She blushed when the driver got out and came to stand beside her. She couldn't believe she'd been so shameless. But realistically, Roy had to be used to things like that by now. This was Henry Vincent's driver. She'd be shocked if the famous guitar player hadn't had Hummer orgies. At the very least.

Instead of calming her desires, the thought actually made her more impatient to get to Henry and Peter. Made her think about sex with them in the limo.

She was twisted.

"In a hurry yourself, I see. Mr. Vincent told me how much you loved your job." Roy was grinning when he pulled out her other bags and set them down beside her. "This is where we part, Ms. Ruskin. Mr. Vincent wants to bring your things in himself so he can show you around. I get the feeling I'm not invited."

He tilted his driver's cap and got back into the Hummer, and she watched him drive away before she turned to face Peter's house.

She stepped back instinctively and her throat started to close. This wasn't a big house. Not even a mansion. This was the set of a sweepingly epic historical…or a horror movie. The sound of organ music or thunder rolling in at any minute wouldn't surprise her.

It was beautiful craftsmanship. Three stories and possibly two city blocks worth of beautiful. There were even—she squinted her eyes as she looked up at the awnings—yep.

Gargoyles. She knew the Faradays had been rich since the states were colonies, but she hadn't been able to wrap her head around what that meant until this moment. The Hummer was child's play. This estate was Jane Austen's Pemberley, complete with a brooding hunk in residence.

*This* was where Peter grew up?

She looked back down the long road they called a driveway again, thinking she could still flag Roy down. Her feet weren't getting cold...they were frozen.

"Holly." Henry jogged down the steps as she turned, a wicked smile on his face. "We were wondering when you were going to show up."

Too late to run. Holly pushed a strand of hair behind her ear, choosing to ogle his rippling biceps instead of looking back at the haunted mansion. "No ninjas required. Hey, are you sure we don't want to go back to my place? I have electricity and running water and I'm pretty sure it's ghost-and gargoyle-free."

He laughed, carrying her bags back up the stairs. "It's an old monster, I know. Trust me, it's better on the inside. He's had so much work done in there you'll think you're at a four-star resort. There's an indoor swimming pool and sauna, a gourmet kitchen, a living room you could go roller-skating in, and at least eight bedrooms...that I've seen. Hell, he even turned the basement into a fully equipped recording studio a few years back. I have a feeling I'll be using it before our research project is over." He winked at her as they reached the door. "That dress is already doing things to inspire me."

She reached out and put her hand on his strong forearm, the feel of his hot skin making her fingers tingle. "Before we go inside, I wanted you to know how great it's been talking to you again. It meant a lot to me."

Henry looked down at her arm and shook his head. "Working on your goodbye already, Betty? How about you open the door for me and give us all a chance to say a proper hello?"

She opened the door and followed him inside. "I was only trying to—"

"Holly. Finally." She saw a flash of dark blue eyes and a smile before Peter had her pressed up against the wall beside the door, kissing her until her toes started to curl. She could feel his impatience, his arousal, and it fueled hers. This was what she'd been dying for since last night.

Her arms wrapped around his neck and she moaned into his mouth when his hand slipped beneath her skirt and caressed her inner thighs as she'd been doing only moments before. This was so much better. His touch. *Yes.* She lifted her leg and wrapped her calf around his, opening herself up for him, inviting him to take more.

Peter lifted his mouth with a growl. "You're soaking wet, Holly. Did you come before you got here?"

"No. I wanted to but…no."

"Are you willing to agree to my conditions?"

Holly bit her lip when his knuckles pressed teasingly against her clit. "Damn, I like the way you say hello. And I wouldn't be here if I wasn't."

"Say it, Holly."

"Yes," she gasped. "I agree. Three months and you set the pace. I'm your willing research slave."

She felt the pull and heard the rip as he tore her underwear and let it drop at it her feet. "That's good. Exactly what I needed to hear. Now I can welcome you properly."

"Thank God."

## Chapter Five

Peter Faraday was a danger to her equilibrium.

He kissed her again, tangling his tongue with hers in a dance that made her wild. His hand was cupping and massaging her sex, his fingers slipping through her arousal as she pushed herself against him greedily. This was crazy. What she was feeling, it was too much. Last night he'd kissed her and it was like something had turned on inside her that she couldn't turn off. Didn't want to turn off.

All she could think about was Peter inside her. Henry and Peter taking her. She wanted him. His fingers. His tongue. His cock. She slid her hand down his chest toward his pants but he caught her wrist in a firm grip.

"No, Holly. We're going to make you come for us first." His skin was flushed with desire, his eyes narrow as he pulled back to study her. "Henry? I got my kiss last night, now it's your turn. Consider it payment for this morning's revelations. Why don't you give her the welcome she deserves?"

Peter moved to her side and she looked away from him in time to see Henry dropping to his knees in front of her, the sunlight shining in from the open door and glinting in his sable hair.

Oh God, the door was still open and she didn't care. She knew what Henry was going to do, what she needed him to do, and she didn't want to stop it.

"Did I mention I love this dress?" Henry murmured, lifting up the skirt until he could see her bare skin. "Jesus, Holly, you have the prettiest pussy I've ever seen. Sweet black curls and pink skin begging for my tongue. Will you hold this for me so I can have a taste?"

She held the skirt and whimpered in surprise when Henry lifted one of her legs over his shoulder and leaned in. Peter wrapped his arm around her, holding her steady against the wall as Henry groaned and opened his mouth on her sex, his tongue curling around her clit, his beard scratching her sensitive lips in a way that made her shudder.

"*Fuck.*"

"That's what you get when you dress like dessert and offer yourself to two starving men." Peter's voice was deeper. Turned on. "You make us want what's under the frosting even more."

"Food again," she gasped. "You two and your—*oh God, Henry.*"

"Can you blame us, Holly? You are delicious." Peter reached behind her neck and untied her halter-top, dragging the fabric down to the snug high waist. "You're... Fuck, Holly it's been too long since I've seen you like this outside of my dreams. Would you like to know how often I've dreamt about these breasts? What I've done to them in my mind?"

Peter dropped his head and covered her nipple with his mouth, sucking hard.

"God," she moaned. "Yes, *oh yes.*"

She dug into Henry's back with her heel and pulled him closer, rocking her hips against his face and leaning her head back against the wall for balance. Henry made a sound of approval, reaching up to cup her ass and tilt her toward him so he could thrust deeper into her than before. God, he was setting her on fire.

*"Yes."*

Peter lifted his head, breathing in rough pants as he cupped her breast and lifted it, flicking and caressing her nipple with his thumb. "Do you like it, Holly? How hungry we are for you?"

"You know I do," she moaned. "You know I love it."

When he scraped his teeth along her neck, she shivered. "I remember how much you loved everything. You were wild with us. I remember how good that sweet little mouth was at sucking my cock as Henry fucked you. How tightly you squeezed me when I was deep inside that ass. The sounds you made when you came for us."

His words were almost like sex, each memory a deep thrust inside her, making her groan as Henry's talented tongue brought her closer to the edge. "I'm close. Fuck, it feels..."

"Tell me what he's doing now, Holly. Tell me how it feels."

She forced her eyes open to look into his. The expression on his face took away what was left of her breath. "Oh God, Peter, I can't...I..."

"Disobeying me already? Tell me."

"He's fucking me with his tongue. It's so good. I need to come, I've been ready since last night, but I don't want it to be over. I don't want him to stop."

Henry made a pained sound and pressed harder against her, moving his tongue faster inside her. It felt wicked. "Oh God. *Oh my God.*"

Peter pinched her nipple and tugged. "Come for him, Holly. I promise it won't be the last time. This is the first time. Come for us now."

She couldn't help herself. She shouted, rocking against Henry's mouth as her climax crashed over her. It was the sexiest thing she'd experienced in years, her men on her as soon as she walked through the door, unwilling to wait before taking her. Her only complaint was it was over too quickly. She shook against them, already wanting more despite her release. Wanting both of them.

Peter lifted her in his arms again and she forced herself to focus as he handed her to Henry. "I'll take her bags upstairs. Go to the living room and make sure she's comfortable. Try and wait for me."

He was leaving? She frowned fuzzily as he climbed the stairs and disappeared. She was still coming down from her climax and he was gone. Didn't he want to continue what he'd started? "What's going on?"

Henry kissed her head and carried her down the marbled hall. There were paintings on the foyer ceiling. Actual paintings. Maybe Peter's mother had been an Austen fan, because this was ridiculous.

"Where is he taking my bags?"

"To his room," Henry answered as they entered the high-ceilinged living room that did indeed look big enough to skate in. "I suppose I should say our room, because we'll all be in there for the next few months."

"We will?" Sleeping together. All of them. Not just wild and wicked sex but morning hair and blanket stealing and the possibility of snoring. "But there are so many rooms."

Henry set her down on the couch, a mysterious expression on his usually open features. "From what little I've gathered, he has an immersive experience planned. Peter rarely does anything halfway. I don't imagine any of us will be getting a lot of privacy, but believe me when I say we won't be too crowded. He had that bed custom made, and you could sleep six comfortably on that baby." He knelt down in front of her, cupping her still-bare breasts in his hands. "Not that I'd mind cuddling with these as I fell asleep. They feel as good as they look."

Oh hell. Holly covered his hands with her own, still reeling from her climax. The calluses on his fingers from a lifetime of playing his guitar were making her squirm. "Henry you were...that was incredible."

He licked his lips. "Only incredible? I obviously need to work on my technique. I blame you for distracting me. You were so sweet on my tongue. So wet. I don't know how Peter stopped last night without letting you come, because there was no way I could have. You might be my new habit, Holly. I already want to do it again. I'm thinking about lying on the floor right here, you straddling my face and taking a little joy ride."

"Henry," she whispered, blushing. "Stop."

"You don't want me to," he rasped. "You've always loved the dirty talk and I was tongue-deep in that pussy when Peter was talking. You loved it as much as I did, and you're as ready as I am for more. You told him you didn't come, but I know you wanted to. Did you touch yourself, Holly? Think about all the things we were going to do and touch yourself before you came here?"

She nodded, pushing his hands down to her stomach, beneath her crumpled up dress. Henry's eyes narrowed. "What are you doing?"

"Showing you." Holly leaned back on the couch and slipped one hand under his. She looked into his eyes and started to touch herself, mimicking Peter's earlier caress. Her knuckles were brushing against his palm, and when he tensed as if he might pull away, her other hand covered his and held it against her. "This is what I did in your Hummer, Henry. How I touched myself, wishing it were you."

He flinched, pulling her hand away and replacing it with his own. She moaned as Henry filled her with one finger, then two, as if he couldn't help himself.

"Holly's grown up into a bad, bad girl," he murmured. "We're supposed to wait for Peter, you know."

She wrapped her wet fingers around his wrist and pressed him deeper inside her. "We are, Henry. We're waiting. We won't—oh, like that—we don't have to do more than this."

THE PLAYBOY'S MÉNAGE

Henry leaned down and bit her shoulder, making her whimper with need. "But I want to. Jesus, what I wouldn't give to bend you over this couch and fuck you right now. You have no idea how hard it's been for me to hold back. When I saw you six months ago. Last night. It's all I've been able to think about."

"Yes," she whispered, too aroused to pretend patience. "Do it, Henry. Right now. I want you to. He'll understand. He told you to make me comfortable."

He snarled and pulled away from her touch. "Not without Peter. That's the deal."

Peter's voice startled them both. "It's good to know you can keep your word, Henry. But I'm here now." He walked over and tossed a box of condoms on the couch beside them. "She obviously wants you to finish what you started and you've definitely shown a lot more restraint over the last year than I would have. It's only fair. Bend her over my couch and take her the way you want to."

Henry got to his feet, eyeing his friend warily. "Peter?"

Peter crossed his arms. "I'm the one setting the pace. This isn't the race it was when we were young and afraid we'd never get another chance. She's not going anywhere for the next few months, and there are certain elements of a ménage relationship we never had the time to explore. This is one of them. Fuck her while I watch. For our research." His voice changed subtly. "Holly? Look at me."

His eyes were so damn blue she felt like she was drowning. She saw something in them that she couldn't turn away from. "Peter?"

"Stand up and take off your dress."

God help her, he was impossible to resist, with his shirt partially unbuttoned and his erection once again straining against his pants. She wanted to tell him to take *his* clothes off, but his command had silenced her. She remembered him being a little aggressive in the bedroom the last time they were together, but there was something she recognized now

295

after her training at the BDSM club. He had *it*. That quality her instructor taught her to recognize, a personality that would make him the perfect Dom. Holly wanted to please him. To obey him.

And she really wanted Henry to fuck her.

Standing up, she undid the side zipper of her halter dress and let it pool at her feet. She started to step out of her shoes but Peter shook his head. "Leave those on and kneel on the cushion."

He moved behind the couch, right in front of her as she followed his instructions. Her breasts pressed against the brown leather and she studied the belt at her eye line, tempted to reach for it. "What now, Peter?"

He caressed her cheek with his fingertips and she leaned into his touch like a cat, needing to be stroked. Needing him. "Now Henry is going to take what you're offering before I'm tempted to show him how it's done."

She heard the sound of clothes rustling behind her. "Far be it for me to ignore an order like that," Henry muttered hotly. "Trap or payback, I don't give a damn. I want her too much."

Peter was still touching her skin, distracting her. He traced a line down her neck and to her shoulder, which was covered in cherry blossoms and dogwood flowers. "Were these for your research, Holly?"

She licked her lips, nodding. "I worked in a tattoo parlor for a book. Receptionist."

Henry gripped her hip with one hand and slipped two fingers inside her again from behind, making her gasp. "Oh lord."

"What do they mean to you?" Peter's fingers pressed into her shoulder hard enough to get her attention. "The flowers—why did you get them?"

Was he kidding? She held onto the back of the couch and rocked against Henry's hand, silently begging for more. "Peter…"

THE PLAYBOY'S MÉNAGE

Henry groaned, removing his fingers and pressing the head of his cock against her sex. "Tell him, Holly. Give the strange man what he wants while I give you— Ah, Jesus, Holly your pussy's so hot and tight."

His cock filled her and she cried out, "Yes, Henry! *God.*"

"Holly."

She shook her head. Tattoos. He was asking about tattoos while Henry was stretching her with his big hard cock. "Empathy," she groaned when Henry started to move. "Impermanence. *Henry, yes.* Yes—oh, renewal. They look similar, mean almost the same thing but they're not—*oh fuck, I can't*—they're not the same."

Henry was moving inside her with long, deep strokes that made her crazy, and Peter's hands were both cupping her shoulders now, his pants the only thing stopping her from taking his erection in her mouth. She was ready to yank off his zipper with her teeth.

"Did you like it?" Peter's voice was aroused. Rough. "Henry says it's like good kink. Some pain and a big adrenaline rush that lasts for hours. Was it like that for you? Did you want more as soon as you were done?"

"I liked it, damn it," she cried. "Peter, *what the fuck* are you doing?"

"Distracting myself," he growled. "So I don't ask Henry how it feels to be balls-deep inside our fantasy girl after all this time. So I don't fill your mouth with my cock or take myself in hand while watching how perfectly you're taking him. How greedy you are for more."

*Yes. More.* "More, Henry." She was moaning loudly now, more than aroused by Peter's words and Henry's— *Oh, yes.* "Fuck me."

"Holly." Henry's thrusts gained force and she held on tighter for balance, loving it. Loving him inside her. Loving the way Peter was watching her as if nothing else existed.

"Let me," she pleaded, her body shaking with every hard stroke. She licked her lips and stared at his erection. "Peter, let me."

He let go of her shoulders and opened his belt with trembling hands, unzipping his pants with a hiss before spreading them open and gripping his erection. He was a beautiful man everywhere. She wanted him inside her too. Just a little closer and she could taste it. Suck him until he came. Have them both again. "Please."

"Is this what you want?" Peter's eyes were wild now. "Henry's holding on by a thread, so lost in you he'd let me do anything. He's had years of practice, baby, years of perfecting his skills, but you make us forget it all. Make us desperate. You always have. And you're close too, aren't you? I can see it in your eyes. Fuck her harder, Henry. Faster. She wants it rough. She can take it."

Henry groaned and muttered her name again as he bent over her back, reaching around her to rub her clit as his hips pounded against her. "Holly, come for me, honey. Let me feel it again."

"Oh God!" she screamed, unable to feel anything but what he was doing to her. Unable to see anything but Peter standing in front of her, taunting her with what was just out of reach. She couldn't hold back. It felt too good. "Henry, I'm coming. God, I'm coming!"

"Fuck, yes," Henry groaned, shouting as he joined her. Holly collapsed in a trembling heap on the couch beneath him, feeling shattered as the powerful climax exploded inside her.

After a few minutes Henry moved, sitting down and pulling her onto his lap. He kissed her as her body came down slowly, her mind taking a little longer to catch up. She leaned into his big, warm body, letting his gentle caresses and his slow, deep kisses soothe her. She'd missed him. How secure she felt when she was wrapped in his arms. She decided in that moment that she loved him with a beard, and she could still spend hours doing nothing more than this—spend *days* kissing Henry and Peter.

Peter. She lifted her head at the thought and looked over her shoulder, but he was gone again. Holly frowned. Why did he keep disappearing? Why hadn't he come?

"Come on, Betty." Henry lifted her off him and grabbed her hand as he stood beside her, gloriously naked. "I think we should go for a swim."

She laughed when he scooped up the box of condoms and started pulling her across the room. "I'm not sure I can walk yet, Henry, and I know my head is spinning. Swimming might not be the best idea you've ever had."

"Trust me. It's a great idea." He raised his voice. "We're going to the pool, Peter. Last one in is a big, hard Dick."

She covered her mouth and snorted. "You really should stop doing that."

"I'll stop when it stops bugging him. Hurry up, beautiful. I want you to see this."

They walked down a long hall toward large double doors made of frosted glass. "You're going to love it," Henry informed her as he reached for the handle. "Peter designed it himself and it's an adult-themed water park, I swear. Grotto, slides, fun with water pressure, it has a little of everything."

"Okay, I'll admit it. Now I'm intrigued."

He stopped and turned toward her, pulling her into his arms. "I'm sorry things got crazy in there, Holly. I wasn't expecting him to…well, I didn't think his retribution would include me getting exactly what I wanted so quickly. I should have taken my time but I was worried the other shoe would drop and I wouldn't get to feel you come around me."

Holly smiled up at him in disbelief. "Are you kidding? That was the hottest welcome I've ever gotten in my entire life. I'm not complaining. *At all.* In fact, I'm hoping we can do it again as soon as I can feel all my fingers and toes."

"And again and again until you're too tired to want more and we're all you can feel. You're going to get everything you want, Holly. I promise you won't regret saying yes."

She wanted Peter. Why was he holding back? "Henry,

did something happen between last night and this afternoon? Is he having second thoughts about this?"

About her?

Henry shook his head, but didn't meet her eyes. "If he was, neither one of us would be here, believe me. I suggest you take a page from my mostly-blank rulebook and just go with it. It'll make the next few months more exciting."

More exciting than having two orgasms as soon as she walked in the door? More exciting than watching Peter watch Henry fuck her? More exciting than feeling Henry inside her again?

She wasn't sure her heart could take it.

# CHAPTER SIX

"What in the hell do you think you're doing, Peter?"

He looked up from his desk to see Henry standing in the doorway, glaring. "Playing criminal mastermind. I'm planning on demolishing the Warren building to put up a parking lot. That is, as far as Dean's uncle knows. He'll eat that up, the sadistic bastard. A juicy bonus on top of the already substantial offer we've made him should his nephew receive a vote of no confidence from the board. If that doesn't make him push the vote up so we can finish this charade, I don't know what will. It's the least we can do for Dean, seeing as you haven't seen fit to give him his car back. You?"

"I'm trying to decide whether your intent is to chase Holly away with your behavior or you've become sexually dysfunctional in your old age. I haven't seen you in action for a while—maybe the gossip is just that. Gossip. Have you given up on sex, Peter? Or is there an issue you're not telling me about? There are pills for that, you know."

"Fuck you," Peter responded without heat. "I haven't heard her complain and you have no reason to. As long as I'm in the room, whether you think I'm asleep or not, you've gotten what you wanted."

And with that thought, Peter's erection returned with a swiftness that stole his breath. He had no problem with the machinery. In fact, it was demanding his attention every hour of every damn day. What *was* he doing? Why was he still holding himself in check? Why had he feigned sleep this morning when Henry dragged Holly out of Peter's arms to fuck her on the bed right beside him?

Jesus, that had been one hell of a way to wake up. His closed eyes had done nothing to stop the mental images that filled his mind with each dip of the bed, each slide of the covers and Holly's muffled screams of pleasure.

He'd had to look, peering through his lowered lashes when Henry's breaths had become soft grunts of mindless pleasure. What he'd seen had nearly brought him to climax without a single stroke of his hand. Henry on top of Holly, her legs stretched over his shoulders and his hips pounding into hers hard enough to break the damn bed. His mouth had hungrily suckled her breasts while his large hand covered her mouth to keep her from waking Peter.

It had been hot as hell and put him through nearly as much torment.

Henry had no clue how much restraint it had taken for Peter not to push him off and take over, not to sink his aching cock deep into Holly's pussy and finally come inside her. Or maybe he did. Maybe he knew and that was the point. His friend had been bending and twisting the rules over the last few days, trying to provoke him. He challenged Peter's directions during their "research sessions" with Holly and took advantage of Peter's presence to stop whatever he was doing and make her come. On those rare occasions when he wasn't between her legs, he was being a general pain in the ass.

"I thought you'd be grateful for the extra time," Peter mused. "I can't imagine what you have to bitch about. You've already broken the world record for the number of times Henry Vincent has fucked the same woman."

Almost two weeks. Peter's balls would be permanently blue if it weren't for Holly's wicked, greedy mouth. Her full, slicked-up breasts sliding over his cock. Her willing hands. Peter had found release with her in every way he could without actually having her. Without giving her the ménage she'd come for.

He'd had a plan when it started, but at the moment he was in such a continuous state of arousal he couldn't for the life of him remember it. He just knew he had to stay strong. They still had time.

Henry blew out a frustrated breath. "For a genius, you are a complete and total idiot. This isn't a wrestling match or a staring contest, Peter. This is Holly. It's heaven dropped right into your lap, naked and ready and wondering why you're hesitating." He stepped further into the room and lowered his voice. "Are you still pissed at me? Is that it? If I'm the cock block, I can disappear for the day so you can have her to yourself."

Peter stood, wincing as the fabric of his slacks rubbed against his erection. "No way in hell. Those aren't the rules of this game, Henry. Holly belongs to both of us for the next two and a half months."

"You have no idea how relieved I am to hear you say it. But you're still pissed at me."

Peter shook his head. "I'm not pissed and I don't begrudge your time with her. I used to, I know, but I don't anymore. I'm being patient. Waiting until it feels right."

He was so full of shit. It had felt right since she'd walked through the door in her cherry-covered sundress. Maybe there *was* something wrong with him. How else could he explain his behavior?

He was telling Henry the truth. In part. Seeing them together so often over the last few weeks, watching or directing from the sidelines as Henry took Holly over and over again, had been strangely liberating. His jealousy had faded enough for him to realize it wasn't about Henry having her, it was about not getting to share her with him. And as his friend had pointed out, that was his insane decision and no one else's.

Henry's lips twitched. "You sound like a virgin waiting for the wedding night. But I'm not here to tease you. I'm here to invite you down to my recording studio. We've gone to a lot of trouble to put something together and Holly wants to show it to you now. Believe me, it's a good surprise."

Peter studied Henry's expression suspiciously. "Why do I sense a trap?"

Henry laughed. "For your own sake, stop being clever long enough to get to the basement. You won't be disappointed."

He shook his head, unable to resist a request from Holly. "Please tell me you won't be singing."

Henry followed him out the door and down the hall. "I won't be doing anything but enjoying the show. Unless otherwise directed."

Peter walked down the stairs and across the house toward the recording studio he'd built years ago for Henry's sporadic visits. Peter had used it himself on occasion when inspiration struck and drew him to the piano, but he knew why he'd made the space. Henry was his family. He'd redesigned every nook and cranny of the old mausoleum, needing to turn it into something the people he cared about could feel welcome in. Needing a home.

He couldn't remember ever really thinking of this place as a home. Not until recently. Hearing Holly's laughter and Henry's guitar, the three of them eating together on the patio outside or talking about her wide variety of occupations in the living room…it felt good. Good enough to get used to.

She wouldn't stay. He knew that. But he still had time to enjoy it while it lasted. To fill his home with life and passion.

Jesus, he was starting to think like one of Henry's songs.

All sap and no spine. He needed to get laid.

He needed Holly.

Peter opened the door to the studio and froze. The sight that greeted him was no longer the Zen room sparsely decorated with stools, microphones and instruments that he'd seen last week when Henry decided to play for them.

They'd temporarily redecorated it in a style he could only assume was bohemian brothel chic.

Most of the furniture had been cleared out to make way for a mattress—no doubt from one of the guest rooms—which was placed in front of the small raised stage where he'd installed the piano. It was still there, but there was a boom box sitting on top of it. Beside it, Peter saw a sex swing with leather leg straps connected to a chain that disappeared into the ceiling.

"What the fuck, Henry?"

The bearded scoundrel hopped up on the stage and rubbed his hands together. "Welcome to Henry's House of Holly and *Wood*." His voice echoed in the small room as he acted the part of lounge performer. "Grab a seat on that comfy mattress and get ready for a one-night only performance by one of this joint's classiest dames. If loving her is wrong, you won't want to be right. Put your hands together for your favorite Burlesque queen and mine, Betty Boom-Boom Ruskin!"

He pushed a button on the boom box and hurried to Peter's side, pressing one hand down on his shoulder insistently. "Sit down," he whispered. "She wants you sitting down."

The door to the recording booth opened and Peter stopped breathing. He sat. Jazz played softly in the background as Holly swayed seductively into view. "Hello, boys." She blew them a kiss and stepped up on the stage, her hands on her hips as she struck a Jessica Rabbit-esque pose. "Happy to see me?"

If he got any happier he'd embarrass himself in a way he

hadn't since he turned twelve and Henry's older brother let him borrow his porn collection. Holly was perfection. From her forties-style hair to her fire engine-red lipstick and thick lashes, she'd gone all out for her role. Sadly, she was wearing too many clothes—a floor-length shimmering ruby skirt that flowed around her like water, a red corset with black piping, long black gloves and a black, sheer scarf skimming her shoulders.

As soon as he got over his shock, he was going to rush the stage and rip it all off.

She fluffed her hair and winked at Peter. "Since this is a private party, I'm planning a very special surprise. More than one, if you must know. I hope you enjoy the finale, because I already know I will."

Holly reached behind her and pushed a button, changing the song to a bawdy striptease classic. Henry clapped and whistled as she started to sway to the music, slowly pulling off her gloves, twirling them and tossing them toward the men.

She turned on her heels gracefully, looking over her shoulder with an expression so mischievous Peter had to smile. He heard a rending sound and one arm crossed over her chest while the other shot up into the air, holding a scrap of red fabric. When she turned back toward them there was still a corset around her waist, but her breasts were bare.

She dropped her arm and Peter saw tassels attached to red hearts covering her nipples. He moaned and started to get to his feet and she stopped swaying, shaking her finger at him as if to scold him. "Not until the finale, handsome."

Peter swore and sat down again, unable to take his eyes off her swinging tassels. She began to dance again, her movements more sensual as she wrapped her scarf suggestively around her wrists as if she were bound before letting it join her gloves on the floor off stage.

"Take it all off," Henry groaned.

Peter silently agreed with the sentiment.

Holly lowered her hands to the waistline of her skirt teasingly. "Remember," she warned in a sweet, siren's voice. "Stay in your seats until the show reaches its big climax."

The same sound he'd heard when she'd taken off the top of her corset filled the room and she ripped off her skirt. It fluttered in the air for a moment before landing right in front of him. Peter made a pained sound. After her striptease there would be a trip in an ambulance, because he was going to have a heart attack.

Holly wasn't wearing underwear, but she wasn't naked. Two straps on either side attached to a red butterfly sex toy. She thrust her hips forward for her dance and he could see it went inside her, and that there was a small stimulator pressed against her clit.

Definitely going to have a heart attack.

She frowned prettily. "Now where is that thing? I know it's around here somewhere?"

"I've got a thing for you," Henry called out with a laugh. Peter punched his arm without looking away from her performance.

She moved to face the piano, giving both men a clear view of her heart-shaped ass. "Aha," she cried victoriously, widening her stance and bending over to pick something up off the stage.

Peter lowered his hands to his pants and started to work on the button and zipper. She was wearing a butt plug, complete with a red, glittering gem.

Henry swore, seeing it too.

She stood up again and faced them, smiling innocently. "Here you go, handsome. For being such a good boy. Enjoy." She threw something at him and Peter caught it instinctively, his mind unscrambling long enough for him to realize what it was. A remote control for her strap-on.

He turned it on and she shivered, her full breasts quivering with the movement, tassels swaying. "Oh," she gasped. "Oh, handsome, you certainly know how to make me shimmy. I think it's time for my *pièce de résistance*. Just let me slip out of my shoes."

She bit her lip when he turned the toy on high and set the controller down, unbuttoning his shirt as he watched her. "Someone's impatient."

But her character was fraying around the edges. Betty Boom-Boom was becoming Holly again in her pleasure. She walked over to the swing, gripped its hand bar and raised one long leg, sliding it into the strap before lifting herself off the ground, setting the swing to rocking.

She adjusted herself, her legs now spread wide by the straps, her skin flushing with arousal as the vibrator buzzed inside her. "I had special request from the audience, so I will finish my performance with an original limerick. *Oh God.*" Her voice was shaking.

Peter stood up to take off his pants while she recited her rhyme. "There once was a man I call Dick, who thought his maneuvers so slick. He promised sweet Holly, he'd lick of her lolly, but never quite did dip his wick."

Henry's laugh was a wicked sound and Peter heard more than saw him stand and start taking off his clothes beside him. "Damn, that's hot. We should set that to music, Betty."

Peter was holding on by a slender, fraying thread. "Was that the finale, Holly?"

She licked her lips. "It was. Did you like it?"

"Henry?" He spoke through gritted teeth. "Do you have the condoms?"

"Behind the boom box."

Peter strode naked to the stage, to her, and shut off the music before reaching for the box and tearing open one foil package. His jaw flexed as he rolled it down his cock and stepped closer to the swing.

Holly was staring at his erection. "Are you finally going to—"

"Dip my wick?" he snarled. "Bury my cock inside you the way I've been dying to for weeks? Fuck your wet pussy while Henry takes out that pretty plug and fills your ass?"

She whimpered.

"Yes, Holly. That's exactly what I'm going to do. Exactly what you asked for." He stepped between her spread legs and bent his head to kiss her while he unhooked the straps at her waist and pulled out the still-vibrating toy. He tossed it over his shoulder toward the mattress and reached down with both hands to pull her closer by her red tassels.

Peter lifted his mouth. "That was a mind-blowing performance, Boom-Boom. Let's see what we can do for the encore."

He dropped one hand to her ass and pulled her slowly toward him, a guttural groan escaping from deep in his chest as he guided her onto his erection. "*Fuck*. Fuck, Holly. Oh God, that's…"

"Peter," she cried, her voice cracking. "*Yes*. So good. You feel *so good*."

He looked into her wide eyes and lost himself. She was beautiful. Fearless. His. He shuddered when the base of his shaft met her slick sex, holding himself still to savor the sensation. He was where he belonged, and it was better than he remembered.

It had been too long. Too many days and nights of denying himself, knowing this was what was waiting for him. He had to… "Henry," he bit out. "If you're joining this encore, now is the time."

He saw him over Holly's shoulder, his gaze focused on her ass. Holly gasped when he removed the plug and Peter kissed her again, unable to help himself.

The moment Henry started to fill her ass Peter could feel it. Feel Holly tightening around him, her body trembling. He lifted his mouth and pressed his lips against her cheek. "Is this the kind of research you were looking for, baby?" he whispered. "Thorough enough?"

She moaned into his ear. "So deep. You're both in me so deep. Please."

"Anything for research," he growled, pulling his hips back before thrusting inside her again. "Fuck, you're gripping me so tight."

Henry lowered his mouth to Holly's shoulder, biting and kissing her skin as he followed the rhythm Peter set, both of them too aroused to be gentle. To go slow.

Peter watched the wonder and pleasure wash over her expression, her moans growing louder and longer with each minute that passed. She let go of the swing with one hand and reached for Peter, pulling him down for another carnal kiss as they pumped inside her.

She pulled back enough to speak against his lips. "I missed you so much. This. I need it. Need to know it's real."

"What do you want, baby?" Anything. He'd give her anything.

"Harder," she whispered breathlessly. "Don't stop. Fuck me so hard I scream."

Henry groaned behind her and Peter knew he heard. He had to hold back, hold on long enough to give her what she needed. "Hang on to me."

Peter gripped her waist and Henry placed his hands low on her hips, both holding her steady in the swing before sharing a speaking look. Then they gave her what they all wanted. Hard and fast. Deep and tight and wet and fucking unbelievable.

"Holly, Jesus, is this what you want, baby? Tell me."

"Yes!" she screamed. "*Fuck, yes*. Yes! *Oh God*, Peter, don't stop. I'm close. I'm close. God, I'm clo—*Oh my God!*"

Her shouts of release made Peter shudder as filled her tightening sex. His body was on fire, lightning striking up his spine as his heart tried to claw its way out of his chest.

He came calling out her name, hearing Henry's release on the edge of his awareness as he buried his face in her neck and shook against her.

Holly. His Holly. Theirs.

*I missed you so much.*

## CHAPTER SEVEN

"I told you I was fine, Chaz. You know how distracted I get when I'm in research mode, but you don't sound good at all. Tell me everything."

Holly wandered through the large house with her phone pressed against her ear, dressed in nothing but one of Peter's shirts while she waited for them to come down. She'd only been up for an hour herself but she had to admit, if Chaz hadn't left her a message she would have stayed in bed and found a creative way to wake them up.

One month and two weeks of wild passion and dirty threesomes. Of more sex than she'd had in years, whispered conversations in bed and playing like carefree teenagers in the pool. Week after week of two charming, insatiable men spoiling her with attention and affection.

She grinned. You'd think she'd be sick of it by now.

"I'm horrible," Chaz groaned. "Bill and I have been fighting for two weeks. It's never been this bad."

Holly frowned as she walked down the hallway that led to Peter's office. "What? You two are the happiest couple I know. You never fight. What happened?"

Her friend sighed into the phone. "I found out he's one of

*her* informants."

"Her who?" But Holly had a sinking feeling she knew.

"Ms. Anonymous," Chaz confirmed, his anxiety making him talk faster. "He'd only tell me she was one of his regular clients, and that he shared information about the Billionaire Bachelors whenever he had any. Friendly gossip is one thing, you and I do it all the time, but this feels cheap, doesn't it? He's strutting around like a cocky rooster, like he's famous for talking trash. You know my sister works at Warren Industries. The last column she wrote basically accused him of throwing the company away to have sex with some floozy in public and said the board of directors was going to vote him out. That kind of talk could have put *Mindy* out of a job. Thank goodness it fell through, but what if it hadn't? How could I face her knowing Bill had something to do with that?"

Peter had told her about it after the fact—how he, Henry and Tracy had helped their friend Dean save his company from being dismantled by his greedy uncle by tricking him into selling off his shares. Holly had been so impressed she'd given them another show, but seeing how she'd only been wearing her bikini at the time, it hadn't take that long to reach the orgasmic finale. For any of them.

Holly felt sick. *Bill* was a source for Ms. Anonymous? Her neighbor? The man she'd spent evenings drinking frozen daiquiris with on her porch, listening to his wild tales about the sordid things he'd heard at the salon and sharing stories Henry had told her just so she could shock and delight him and Chaz?

Thank God she'd never mentioned where she heard those rumors. Thank God Bill never found out she'd gone to school with them. But sweet Jesus, he'd probably told that tabloid tart everything he knew. Every word she'd said. Which meant she was guilty by association.

She knew Peter wasn't a fan of Ms. Anonymous after her last column. Neither was Henry. Damn it, what was Bill thinking?

"Son of a bitch, Chaz."

"I know!" he cried. "I tried to make him see reason. We've done a thousand things over the years we might laugh about with friends but wouldn't want showing up in the papers. Remember those pictures? Good lord, his mother's head would explode if they'd ever gotten in the paper. The Bachelors provide a lot of material, sure, but they're just men like us. They have families and people who look up to them. I never thought Bill could be spiteful."

"He got carried away," Holly defended instinctively, even though she wanted to punch Bill in his attractive nose. "I'm sure he thought it was good for business, having Ms. Anonymous coming to him for information. She might be a great tipper."

"Well, I'm going to show up at her next appointment and pull out her gray roots one at a time for turning my loving husband into a rat."

"Chaz," she soothed, moving around Peter's office and running her fingers along his bookshelves. "Take a breath, honey, and listen to me. You're right. Harmless gossip about European orgies is one thing, but we both know people employed by Warren Industries. And I have it on good authority that those men aren't being portrayed in the best light. You know some of the people I've written for. They talk."

"What am I going to do, Holly? I love him, but I'm so disappointed. Is this what the future will be for us? Him scrounging in the mud to feed her vulgar rumors and not caring what I think about it?"

*Is this what the future will be?* She knew the danger in that question. Her mother's stupid relationship stages. Granted, it had taken Chaz and Bill ten years to reach it instead of a few months, but Holly could hear it in his voice.

She couldn't let that happen. Chaz and Bill were one of her success stories. One of the couples she looked to for hope that maybe, somewhere, people had happy endings.

"This is a fight, Chaz, that's all," Holly insisted. "He's being stubborn. It happens. He'll see reason and beg your forgiveness soon enough."

"I don't think so, Holly."

"I do. I've got a plan, but since I'm a little tied up at the moment I'll need your help to make it work."

"A plan?" Chaz sniffed, sounding hopeful. "I like the idea of him begging. What do I have to do?"

Holly looked around and lowered her voice. "You have to play the good, supportive husband and find out who Ms. Anonymous really is. She pays to have her hair done, right? Uses a credit card? As soon as I know how to get ahold of her, we'll have a nice long chat. We do have a lot in common, you know. We both write anonymously." And they were both fascinated by Henry and Peter, though the gossip's way of expressing it made Holly want to whip her with a leaky fountain pen. "When it's done, I can promise you Bill will *never* do her hair again."

Chaz chuckled in relief. "I knew you'd make me feel better. Mission accepted. I think I'll take a batch of my famous walnut chocolate chip cookies to the salon today. My baby has to eat, right?"

"Hello, Nancy Drew. Call me as soon as you know. Love you, Chaz."

"Love you, Holly."

She hung up and slipped the phone into the pocket of Peter's shirt, walking out of his office and staring at the closed door at the end of the hall. She hadn't been in there yet, and she needed something to distract her. She started toward it, her mind racing.

Damn Bill. Damn Ms. Anonymous. Holly laughed wryly. While she was at it, she could damn herself as well. How was she any better? She got paid to write tell-alls and scandalous autobiographies. Sure, there were one or two important books mixed in with the rest, but in the end the only difference was she got permission to publish other people's dirty little secrets.

Not exactly the great novelist her professor predicted bragging about.

She opened the door and every disturbing, anxious thought in her head disappeared. This wasn't another bedroom. It was an artist's loft. Ribbons of early morning light streamed through a narrow skylight and lit up the paintings and framed sketches on the wall as well as the table of smaller busts and sculptures.

She stepped inside, taking it all in. The closest painting was of a woman's hand resting on her naked hip. That was all. The detail and soft brushwork were so skilled she could almost see the pores on her skin, the fine hairs on her forearm. It was beautiful.

It was Peter's. These were his work, there was no doubt in her mind. She looked at everything more carefully. They were all pieces of a woman. Long legs tangled in sheets. The delicate shell of an ear leading to the nape of a neck. One of the paintings had a woman bending over in the shower, her leg on the rim of the tub as she ran a washcloth over her body. Holly could see the dark hair upswept in a messy bun, could see the line of her spine and the shape of her thighs.

Even the tattoo on her ankle was clearly visible. A broken heart.

She lifted her hand to her mouth in shock. He'd painted her. Why? When? Had these all been done in college? They must have, because the flowers tattooed on her shoulder weren't anywhere to be found.

Her gaze fell on the chair in the corner, open sketchpad beside it. She moved closer and studied the drawing. This was new. She could see the tattoos on the sensual woman clearly as she rode her bearded lover, her legs wrapped around his waist. His sleeved arms supported her, knuckles white as he held himself back, letting her set the rhythm. They were lost in each other, unaware of anything else.

Unaware of the artist.

Peter had drawn this? She remembered the moment, and the one that followed it. She'd looked over her shoulder and begged him to join them. He had. They'd come together that night with an intimacy, a tenderness that none of them had expected. All of them wrapped around each other, a part of each other. She'd never felt so connected to anyone. Henry, too, had admitted to her that what they'd shared, the three of them together, was like nothing he'd ever known.

But that wasn't what Peter had drawn. He'd left himself out of the picture. An observer. Did he still feel that? Was he still holding back?

She reached down to turn the page, to see what else he'd captured with his detailed eye when the sound of the door opening made her whirl around in surprise. "Peter."

Holly moaned softly. He was naked and aroused. How was she supposed to think with that kind of distraction? "These are beautiful."

He clenched his fists at his sides. "It's something to keep my hands busy."

Her heart was racing. She knew she'd exposed him, made him feel vulnerable. She moved closer to him until she was standing beside the table, her hand reaching out to caress a small sculpture of her naked body. "I can't help being flattered. I do love your hands. I wish I could see things the way you do." She forced a smile. "I bet you have vaults filled with paintings of naked women you've known. You certainly have enough material to be inspired by."

He frowned. "Do you think I took them down before you got here? That you seeing this was something I planned?" He shook his head, running his hands through his hair and watching her with those impossibly blue eyes. "I suppose that's better than you thinking I'm obsessed with you, isn't it? That yours is the only face I see when I need comfort. Me being a lewd, manipulative playboy is easier to swallow."

She backed away, holding up her hands. "Peter? I was

just—"

He reached out and gripped her shoulders. "You just want to ignore what's right in front of you. You want your memorable ménage with the royal rocker and the rebel. Material for your research."

She gasped when he dragged her toward him and pressed his lips hard against hers. He was angry and hurting, she could feel it. He was also undeniably hard. Her body reacted, unable to help responding to his. Unable to resist rubbing herself against his erection, begging for more.

The need that consumed her was overwhelming. Peter pulled back and looked down at her, his cheeks flushed and lips full, so beautiful she suddenly wished she could draw. If she could, she would draw him right now. That expression of carnality and desire.

He let go of her shoulders and grabbed onto the fabric of the white shirt, buttons flying and rolling along the floor as he tore it open and pulled it off of her, phone and all.

"Peter…" She thought of Henry not being here. Of the rules Peter had made. But she couldn't deny how turned on she was. Couldn't deny how much she wanted him.

"I know," he snarled, responding to her expression. "But I need—"

He didn't finish his sentence, pushing his art to the side before lifting her onto his worktable and spreading her legs. Holly groaned when he lowered his mouth to her breasts, his fingers gliding down her stomach to slip through her curls and inside her. "Oh, Peter."

He was sucking on her breast, pressing her clit with his thumb. Two fingers thrust into her sex and pressed against that special spot he knew she loved, and she whimpered. "Yes. Peter, oh that's good."

He looked up at her. "You did say you liked my hands."

"I love them."

"I need more," he growled. His took away his touch and picked her up, whirling her around until she was bent facedown over the table, her breasts pressed against the wood and her toes barely touching the floor.

"Peter, what are you— *Oh my God.*"

He filled her with his cock, one hand between her shoulder blades, holding her in place. "I need this, baby. I won't come, I swear. Fuck, I can feel everything." He pumped his hips and shuddered. "It's so good, Holly. You're so wet for me. Just for me."

Holly was on fire. She couldn't think, couldn't hold back. She wanted him more than she wanted to be safe. "Feel me, Peter. Feel how much I want you."

He groaned as if he were in pain and slung his hips against her with deep, powerful thrusts. "Holly," he whispered raggedly. "My Holly. You have me, baby. Take it. Fucking take it all."

She reached for the edge of the table, holding on as it started to rock with the force of his movements. So deep. He was so deep inside her. Her eyes were open and she could see an image of her face mid-climax on the other side of the room. He knew her. He knew how to bring her that kind of satisfaction. "*Peter.* Peter, make me come for you. Don't stop. Don't ever stop."

When her climax came it brought tears to her eyes, blurring her vision and making her blood pound in her ears. He was everything. Everywhere. Peter. She barely heard his shout as he pulled out of her body, but she felt the warmth on her hip as he came.

She was shaking so hard she felt like she might shatter. When she regained her ability to think, Peter was rocking her in his arms and apologizing over and over again. Why? Why was he sorry for that?

He hadn't worn a condom.

She stiffened in his arms and he held her tighter. "I know. I swear to you, Holly, I've never in my entire life been that careless. I don't know what happened. You were here, in this room and I…I lost control. I'm so sorry."

She believed him. Peter was too smart to be that reckless. Except he had been. He'd almost...what if he had come inside her? What if he hadn't been in control enough to pull out in time? Just because he was healthy didn't mean she couldn't have gotten pregnant.

Holly started to shake again at the thought. A baby. She couldn't let that happen. Babies came with happy endings, the kind she didn't have.

"Holly, talk to me, please."

The loud knock on the open door made them both tense in surprise. "Remember me?" Henry's voice sounded strained, so much so Holly was almost afraid to look at him. "Peter, we've been ordered to make a morning appearance and save Dean's bacon again. Get dressed—Roy and Tracy are waiting outside."

"Fuck," Peter swore. "Henry, man I'm—"

"If you say you're sorry for breaking your own rules, I'll have to kill you. Dress. Now. And consider us even after this. My guilt is gone."

Henry turned away without acknowledging her presence and Peter kissed her forehead before releasing her reluctantly. "Holly..."

"Go." She bent down to grab the torn shirt, covering herself as best as she could. She wanted to go to Henry and make sure he was okay. She didn't want to feel guilty for what had just happened. Not when it had made her feel so special. So treasured. "Your friends need you."

He didn't move. "Promise me you'll be here when we get back, Holly."

A feeling she didn't want to explore gripped her heart and squeezed. "We still have a month and a half, Dick." She smiled when he raised one eyebrow at the nickname. "I'm not going anywhere."

The smile that lit his eyes made her breath catch, and then he was gone, leaving her alone in the room filled with pieces of her. She hoped it wasn't a preview of what would be left of her when their time was up.

# CHAPTER EIGHT

"Still pissed?"

"What do you think?"

Peter sighed and pressed his fingers to the bridge of his nose. They'd dropped off Tracy after their group intervention with Sara and Dean, and Roy was taking them back to his estate. Back to Holly and the mess he'd left behind.

"Can we talk about this, Henry? I wasn't planning it. I didn't mean for that to happen."

Henry pulled off his sunglasses and stared at him. "Which part? The part where you were fucking Holly without protection? Or the part where you were fucking Holly without me around when you wouldn't let me do the same?"

"Both." When Henry shook his head, Peter leaned forward, his hands between his knees. "I don't know what came over me. I deserve whatever you have to say, but I really need you to say something. You're my best friend, man. Will you have the fucking decency to tell me off? Yell at me. Punch me. Tell me you want equal time. You offered to leave me alone with her a few weeks ago. Is that what you

322

want me to do?"

Henry pressed his head back against the seat. "Man, you are dense, aren't you? I don't want to yell at you. Okay, I do, but only because I'm still hard as a fucking rock from catching the tail end of the show. Sexual frustration makes me grumpy. And you should have used protection, idiot, because nothing sends a girl like Holly running quicker than a baby scare...unless it's an engagement ring."

A baby. A baby with Holly. Jesus, he was a sick, sick man. The idea of her carrying his child didn't send him running in the opposite direction. It made him desperate to have her again. Made him blissfully fucking happy. "Fuck."

Henry pointed at him. "That. I saw that. And that's why you're dense. We both know why you did it. We both know how you feel. At least, I do. Hell, I might be the only one in our trio who really knows what's going on. Who's willing to embrace what's happening. With great power comes great responsibility, I suppose."

Peter snorted. "Really? I think you've been reading too many comics, buddy."

"You love her. You always have, and it's only gotten stronger since she's been with us. That's why you held back, and why you didn't hold back. Why you've been acting like a bipolar lunatic for close to two months now. You. Love. Her."

He couldn't deny it. He loved Holly. Completely. And Henry was right—looking back, he couldn't remember a time when he didn't. Holly had her own reasons for running, but his were clear. She was in his heart, and when she left she'd taken part of him with her. Without her there'd been nothing to do but keep moving from place to place, woman to woman. No reason to stay.

She wasn't going to stay.

"What about you?" He challenged Henry. "Since you seem to know so much about how I feel."

"I love her too. As much as you do. It's insane how

much." He laughed without humor. "Last year, when my littlest nephew got sick and I left the tour for a few weeks? I saw it. My brother and his wife and children have something I want. I don't mean marriage, picket fence, and a dog. I don't mean the perks that come with being in the royal lineup. They're a family. The love between them connects them, makes them more than they would be alone. It's beautiful and I don't want to live without it anymore."

Peter studied Henry. "That's why you started writing to her?"

He nodded. "I thought about it, about how long we've been wandering without her, and I was tired of waiting. I thought about you too, you know. I knew how you felt about her, knew it couldn't work without all of us, but I thought you weren't ready to admit it yet. It took me until now to see that I was wrong. You've been ready, you just had no idea what it was you were ready for. Dense."

"What was it?"

Henry's smile was almost sad. It made Peter uncomfortable and hopeful at the same time. Bastard. "Family, Peter. Love and family. You, me and Holly."

"I may not be as clever as you are, Super Henry," Peter responded sarcastically. "But even I know that's an unusual equation that rarely equals a family. Certainly not one that would be accepted by the masses that read the tabloids."

"You don't care about that, Peter," Henry snorted. "All you care about is what Holly will think."

"There's that too. You said it yourself. She'd run if she caught the scent of commitment. You and I can love her all we want, but in the end, she'll be the deciding factor. As far as she's concerned, this is a research project with a safe time limit."

Henry made a face. "Sorry about that. It was a desperate addition to the plan."

"Why are you sorry? It was my idea."

"So you think."

THE PLAYBOY'S MÉNAGE

Peter glared at Henry. "That was *your* plan?"

He shrugged. "Well, I wasn't expecting her to throw down like that. It stunned me for a minute, I have to admit. But yes, my devious master plan was to find something she'd want to write about and research for three months that would put her in our immediate vicinity long enough for us to seduce her."

"Good plan."

Henry sighed. "I thought so. But now we've only got six weeks left to convince her she can't live without us."

Peter's fist clenched. The idea of their project ending, of her leaving, put a knot in his stomach and a bottomless hole in his heart. "How the hell do we do that, Henry?"

"You're the genius. You figure it out."

The car stopped and both men were still lost in thought when Roy opened the door. He smiled in concern. "I thought you'd be happy to know I got a phone call as I was pulling into the drive. Andrew says he got a heads up from accounting that Mr. Warren got on the elevator with Ms. Charles slung over his shoulder like a weeping sack of potatoes. So the plan worked."

Peter grinned at Roy. "That *is* good news. About time someone had some."

When he and Henry got out of the limo, Roy took his hat off and held it in his hands, waiting.

Henry tilted his head. "What is it, Roy?"

"I just wanted to tell you that you're a good man in my book, Mr. Vincent. You too, Mr. Faraday. You did a great thing today. I'm honored to work for you, and I wish you both the kind of happiness Mr. Warren must be feeling at this moment. You deserve it."

"Thank you, Roy." Henry reached out to shake his hand. "We're working on it, believe me. And it looks like Mr. Faraday might cry, so be on the lookout for a big, fat summer bonus from me for that alone."

Roy snorted and slipped his hat back on. "I think I'll

drive back to Mr. Reyes' hotel and see if he'll be wanting a lift to the airport tomorrow."

"Good man."

They watched him drive away, both grinning like idiots. "He was carrying Sara over his shoulder. At the office." Peter didn't know Dean had that much rule breaking in him.

Henry nodded. "And they lived happily ever—"

"Shut up."

"I know. I don't want to jinx it either."

They heard the front door open and Holly's voice call out to them from behind it. "Is Roy gone?"

"Yes," Peter called back. "Why? Are you hiding from Roy?"

The door opened wide and Holly came out to stand on the front steps wearing a smile...and very little else.

"Jesus, Betty," Henry groaned.

Her hair was in pigtails. She had on pink sneakers and white ankle socks, and was carrying a small backpack over her shoulders. That was all. The sun was shining through the trees onto her bare skin, and Peter knew he was never going to forget this image. Before he died, the last thing he would see was Holly standing naked in the sun.

"I was just thinking." She shrugged and her breasts jiggled in a way that made Peter's heart stutter. "It's a beautiful summer day and we've hardly been out of the house, which is insane and sad when you think of how many acres this estate has. When I saw the gardeners leave, I thought it would be safe to have a picnic."

"I am hungry," Henry assured her, stepping closer. "We both are."

Her smile grew. "Good. Because I packed everything we'd need, including condoms, in case anyone's wondering. Now all you have to do is catch me."

Without another word she ran down the steps and around the house, and both of them moaned at the sight.

"Six weeks?" Peter muttered.

"Think fast, Dick."

Henry started running and Peter swore, taking off after them. He caught up to her by the pond, picking her up and spinning her around as she laughed in delight.

He set her down as Henry caught up to them, swearing a blue streak. "You two are fast."

Holly moved closer to him and caressed his arms. "Faster than you. All these sexy muscles are weighing you down."

"Think they're sexy, Betty?" Henry flexed playfully, wrapped his arms around her and cupped her ass in his hands. "Being slow did have a few perks. I had the best view."

Peter saw relief flit briefly across her expression before she reached up to kiss Henry's lips. She'd been worried he was upset with her. If she only knew the power she had over both of them. But now wasn't the time to tell her.

It was the perfect time to show her.

"Is there a blanket in that backpack?"

Holly slowly ended the kiss and nodded. "A sheet. I took it off one of the guest beds."

"That'll work for Henry," Peter said absently as he pulled the straps of her backpack down her arms and unzipped the bag. "His muscles will cushion him."

Henry chuckled. "The boss is back." He pulled Holly close again. "Sounds like you're going for another ride."

"I certainly hope so. I didn't get all dressed up for a game of horseshoes." Holly helped Henry out of his clothes while Peter spread the sheet over the grass, digging through the backpack for the box of condoms and using them to hold the cotton in place.

When he turned back around, Henry was kissing her again and she was kicking off her sneakers. She was so damn sexy. He had to get his hands on those pigtails. "Holly, let Henry lie down so you can give him a taste of your...picnic."

She laughed against Henry's lips and he pulled back to

share a wicked smile. "I did mention I was hungry."

Peter watched him lie back on the sheet and hold up his arms to guide Holly down until her knees were on either side of his head. Henry didn't hesitate, his hands gripping her ass as he rocked her pussy against his mouth. Holly gasped and looked up at Peter with desire in her eyes.

He smiled. "I'm hoping you're hungry too." He tore off his shirt and reached for the zipper on his pants, stepping out of them before moving closer to her mouth.

Holly nodded, moaning. "Please."

He guided the head of his erection to her lips, groaning when she opened her mouth and took him in. "That's good, Holly. God, I'll never get enough of your mouth."

He stepped closer, watching her lips stretch around his cock as she took more of him, loving the vibration of her moans when Henry thrust his tongue deep inside her.

Peter gripped her hair in his hands and wrapped the strands around his fingers. "I caught you, baby," he rasped. "We're all going for a ride."

Seeing the approval and need in her eyes, he growled, unable to stop himself from rocking his cock deeper into her mouth. She took everything, sucking him so hard he saw stars and swallowing when he hit the back of her throat.

"Fuck. That's right, baby. Take it all. Suck my cock. Jesus, you're driving me crazy, Holly. So good. So fucking good."

Her muffled shout and the edge of her teeth scraping along his shaft made him groan, release his grip on her hair and pull out as Henry made her come.

"Oh God," she cried. "*Yes.*"

Peter dragged her into his arms, though Henry resisted, and held her quaking body against his. "Condom, Henry. Now."

"Damn it," Henry snarled, sitting up and ripping open a foil packet with unsteady hands, rolling it onto his erection. "I'm still hungry."

She shivered at that and Peter held her tighter. "I know the feeling."

When Henry was ready Peter guided Holly back down to the ground, this time straddling his friend's hips. Kneeling behind her, he whispered in her ear, "Take him, Holly. Take him so I can take you."

"Yes," she moaned, lowering herself onto Henry's erection.

"Oh fuck, Betty," he gasped. "You're still coming. You feel fucking amazing."

She nodded raggedly. "So do you."

Peter reached for a condom, finding a bottle of lube in the backpack as well. "Smart girl."

Wild girl. She was rolling her hips against Henry's, bucking his hold when he tried to control her movements.

"If you don't slow down, this will be over before Peter can join us, Betty."

She stilled, trembling. "Peter needs to hurry."

Peter smiled, his face tight with need. "Holly needs to listen or she might get spanked."

Henry laughed. "She likes that idea, Peter. Not sure why we haven't thought of it before."

"Later," Peter groaned, crawling between Henry's legs and gripping her ass in his hand. "And you know I won't forget."

He poured the lube between her cheeks, rubbing it in sensually until she was pressing against his fingers. He couldn't wait any longer, and then he was there, his cock pushing past the tight ring of muscles to feel that bruising grip he'd become addicted to. She was so tight.

"Oh my God," she cried. "Oh my fucking God that's— yes. Deeper. Fuck me de—"

Peter reached up and covered her mouth with his hand, the one slippery with lube digging into her hip to hold her close. "Baby, I can't think of anything that gets me hotter than the sound of your screams. But out here, I don't want to take the chance someone on the street will call the police and spoil our fun." He pushed deeper inside her, making her groan against his hand. "Oh, that's better. So good. And I know you like it. I saw your face that morning in bed when you and Henry thought I was sleeping." He pulled back and thrust deep and both Henry and Holly moaned. "You like being a bad girl, don't you? Like thinking you're getting away with something. An outdoor ménage, where anyone walking buy could see my cock filling and stretching your sweet ass while Henry fucks your pussy."

She was shouting against his palm, her hands covering his but not pulling it away.

"You love it, Holly. I know you do. I know what else you love." His hand left her hip, trusting Henry to hold her as he reached up to cup her breast, squeezing her nipple hard between his fingers. She shuddered and Peter stopped talking.

He hoped that Henry could follow the pace he was setting, because he wasn't sure he could stop. He loved her ass. Loved taking her like this.

Fuck, he loved her so damn much it was killing him not to tell her, killing him to hold back while he waited for her to come again.

"Jesus, that's good," Henry growled. "I can feel how wet you are. Take what you need, baby. Anything you need."

She cried against Peter's hand and he curled his body around hers, pumping faster, knowing she was close. Knowing he might scream himself if she didn't come.

"Yes," Henry moaned. "I'm coming with you, baby. Fuck."

Peter closed his eyes and let it overtake him. The storm of fire and lightning, the shuddering thunder and howling winds. His body felt like it had been thrown against the rocks. Battered but victorious.

Home.

Six weeks. Five weeks, six days and seven hours to make

her stay and get everything he'd ever wanted.
He hoped it was enough time.

# CHAPTER NINE

*Three weeks, six days and sixteen hours.*

Peter opened his eyes and knew right away that something was wrong. Holly wasn't in his arms and Henry wasn't passed out on the other side of the bed. The sheets were cold.

He got up, went to the bathroom to splash water on his face and reached for the pants still crumpled on the floor, slipping them on before walking down the hall. It was too quiet. He hated the silence now more than ever. Two months had spoiled him forever. Laughter and screaming, the clattering of dishes or the sound of music—that was life to him. That was what made him happy.

And he had been happy. Maybe for the first time in his life.

"Holly?" he called down the stairs. "Henry?"

No one answered.

Where were they? He took the stairs two at a time and headed for the living room, looking for dishes or signs of life. "What the hell?"

They weren't in the kitchen either.

Peter walked toward the front door, and that's when he

saw it. The envelope with his name and Henry's scrawled in shaking script. It had already been opened.

He pulled out the folded piece of paper and saw what the envelope had been covering. A page from his sketchpad with an image of Holly's profile and the question he'd written beside it months ago.

*Ms. Anonymous?*

"Fuck." His heart started pounding, breaking, as he read the letter.

*For Peter and Henry,*

*I thought writing would be the best way to do this, but now I'm not sure. How will you know by looking at a flat piece of paper that I'm sincere when I tell you that these were without question the best two months of my life? Being with you gave me more joy than I will ever be able to express. Everything was perfect, so perfect it scared me. Maybe that's why my vain peek through Peter's drawings last night had to happen, so I could remember that nothing is the fairytale we wish it could be. Fairytales are overrated anyway.*

*Don't be upset, Peter. I don't blame you at all for wondering. It makes sense that you would think I was Ms. Anonymous. For the record, I'm not, though I did discover a few weeks ago that one of my friends was a source for her column. In a way, you weren't wrong to be suspicious.*

*Finding it did give me the push I needed to make my decision. Another month would only make this harder for me, and since it already feels impossible to walk out those doors, I don't think I can keep my promise to stay.*

*What we have is special, but things like this don't last. They can't. I know I said this seventeen years ago, but it's still the truth. I was lucky enough to know what it was like to love both of you, to know what it felt like to be yours. That's more than most people get in a lifetime.*

*I hope you understand.*

*Holly*

He crumpled the note in his hand and forced himself to keep breathing. He'd done this. One stupid question he hadn't thought about since that conversation with Henry. He hadn't fucking cared one way or the other.

She was gone again. Running again. Giving him the same bullshit line and disappearing from his life again.

Not this time. Peter wouldn't let her go without telling her how he felt, how they both felt about her. There was no way in hell he was going to let this letter be their goodbye.

They all deserved better than that.

He looked for his keys but they weren't where he'd left them. Peter heard his angry shout as if from a distance, watched himself throw the small table across the foyer. Saw the legs crack against the wall.

He studied the carnage and took a deep breath. Henry had taken his car, which was fine since he had three more in the garage, but it still felt good to break something.

He walked barefoot over the gravel and opened the garage, grabbing the first set of keys on the wall and climbing into the black jaguar. He turned on the music to drown out the silence, reminding himself not to speed, not to do anything that would delay seeing Holly face to face and making her look into his eyes and tell him what was between them wasn't real.

Peter could feel himself wanting to shut down. The pain was too intense, bringing all his insecurities to the surface and making him want to run again. Logically, he knew this was about her issues, not his. Emotionally, he couldn't help but wonder what there was about him that was unlovable. That ensured he would be alone.

Didn't he show her how he felt? Had he done it wrong? He wasn't as open as Henry. It wasn't as easy for him to share his heart. But she'd seen that room. Been surrounding by the evidence of his emotions. Surely, she knew.

When he turned on her street, his bright yellow sports car

was parked in front of her house. Peter parked beside it in the middle of the road. Let someone complain. He wanted them to. He'd never been in a street fight with hipsters before.

Her front door was open. As he walked toward it, the two men standing on the porch next door stared at him with matching expressions of shock and recognition. He looked down at himself, realizing for the first time that he was in nothing but a pair of wrinkled, unbuttoned pants.

"Fuck it," he growled, not giving them a second thought as he walked up the steps.

He stopped before he went through the door. Henry was talking.

"I'm the one who suggested it, Holly. He didn't believe it. Especially after I told him about your mother."

He heard her gasp. "What the hell do you know about my mother, Henry?"

"Most of it," he responded. "I know what happened right before winter break. I've heard things since, but that's not important."

"But it is." Her voice was ragged with unshed tears. Peter wanted to pull her into his arms and kiss her, then shake her until her teeth rattled for putting them through this. "Don't you see it, Henry? Look at what I want. Not one man like a normal person. *Two*. My mother was never satisfied with any one man or any amount of money. And I haven't been satisfied, either...not with any of the men I've dated."

"You were satisfied with us."

"For two months, with no obligations or awkward introductions or photographs of the three of us showing up in a magazine. It wasn't real life."

Peter had heard enough. He banged on the door as hard as he could and stepped back, looking over at Holly's neighbors. "You know me?"

They nodded.

He forced his most charming smile in their direction.

"I'm assuming from your interest that you're friends with Holly and, I believe, one of you also knows Ms. Anonymous. Is that right? You can tell me. I'm unarmed. I'm not even wearing shoes."

The shorter redhead pointed to the man with the goatee beside him.

"Good. I'd like to send her a message. Do you think you can help me with that?"

"Peter?" Holly walked out onto her porch, disbelief in her eyes. "What are you doing? Where are your clothes? Come inside."

He ignored her, looking at the redheaded man instead. "You strike me as a romantic. Do you believe in love?" He nodded and Peter continued. "Then you should be able to give me an informed answer. Say you fell in love in college. Madly in love for the first time in your life, and then for seventeen years—even after your lover left you because they claimed what you felt wasn't real—you kept on loving them. So much that you went with the obvious ruse of research to have them back in your life again, if only for a few months. And it worked, and those months were glorious, but then your lover disappeared again, still doubting what you had could survive in the harsh light of reality. Imagine how crushing it would be to receive a blow like that a second time, all those years later. To wake up thinking everything was finally right with your world, only to find they'd slipped out the door and left you a Dear John. But you still picked yourself up and drove across town without shoes to declare your feelings to anyone who would hear you. Would you be a jackass, or a man in love?"

Goatee man put his arm around the redhead. "Is there a difference?"

Peter pointed at him. "I still need to give you that message."

He felt Holly's hand on his chest and tensed, arming himself for the pity he would see in her eyes.

It wasn't pity. She was crying. He swore, covering her hand with his. "Holly—"

She shook her head. "Stop, damn it, just stop. You *love* me?"

"What gave me away? And yes. Unconditionally. Hopelessly." Peter raised his voice. "Henry does too, by the way."

The redhead gasped and covered his mouth. "Hold on. *That's* who you were in love with in college? That was your three... Oh my *God*."

Holly muttered under her breath. "Chaz, don't start. And if Bill says anything—"

"He won't," Chaz insisted. "Pretend we're not here."

Henry laughed behind her. "Too late for that."

Peter squeezed Holly's hand. "That was a stupid letter."

"I know."

He didn't think she did. "I heard you two talking. You are not like your mother. You're independent, strong, and loving. You've climbed mountains and gone swimming with sharks. You don't need anyone to give you validation. You're not her." His throat tightened. "And I'm not my parents. I don't want to be like them, Holly—stiff and loveless and alone at the end because they were too concerned about how things looked to experience life. Too concerned with what other people would say about them to love their child."

"I can't say anything bad about my parents," Henry murmured, almost apologetically. "They taught me that love is all that matters, whatever form it takes."

"Hear, hear," Bill cheered before Chaz shushed him.

She sobbed, staring up at Peter with something that gave him hope. He kept talking. "I don't know why you keep saying this isn't real, or it can't last. We've loved you for most of our lives, and knowing you now? I didn't think it was possible, but I love you more."

"Betty Boom-Boom or Holly," Henry agreed, moving

closer to cup her shoulders. "Whatever hat you're wearing, you're the missing piece of our hearts."

"I think Broken Heart Baby is about Holly, Bill," Chaz said in a loud stage whisper.

"Everything is about Holly, Bill," Henry confirmed without taking his eyes off Holly's. "It always has been. It can't get more real than that. Don't make us wait another seventeen years before you finally give us a chance. A real chance."

Holly reached up to touch Henry's hand while still clinging to Peter. "I don't know what to say."

Chaz whistled, drawing their attention. "Holly, I adore you, but get your cute head out of your ass. When something like this happens…and it never happens outside of the movies, so pay attention…you say yes."

Holly smiled through her tears. "Yes."


*One year, three weeks and two time zones later…*

"I can't believe you really did it."

Peter glanced lazily over his sunglasses at Tracy's wife, Alicia. "Did what?"

The blonde leaned back against her giant of a husband, cradling her rounded belly protectively. "Bought a whole island so Holly could do research for a book by that reality show survivalist."

Henry handed him a beer and sat down in the lounge chair beside him. "It's her last hurrah as a ghostwriter before her debut as Betty Holly, author of the already-bestselling women's fiction series, *The Dominatrix Detective*. I came up with that title, you know. And her penname."

"Everybody knows," Peter sighed. "You've told them all fifty times since we got here."

Sara laughed, tilting her head when Dean started rubbing her shoulders. "He's proud of your girl, Peter. We all are.

And she knows how to do everything. After she saved my wedding? I'm in her debt for life."

"Don't forget how she rescued my first flailing attempt at putting together a fundraiser. I don't know what I was thinking. A New York girl trying to wrangle rodeo clowns?" Alicia blushed and Tracy kissed her cheek tenderly. "Holly is a good woman to keep around."

Dean stopped massaging his wife long enough to reach for his glass and lift it. "Definitely worthy of the island, as well as the house and runway you built so we could join you."

Tracy nodded. "Especially when it gives us all a chance to enjoy a private vacation and celebrate the end of an era. Speaking of, do you have another copy of that column? I want to read it again before I toss it in the fire."

Peter reached under his chair, grabbing one from the top of the pile. The last Ms. Anonymous column. Peter and Bill had several long talks and participated in one or two plots to bring that about. In the end, they'd managed to convince her that setting her sights on greener pastures might be the way to go. There were a couple of bachelors causing a lot of mayhem in California. Granted, they were only millionaires, but they were fresh meat and they didn't know who she was. They hadn't discovered anything about her that might embarrass her if it were made public. Peter had.

He'd also erased the evidence from existence in front of her with a simple computer virus, letting her know that he would never stoop to that level. And then he'd asked her if she believed in love. She assured him she didn't, but to her credit, she'd agreed to put a stop to her snooping and get her hair done at another salon. She'd also found a way to exit gracefully.

The Billionaire Bachelors Bow Out.

That's right, dear readers, the country's most eligible bad boys have hung up their No Vacancy signs and announced to the world that they are bachelors no more. Our rocker, rancher, rebel and reformed rogue have all found their special Cinderellas and been living in marital, or at least conjugal, bliss for long enough that even I must admit defeat.

Since there can be no Ms. Anonymous without her boys, this will be my last column. You can use it to wipe your tears or line your child's hamster cage, but either way, this goose is cooked.

Will our handsome heartbreakers really live happily ever after? Only time will tell. But since this is my last hurrah after years of following their every wild escapade and doomed romance, I feel like I should give you my honest opinion on the matter.

I sure as hell hope so.

Peter smiled and pushed himself to his feet. "I think Holly should be done making fishing nets out of coconut husks by now. It's almost time for dinner."

Henry stood too. "I'll go with you."

As they walked away from the beachside gathering and into the shade of the palm trees, Peter glanced at Henry. He'd been acting strange for days. "What's going on with you? Was it a bad idea for me to invite them to join us?"

"Of course not." Henry shook his head. "It's been a while since we've had this much time together. And Holly loves Sara and Alicia."

So did Dean and Tracy. Those were two happily married men. Thanks to Alicia, in a few months they'd all be honorary uncles to a baby cowgirl. Peter and Henry were already planning to spoil her rotten…and protect her from lewd playboys and lustful musicians until she was old enough to protect herself.

Henry still had something on his mind. "It's okay that they're here. *But*?"

"I think we should do it, Peter. What we talked about? The timing couldn't be better."

A knot formed in his stomach and he finished off his beer

in one, long gulp. "Are you serious?"

"I am. We're a family, Peter. We fit. She knows that now."

"But what if she says no?"

"She won't. She'll say yes and then we'll tell her what we've agreed on. You'll marry her legally, then we'll have another ceremony at home for the three of us, only family and friends allowed. And they lived happily ever—"

"Shut up."

Henry chuckled. "No jinxing. I forgot."

Peter rubbed his neck. "You really are a sensitive musician. Aren't you?"

"Fuck off. It's not just me. You know how much my mother loves weddings."

And they loved Holly. Their bachelor days were over for good, and Peter couldn't be happier. He also couldn't think of anything he wanted more than he wanted to marry her.

A sudden image of Holly holding his baby appeared in his mind. Okay, he could think of one more thing.

They saw her on the small beach before she heard them approach. She was cussing like a sailor and throwing coconuts into the sea.

Peter laughed so hard tears came to his eyes.

"Hey honey?" Henry called. "You shouldn't do that. That coconut could be the only thing between you and dehydration."

Holly whirled around, her nose sunburned a bright red and her bikini making Peter's mouth water. "Is it dinnertime already?"

"Almost," he responded, striding up to her and pulling her into his arms. "But first, we're hungry."

He kissed her, tasting salt and sea on her lips and moaning when she pressed her breasts against him. When she went for the button on his shorts, Peter lifted his mouth. "Holly, wait, we wanted to talk to you."

"Sex now," she demanded. "Talk later."

"Being stuck on a deserted island just got hotter," Henry murmured, leaning against a nearby palm tree. "Don't let me stop you."

"Pocket," Peter growled. "In my pocket."

She reached into his pocket and pulled out the condom, pushing down his shorts and rolling it onto his hardening erection in a way that made him grit his teeth. She drove him crazy.

Holly wiggled out of her bikini bottoms, still in his arms.

He fell to his knees and she wrapped her legs around his waist, crying out as his cock filled her. "Yes."

"Baby, slow down," he groaned. "Let me love you."

"You do love me," she gasped. "I've been lost on a desert island. No one to touch me. No one to fuck me. Oh God, Peter, fuck me."

He dug his fingers into her hips and gave her what she wanted. Hard and raw with a desperation he couldn't contain. He dipped his head to bite her nipple through the red bikini top, making her shout in surprised pleasure. Holly arched her back, taking everything.

Giving everything.

"Love you," he moaned against her breast. "I love you, Holly."

"*Yes.* I love you so much. Fuck, I'm coming. Peter!"

He felt her orgasm take her and, like a moth to a flame, he joined her in the blaze. She was irresistible. His Holly.

They clung to each other, trembling in the aftermath, kissing whatever bare skin they could reach. Peter never wanted to let her go.

He wasn't given a choice when Henry unceremoniously plucked her out of his arms. "Not cool, man."

Holly laughed when Henry threw her over his shoulder. "Are we going to dinner now?"

Henry smacked her bare ass. "Not for a while, and it's all your fault. I want *my* desert island sex, and then the three of us need to have that talk."

Peter watched his best friend carry their lover into the clear blue ocean water, his fingers buried between her thighs, and shook his head.

This was his life now.

He smiled. *This was his life now.* Surrounded by friends, loved by a woman like Holly…a woman who would either say yes to marrying them or find herself handcuffed to the bed until she had no choice but to give in.

It didn't get much better than this.

# THANKS FOR READING!

I truly hope you enjoyed these books. If so, please leave a review and tell your friends. Word of mouth and online reviews are immensely helpful to authors and greatly appreciated.

To keep up with all the latest news about RG's books, release info, exclusive excerpts and more, check out her website RGAlexander.com. Stop by her group blog, Smutketeers.com to enter the frequent *contests* and *free book giveaways* each month.

Friend me on Facebook to join **The Brass Chattery** for contests, and smutty fun.

# More Hotness from R.G. Alexander!

## Big Bad John
### Book 1 in the *Bigger in Texas* series

*Kinda broad at the shoulder and narrow at the hip...*

Trudy Adams never planned on going home again. Not to that sleepy little Texas town where everyone knew her business and thought she was trouble. She ran away to California years ago, and now, after what has felt like a lifetime of struggling, her lucky break might finally be around the corner.

And then she got that email.

John Brown has been waiting patiently for Trudy to return, but his patience has run out. He's had years to think about all the things he wants to do to her, and he's willing to use her concern for her brother, her desire to help her best friend get her story, and every kinky fantasy Trudy has to show her who she belongs to.

The explosive chemistry between them is unmistakable. But will history and geography be obstacles they can't overcome? When Trouble makes a two-week deal with Big Bad...anything can happen.

**Warning:** READ THIS! BDSM, explicit sex, voyeurism, accidental voyeurism, voyeurism OF voyeurism with a sprinkle of m/m, exhibitionism, ropes, cuffs, gratuitous spanking, skinny dipping, irresponsible use of pervertables...and a big, dirty man who will melt your heart.

### Available Now!

## THREE FOR ME?

*Three men, a tomboy…and one erotic game that could change everything.*

Simon, Eric, Rafael, Lee…and Charli. It's never mattered that Charli is the only girl in the crowd. She's always been a tomboy, anyway. Just one of the guys.

Between work and Couch Potato Thursdays, life is pretty full. Sure, no man alive can get through the friend gauntlet, but thanks to her boys and her toys, she's got plenty of fantasy material. It's a win-win situation. Until Lee has a destination wedding in Cozumel—and Charli's "best man" duties take a kinky turn.

Through what looks to be foul play by Lee's new brides, Charli finds herself on a decidedly decadent shore excursion, playing "The Race Erotic". With each sexy challenge, it becomes clearer that down deep, she desires not one, not two, but all three of her remaining single buddies.

They're the only family she's ever known. She can't imagine living without them. Will she have to choose? Or will the final score be three to one?

**Warning:** Naughty costumes, kinky toys, a boy, a girl…two more boys, all doing unspeakably dirty things to each other.

### Available Now!

# OTHER BOOKS FROM R.G. ALEXANDER

**Fireborne Series**
Burn With Me
Make Me Burn
Burn Me Down-coming soon

**Bigger in Texas Series**
Big Bad John
Mr. Big Stuff-coming soon
Book 3-coming soon

**The DD4 Series**
Dirty Delilah

**Billionaire Bachelors Series**
The CEO's Fantasy
The Cowboy's Kink
The Playboy's Ménage

**Children Of The Goddess Series**
Regina In The Sun
Lux In Shadow
Twilight Guardian
Midnight Falls
Eternal Guardian

**Wicked Series**
Wicked Sexy
Wicked Bad
Wicked Release

**Shifting Reality Series**
My Shifter Showmance
My Demon Saint
My Vampire Idol

## Temptation Unveiled Series
Lifting The Veil
Piercing The Veil
Behind The Veil

## Superhero Series
Who Wants To Date A Superhero?
Who Needs Another Superhero?

## Kinky Oz Series
Not In Kansas
Surrender Dorothy

## More Than Mènage
Truly Scrumptious
Three For Me?
Four For Christmas
Marley in Chains

## Anthologies
Three Sinful Wishes
Wasteland - Priestess
Who Loves A Superhero?
A Kinky Christmas Carol - Marley in Chains
Midnight Ink - Boxed Set

## Bone Daddy Series
Possess Me
Tempt Me
To The Bone

## Elemental Steam Series Written As Rachel Grace
Geared For Pleasure

# ABOUT R.G. ALEXANDER

R.G. Alexander (aka Rachel Grace) is a *New York Times* and *USA Today* Bestselling author who has written over 30 erotic paranormal, contemporary, sci-fi/fantasy books for multiple e-publishers and Berkley Heat. Both her personalities are represented by the Brown Literary Agency.

She is a founding member of The Smutketeers, an author formed group blog dedicated to promoting fantastic writers, readers and a positive view of female sexuality.

She has lived all over the United States, studied archaeology and mythology, been a nurse, a vocalist, and now a writer who dreams of vampires, witches and airship battles. RG feels lucky every day that she gets to share her stories with her readers, and she loves talking to them on twitter and FB. She is happily married to a man known affectionately as The Cookie—her best friend, research assistant, and the love of her life. Together they battle to tame the wild Rouxgaroux that has taken over their home.

Sign up for the Smutketeers Newsletter
**http://eepurl.com/OBKSD**
for updates on contest giveaways and New Releases.
All for Smut and Smut for All!

### To Contact R. G. Alexander:
www.RGAlexander.com
www.RachelGraceRomance.com
www.Smutketeers.com
Facebook:
http://www.facebook.com/RachelGrace.RGAlexander
Twitter: https://twitter.com/RG_Alexander

Printed in Great Britain
by Amazon